Warlord

"You're talking about surrender to a Phrenorian warrior of the Empire?" Zhoh's *chelicerae*
twitched. "The only reason we understand that
concept is because we crossed paths with humans.
We don't even have a word for that in our language."

"I hear you don't have a word for *mercy* either."
Sage shifted slightly, trying not to get noticed.

Two other Phrenorians stood to one side of
Zhoh. Both held their assault rifles at the ready,
but neither appeared too eager to use them.

"But mercy is something I'm willing to offer,"
Sage continued. "You just need to let the woman
go and lay down your weapon."

"What would you do if our situation were reversed?" Zhoh asked. "Would you accept . . .
mercy?"

"No," Sage stated flatly.

By Mel Odom

The Makaum War

MEL odom

warlord

THE MAKAUM WAR: BOOK THREE

HARPER Voyager
An Imprint of HarperCollins Publishers

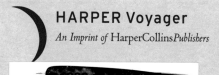

WARLORD. Copyright © 2020 by Mel Odom. All rights reserved. Printed in the United States of America. No part of this book may be used or reproduced in any manner whatsoever without written permission except in the case of brief quotations embodied in critical articles and reviews. For information, address HarperCollins Publishers, 195 Broadway, New York, NY 10007.

First Harper Voyager mass market printing: February 2020

Print Edition ISBN: 978-0-06-228453-2
Digital Edition ISBN: 978-0-06-228454-9

Cover design by Amy Halperin
Cover illustration © Gregory Bridges

Harper Voyager and the Harper Voyager logo are trademarks of HarperCollins Publishers in the United States of America and other countries.
HarperCollins is a registered trademark of HarperCollins Publishers in the United States of America and other countries.

FIRST EDITION

20 21 22 23 24   QGM   10 9 8 7 6 5 4 3 2 1

For my wife, Sherry, who keeps my world bright.

ACKNOWLEDGMENTS

To David Pomerico and Kelly Lonesome, editors who stood by me.

To Ethan Ellenberg, my agent, who has always been there.

To my son, Chandler, who came up with the name for the world in the beginning.

To you steadfast fans, who wouldn't give up on the trilogy while I was being reconstructed.

warlord

ONE

Taking refuge in the shadows that draped one of the squares, stocky outbuildings dotting the bazaar grounds, Master Sergeant Frank Sage studied his target.

No matter how carefully he'd set up the attack, no matter how much he'd reworked the assault force—balancing between strength and stealth, and moving quick so that rumor of the attack didn't get there ahead of them—he figured operations were about to go sideways. That was what happened when even the best plans met enemy forces. During engagement, the trick was to stay alive and keep his troops alive too.

He focused on remaining calm, relying on training and combat experience. Those were skills he had that most of the other soldiers around him lacked and he was uncomfortably aware of their absence.

Despite the police action they'd been involved with

over the last few months, too many of the soldiers at Fort York were green when it came to fighting. Most of them had only handled the rough trade from the bars and the developing criminal element shipping in from offplanet and those learning illegal tradecraft among the local population. A burgeoning economy in a primitive setting transformed Makaum into an Old West boomtown. There hadn't been a sheriff to keep the peace.

That had recently changed. The Terran military had stepped up to bring things under control. The speculators from a dozen different worlds operating in the black market hadn't appreciated the interference, but they didn't want to gun up against the Terran soldiers, so they backed down more often than not.

Tonight the adversaries would be a lot more experienced and callous than common criminals and junkies. They wouldn't pull punches and they wouldn't hesitate to kill.

Sage pushed that thought out of his mind. His troops were committed now, and lucky to have come this far without being discovered by their opponents. That would give the Terran military a slight edge because they would choose when things would go down. Getting discovered early would have forced them to gain access to the areas they already controlled.

Strictly speaking, the Zukimther mercs guarding the three-story building in the center of the bazaar weren't hostile combatants. Like many of the other alien traders that had come to Makaum in the hopes of making a quick credit, they made efforts to stay away from the Terran and Phrenorian military forces located onplanet. The Zukimther mercs were, however, dealing in explosive contraband that Sage intended to take off the market because things onplanet had become volatile.

Hostile entrepreneurs, Colonel Halladay had called

the Zukimther mercs during the briefing prior to the op. The warriors were identified as undesirables just as the corp drug labs had been. Intel on the Zukimther mercs suggested—*strongly*—that the warriors wouldn't surrender without a fight. Past history combatting them on other worlds assured Sage of the same certainty.

With the backing of the Quass, the Makaum ruling body, Terran military Charlie Company was there to serve cease-and-desist orders on all transactions. The surviving Zukimther would be kicked offplanet on the first ship bound out of the system.

"Snipers in position." Sergeant Kjersti Kiwanuka sounded cool and distant over the comm. She was heading up the long-range gunners that would back the engagement, taking out the first Zukimthers who aggressively resisted and threatened Terran soldiers. And the mercs would react aggressively because violence was hardwired into their DNA. After the initial firefight opened up, Kiwanuka and the snipers would settle into overwatch, picking targets as they could.

Using his helmet's 360-degree HUD, Sage pinged the snipers' positions and lit them up on his faceshield. All eight of them occupied positions in the ruins of multistory buildings that ringed the marketplace's walls.

Other structures held central locations within the rectangular area. Dead trees snaked through the structures, proof that the newest generation of squatters in the area used defoliants against the constant encroachment of jungle that covered the planet. Makaum was aggressive down to its core.

The present squatters in the bazaar killed the trees and plants. They just didn't clear away the debris, only succeeding in slowing down the growth and leaving piles of dead foliage behind. Makaum natives would have worked with the growth and shaped it into useful parts of the structure, and they would have hauled off the detritus for use as fertilizer. Before the arrival of offworlders, the Makaum people lived simple and clean, and Sage respected that.

"Roger that, Sniper Leader." Lieutenant Hadji Murad, Operation Lynx's OIC, sounded tense.

As officer-in-charge, Murad was still as green as most of his troops. He was a good guy. Sage liked the man, and one day Murad would make a good officer. If he lived. Living long enough to become adept at command was always the problem with green lieutenants and the sergeants who had to get them there.

"Confirm sniper readiness," Murad said.

Sage peered around the building's corner and looked at the Zukimther warrior standing only a few meters away.

The merc was almost three meters tall and massive. His body was corded with natural armor. Twin ridges of bone ran up from his eyebrow ridges, over his hairless head, and to his shoulders. More bone, all of it as durable as steel, overlaid major arteries in all four arms and both legs.

The Zukimther tended not to wear armor because their thick yellow skins splotched with brown patches were as dense and hard-wearing as most composite alloys. They figured it saved credits. And there was a pride issue. Broad belts containing tactical gear and weapons crisscrossed the warrior's huge chest.

Three of Makaum's five moons showed pastel green, yellow, and pink crescents in the sky. Cloud cover rendered the moonlight feeble and thin. Shadows pooled in inky darkness. The weak light bathed the loose circular pattern of the bazaar.

In the days before the planet had been discovered by space-faring races and opened up for trade, then exploitation, by the Phrenorians, the bazaar had served as a community place for the Makaum people to trade and share news. The technology they'd had at that point had been minimal. No vids. No sensies. And the drug trade had been limited mostly to wine and natural herbs. Overindulgence of either was punished.

The arriving merchants brought drugs and offworld alcohol as they built up the area, raising buildings of plascrete as they'd needed them, with no regard to style or design. The buildings occupied loose concentric circles around the old Makaum building in the center. The planet's fierce vegetation tore through the plascrete in short order if it wasn't kept in check with defoliants, but the Makaum structures remained for the most part because the natives had worked with nature instead of seeking to overpower it.

Traders moved into and out of the building as they wished. As a result, keeping up with who was where at any given time was an almost impossible task even with intel provided by friendly shopkeepers and the local snitches. The crooked alleys and truncated streets provided lots of cover and ambush points. All of this was surrounded by the tall walls where Kiwanuka and her snipers had dug in.

Holding his position, Sage accessed the vid feeds from the other members of the assault team. The images lay ghostly pale over his own view and fed through quickly as he assimilated them. Charlie Company had rolled out six four-soldier fireteams in conventional armor with two four-soldier fireteams in powersuits lying in wait. Plus Kiwanuka's snipers.

If the heavy cavalry showed early, the Zukimther mercs would set up inside the building and be harder to dig out. Sage hoped to circumvent that.

Sage held his Roley rifle loose and ready. "Lieutenant. I confirm seventeen tangos in sight."

Those Zukimther showed as thin, translucent triangles

on his faceshield, read in by thermographic imaging programmed to identify their heat signatures.

"Confirm that, Master Sergeant." Murad's voice sounded dry and cracked a little. "Seventeen tangos visible."

Word on the street was that the Zukimther mercs were twenty-seven strong. Plus or minus two. Satellite imagery and Kiwanuka's soft recon before sunset had confirmed that. "The other ten are probably in their racks or on downtime."

"Affirmative."

"It's not going to take them long to join the party once we open this up." Sage had been clear about that in the briefing but he wanted everyone to remember that now.

"I know."

Sage kept his voice level but firm. "Waiting for your go, sir." He knew he had to lead Murad into the engagement and not push. "Let's button this down and get everybody back home."

That was the plan, but Sage knew there was a good chance that some of the soldiers wouldn't make it back to Fort York alive or in one piece. He'd already regretted that as he'd geared up, but that was out of his mind. Now, he focused on controlling the situation and nullifying any threat to his soldiers.

"Roger that. Changing channels." Murad switched to the command frequency and Sage rolled over with him. "All right, soldiers, let's shut this place down. On my mark. Go!"

As far as command voices went, the lieutenant was coming into his own. He sounded confident and ready, strong and motivated.

Smoothly, letting the training take over, Sage rounded the building in a single flowing motion and leveled the Roley. The combat rifle fired depleted uranium rounds as well as gauss blasts and laser bursts. For tonight's action, he'd also equipped it with a gel-grenade launcher slung under the barrel.

"Terran military. Put your weapons—" Sage wasn't sure if the Zukimther merc heard the public address speaker from his suit or if the warrior had heard him approach.

Either way, the merc went for his weapons before Sage finished speaking. The big alien filled two hands with an Yqueu 20mm assault rifle and his two other hands with Kalrak plasma pistols. Sage's comm juiced and tried to open a channel, but the damper in his AKTIV-suit immediately blocked that attempt. They'd already dialed in the Zukimther frequencies prior to the op.

Sage held his weapon steady and spoke in a firm, nonthreatening manner. "Put your weapons—"

The assault rifle swung and pointed dead at Sage, but he managed to throw himself to the side before the stream of 20mm rounds and plasma bursts ripped through the air where he'd been standing. The impacts chopped fist-sized holes in the wall as the detonations and impacts rolled over the bazaar. If Sage hadn't been in his suit with the aud dampers in play, the vicious blasts would have deafened him.

Rolling to his feet and coming up effortlessly, the reticule on his faceshield locked on his target while a secondary reticule tracked another Zukimther turning toward him, Sage squeezed the trigger on the grenade launcher. The Roley twitched slightly as Sage compensated for the recoil.

A trio of blue gel-grenades sailed through the air, stuck to the merc, and smeared only slightly as they grabbed traction and settled. The initial kinetic force of the impacts staggered the huge warrior and he roared in delight, thinking that he had escaped injury. Then the grenade blasts punched him backward, knocked him off his feet, and wreathed his upper body in an incendiary cloud. Red and yellow flames chewed into his flesh, digging past the armored hide.

Sage's helmet automatically filtered the bursts of light and the sudden thunder, dialing all of it down to something he could handle. Voices of the men and women in his unit echoed around him as they called out to each other.

Roaring in pain, the Zukimther rolled on the ground as he tried to smother the clinging flames. He dropped his weapons and clawed at the mud from the recent rains, smearing fistfuls of it over his body to extinguish the fire.

Sage couldn't believe the warrior wasn't dead, but from the severity of the wounds, he knew there was no way the Zukimther was going to live. Aware of the approaching second Zukimther, Sage stepped up to the merc he'd put on the ground, aimed the Roley at the base of his opponent's thick skull, and fired a short mercy burst.

The depleted uranium rounds cracked the thinner segment of the skull, then penetrated and killed the Zukimther, putting him out of the agony he'd been suffering. Still in motion, Sage pulled his assault rifle up, aimed at his second target, and fired as soon as he had target lock.

Howling like some mythical monster, the second Zukimther warrior fired short 20mm bursts at Sage that slammed into the hardsuit and knocked him backward. Sage aimed just above the muzzle flashes that tracked him and returned fire.

Warning! the suit's near-AI spoke softly. *Seek cover. Armor is taking critical damage.*

Sage ducked away to the right, heading for the crumbled remains of a building's foundation covered in vines and brush. He avoided the deadly hail of rounds as he ducked behind the structure, and he was glad to see the grenade launcher was once again charged and ready for use. He knelt behind the short broken plascrete wall that remained from the building that had fallen into ruins.

"This is the Terran Army!" Murad called over a loudhailer. "Put down your weapons!"

The merc coming for Sage fired on full-auto while at a dead run, and his accuracy kept the sergeant pinned behind the wall that fell in smoldering chunks as the large rounds cored through the building material.

"Master Sergeant!" a hoarse voice yelled.

The three men assigned to Sage's personal fireteam broke cover and came out firing.

As the Zukimther turned toward the new threat, Sage yelled, "Stay with cover! Hit him with gel-grenades! Move! Now!"

The three soldiers fired their weapons but missed their target and scattered explosions all around the big merc. One of them almost hit Sage. Cursing as dirt, rock, and broken plascrete slammed against him, Sage went to ground.

The men realized the danger they were in when the Zukimther leveled his weapons at them. They pulled back immediately, but one of them got hit by return fire and went down. Another soldier reached out, laid a glove on the downed soldier, and juiced magnetism through the glove, taking hold. The soldier reared back and pulled the fallen one to cover just ahead of another burst of fire that chopped into the ground.

"Kiwanuka!" Sage bellowed.

"Copy that, Master Sergeant," Kiwanuka answered coolly. "We have you in sight and we are working on a solution."

Popping up, Sage aimed a burst of depleted uranium projectiles at the merc's back that made the alien stumble and tore through his hide in several places. As the Zukimther wheeled around, Sage plastered the merc's chest with gel-grenades. The last one adhered to the Zukimther's chin.

The Zukimther roared defiantly and unleashed a salvo of rounds that chewed into the foundation where Sage took cover. Then the charges draping his body exploded, and the one on his chin snapped his neck. Incredibly, the merc stood there for a moment as blankness filled his eyes and his heart stilled, then he dropped to his knees and fell face forward.

Four other Zukimther mercs rallied and started for him, but they were briefly targeted by Kiwanuka's sniper team. The Zukimther dropped and Sage knew most of them wouldn't get up again.

"Are you clear, Master Sergeant?" Kiwanuka asked.

"I've still got tangos on my twenty," Sage replied.

"We're having trouble seeing through all the dust and debris. For the moment we're blind."

"Understood."

Another volley of 20mm rounds dug into the foundation fragments and chased Sage out of his temporary cover. Duckwalking rapidly along the low wall, pursued by the rounds, Sage popped up ahead of the enemy fire and took aim. When he squeezed the trigger, depleted uranium rounds dug into the nearest Zukimther's chest and penetrated far enough into the merc's hide to draw thick, orange blood, but not far enough to disable the alien.

Twenty-seven meters behind the merc bearing down on Sage, a hailstorm of 20mm rounds caught two soldiers. The continued ballistic assault shredded the AKTIV-suits and left the flesh beneath unprotected. Corpses hit the ground and lay still as KIA stats flared to life on Sage's faceshield.

Privates McKendle and Birchart, both of Texas, were going home in body bags.

Sage shoved the thought of the loss of young lives away

and concentrated on the battle. He squeezed the launcher's trigger before the Zukimther could regain his balance. A tight cluster of gel-grenades hugged the merc's chest over his heart, but he still charged Sage's position.

Sage ducked behind another pile of ruins once his opponent had gotten close enough to leave him in the blast radius of the grenades. He held his position and waited, listening to the dulled thunderclaps of the charges exploding.

Blood and splintered bone spread over the immediate vicinity and coated the AKTIVsuit's armor. Holding his position, Sage fit his left hand to the grenade launcher's loading gate and linked his armor up, pumping in fresh explosives from his ammo backpack through his wrist reloader. The Armored-Kinetic-Tactical-Intelligence-Vestment suit packed ammunitions throughout its frame.

"Master Sergeant," Murad called. "There is movement in the building ahead of you. Looks like the tangos are putting some kind of machinery into play. We're unable to confirm."

"Roger that," Sage replied. "I'll take a look."

Up again, Sage glanced at the battlefield. The Zukimther had staggered back toward the central building they guarded during the initial attack, but now they pushed back, cut into the Terran soldiers, and drove them into small groups like pack predators closing in on prey. He couldn't clearly see the building's windows either from where he was.

Sage didn't know what the mercs hoped to accomplish by withdrawing to the building because it wouldn't stand, then two 100mm cannons opened fire from the target building's second floor. The weapons *whumped* as they launched their lethal payloads. Almost immediately, two pockets of Terran soldiers vaporized and only smoking craters marked where they had stood.

TWO

Where did they get those big guns?" Murad demanded. He wasn't calm or confident now, but he wasn't panicked either. Yet. "No one said anything about the Zukimther having cannons!"

Cursing, ignoring the lieutenant's question, Sage ran toward the nearest Zukimther, who was driving three soldiers back into a corner filled with foundation remnants. Wondering how they'd missed the intel on the mercs' weapons wasn't nearly as important as figuring out what to do about it. Murad would learn to ignore curiosity while engaged. Figuring out how surprises happened and where to place the blame was amateur thinking. Survival was key.

Stumbling over the uneven terrain, two of the soldiers dragged a wounded third. One of the standing soldiers wore armor with a dark scarlet *ypheynte* marked on the chest that only showed up with the faceshield's enhanced vision capabilities. The insect reminded Sage of a Terran dragonfly but was one of the creatures revered by the Makaum people because of its ability to survive hardship.

The domestic recruits to Charlie Company had taken to wearing *ypheynte* graphics after the recent attack during the Festival of the Beginning that had left so many innocents dead and injured. Colonel Halladay had tried to prevent the adoption of the insignia, and had even pointed out that the added graphic wasn't official, but the local recruits wouldn't give it up even after the colonel told them it marked them as targets for local dissidents and offplanet gunmen.

The young men and women hadn't cared and had stood by their chosen colors. The colonel had given up that fight in short order because the Makaum scouts now in the muster were valuable in the field as well as for public relations, especially since the local population was divided between supporting the Terran military and the Phrenorian Empire.

On the run, Sage lined up a shot, aiming for the Zukimther's head because that would at least disorient the merc. Just as he squeezed the trigger, two 20mm rounds slammed into his stomach and right thigh, hurling him through the air. He went with the momentum, turning the fall into a roll that brought him to his feet again. His senses swam for a moment and pain wracked his body. The armor had saved him, but the hydrostatic shock had penetrated with bruising force.

Do you require centering? the suit's near-AI asked. *I have a pain and focus suite ready.*

A screen of available stims flashed in the lower right quadrant of Sage's HUD.

Sage ran, crouching down to provide a smaller target.

Stims kept a soldier up and moving, but they tended to take the edge off and turn reflexes sloppy. On the battlefield, a split second made the difference between life and death. "No."

The Zukimther who had shot him laid down quick bursts of 20mm ammo that dug craters and plasma bursts that blistered patches of ground into glass. His attention drawn by Sage's previous attack, or maybe warned by one of his team, the second Zukimther swiveled around and brought his weapons up. Together they would catch Sage in a lethal crossfire.

Hoping his armor would hold up long enough to get to cover, he fired the grenade launcher at the opponent closest to him. At the same time, the other Zukimther's head suddenly exploded, cored through by one of the sabot rounds fired by the team's snipers. The ammo had been designed for use against heavily armored powersuits and troop transports, but it worked equally well against the Zukimther.

Sage's trio of gel-grenades landed on the first merc's chest and thighs. Moving at the speed he had been, Sage hadn't had time to do anything other than aim for center mass. Before the grenades detonated, the Zukimther's head snapped back as a sabot round drilled through his eye, then the delayed charge emptied his brain pan.

Sliding into cover behind huge chunks of plascrete, Sage took a moment to reload his weapon. One of his team skidded into place beside him. The soldier's AKTIVsuit glowed cherry-red in spots and smoked from plasma charge hits.

Sage's AI identified her as Private Remedios Escobedo from Rio de Janeiro.

"How is Raetsch?" he asked her. Raetsch was the wounded man.

"Stable, Master Sergeant. Private Chouteau is making sure he stays squared away."

"Good." Sage hoisted his rifle and took a measured breath. He glared at the Zukimther reinforcements taking the field. The mercs had evidently added to their number. More than the estimated twenty-seven were in play.

And they had those cannons too.

Sage looked at Escobedo. "Are you ready?"

Escobedo took a fresh grip on her assault rifle and rose into a crouched position, like a runner in the blocks. "Roger, Master Sergeant. Confirm ready."

The 100mm cannons blasted again. The explosive rounds demolished one of the crumbling buildings soldiers had taken cover behind and spilled tons of plascrete over them. Smoke rolled over the area and concealed most of the destruction, but Sage spotted soldiers struggling to get out from under the rubble. Other soldiers weren't moving.

"Good, because we're going into the building after those guns." Sage peered around the cover and noticed the Zukimther mercs had spread out around the base of the building and started taking cover.

Kiwanuka and her snipers were taking their targets down. A half dozen Zukimther corpses lay across the battlefield. Most of the bodies were headless. Others had their chests blown open.

Unfortunately, the snipers' successes had been noted by the Zukimther forces as well. The next salvo from the 100mm cannons smashed into the wall surrounding the bazaar. As the din of the explosions rolled over the area, a section of the wall spilled to the ground in jagged chunks. One of the snipers came down with it and got buried in the avalanche.

"Sage," Kiwanuka called over the private channel

he'd set up with her. "They've got my people in their sights. We hadn't counted on long-range weapons like this. We can't stay stationary and hold overwatch."

"Copy that. Get moving. I'm going to try to take out those cannons." Sage switched frequencies. "Lieutenant Murad."

"Copy, Sage," the lieutenant replied. He was on the move sixty meters away to the right, closing in on a group of Zukimther.

"Maybe it's time to bring in the powersuits, sir."

"Roger that." Murad switched to the powersuit frequency. "Sergeant Ekonomou, bring your team in."

"Copy that, sir. Oscar Team is on the move."

Ekonomou was young, but he'd seen action against the Phrenorians before getting a medical evac from the last planet he'd served on. After he'd had new legs and an arm vat grown, Command had reassigned him to Makaum to finish out his rehab with "light" duty. Like Sage, he'd wanted to get back into the Phrenorian War.

On Sage's faceshield, four of the eight purple pixilated images of the powersuit squads lurched into action while four others held back to protect a retreat if necessary. Also, jamming the battlefield with the big units while the foot soldiers were scattered didn't work well. The powersuits needed room to move.

Eight meters tall and three meters wide, covered in heavy black polycarbonate armor, the powersuits were dreadnoughts in the combat area. They stood in blocky humanoid shapes and moved on tree-trunk-thick legs. At forty-plus tons, they had plenty of speed, but lacked adroitness because stopping that much tonnage quickly was a problem. The powersuits bristled with weapons, from 20mm cannons to flamethrowers to missiles.

Ekonomou led the powersuit charge, lifted a thick arm, and crashed through one of the U-shaped arches over an entryway choked with brush and brambles only partially cut back. Plascrete chunks scattered like chaff before him and the heavy clank of the articulated joints rattled like a basso tambourine.

A Zukimther merc opened up with his 20mm machine gun thirty meters in front of Ekonomou. The power-suit's ablative armor exploded in response but left thinner protection in its wake. Ekonomou raised his left hand and sprayed a roiling blast of napalm over the merc.

Covered in fiery liquid, the Zukimther squalled in agony and abandoned his position. He managed only two steps before the fire filled his lungs and his corpse collapsed to the ground.

As Ekonomou raced across the bazaar, Terran military soldiers hurried out of his path so they wouldn't get stomped during the confusion. Even with the power-suit's HUD tracking and sorting friendlies and foes, moving that much tonnage quickly was problematic even under the best of conditions. Traversing a landscape pitted by craters and ruins made the situation even worse.

Corporal Jasper tried to take his powersuit over a collapsed building, got almost to the top, then sank into it like it had turned into quicksand. He fought against the structure's remnants and shoved off huge pieces as he tried to extricate himself.

A Zukimther merc took advantage of the corporal's plight and fired a steady stream of plasma and 20mm ammo at the polycarbonate bubble that protected the driver's head. Cracks and chips appeared in the soldier's helmet. Jasper picked up a large section of wall, heaved it at his opponent, and buried the man in a pile of rubble when the projectile shattered on impact.

Ekonomou fired on the move, riddled pockets of

Zukimther mercs with 20mm rounds, and laid down suppressive fire to protect the soldiers pinned down by enemy weapons. He rocked back and looked up at the windows where the 100mm cannons were, then fired two missiles from the pods on his shoulders.

The missiles streaked 150 meters, halfway to the main building where the Zukimther had holed up, before they met with anti-aircraft fire that detonated them early. The two bright yellow explosions triggered twin concussive waves that swept across the battlefield and indiscriminately rained down flaming debris over all combatants. The flashes of light caused temporary blindness as Sage's HUD tried to compensate.

Sage took cover and pulled Escobedo with him just before a wave of fire crashed against the broken wall where he'd set up. He waited a heartbeat, then looked at Escobedo.

"You still with me, Private Escobedo?"

"Yes, Master Sergeant." She sounded a little shaky and seemed to be having trouble focusing, but she kept it together.

"Good. Because we've got some work to do." Sage slapped her on the shoulder, causing her to reset herself, making sure she was reacting, not frozen up. "Let's move."

Breaking cover, Sage ran for the main house. Escobedo sprinted behind him, covering his six.

"Kiwanuka." Sage swiveled the Roley and blasted a Zukimther who spotted him and swung his weapon toward him. The depleted uranium staggered the merc back, leaving him open to a trio of gel-grenades that plastered his chest.

"I have your six," Kiwanuka replied calmly.

An overlay of her screen tinted Sage's faceshield, letting him see what she was seeing, which was a

Zukimther taking cover behind a building out of sight to the left. The merc stepped forward, intending to blast Sage when he came into view.

"You have an active tango at your twenty," she stated.

As the Zukimther covered with gel-grenades exploded, the other merc staggered to the side and blood trickled from a hole in his temple where Kiwanuka's sabot round had entered. Before the Zukimther could instinctively cover his wound with a hand, the delayed charge exploded within his skull and caused him to lurch.

Coming up on the falling dead merc, Sage pushed a hand on the toppling corpse and vaulted across while Escobedo ran out wide around it. Sage threw himself forward and gained ground while the powersuits attracted most of the Zukimther attention.

The enemy cannons fired again, and this time the payloads took out the wall where Kiwanuka held her position. Sage didn't know if she'd gotten away or not and he had to resist the temptation to go back for the sergeant.

She's a professional. She knows what she's doing. You've got green soldiers out here who need your attention more. Sage focused on the building.

Ekonomou fired another three missiles. More anti-aircraft fire took out two of them, but the third missile got through. The projectile smashed into the third floor, penetrated the wall, and filled the room with an explosion that leaked flames out all of the windows.

Before Ekonomou had a chance to set himself again, the 100mm cannons fired twin rounds that punched through the polycarbonate armor and tore the powersuit to pieces. The armor died instantly and all of Ekonomou's readings went off-line with it. Sage didn't know if the man was alive or dead.

Focus, Sage told himself.

Around him, 20mm cannon fire dug divots in the ground and slammed into fractured plascrete. He concentrated on the doorway ahead and knew the Zukimther might have planted anti-personnel mines there because it was something he would have done if he'd held the position.

And there was the fact that none of the Zukimther mercs had tried entering the building once they'd charged out to meet the attack. Something kept them from seeking cover there.

Sage brought the Roley to his shoulder and put two gel-grenades on the door, then plopped two through the doorway. The explosions widened the doorway and lit up the room briefly before triggering more explosions from the charges set within.

Without hesitating, Sage entered the burning opening, leaped up the steps leading to the entrance in two long bounds, sprinted to the door, and took cover. As soon as Escobedo joined him on the cracked wraparound stone porch, Sage lowered the Roley into position and whirled around the door.

When he stared into the flames, his HUD automatically shifted into thermographic. The vision filtered details better when fire clung to the walls than the low-light capability. One dead and one dazed Zukimther lay sprawled on the floor amid shattered pieces of worn furniture.

Sage moved into the room and dropped down into a semi-crouch with the Roley leveled and ready. Escobedo was at his heels and selected a covering field of fire three steps to his right.

Some of the Zukimther gunners outside in the bazaar spotted Sage in the building and hammered the area with rifle fire. The 20mm rounds chopped into the building and destroyed what wasn't already broken. The rounds ricocheted from Sage's armor, which was taking a beating, already flashing red in several areas on his HUD report suite as his protection grew steadily weaker. Then the Zukimther barrage thinned out as the Terran military troops reorganized and turned up the heat under Murad's orders.

Sage grinned mirthlessly. The lieutenant was developing quickly, figuring out survival was aided by enemy units dying as fast as possible. Combat did that to a soldier as long as it didn't get him killed.

Moving quickly, Sage pushed through the debris and bodies till he reached a plascrete stairwell that led up to the next floor. Keeping the rifle at the ready, following the sights of his weapon, he spotted a Zukimther ahead and above him.

Firing the Roley one-handed, Sage ran up the steps, knowing he couldn't blast the man out of his path. Bullets ricocheted from his opponent's thick skin and kept him off balance. Too close to use the gel-grenades, Sage allowed the Roley to hang from its shoulder sling while he drew the Smith and Wesson .500 Magnum from his hip. Leveling the pistol only centimeters from the merc's left eye, Sage pulled the trigger as his opponent tried to dodge.

The large caliber round tore through the soft tissue and had the same effect as the snipers' sabot rounds, evacuating his combatant's skull. As the Zukimther sagged, Sage grabbed the big merc with his free hand and yanked him toward the edge of the stairs. The stairway railing held for just a moment under the Zukimther's weight, then tore free and dropped the corpse to the floor below.

Sage holstered the Magnum and brought up the Roley again. Two more stories up, the cannons belched flames and death again, filling the hallway with light from the room where they were located. The overlay on Sage's HUD revealed a cluster of soldiers flying backward from the detonations in the bazaar.

Immediately, injuries queued up on his faceshield. He dismissed them because ending the threat would save more lives than dealing with the fallout at the moment. He rushed up the stairs leading to the third floor, getting the most from the suit's augmented strength and speed.

Just as he turned onto the next narrow set of steps, an explosion ripped into the wall where he'd just been. Caught by the concussive wave from the blast, Escobedo slammed back against the wall behind her and dropped under the remnants.

Peering through the smoking haze that remained of the barrier, Sage took a step back, crouched, and spotted the merc who'd targeted the wall. Sage swung his rifle up. Coolly, he put two gel-grenades over the merc's face and dodged back just ahead of the fire that ripped through the space he'd just been.

The gel-grenades went off and knocked the Zukimther backward and down as he grabbed at the explosive, succeeding only in spreading around the combustible material.

Sage moved back to Escobedo, placed a hand on her armor, and read the injury report assessed by her suit's near-AI. There was no immediate threatening damage. "Private?"

"I'm all right, Master Sergeant. Just had the wind knocked out of me."

Gripping her hand, Sage pulled the young soldier to her feet. "Let's go." Trusting her to make her way, he continued up.

On the fourth floor, he whirled out of the stairwell and spotted the two Zukimther guards there. He sprinted toward them and triggered two gel-grenades at the one on the left. The explosives went off an instant before Sage threw himself into a feetfirst slide toward the second merc.

The first merc blew up, dead or heavily concussed, but remained standing unsteadily. The grenades had plastered the Zukimther's lower abdomen and opened traumatic, possibly lethal, wounds.

Recognizing the danger speeding toward him, the second merc brought up his weapons and opened fire. Two of the plasma bursts splashed across Sage's upper body for just an instant, then he drove both of his feet against one Zukimther's left knee. The merc's joint shattered with an audible crack and the splintered bone tore through flesh like a jagged spear.

His forward momentum slowed by the tree-trunk-thick leg he'd collided with, Sage pushed off his opponent's broken limb and rolled to his feet. The Roley came smoothly to Sage's shoulder and he opened fire immediately from less than a meter away. Gel-grenades slapped against the Zukimther's face and covered both his eyes. Without pause, Sage slammed his shoulder into the merc and shoved his opponent back into the room with the cannons.

With the merc blinded and seconds away from death, Sage took cover behind the plascrete wall, shoved his arm up to the grenade launcher loading gate, and pumped in more ammo.

Alert, Master Sergeant, the suit warned. *Gel munitions running low.*

The gel-grenades inside the room detonated and Sage whipped around through the doorway as sections of the plascrete ceiling and wall spattered over him.

Sage continued forward, stepping quickly as the 100mm cannons fired again. "Acknowledged."

The overlay on his faceshield revealed a double-punch along the bazaar's surrounding wall that brought down a large section in a tumble of plascrete chunks. One of the snipers came down with it.

Escobedo opened fire behind him. A quick check in that direction let Sage know Zukimther reinforcements had entered the building after them. He concentrated on the cannons.

Thirty-two meters away, the cannons filled a large section of the floor. The Zukimther mercs had removed most of the walls to make room for the weapons. That left a lot of open space.

Four Zukimther operated each cannon. One sat in an attached seat on one side of each gun and used a cyber-assist helmet to lock in on targets. The other six mercs loaded the big weapons from munitions crates at the back of the room. At the moment, they turned their attention to Sage.

Ignoring the Zukimther, Sage aimed at the base of the cannons. Bolts as thick as his leg ran through the floor to anchor the big weapons. Cracks spread out from the bolts and showed the growing weakness of the floor to handle the recoil of the cannons.

One of the cannons fired and the sliding action compensators negated part of the recoil to ease the brunt of the movement. The merc sitting in the attached seat whipped back with the gun, jerking so hard that Sage didn't know how the operator survived the whiplash.

Triggering the grenade launcher, Sage covered the floor between the big guns with gel explosives. The reservoir emptied quickly on full-auto and left a crooked trail of grenades plastered to the floor.

Plasma bursts and 20mm rounds hammered Sage and drove him back.

Armor is at critical levels. Seek shelter.

The AI's voice remained steady, but the faceshield held a red tint that grew in intensity as Sage took further damage while withdrawing from the room. He whirled and blasted depleted uranium rounds into the two Zukimthers who had engaged Escobedo. She plastered the lead merc and the stairway with gel-grenades.

Sage slapped a magnetized hand against her shoulder, set himself, and yanked her back with him to a gaping hole blown in the wall at some point. "Private. We're leaving now."

He didn't know if the hole was large enough, but there was no other exit point. And the gel-grenades were counting down on his faceshield.

3 . . .

2 . . .

Sage crossed his free arm over his face, dragged Escobedo behind him, and slammed into the opening. He didn't fit. For just a moment, it held against him.

1 . . .

The sudden din of the gel-grenades going off caused his aud filter to muffle all exterior sounds. The only noise that reached him was the conversation of his team, and that was confusing because there were soldiers down, dying, wounded, dazed, and scared.

The blast smashed Sage and Escobedo through the wall like a cork from a champagne bottle. He got a brief glance at the ground four stories below him as it came up fast.

He hit face-first, unable to balance while holding on to Escobedo. She crashed into him almost at the same time and drove him to the ground. His senses swam as he struggled to remain conscious.

THREE

Gazing down on the dead body of his former commanding officer lying in the *lannig* receptacle, Captain Zhoh GhiCemid tried to summon up some sense of loss. The effort wasn't working and that left him dissatisfied. He had to sell himself to the Phrenorian Prime War Board in only *engits*.

During that interview, in addition to thinking that he felt his commanding officer's loss, he had to convince them to believe he was capable of handling the situation on Makaum and that the situation on the planet was growing more dire.

In fact, the state of affairs on Makaum truly was getting more dangerous to the Empire's goals. And to Zhoh's own. He needed the War Board to believe part of the reason he wanted to assume command of the Makaum forces was to avenge his fallen general.

If his personal stock had been in better shape, Zhoh could have gotten by with merely wanting the now-vacant position to improve his standing among the warriors. Once not so long ago, he had been a respected and higher-ranking officer, a colonel about to make brigadier general.

Now he was a captain and was *kalque*, one without a future in the Phrenorian Empire. He had endured the designation for the last two months. Now he was in position to reverse his bad fortune.

There was no loss in Zhoh's heart over General Rangha's death. From the beginning, even before he had met the general, he had despised Rangha. Zhoh was the one who had put the general in his crypt. If he had been true to his own wishes, Zhoh would have taken credit for the assassination and allowed others to learn of the general's lack of honor in becoming a black market munitions supplier.

Better still, Zhoh would have challenged Rangha over the matter when it had come to his attention. He would have issued *Hutamah*, a personal call to combat for honor, and killed him with a *patimong* instead of the Kimer pistol he'd wielded only a few nights ago. Then he could have eaten the general and excreted the weakling's remains on the nearest dung hill.

General Rangha HatVeru lay in state in waters from their homeworld. Normally those waters would offer comfort during *lannig*, the times when a Phrenorian molted and split his exoskeleton as he outgrew it. Females molted as well, but their growth was not so aggressive or often because they served primarily in support positions in the Phrenorian civilization. In the military they functioned to keep warriors equipped and healthy, and they had skills as science officers. They also served in security positions on base. Other than that, they bore the young, at home and on the battle-field, to further the Empire's future.

With his primary appendages wrapped over his thorax, and both sets of secondary appendages wrapped as well, Rangha's body didn't show the wounds where projectiles had ripped under the hard surface of his exoskeleton and killed him. His lesser hands lay curled into balls like wilted blossoms, the thumb and three fingers tight against each other. His *chelicerae* lay curled peacefully against his face, as if he was only sleeping.

Rage quivered through Zhoh. The general deserved no peace even in death. Zhoh wished he could have desecrated the corpse and provided no place for his remains to rest.

Zhoh leaned over his primaries, rested the huge claws at the end of his largest set of arms on the container, and stared with disgust at the general's body. He re-gretted killing Rangha, only because the being's death had come too quickly. And he had accomplished it in a fashion that lacked honor because Rangha was *Laliwu*, of a preferred bloodline. With that designation, Zhoh would never have been able to even openly mock the man, let alone deliver physical harm. Rangha had been protected from lesser castes.

Normally Phrenorians prided themselves on the purity of their exoskeletal colors. Blue and purple were most desirable. Those who wore those hues received special dispensation for that feat alone so that Phrenorians could breed true.

But being of *Laliwu* heritage meant that the family bloodline was secure because an ancestor had fought bravely in some great battle. Rangha's ancestor had lived over four hundred years ago, had made a great name for himself in battle, had eaten the flesh of his enemies, and collected their skulls.

Rangha only had to breathe to maintain that privilege his ancestor had provided.

The Terrans, even the greenest soldier among them, had more right to respect than the dead thing that lay before Zhoh.

"*Triarr*, it is almost time."

Drawn by the announcement, Zhoh straightened and looked at Mato Orayva standing only a couple meters away. Bound by blood, they had been friends and allies since before they had first taken up arms in defense of the Empire. Their mothers had been sisters, which was why Mato was allowed to address Zhoh as *triarr*— "family of my family."

Mato's father was Raltu Eytuk, a warrior known for his bravery and for his coveted purple hue. Mato's coloration reflected that of his sire. He stood tall and ready in his armor and weapons, a perfect Phrenorian warrior in his glory.

Zhoh glanced at the others in the communications room. "I am ready."

Computers lined the walls and left open the holo space at one end of the room. A nascent fog covered a vague, intangible doorway that signaled the entrance to the holo. Rangha's honor guard stood at one end of the room to watch over their fallen commander's remains. Zhoh faulted them for their inefficiency—they hadn't been there when he'd slain Rangha after all—and for the waste they continued to be by guarding the general's body. A war waited to be waged and won, as well as glory and wealth and power.

The communications officer glanced over to Zhoh

from his seat at the holo controls. "Captain. When you are ready."

Zhoh nodded. "Execute transmission."

The lieutenant turned his attention to his computer and his secondary hands flew over the keyboards. Zhoh didn't understand much of the way the interstellar communicator worked, but he knew the connection made through wormwave technology in a manner similar to the Terran Alliance's Oakfield Gates.

A spot of white light came to life in the center of the nascent fog, then it spread outward to form a disk large enough to encompass Zhoh. He ran his lesser hands over his thorax armor and his weapons, and briefly touched the Kimer pistol at his hip and the *patimong* sheathed down his back. He clacked his primaries, irritated that his unease had grown, and stepped into the fog.

27619 Akej (Phrenorian Prime)

Zhoh experienced only a moment of disorientation before striding into the War Board Command Center. He wasn't really there, of course. He was still at the Phrenorian base on Makaum. But he had been in the command center before and the holo's replication was faultless.

Thick slabs of orange-red *daravgane* stood out on the floor, reproducing the symbols for courage and skill and cruelty to enemies. Harvested at great risk from the primordial creatures that lived in the deepest parts of the Phrenorian seas, the resin symbolized the strength and conviction of the Phrenorian warriors.

Zhoh stood in the center of the floor. Across from him, seven members of the *Seraugh*, the commanders of the military, sat on tall *daravgane* seats. The warriors wore full armor and carried a mix of traditional weapons—*patimongs* carved from *daravgane* and tempered by fire and acid, beam weapons, and slug-throwers. Ceremonial capes so darkly purple they were almost black hung from their broad shoulders to the floor. Their *chelicerae* twitched only a little as they focused their gazes on him.

None of them wanted him there, but he had a right to make his claim known. Even as a *kalque*. The thought lay bitter in Zhoh's mind and he pushed it away. Unless dealt with, the memory would only scar over, though, and remain festering as it had been doing.

"Greetings, my commanders." Zhoh clasped his primaries behind him and kept his tail still. "May your strength always prevail, your appetites for the flesh of your enemies always gnaw at your stomachs, and you continue to add skulls of the vanquished to your war chests."

Although the *Seraugh* had no leader and all members sat as equals, Belnale was currently the most senior among the group. "Captain Zhoh, you are punctual."

He was large and broad, covered in a latticework of scars. His left primary had been lost in battle and now a black cybernetic limb replaced it. He kept the artificial arm wrapped in the folds of his cloak. He was sensitive about the loss.

Every Phrenorian who had lost something of himself in battle reacted the same way. Belnale's face hung slightly askew as well. A grenade nearly destroyed his mouth in combat and surgeons had barely managed to return its function to him.

The observation of his punctuality was not lost on Zhoh. Of course he could not be late. That would have been inexcusable. But neither had he waited like a dim-minded *etsayash* in a cybernetic queue to be brought onto the floor at their leisure.

Most of the warriors on the War Board didn't care for Zhoh and the captain was acutely aware of their displeasure. He had raised himself up in their gloried ranks through his own strength and bravery as he was supposed to, but the unacceptable nature of his offspring had pushed him out of favor and gotten him assigned to Makaum. That posting, especially under Rangha and since he hadn't had the decency to die in battle, should have been the end of his career.

Only the war against the Terran military had slid that direction, and the resources on Makaum would be key to the continued struggle in just a short time. A chance lay with the planet for Zhoh to regain all that he had lost and he was not going to miss that.

"Events on Makaum are fluid at the moment, as I'm sure you are all aware." Zhoh kept his voice well-modulated, choosing to show confidence instead of polite loyalty. If he was to regain everything he had lost in the Empire, he had no choice other than to be a warrior in all things. He would not curry favor. He would insist on respect. "There are many things there that require my attention."

"Then you should devote your energies to those things," Belnale stated.

"If I did, I would be remiss in my duties."

"How so?"

The question was asked, but Zhoh knew they were aware of why he wanted this meeting. Their prejudice against him reduced him to asking for their consideration. Instead, they should have been pursuing him. "With General Rangha gone, the troops on Makaum need firm guidance."

"There is a command structure in place on that planet."

Zhoh spoke a little more fiercely now. "At best, it is only nearly good enough. If you would hold Makaum, you need to put the right warrior into power."

Belnale shifted on his seat. His spiked tail coiled around his left leg. His face remained implacable, but the stink of angry pheromones radiating from most of the members on the board filled the air. On the end, the youngest warrior, Ashvor, raised his deep red *daravgane braest* and would have protested Zhoh's summation if Belnale had not looked at him. The spear's three blades gleamed as they caught the light.

Ashvor was older and larger than Zhoh, deeply purple and blue. Burn scarring showed on the right side of his mouth. Only gray stumps of his *chelicerae* remained there. He was skilled in personal combat, but Zhoh was certain he could kill the warrior if a personal challenge was offered. If that was what it took to reclaim his path.

"Careful, Captain Zhoh," Belnale rumbled. "You don't want to risk offending any warrior present. We all choose who commands on Makaum."

Zhoh looked at them, not backing down. "No, I would never insult any of you great warriors. But I realize that losing our presence on Makaum would be the greater insult. To me and to you and to the Empire. We need this planet and its resources to continue the war with the Terrans."

They should realize that too, but he was going to remind them of the stakes.

"You requested an audience of us. Why?" Belnale asked as though not everyone in the command center already knew.

Despite his personal control, Zhoh knew pheromones leaked from him that betrayed his uncertainty about their decision. "I have come to stake my claim for command of the Phrenorian forces on Makaum."

The board could easily refuse his request. Those abominations Sxia had borne him instead of healthy offspring had cast a permanent stain over him. The efforts of her father, Blaold Oldawe, to blame him and push any doubts from his daughter and bloodline had further torn away what honor had remained to him.

Belnale's tail twitched in predatory anticipation. The spiked tip glistened blackly. It was obvious he looked forward to the coming events. "Colonel Echcha Ler'eti has seniority over you, as do the two other colonels on Phrenoria. Three warriors currently onplanet outrank you."

Knowing he had staked his life on his brazen claim, Zhoh raised his voice, making his words stronger. "I am the better officer. I have had more combat experience than any of those warriors. You need someone who can hold this world and improve our command of it. I am that warrior."

He wanted to tell them that choosing Echcha over him would be a mistake, but he could not insinuate that they did not know what they were doing. Bruising their honor during this encounter was possible and permissible, but he could not directly challenge their ruling.

"Colonel Echcha believes that he can do the same. We talked to him only a short time ago."

"Colonel Echcha means well, but he lacks the experience to make this operation a success. He is mistaken about his own abilities."

"General Belnale," a deep voice roared, "I demand satisfaction. I want to face this *kalque* who has disrespected me."

Zhoh recognized Echcha's voice and was not surprised the War Board had allowed the colonel to listen in. Belnale, at least, had known what Zhoh would request,

and the old warrior had set events into play so that everything could be dealt with at once.

Belnale raised a hand.

Immediately, Echcha's holo formed in the room as
well. He stood only a few meters away. He was taller
than Zhoh, more massive, filled out with corded muscle.
His color was primarily purple, but there were pools of
blue and green as well. His position guaranteed him the
privilege and power that his color did not.

With a sudden shift, Echcha lashed at Zhoh with his
tail and his *patimong*, driving the points of both into
Zhoh's face. Zhoh didn't move. The weapon and the
tail dug into his replicated image but didn't touch him.

Cursing, Echcha pulled away and sheathed his
weapon. His tail coiled restlessly behind him. His anticipation of causing Zhoh to flinch backfired on him.

Echcha glared at Zhoh, and his pheromones, even
through the holo, carried the scent of angry disgust. "I
claim *Hutamah*. This diseased *selydy* would be better
cleaning dung heaps than he would be at pretending to
be a warrior."

Zhoh almost reached for the *patimong* but stopped
himself at the last moment. Echcha was back at the
base, in another area. He wasn't in that room.

Zhoh kept his voice soft and level. "I would ask that
Colonel Echcha's request be allowed."

He was surprised at Echcha's instant demand for
personal combat, but it would settle things once and
for all for the command on Makaum. Provided Zhoh
lived.

Echcha's *chelcirae* flexed, springing out and collaps-
ing like they were practicing ripping into Zhoh's face.
"Have you grown embarrassed of living?"

Zhoh fixed his gaze on Echcha. "I have grown tired

of lingering in the shadows through no fault of my own. I will have my future and my respect back."

"You will find yourself resting upon a dung heap shortly."

Zhoh ignored the threat. "I would also ask that Lieutenant Colonels Nalit Ch'achsam and Warar Tindard serve as Colonel Echcha's seconds in the *Hutamah*. That way all possible resistance to me taking command of the army on Makaum will be dealt with at once. One after the other if need be."

Belnale hesitated, and Zhoh wondered why, but Ashvor spoke into the silence. "I agree with the *kalque*. Let Colonel Echcha have his *Hutamah*, and let Warar and Nalit serve as his seconds if they so choose." He shifted on his seat and took a fresh grip on his trident.

Two of the other warriors agreed with Ashvor, then a third. A majority had already formed. The remaining two warriors added their votes as well.

Belnale sat back in his seat and one of his lesser hands played over the hilt of his *patimong*. "It will be as you wish, Colonel Echcha, but it will be done quickly. You have one *taimor* to arrange combat. We will view the *Hutamah*."

Echcha clacked his primaries as he looked at the *Seraugh*. "I look forward to ridding you of this embarrassment to the Empire, then to serving you longer as your general in delivering this bountiful world to you." Then he faded from the holo.

Ashvor looked at Zhoh. "No brave words, *kalque*?"

Zhoh swept his gaze over the assembly. "No. With your leave, I will rejoin you shortly to accept my command." He stepped backward. "Then we will all feast well on our enemies."

28003 Akej (Phrenorian Prime)

When Zhoh blinked, he was back at the base on
Makaum. Emotions shifted restlessly inside him and
anticipation rose to the top, followed swiftly by fear,
and then anticipation again in an endless cycle. He
calmed himself, but he could think of little besides the
coming confrontation. He had not expected things to
happen so quickly, nor to gravitate to all or nothing
stakes.

Then again, that was the only way his true future
could be forged.

Mato watched Zhoh. "*Triarr.* I would serve as your
second during the *Hutamah.*"

Zhoh glanced around the communications center.
None of the warriors there would stand as his second.
Not even his bonded warriors in the Brown Spyrl would
risk themselves as Mato was going to. "Of course. I
would have no other."

A second in the *Hutamah* was there to administer a
killing blow to prevent suffering, but the second could
also be killed if the opposing victor so chose to take
further satisfaction in his victory.

Mato's confidence was infectious. "We will triumph.
This moment is *lannig.*"

"And *lannig* changes everything," Zhoh finished. "I
could end up facing all three of them."

"Then it would be best to kill Echcha and the next
two swiftly, *triarr.* We have a war to win here."

FOUR

The thunder of battle and screams of the wounded and dying clamoring inside his skull, Sage tried to sit up only to have a strong hand press against his chest and shove him back down. He reached for the hand, searching for a hold that would allow him to break the fingers or the arm attached to the hand. Then his vision clicked in and he saw Captain Karl Gilbride standing over him in blue surgical scrubs.

The medical officer smiled, but his hand was firm. "Easy, Master Sergeant. You're among friends."

Gilbride tended to be obstinate and autonomous. In his early forties, he was only a little older than Sage. A surgical cap covered most of the captain's brown hair. His gray eyes were attentive and bloodshot. Perspiration threaded through the stubble darkening his cheeks. A surgical mask lay crumpled around his neck and hung from the elastic bands. Blood stained his scrubs.

Ignoring his heart hammering inside his chest and the suddenly awakened pains and aches that laced his body, Sage relaxed a little. He winced as he shifted because familiar pain threaded through his body and let him know a swarm of nanobots were within him repairing damaged tissue.

Gilbride took his PAD from the thigh pocket of his scrub pants and tapped the unit to life. He scrolled through the information contained on the screen with quick, practiced flicks. "You're going to need some more pain meds while the repair work is being done. And you're going to need bed rest."

"I'm fine." Sage tried to focus, but his thoughts still swam elusively. He remembered the action at the bazaar in a crazy quilt of images and sound bites that didn't quite jibe as a continuous thread. They'd shut the Zukimther mercs down, confiscated the munitions they'd been selling, and even took the 100mm cannons into custody. He received that information on-site when he'd carried Escobedo to the medics.

They'd achieved the mission's objective, but the cost had been high. A third of the team had died, and another third was somewhere here in the fort's medical wing. He didn't know how many of them were critical. Instinctively, he tried to pull up the information but realized when he got no response that he wasn't wearing the AKTIVsuit.

"You say you're fine," Gilbride said agreeably, "but that's not what your body is telling me." He made a couple final taps on his PAD. "I listen to your body, Master Sergeant. And to the nanobots. They never lie to me."

"I've got things to do."

"Those things are getting done by people perfectly capable of getting them done without you. For the moment, Colonel Halladay's orders are for you to rest, so you're going to rest. You've been running on empty since the festival, not sleeping, not eating, and not taking care of yourself. You've burned through a lot of energy. Now you're going to pay it back."

Stubbornly, Sage grabbed the bed rails and tried to pull himself up. The assassination at the festival had caught them unawares. He'd been trying to climb from behind the eight ball since then and get ahead of the curve. Makaum was in the throes of social unrest fed by fear of the Phrenorian War igniting around them. There were too many things to do. He still didn't know everything that had happened at the festival. The assassin that had killed Wosesa Staumar and General Rangha was still in the wind. The Makaum people were split down the middle as to whether to trust the Terrans or the Phrenorians.

Sage heaved himself up to a sitting position only to find out his legs were strapped down. His head spun and his vision blurred as he reached for the strap releases. "I can't stay here. I've got to get moving."

Gilbride shook his head and smiled agreeably. "You're not doing anything for the next few hours, Master Sergeant. Those are the colonel's orders, and he outranks us both. Good night." He gave the PAD a final tap.

The collar around Sage's neck pulsed and he grabbed for it too late. Meds swam through his veins. A warm lassitude swelled inside his head and strength left his arms. Feeling betrayed, he fell back onto the bed and blackness enveloped him.

The nightmares came then, slamming into him furiously. One moment he was on Makaum fighting the drug traffickers in the jungle and the Makaum terrorists in the red light district, then he was on Nogdria 7 trying to get the local populace to safety from invading Phrenorian kill squads after the (ta)Klar had undermined Terran efforts to shore up the defenses. He'd lost his legs there and spent three months regrowing them. After that, Command assigned him to Terra to run boot camps and turn out cannon fodder for six years.

Finally he'd created enough problems trying to return to the war that Command had seen fit to put him on Makaum. The planet had been an out of the way place, and they'd intended for Sage to disappear into the Green Hell.

Now the war was coming for Makaum. The Phrenorians had their secret base out in the jungle. A stockpile of weapons and war vehicles could be inside—*were* inside, Sage felt certain, though he still couldn't prove that. Learning what was in that base remained a priority.

He felt a twinge of guilt about his desire to get back into the war, thinking that maybe somehow his aspiration to do so had acted like a lightning rod and pulled the war to the planet, had brought death to so many people. The rational part of him knew that wasn't true, but that part of him wasn't in control at the moment. Now, he was prey for his fears.

The meds kicked him down deeper and took him back. Before he'd gone to space to fight Phrenorians, he'd grown up in Sombra de la Montaña. The Shadow of the Mountain. It had been one of those small Colombian villages on the outskirts of Bogotá where the United States military had battled the narco-barons. Space travel had been new then, but the drug trade had still been deadly because the future never gave way easily to the past. In so many ways, Makaum resembled that village and became a lodestone for Sage's memories.

In the nightmare, eight-year-old Frank Nolan Sage ran for his life as helicopters peppered the mountainside with machine gun fire and rockets. Explosive rounds opened up craters around him and ripped trees out by their roots. He screamed for his mother. His father was somewhere out in the jungle fighting with his military unit against the narco-troops.

Rounding a tree, Sage spotted a savage figure lunging for him, then he felt a strong, chitinous claw suddenly close around his neck before he could get away. His forward momentum came to an immediate halt as his feet left the ground. He gripped the pincers and tried to pry them loose, but it was no use. The Phrenorian held him and he dangled helplessly.

The alien's six black facial eyes stared down at him with bestial intelligence. For all the armament it wore, this Phrenorian was stripped of intellect down to pure lethal intent, a predator on par with the jaguars and anacondas that hunted in the South American jungles. The alien opened its mouth and the *chelicerae* wiggled like tentacles as they flared wide as well.

The Phrenorian ducked his head forward and the *chelicerae* bit into Sage's face. One of them punctured his left eye. Poison flooded his features and set them on fire.

Sage yelled, and the meds took him more deeply into the black so the nightmares could no longer reach him.

FIVE

Jahup walked along the street with the Roley at the ready, cradled across his body as he'd been taught, which wasn't much different than how he'd trained to hunt in the jungle. Since there was no tree canopy, the sky was bigger in the sprawl, but the density of potential predators was much greater.

The Terran AKTIVsuit drew a lot of attention from nearby people and marked him as an outsider and unwanted. Martial law had been declared in the sprawl and sanctioned by the Quass after the killings during the Festival of the Beginning, and most offplanet businesses weren't happy about the restricted hours.

Neither were most of the Makaum people who liked socializing at night. Emerging from the jungle to set up a civilization after the generation starship had crashed onplanet had been a necessity, but now it was a freedom they wanted to keep. They didn't understand that massing at night, when nocturnal predators could kill from the shadows, was dangerous.

His grandmother had been one of the first to sign the martial law measure into the few guidelines the community had. Many of the people argued against the Quass—and his grandmother—showing such a heavy hand. So their dislike for him came from both sides: the military and the fact that he was the Quass's grandson.

The hateful looks didn't bother Jahup much. Makaum was no longer safe and he knew he was doing what he could to protect his friends and neighbors. His presence there in the AKTIVsuit was a grim reminder of that. Many of his people hated the Terran military, and a lot of the offworlders didn't want any kind of police or military control around their businesses.

He was glad the faceshield disguised him. Most of the Makaum people along the street and in the offworlder bars knew him. It was one thing to be reviled, but it was another for the attacks to become personal.

Before he'd agreed to fight with the Terran military, he'd belonged to one of the hunter bands. He'd helped feed his people by going out into the jungle and bringing back meat. He hadn't exactly been a hero to them then, but they had respected what he was doing. Out there, people knew he was risking his life to bring them what they needed. Serving the Terran military didn't translate quite so neatly.

All of the Makaum had valued him as a hunter. Now some of those same people who had gifted him with food and craft items after hunts looked away from him as he passed. They thought of him with the same dislike they reserved for the Terran soldiers. To them, he was an oppressor, a living symbol of all the freedom they had lost.

The judgment wasn't fair. Those people blamed the Terran military for their problems when they'd actually given away their innocence and autonomy so willingly in the early days after planetfall. People had helped the offworlders rip away chunks of the jungle to plop down shops, manufacturing plants, and bars that lined either side of the cracked plascrete streets that had been quickly laid to support those endeavors. The Terran military had arrived later.

Cracks pitted the plascrete in several places, and in many of them tree roots had pushed through the buckled surface. Someone had sprayed defoliant on the new growth recently and the orange foam glistened wetly in the morning sunlight.

"You're being awfully quiet."

Startled, Jahup almost turned his gaze from the street, then remembered the 360-degree view afforded by the faceshield. The suit's tech had taken some getting used to, and some habits were proving hard to break. Like looking to the side to see his patrol partner.

Jahup hoped Tanest would leave him with his thoughts, but he knew that was too much to ask for. She reminded him of his little sister, Telilu, because of her prying and tendency to natter on about anything that caught her eye. "I'm just thinking."

Tanest was curious about things. That trait had made her a good hunter, but not always a good friend. And sometimes even as a hunter she had a tendency to poke a *cudide's* nest, arousing the stinging, finger-long insects to battle just to see what would happen.

She was a couple years older than Jahup, but he was half a head taller and broader. She was slender and agile, and easy to look at. Her dark hair, only showing a light green cast to it, fell past her shoulders and framed an oval face with a slightly turned-up nose.

After Jahup had joined the Terran military, Tanest had quickly followed, but it was her own curiosity about the offworlders and their tech that had pulled her in. She wore a *kifrik*, with all eight legs on display, on her Velcro shoulder flashing.

Three years ago, she'd been bitten by a young *kifrik* and the concentrated poison had almost killed her. Once she'd recovered, the wound had healed slowly and left behind a slightly raised web of scarring on her right forearm. Instead of being upset about the ravaged flesh, she'd had the scar tattooed, showing it in bolder relief rather than trying to hide it.

Jahup had liked that. Scars were acceptable things for hunters.

"Thinking about what?" Tanest asked.

Jahup considered pulling rank on her and ending the questioning. He'd been made a corporal only a week before, after his action during the festival and because of his scouting ability and knowledge of the jungle. Tanest remained a private.

Using authority on Tanest wouldn't work, though. She'd find some way to circumvent it. She was crafty like that.

"I'm thinking about last night." Jahup had taken part in the attack on the Zukimther mercenaries. Images of the wounded and dying soldiers, some of them people he'd grown up with, haunted his thoughts.

He felt dead on his feet now, propped up only by the low-level stims his suit insisted on providing. As a result, he felt like he was vibrating inside. If he could have remained in his barracks, or returned to his grandmother's house, he would have done that instead of going on patrol, but manpower was thin.

Colonel Halladay had wanted boots on the ground in case anyone wanted to strike back after what had

happened with the Zukimther. That action had shut
down a lot of avenues for gunrunners on Makaum for a
while, but someone would rise to take their place.

The Makaum people had understood the law of
supply and demand long before the offworlders came
with their drugs and tech.

His grandmother's home would have been Jahup's
choice for resting. He'd grown up there after his parents
had died and he still had a room there. He'd always felt
safest under that roof.

"Last night is over." Tanest's tone was firm. "That's
one of the first rules of being a hunter and you know
that. You don't worry over missed shots. You don't
worry over close calls. You learn from them, figure out
what you did wrong, and study that so you don't make
the same mistakes."

Jahup magnified his view and pulled in the image
of the technology shop to his left across the street.
He wasn't much of a game player. Even before becoming part of the Terran military, he hadn't had
much time to play. But he'd heard good things about
some of the VR software, and he'd watched soldiers
playing in the common areas. "Master Sergeant Sage
didn't make a mistake."

"Did I *say* the sergeant made a mistake?"

It took Jahup a moment to realize that she hadn't said
that. The question had restlessly circulated through his
own mind. Three soldiers who had died last night had
worn the *ypheynte* image on their armor. None of them
had been much older than he was. They were friends
that he wouldn't be getting back, and there were more
yet to lose. Sometimes an occasional hunter was lost,
but never in groups.

He didn't know why the deaths bothered him so
much. He'd lost people out in the jungles, hunters he'd

been training, and older hunters who should have stayed out of the wilderness because their time had passed. Nothing on Makaum had been easy. Nearly everything killed to eat, and all of them were proficient at stalking prey.

But making meat, feeding the populace, that was a clear-cut goal that was attainable. Fighting against the encroaching black marketers, especially when people wanted what they had to sell, seemed . . . unwinnable.

"Well, did I?" Tanest asked. She sounded irritated.

"No," he conceded. "You didn't say that. I'm just tired."

"Oh? I figured maybe you were thinking about Noojin."

That was a sore point and Jahup was certain Tanest knew it and had mentioned Noojin just to needle him. Even before the assassinations during the Festival of the Beginning, Noojin had decided to give up her position in the Terran military. He still didn't understand that. Moreover, she'd seemed disappointed he hadn't quit the military with her. It was the first time they hadn't been on the same side of a problem facing them.

"Why would I be thinking of her?" Jahup asked.

"Because usually she watches your back when you're in a dangerous situation. And now it's dangerous and she's not here."

"We have our own paths to follow."

"Not until lately. You two have been like two *iani* in a husk. Always together."

"Not true." Jahup said that, but he knew that Tanest was speaking nothing but the truth. Noojin had been his constant companion. Both of them had lost their parents and had been mentored by Quass Leghef. He and Noojin had been close. He hadn't known how truly close until she was gone from him.

Since the festival night, he had only seen her twice and talked to her not at all. He told himself that her absence didn't matter, that he was as fully capable of being without her as she was being without him. He preferred to walk his own path, and actually had. She had chosen to join him.

"So you two aren't together anymore?" Tanest asked.

Suddenly, Jahup knew what the young woman was truly hinting at. Under the faceshield, his face burned, and he was glad Tanest couldn't see him. "We were never *together*. Not like that."

She adjusted her armor, making him even more aware of those curves the AKTIVsuit partially hid. "Good. Maybe I can talk you into a drink after we get off patrol."

Feeling irritated and confused, and maybe a little attracted to the idea of spending time with Tanest, Jahup tried to figure out what to say. Before the offworlders arrived, there had been few places to socialize other than homes. Everything young people did together was more or less chaperoned because children needed structure in their community. Resources remained scarce. And there hadn't been a lot of free time.

Things had changed.

He and Noojin had gone to a couple of the clubs. That was where he'd first seen Master Sergeant Sage in action. Sage had brought in the corpse of a dead bash-hound and laid it at the feet of one of the corp execs, and accused DawnStar of setting up drug labs in the jungle.

Jahup's anger and confusion about Noojin swirled inside him, and he thought maybe it wouldn't be so bad to have that drink with Tanest. She was attractive. A lot of the other males his age—and older, judging from the stares of the offworlders—would have loved to have a drink with her. Many of the soldiers at Fort York had tried to spend time with her.

He turned to her, thinking maybe he'd be a little coy, not too quick to agree to drinks. Then his faceshield pinged red.

Alert! Hostile weapon detected!

Vector lines led Jahup's line of sight to the bearded man raising a Rudra Tech plasma burster from behind his leg 17.4 meters away. Judging by the spidersilk clothing and the slightly green tint to his coloring, the man was a local, not an offworlder, and for a split second the feeling of betrayal hit Jahup more than fear.

The small, blocky pistol filled the man's hand as he pointed the blunt muzzle at Jahup. The sidearm was an illegal civilian weapon on Makaum because it was so powerful. The plasma burster was capable of burning through the AKTIVsuit with a direct hit.

Already moving away from the threat, Jahup twisted, threw an arm around Tanest, and headed both of them into a narrow alley filled with shallow pools from the morning's rain.

"Get down!" Jahup yelled. "Get—"

In the 360-degree view, the plasma fireball from the weapon's barrel spread into a meter-wide conflagration and grew larger as it streaked for him. The immense heat soaked through the armor and nearby bushes and fingerling saplings that had reached through the broken plascrete caught on fire. The leaves and branches turned to gray ash immediately.

Then the fireball struck Jahup between the shoulder blades and lifted him from his feet as a wave of intense heat seared his senses.

SIX

"Μay I offer you a warm-up, Staff Sergeant?"

Caught off guard, Kjersti Kiwanuka glanced up at the private standing a short distance away.

The young man held a coffeepot in one hand. He looked tired and Kiwanuka had at first believed the hollow look in his eyes was from fatigue. Then she noticed the synth-skin that covered much of the private's left hand. Memory kicked in and she recalled that he was on the disabled list from prior action against a biopiracy group.

Kiwanuka scooted her cup toward the table's edge. "Sure. Thank you, Private."

He poured. "My pleasure. Can I get you anything else?"

"No, I'm fine. Thank you."

He hesitated for a moment and she knew it was because they hadn't met. She knew she was striking-looking and had no false modesty about it because soldiers of both sexes had hit on her a lot in the clubs. Her platinum blond hair and smooth dark brown skin guaranteed attention.

Her father was a diplomatic attaché in Uganda, and some whispered he might be the next president once the man currently in office stepped down. Or was assassinated. Things in that country had always been restless.

The hair color came from her mother, who was Norwegian and had been a medical doctor. She and Kiwanuka's father had met while she was on a relief mission. Both of them were intellectuals and liked having power. Neither of them understood their daughter.

When she'd enlisted in the Terran military, Kiwanuka had drawn the ire of both parents. She hadn't cared. She'd had to get away, and offplanet with the military had seemed to be the best way to go because she was able to leave on her own terms.

"Was there anything else you need, Private?" she asked. She picked up the cup with her bionic hand.

After getting wounded during an ambush her team had been led into by an incompetent lieutenant, she'd lost her right arm and some friends. The lieutenant had lost the face he'd been born with when she'd attacked him for his carelessness. Lieutenant Swarton was out there serving somewhere in the war while she'd cooled her heels on Makaum as a disciplinary action. She was lucky she hadn't received a quick exit from the military with a section eight classification.

"No, Staff Sergeant." Looking a little self-conscious, he wandered away to take care of other soldiers at breakfast.

Seated at the table she'd commandeered for herself, Kiwanuka struggled to stay awake and find the right words for the reports she was working on. Colonel

Halladay had stressed the importance of getting them exactly right.

"Colonel Halladay," someone barked. "Good morning, sir."

Surprised, Kiwanuka slid out of the chair, stood by the table, and saluted the colonel. She hadn't ever seen him in the enlisted mess. Officers never came here because they had their own cafeteria. Slipping her cover from a thigh pocket, she pulled the hat into place even though she wasn't required to wear it inside a post building. Her hair hung in disarray from the shower she'd had earlier. Maybe the private had been looking at that.

Colonel Nathan Halladay wore an AKTIVsuit. All soldiers did now because the fort stayed on Orange Alert, ready for hostile aggression. His helmet hung at his hip, but he wore a military cover over his neatly clipped brown hair where strands of gray were starting to show. Clean-shaven and meticulous, Halladay looked more like a schoolteacher or a salesman than a battle-hardened soldier.

Mentally, Kiwanuka backed off on the harsh view. Halladay hadn't seen much action because he'd served General Howard Whitcomb as a lieutenant and had risen through the ranks under the older officer. Scuttle-butt had it that Halladay was somebody's golden boy and had been given the cushy assignment as the general's aide. Kiwanuka didn't think there was any truth to that, but she didn't know what the true score was.

"At ease, people," Halladay said without breaking stride as he made for Kiwanuka. He stopped in front of her and returned her salute. "At ease, Staff Sergeant."

"Yes sir." Kiwanuka automatically fell into parade rest and didn't know what to do next. Sage seemed to be at ease with officers, but that wasn't in her wheel-house. She'd grown up in her mother and father's world

of privilege, and those in power were always acknowledged.

Halladay motioned to the table. "Sit."

She did, and to her surprise and consternation, he
joined her there.

She stared at him.

"Is something wrong, Staff Sergeant?"

"No, sir. You're . . . sitting there."

"I am."

She'd prepared for a full-on Phrenorian assault, a ter-
rorist attack, and even for soldiers with inane questions
about field orders for today. But she wasn't ready for an
officer to sit at breakfast with her. She knew the other
enlisted were staring. "Well, I wasn't prepared for you
to be sitting there, sir."

Halladay's green eyes twinkled a little. "I understand,
Staff Sergeant. I didn't mean to make you uncomfortable."

"I'm not uncomfortable, sir."

"I can see that by how relaxed you are."

Kiwanuka suspected he was being a little facetious,
and maybe having a little fun at her expense. "Perhaps
I'm a little caught off guard, sir. And I'm wondering
what you're doing here."

Halladay gestured to her PAD. "I came for that report."

"I'm sorry, sir. I thought I had another"—Kiwanuka
checked the time by accessing her suit's hologram HUD
that supplemented the helmet—"forty-three minutes."

And she did have those forty-three minutes according to her last communication with him. If something
had changed, she'd received no notification.

"You don't. I need the report now. Please."

Kiwanuka wanted to protest. She was used to being
perfect, to being on time and completely correct in all
her assigned tasks. Writing after-action reports wasn't
one of her best abilities. "The draft's still rough, sir."

"Bring it up for me."

Picking up her PAD, Kiwanuka opened the report and handed it over to Halladay. He scanned it quickly.

Halladay handed the PAD back to her and lifted his own PAD. "Staff Sergeant, this is a little rough, but it's fine. Send a copy to my device manually. I don't want this on the Net."

That surprised Kiwanuka because news of last night's takedown had spread all over the fort.

"Sir, I'm sure with a little more work I can improve on what's here."

"I appreciate your diligence, but I need it now, Staff Sergeant."

Kiwanuka's anger flared up then, and she suddenly felt like she was in front of her father. He'd always been demanding and unrelenting. In his eyes, she'd always been found wanting.

Trying not to sound irate, Kiwanuka pushed her PAD against the colonel's, and tapped the screen to send the file to the colonel's device. "Of course, sir."

"Thank you, Staff Sergeant." Halladay sat there and didn't leave.

"Was there something else, sir?"

"I'm taking a moment."

"Of course, sir."

"I'm going to need you to help me."

"I'll be happy to, sir." Kiwanuka hated making that blanket statement because it could be false, and after pressuring her as he had, he didn't deserve a favor. Taking on the Zukimther mercs had been fine. She'd known what to expect. Dealing with Halladay on a personal issue was an unknown.

"I'm about to go ambush the general," Halladay confided, "and I don't know how that's going to go."

Questions bubbled up inside Kiwanuka, but she

knew she couldn't ask them because it wasn't her place.

"I'm going to recommend—*vigorously*—that we send for reinforcements. I don't see how that's going to be a successful argument, but I have to do it."

Kiwanuka didn't know how it would be fruitful either. General Whitcomb had pretty much maintained a hands-off policy toward the planet since he'd been assigned there. He was just clocking out his final months shepherding Fort York, looking for an easy end to a career.

"So if I come back here in a less-than-optimum mood," Halladay said, "I want you to understand."

"Me, sir?" The question was out of Kiwanuka's mouth before she could stop it.

"Yes. Either way this ambush goes, I'm going to need you to help me with damage control among the troops."

"Yes sir," Kiwanuka answered, but she was wondering what was going on. Halladay and Sage had gotten tight over the last few weeks. She had operated on the periphery of things.

"Because you're going to be in the middle of whatever situation results."

Kiwanuka had no intention of stepping into a conflagration like a war between a general and his XO. Executive officers could weather a storm like that. A staff sergeant couldn't. She was already on thin ice from bashing her lieutenant when she'd lost her arm in combat. She didn't want to lose the military and had no idea of what she would do if she did. "*Me*, sir? I don't want to rock the boat, sir."

Halladay frowned. "I'm going to rock the boat. I'm just afraid some of the fallout is going to land on you."

"Sir—" Kiwanuka took a breath. "With my record, the general's displeasure could be detrimental to—"

"I've got your back, Staff Sergeant. Nothing's going to touch you that will leave a mark. It's just that General Whitcomb might not be happy with you and that could be somewhat . . ."

"Less than optimum, sir?"

"Yes. Definitely less than optimum."

Kiwanuka figured she could live with that. Unless the general decided to pop into the enlisted mess some morning and make a scene. That didn't seem likely to happen because General Whitcomb hadn't left the DawnStar Space Station since he'd made his one appearance at Fort York the day he'd taken command.

"All right, sir. I can deal with that."

"Good. Of course, I'm going to expect you to have my back too."

"Against General Whitcomb, sir?" Kiwanuka shook her head. "I'm not in a position to—"

"With Master Sergeant Sage."

Deciding she liked where this was going even less than the previous conversation because her relationship with Sage was day-to-day and they liked each other— maybe a lot more than they should—Kiwanuka leaned back in her seat and crossed her arms in front of her.

"Begging your pardon, sir, but my working relationship with Master Sergeant Sage is not up for debate."

Halladay smiled grimly. "I know that, but he's not going to be any happier with me than the general is."

Kiwanuka cocked her eyebrow suspiciously. "Where is Master Sergeant Sage?"

"In the infirmary."

That worried Kiwanuka. During the attack on the Zukimther, she'd seen Sage go down, but he'd gotten back up again. "The last I'd heard, Master Sergeant Sage was only shaken up, sir. Has his condition changed?"

"No. I've given Captain Gilbride orders to keep Sage

out for a few hours. In addition to being shaken up, the master sergeant is in danger of exhausting himself. He needs some rest, even if I have to order it for him."

Kiwanuka knew that was true. The last few days, Sage had hollowed out his reserves while trying to keep the fort's defensive systems operating at peak performance and getting the troops ready for anything that might come. In addition to that, the police action enforcing martial law in the sprawl had taken up even more time and energy that Sage hadn't had.

Halladay paused. "It's for his own good because I know he's going to be needed more later, and to keep him out from underfoot while I deal with the general. The general is under the impression that Sage will be with me and is looking forward to getting Sage in line with *Charlie Company policy while on Makaum.*" He said the last like it was a title of an MOS handbook. Then he rubbed his chin. "Having the master sergeant in the general's office is . . . *problematic*, to say the least. Like walking through a minefield. Sage wears his heart on his sleeve. Even when he's being polite you can tell what he's thinking. The general doesn't like anyone in his office who is thinking anything other than what he wants them to think."

Kiwanuka figured leaving Sage out of that meeting was probably the smart thing to do. Makaum needed a firm hand right now, and—as long as he was onplanet—Sage was going to use one. If he was asked by the general what was needed, he would tell the general that. She felt a little relieved because there was nothing Sage could hold her accountable for concerning getting left out of that meeting. "That sounds fine, sir."

Halladay tapped his PAD and dropped a file on to Kiwanuka's device. "Here's where it gets sticky for you. I've just received some information from Mr. Huang regarding the assassins who killed Wosesa Staumar at the festival."

Mr. Huang operated a noodle shop in the sprawl, but he was also a trader in secrets and gossip. The Terran military, and others, had used Mr. Huang and his large, colorful family as spies on other planets before Makaum. The man had an uncanny knack for being in the right place at the right time.

"I thought we were at a dead end in our pursuit of the assassins, sir."

"We were. Now we aren't. Mr. Huang has managed to locate at least one of the people who were involved with the shooting." Halladay leveled a forefinger to her PAD. "The intelligence we received is in that file."

Tapping her PAD, Kiwanuka opened the file. Its contents were slim, just a few images and a paragraph of information.

The subject of the images was a Voreusk female. At least, Kiwanuka thought the alien was female. With the Voreusk, it was hard to know the difference. Sometimes only another Voreusk could tell.

Kiwanuka assumed the alien was a female because she was surrounded by males of a half dozen different cultures who were showing evident interest in her as she stood at one of the ramshackle bars in New Makaum, which was essentially the sprawl's red light district.

At least two meters tall, nearly half a head taller than the humans around her, the Voreusk was covered in fine reddish-orange feathers that deepened more toward red at the center of her body. Her head was vaguely wedge-shaped, large round eyes set wide over a curved beak. Clad in a grease-stained mechanic's jumper that had worn cuffs and patched elbows, the alien leaned an elbow on the bar and hoisted a tankard in her other hand. A fluff of pale orange feathers stuck out from the crown of her head.

Kiwanuka read the intel on the one-sheet showing on her PAD. "Says here that Darrantia is a ship's mechanic with a history of making repairs using other people's parts. She hasn't done anything criminal on Makaum, sir."

"According to Mr. Huang, Rakche Darrantia is serving aboard a ship called *Kequaem's Needle*. Have you heard of the name?"

Kiwanuka had to think a moment. "No, sir."

"Well, I have. It's from a Fenipalan drinking song, a satirical lament about how Black Opal Corp gutted a world called Fenipal a few years back."

There were a lot of worlds out there left gutted by the corps. "If you say so, sir."

Halladay looked pained. "I do. General Whitcomb was stationed at Fenipal for a time when I was still just a shave-tail lieutenant. The Terran Alliance sent us in to help keep the peace after things there got out of hand. By that point, there wasn't much we could do. The planet was in shambles."

Kiwanuka nodded, thinking that General Whitcomb had a history of assignments filled with too little, too late. Makaum was just another bead on the string.

"Mr. Huang insists that Darrantia is part of a mercenary crew that specializes in assassination, as well as smuggling and other illegal enterprises. The ship's captain is supposed to be a ghost, a guy who can walk in anywhere and kill a target, then disappear."

"Sounds like our guy, sir."

"I want you to go collect Darrantia, Staff Sergeant, and bring her here so we can talk to her."

"She hasn't broken any laws, sir."

"Trust me, you'll find stolen goods on her."

"And how do you know that, sir?"

Halladay checked the time on his PAD. "Because one of Mr. Huang's family members is going to sell them to her this morning. You've got an hour to get a team ready and bring her in."

"Sir, shouldn't Master Sergeant Sage be involved in this?"

"No. I want the master sergeant off the firing line on this one. He's already hit the general's radar way too often lately. This thing could get messy. If it does and Sage is involved, it will make my job harder." Halladay grinned. "Now do you see why we're both going to be taking heat over this?"

Kiwanuka did. Sage would be upset that he wasn't there to bring Darrantia in. Of course, he would be even more upset if the Voreuskan got away.

If the alien was truly involved in the assassination.

Then again, Mr. Huang seldom had bad information.

"Good hunting, Staff Sergeant. Try not to get yourself killed. That would leave only me for the master sergeant to be annoyed with."

Realizing Halladay was out of his chair, Kiwanuka stood and saluted him. "Thank you, sir. Of course not, sir. Top of my to-do list every day is to save my own life."

Halladay smiled. "Good. Keep me updated."

"Of course, sir."

Halladay walked away and Kiwanuka ignored the curious stares turned in her direction as she gathered her things to prepare for the mission she'd been given. The colonel was right. No matter how the arrest went down, Sage was going to be properly ticked at being left out of the loop.

So you'd better have Darrantia in hand when he finds out.

SEVEN

Red Light District
Makaum Sprawl
1058 Hours Zulu Time

*G*et up, soldier! Move or you're going to lie there and
die!

The AI no longer spoke in the dulcet feminine
voice inside Jahup's head. The new voice belonged to
Master Sergeant Sage. Jahup had programmed that in
for emergency situations, thinking that he would react
more to Sage's voice than any other.

Feeling chems racing through his body to clear his
head and take away the pain wracking his body, Jahup
rolled over onto his back and pulled the Roley up. The
reticule tracked the movement on his faceshield and
showed him what he was going to hit when he squeezed
the trigger. It came to rest on the center of his attacker's
face.

In that second before firing, Jahup realized he knew
the man. His name was Oeldo and he was one of the

farmhands who worked in the *corok* fields. The man was old and stooped from his labors, his back no longer straight, and his stomach bulged from too much time spent with a wine flask. His bearded cheeks and nose showed burst blood veins, and his eyes were phlegmy, like they had gone bad inside his head and were just waiting to ooze out.

"It's you, isn't it, Jahup?" Oeldo bellowed.

Pedestrians on both sides of the confrontation fled either down the street or took shelter in some of the shops. On the ground beside Jahup, Tanest lay face-down and still on the cracked street.

Oeldo took a step forward, almost stumbling. His hand holding the weapon shook. "I know it's you. You took my son out into that jungle and you got him killed, got him eaten by a *kifrik*."

Luek's death had been unfortunate. The young man volunteered to become a hunter, and Jahup had suspected it had more to do with his father's drinking than a desire to make meat for the village. Family problems couldn't follow hunters into the jungle, but a hunter had to make sure they got left at home. Luek had never seen the *kifrik* that had dropped from the canopy and killed him.

Slowly, Jahup got to his feet. He kept the Roley pointed at the man's center mass. "Oeldo, you need to put that weapon down."

The old man swayed a little. "No! I'm going to have my revenge on you, boy. You took my son from me. My only family. And now you've joined up with those offworlders to try and take our world away from us."

"Corporal Jahup, this is Corporal Vaughn. We're on our way to you."

Jahup knew his suit AI had sent for support. Vaughn was patrolling the next area over. "Roger that, Vaughn."

He watched Oeldo and spoke to the old man. "I want to check on my friend. I don't think you meant to shoot her." He wanted Vaughn to arrive and take command of the situation. Too many people were watching, and Jahup didn't want things to get worse. "I'd like to make sure she's okay."

Oeldo glared at Jahup over the weapon. The man took the burster in both hands now, fighting to keep it steady. "You're not going to do anything! I'm in charge here!"

"Jahup," Vaughn transmitted, "you need to drop this guy."

"I don't want to kill him."

"Negative, soldier. You don't want to die. You don't want your partner to die. He is a threat and that weapon can cause a lot more damage in that crowd even if he misses you. Shoot him."

Even though he was aware of the wall slagged and burning behind him because it had taken the brunt of the burst, Jahup ignored the command. Vaughn held the same rank he did. He wasn't in command.

"Oeldo, please," Jahup said, "put the weapon down."

"You put yours down!" the old man shouted.

Even before he'd been accepted to the Terran military and told never to surrender his weapon, Jahup wouldn't have made himself defenseless. He'd hunted in the jungle too long for that kind of thinking to be acceptable. "I can't do that."

Farther down the street, Jahup spotted Noojin standing in the crowd. She wore bloodstained hunters' leathers and carried her bow in one hand. Leaves were still caught in her short-cut dark hair that lay close to her head and was no longer than her jaw. Dirt smudged her face and her eyes were dark and hollow from lack of sleep.

Jahup wished she wasn't there because he didn't want her to get hurt and he thought the confrontation with Oeldo was going to end badly. At the same time, he was scared and angry that she had gone off to hunt without him there to watch over her. He'd suspected that was where she had been the last few days since he hadn't seen her.

"Jahup, shoot him!"

Tracking Vaughn's movements on his faceshield, Jahup knew help was less than a minute away. Moving slowly, Jahup walked away from Tanest but didn't close the distance between himself and his attacker.

Oeldo's hand tightened on the weapon. His knuckles whitened with pressure. "You're going to burn, boy."

Jahup kept moving and Oeldo moved with him, turning so that his back would be toward Vaughn when the Terran arrived. "Oeldo, please. Don't do this. We can talk."

Oeldo rubbed his mouth on his shoulder. "There's no need to talk. You killed my boy, and now you're killing your people for the offworlders."

"That's not true."

Behind Oeldo, the crowd had grown. Many of them were Makaum, and some of them were offworld media people who had their recording devices in hand. They were an oddity. Jahup still couldn't imagine vid of him being shown on other worlds in other galaxies. That made everything seem far too big.

"Time for you to die, boy! *Freedom for Makaum!*" Oeldo pulled the trigger.

A bright ball of flame erupted from the stubby weapon and streaked for Jahup. He dove to the side, rolled, and shifted the reticule from Oeldo's center mass to his shoulder, hoping to wound the man, not kill him.

The bullet struck Oeldo in the shoulder and staggered him. Clinging stubbornly to his weapon with his other hand, the old man fired again. This time the blast smacked into the top floor of a two-story building meters away from Jahup.

Flaming slag ran down the side of the building onto a group of bystanders. Screams of pain and agony filled the street on the heels of the rumbling destruction.

Vaughn yelled curses inside Jahup's head. Jahup tried to line up his second shot, but a pile of molten rock poured over him and knocked him to the ground.

Get up, soldier!

As Jahup forced his way to his feet, heat waves distorted his vision. Broken and molten plascrete tumbled off him. He wiped away debris wreathed in flames from his faceshield, but that only made his vision worse. Even with the AKTIVsuit's cooling system working at full strength, he felt like he was baking alive.

Alarm systems pinged and whistled inside the suit. Jahup didn't know what all of it meant other than he was in deep *awivor*. He tried to track Oeldo, but the targeting system was suddenly erratic and the reticule blinked into and out of existence across his vision. Vaughn's voice crackled across the comm but the transmission was too staticky and cut out often.

Cooling systems unable to combat heat. Automatic armor evacuation in progress. 10 . . . 9 . . . 8 . . .

Blearily, Jahup tried to focus. There was a way to stop the auto evac of the armor, but he couldn't remember it. Perspiration covered his body. His eyes teared up. He tried to manually aim his weapon, but there were too many people behind Oeldo. If he missed, he might hit a bystander instead.

. . . 7 . . . 6 . . .

Still howling threats and curses, Oeldo readied his

weapon again. Then the man staggered and looked down in surprise at the arrow jutting from his chest. Dropping his weapon, he grasped the arrow with both hands and looked over to where Noojin stood with another arrow already nocked to the string.

Her face was stone cold, but even at this distance Jahup could see the pain and shock in her eyes. Her lower lip trembled, but her hands were steady on the bow.

. . . 5 . . . 4 . . . 3 . . .

Oeldo took one step backward, then he collapsed onto his back. His hands slid away from the arrow and he stared sightlessly into the sky.

. . . 2 . . . 1.

The armor jerked and vibrated and jarred Jahup inside it.

Unable to engage automatic evacuation at this time. Systems compromised. Distress beacon activated. Get out of the armor.

Jahup dropped his assault rifle and fumbled at the armor's release points, but they wouldn't respond to his frenzied attempts. He couldn't breathe. His lungs moved and he tasted smoke, but no oxygen was in the air.

Oxygen supply stopped because it is flammable and will result in death. Get out of the armor.

Jahup tried the release again but only got the same non-response. Panic rose in him as his lungs struggled to fill and only found the same dead air. The suit had sealed to protect him from the fire; now it held him captive. The armor was killing him.

His vision dimmed, growing smaller and smaller till only a pinprick remained.

Noojin was there.

He reached for her, wanting to tell her that he couldn't breathe, wanting to tell her that he was sorry

they weren't getting along, wanting to tell her his lungs
hurt, wanting to . . .

1106 Hours Zulu Time

Kneeling beside Jahup, Noojin peered into the AKTIV-
suit's faceshield and tried to see him within, but the
pressure-treated polycarbonate didn't allow that. She
knew he was inside because she knew the way he moved
and because he wore a coiled red *omoro* on the right
side of his helmet. He'd gotten that after he and Master
Sergeant Sage had encountered one of the large tree
snakes on a recent scouting expedition into the jungle.

When he reached for her, his hand still covered in
flames from slagged plascrete, she broke out of the
shock she was in and dodged back almost too late. The
heat singed her hair and burned her face. Pain bit into
her and she almost got angry.

Weakly, Jahup reached up toward his helmet and
writhed on the ground.

He's burning! As soon as the thought entered her
head, Noojin shot to her feet and looked around.

Now that the attack was over, the crowd grew
braver, drawing closer to see what was going on.
They'd divided almost equally between Oeldo with
an arrow in his chest—*Don't think about what you've
done now, Noojin!*—and Jahup lying there on fire. All
of them drew to the spectacle of impending death like
a storm of *krayari* beetles to rotting flesh.

Noojin shoved through the crowd, throwing elbows
and knees into those who didn't move quickly enough.
"Get out of the way!"

Curses and protests spilled out behind her, but the

people in front of her—including a huge Lemylian over twice her size—got out of her way more quickly.

Inside the clothing store across the street, Noojin gazed around wildly. The store was operated by a Makaum family she barely knew. The family had signed on with a subsidiary of DawnStar to sell off-world fashions that had grown popular on Makaum. Several of Noojin's friends wore the clothing, and all of them complained of how substandard they were. They didn't stop wearing them, though.

The male clerk came over to Noojin, switching his attention to the street, then back to her. "What happened out there? Did someone get shot? Did the Terrans kill someone else?"

Ignoring the man and running to the counter area, Noojin spotted the red fire extinguisher tank clipped to one of the shelves. One of the rules the Quass enforced was having firefighting equipment on hand. Fire was the chief fear of Makaum people because it could rip through the whole sprawl once it got established.

Ducking under the counter, Noojin grabbed the fire extinguisher and freed it from the clips.

The clerk rushed at her. "What are you—?"

Noojin ducked his outstretched hands and ran for the door. With the arrival of the offworlders and the construction of so many plascrete buildings in the sprawl, everyone had learned quickly how careless the new-comers were with fire. Extinguishers had enjoyed a big market from the beginning.

Noojin brandished the fire extinguisher like a battering ram. "Out of the way! Out of the way!"

A tall, spindly Nygend stood his ground stubbornly. Leathery purple skin covered his too-thin body. A snarl twisted his lips and revealed hooked canine fangs. He held out a large, three-fingered hand that looked more like a *swonal's* clawed foot and could have wrapped Noojin's face with ease.

"Stop pushing, *anof.*" His voice came from a small, flat translator grafted under his chin, which meant he was probably a merchant who had to deal with different languages on a regular basis.

Noojin didn't know what an *anof* was, but she didn't like the alien's physical attitude even though the translator made him sound pleasant. The computerized voice was bait, like the dangler on a *lerildo* at the edge of a creek.

Pulling the extinguisher back, Noojin drove the bottom into the alien's face with all her strength, not willing to take chances. As the alien fell, she couldn't believe what she was doing because of Jahup. He was going to hear about it when he, if he—

Let him be alive!

Other pedestrians who had heard the clunk of the extinguisher meeting flesh got out of Noojin's way, parting like a river surface when a *jasulild* chose to breach for an attack on an *ildyr* that flew too close to the water.

Jahup wasn't moving when Noojin reached him, and fire still covered him. Almost sobbing, her hands not obeying her quickly enough, she managed to ready the extinguisher and direct the chemical spray over him. She started at his head and came down to his feet. Instantly, the foam swelled and turned bright blue as the chemicals sought out the flames and quenched them.

When the extinguisher emptied, Noojin tossed it aside and threw herself on her knees beside Jahup's head. She brushed at the foam and knocked it from his faceshield.

"Jahup!"

He lay so still she couldn't bear it. Memories of all the mean things she'd said to him came back at her. She hadn't talked to him for days. She'd ignored him when he'd tried to speak to her. How could she do that to him?

Her hands grew slick with the foam. She leaned close and tried to peer through the fire-blackened faceshield. For a moment, she thought she saw him lying there like he was sleeping, his eyes closed. Then she grew just as certain that he was dead.

"Jahup!"

She seized his helmet and tried to find the manual catches, but the foam made everything slippery and the surface burned her hands. She wanted to scream in frustration.

Hands closed around her shoulders and pulled her away. She fought against them, but they were too strong. Then she realized an armored soldier was holding her.

"Easy, Noojin. Take it easy. Same side, remember?" Corporal Vaughn cleared his faceshield so she could see him.

He was probably five years older than her and was from some place called Ireland back on Terra. His skin was a warm brown and he had an accent that was pleasing to the ear.

Noojin nodded. "Jahup was on fire. I put it out."

Another soldier was kneeling beside Jahup and working on him. "His suit isn't responding. It's shut down."

Vaughn released Noojin but didn't take his hands back. "Stay here. Understood? Stay here and let us do our job."

Trembling, sick to her stomach, not knowing if it was because Jahup might be dead or if it was because she'd killed a man so cold-bloodedly, Noojin nodded. She wrapped her arms around herself and somehow stayed back.

Vaughn placed a hand on Jahup's scorched chest armor. "His oxygen is off. Suit shut it down to prevent possible combustion, mate."

"The manual releases aren't working." The other soldier tugged on Jahup's helmet to prove his point.

"Okay. I have an idea. Give me room, mate."

The younger soldier stepped back. His faceshield was still dark and Noojin couldn't see his face when she grabbed him by the arm.

"Is he all right?"

The soldier pushed at her hand to free himself. "Step back, miss."

"It's okay, Tyler. She's one of us. Out of uniform this morning, is all." Vaughn extricated a drill bit from his waist kit and attached it to one of his fingers. "This is one of her mates."

Tyler stopped pushing and cleared his faceshield. He was older than Noojin, but he was still young. Heavy beard growth showed on his cheeks and he looked worn. "Sorry. Jahup's med suite is dead. I can't get any readings. I don't know how he is."

Noojin held herself together with effort, reminding herself of how many times Jahup had disappeared in the jungle when things had gone wrong on a hunt. She hadn't known where he was or what condition he was in during those times either.

Except those times she hadn't seen him lying somewhere so lifeless.

EIGHT

have the target, Echo Leader. Can you confirm?"

Kiwanuka stood in the shade of a large hangar and tracked Rakche Darrantia's progress across the tarmac. The Voreusk mechanic piloted a battered open-bed crawler through the cargo handlers waiting to load suborbital transfer ships with goods taken from Makaum.

Kiwanuka left the hangar and strode across the tarmac. It wasn't unusual to see Terran military working security there these past few weeks. "Echo Leader has the target, Echo Six. Let's close it in."

Guarding the spaceports was another reason they'd been spread so thin. Fort York had been placed there to create a presence and up the ante for the Phrenorians and (ta)Klar, either of whom would have drained Makaum in one way or another. Now Charlie Company was taking care of so many things that they were hard-pressed to take care of themselves.

With as much cargo as the planet was exporting, the populace would have been rich. With the way boom economics worked, though, prices in the shops and bars ate through those profits. When all the dust settled, there would be a few people made wealthy by the trade, usually the greedy ones on a planet who could wheedle their way into power among their friends and neighbors. Once the boom was over, those wealthy could choose to stay, but most of them left their birth planets and the poor were left with the remnants of what those worlds had been.

The behavior wasn't anything new. Kiwanuka had seen it happen to emerging countries in Africa, and on some of the planets where she'd served. War with the Phrenorians could be profitable for a neutral planet in the right place.

Of course, that planet didn't get to remain neutral for long once the Phrenorians claimed them. From boom to bust, from wealth to slavery, all of that happened as soon as treaty or force pulled the Terran military out of an area.

Kiwanuka didn't want that to happen to Makaum. The people here were innocents. The planet was a good place to live. In Kiwanuka's experience, it didn't seem like a lot of those populated worlds still existed unspoiled. She knew that was something she shared with Sage. Both of them came from places filled with violence, and they both wanted to make a difference here.

Thinking about Sage made her feel guilty because he would have wanted to be here so she stopped and focused on Darrantia.

Kiwanuka took a roundabout path in Darrantia's direction. The mechanic had piloted a small suborbital down from her ship, which had not turned up in the logbooks yet. Kiwanuka didn't have access to all of them. That was where Corporal Veug, the electronics intelligence specialist assigned to her team, was going to come in.

"Echo Four," Kiwanuka said, "tell me you have something."

"I'm trying." The frown was evident in Veug's tone. "Whoever hardened the encryption on their comm software was really good."

Darrantia stopped her crawler by a suborbital bearing a Cheelchan flag.

Kiwanuka's hackles immediately rose because Cheelcha was a planet of outlaws. Their primary vice was smuggling. They hammered out cheap ships, staffed them with cutthroat crew, and went after every illegal cargo they could get their hands on.

She cursed. She and Sage had already had one encounter with a Cheelchan crew when they'd pursued Ellen Hodgkins offplanet. In addition to being smugglers, the Cheelchans had a strong sense of community. They talked to each other. A lot. Word about Hodgkins's apprehension had had plenty of time to spread.

Four Cheelchan crewmen stood outside their open cargo bay like they had nothing better to do. Wearing dark maroon jumpers, they looked like most of the other support crews at the space dock, busy but not too busy. Kiwanuka knew they would be better armed than most other crews.

Darrantia walked over to the group and entered the conversation.

"Echo Four," Kiwanuka said, "can you get me aud on that conversation?"

"Roger that, but they may know as soon as I light them up."

"Affirmative. In about four more steps, this isn't going to be a surprise anymore anyway. Light them up."

Almost instantly, a laser eavesdropper from Veug's position touched Darrantia and her crowd. All sound waves in the area transmitted back along the laser beam.

". . . got it in the back," Darrantia was saying, jerking a thumb over her shoulder toward her crawler, "but the price has gone up."

One of the Cheelchans folded his arms and spat in disgust. He shook his head. "We offered what we offered. If you're not going to take it, we'll look somewhere else till we can find the price we want."

Darrantia shrugged. "Sure. It's no pinfeathers off my hump, but you guys are going to lose credits while you're sitting here."

The Cheelchans looked at each other. Finally, the one doing the talking cursed. "Fine, thief. We'll pay your price."

Darrantia smiled with that narrow mouth Voreuskans had. "No need to get a bad attitude. It's not my fault you can't make friends."

One of the other Cheelchans pulled a device from his jumper pocket and nudged his superior with a shoulder.

"Okay, Echo Leader," Veug said, "we're blown."

"That's fine. Let's close it up." Kiwanuka strode straight at the group and slipped the sling on her assault rifle around so she could grab it quickly. "Remember, I want the target alive, and I don't want this turned into a bloodbath."

There was already enough bad press coming from the dustup Jahup and his partner were in only minutes ago. Kiwanuka had stayed in the loop only tangentially.

Slowly, probably practiced from years of harassment on dozens of planets, Darrantia turned around to face

Kiwanuka and looked casual. She put her hands in her pockets. "Good morning. Is there something I can do for you?"

Kiwanuka looked up at the alien and felt like she was being eyed by a predatory avian. "Staff Sergeant Kiwanuka of the Terran Army. We're going to search your cargo."

"I'm not subject to Terran authority."

"No, but this spaceport is."

"This spaceport is neutral territory."

"Not anymore. We've been tasked with keeping the peace."

"I'm peaceful. I haven't been anything but peaceful." Evidently Darrantia had a sense of humor that matched her confidence.

Kiwanuka produced a set of wrist restraints and dangled them from her left hand. "Turn around and put your hands behind your back."

Darrantia acted like she couldn't believe it. "You're arresting me? For what?"

"Receivership of stolen goods for starters. We'll work out the list as we go. Now turn around or the corporal here will shock you into insensibility."

Veug pressed the activation stud on his shokton and blue electricity crackled along the baton.

Kiwanuka didn't like the fact that she couldn't read the alien's face, but the Voreuskan's body language had definitely tensed.

"However you want to do this," Kiwanuka said, "you're coming with me."

"All right." Removing her hands from her pockets, Darrantia pitched a small sphere toward Kiwanuka's feet.

Before Kiwanuka had time to react, could only begin to curse herself for being so careless as to be so close to the Voreuskan without taking physical control of her, the sphere exploded.

Red Light District
Makaum Sprawl
1112 Hours Zulu Time

The drill at the end of Vaughn's gloved finger shoved against Jahup's faceshield whined in a high-pitched shriek as it bit into the material. Smoke wound up from the contact and, for a moment, Noojin feared that the fire would reignite.

Seconds later, Vaughn pulled his hand away. For a space, nothing happened. Then a lingering wisp of smoke curled in through the hole in the faceshield.

Vaughn stood. "He's breathing. That's a good sign."

A moment later, a cargo crawler with flashing lights and a blaring horn rounded the end of the street and tried to get through the crowd. Most of the pedestrians got out of the way, but several Makaum men remained in the street and blocked the way.

"Move." Vaughn's PA-assisted order reverberated between the buildings. "Let the emergency vehicle through."

One of the men stepped to the front of the group. His expensively tailored Makaum clothing made him stand out from the others. He wore royal green and emerald silks. He was tall and fair-haired, something that wasn't often seen on Makaum, and wore a short beard that made him look only slightly older than he was. He was handsome, but there was a cruel arrogance to him.

Seeing him better now, Noojin recognized him

as Throzath, the eldest son of Tholak. Tholak was a member of the Quass and had always been jealous of Quass Leghef's popularity among the people.

Throzath glared at the Terran military soldiers and ignored the way the medical crawler bleated at him. "I choose not to move. This is our home, offworlder." He pointed to Oeldo's body lying only a short distance away. "You come here and shoot our people down in the streets and expect us to kiss your boots."

The men and women around him hurled curses at the Terran military.

"We're not going to take it anymore," Throzath said. "We're going to arm ourselves and defend ourselves the way we've been doing since we first landed on Makaum."

Around him, his band of followers cheered and incited the surrounding crowd to join in. Many of them did, and it wasn't just the Makaum among them. Offworlder shopkeepers and workers joined in as well. All of them had something to gain if the Terran military presence was pulled back to just the fort and the soldiers could no longer monitor them as closely.

Throzath spread his hands and smiled. "If you want to get your *soldier* out of here, ask us to allow it. Or maybe you want to shoot more of us this morning."

Vaughn hesitated, and Noojin guessed he was in contact with the fort seeking direction.

Thinking about Jahup lying there, maybe cooked to the bone inside the heated armor, Noojin scrambled over to where Tanest's Roley lay. She wasn't moving either, but Tyler had checked her and seemed satisfied she was all right.

Noojin picked up the Roley and pressed the code into the keypad that released the weapon's operation. Her unarmored hands were small on the rifle, but she checked the load manually, saw that it was full, and strode out into the middle of the street from behind the two Terran military soldiers.

Several nearby pedestrians saw her and pushed back into the crowd to get clear of the situation.

Grimly, Noojin fired a short burst into the air. The rapid-fire detonations quieted all conversation. Silence rolled in like a tide. Looking straight into Throzath's eyes, Noojin leveled the rifle at him.

"Get out of the way, Throzath. Otherwise I'm going to shoot you where you stand. After that, I'm going to shoot anyone following you who's still standing there." Noojin couldn't believe the calm that had settled over her, and she knew she meant every word she said.

Tyler took a step toward her, but Vaughn held the young man back with a hand.

Throzath smiled, looked at the crowd, and sought support. After he saw they were still there, he turned back to Noojin. "Do you really expect me—"

Noojin squeezed the trigger.

Blam!

The bullet cored through Throzath's left leg and struck one of the men behind him. The man went down, howling in surprise and pain. The bullet had flattened somewhat when it had struck Throzath and had spread its residual velocity across the second man.

Noojin had seen the same effect in the jungle when they were taking meat from a flock or a herd. Lining up shots had been necessary when gunpowder and bullets had been hard to come by.

White-faced and incredulous, Throzath looked down at the hole in his pants and the blood that stained the spidersilk in a growing pattern. He tried to take a step and his leg gave way beneath him.

Noojin aimed the rifle at one of the men beside

Throzath. "Have your friends pick those two up and get them out of the street or I'll shoot you next."

The man turned to his friends and spoke rapidly. A half dozen of them lifted Throzath and the other wounded man and carried them away. The street cleared quickly after that.

Tyler reached for Noojin. "Maybe you should let me have that weapon."

Vaughn waved to the med crawler. "Let her keep it in case she needs to shoot someone else. Go secure that illegal weapon before it disappears."

Noojin hadn't even considered the whereabouts of the burster. She glanced over her shoulder and saw that the weapon still lay only centimeters from Oeldo's hand. She winced at the arrow sticking up from the old man's chest.

Oeldo had always been around the sprawl, always looking for a handout. Noojin had given him coins when she could spare them even though she'd known he was only going to spend them on wine and waste the day in a drunken stupor. He'd been drunk the day of Luek's funeral too, but everyone had forgiven him then.

Now Oeldo was gone. And she had killed him.

With effort, Noojin blew out her breath and put that thought away. She watched over the soldiers as medical personnel got out of the crawler with bot-driven gurneys. The gurneys lowered themselves to the ground, then used mechanical arms to assist the soldiers in getting Jahup and Tanest on board.

Vaughn strode over to where Throzath sat on the sidewalk in front of an electronics shop. Not as many of his friends were around him now and a few left as the soldier approached.

"If you want, we can take you to the fort and have a doc look at you," Vaughn said.

Throzath glared up at Vaughn. "I'm fine."

"Sure."

Shifting his glare to Noojin, Throzath said, "This isn't over."

Vaughn took a step and put himself between Throzath and Noojin. "For your sake," the soldier said to Throzath, "it had better be. The next time she shoots you, I don't think she'll be as generous."

Unwilling to let someone else do her fighting for her, especially after the way Velesko Kos had manhandled her not so long ago, Noojin stepped to the side so she had a clear field of fire again. She pointed the rifle at Throzath. "I'm a hunter. You should remember that. In the jungle, we don't let even a wounded *cebsay* live to attack again another day."

A *cebsay* was a small, vicious lizard capable of running on its back legs. It was also known for its coward-ice because the creature only attacked when it was in a swarm.

"This isn't over for me either, Throzath." Noojin's voice was cold and full of promise. "If I see you even *look* at me like you're going to hurt me, I'll gut you where you stand. Do you understand?"

Dropping his gaze, Throzath looked away but didn't say anything.

"If you ask me," Vaughn said, "I think he understands just fine." He looked at Noojin. "They've got room for one more on the crawler, Noojin."

She nodded and went to the vehicle, still holding on to the rifle.

NINE

Tangler wires leaped from the sphere and wrapped Kiwanuka's legs, pulling them close together. Others lashed Veug to her and they went down in a heap.

Darting from the reach of the tangler wires, Darrantia sprinted to her crawler, reached in the back, and took out a package wrapped in protective film. It was no bigger than both the alien's fists pressed together. She turned and tossed the package to the Cheelchans.

"My treat," she said as she slid behind the crawler's controls.

One of the Cheelchans caught the package and looked at the others in confusion. He said something, probably a curse from the tone, but the translator didn't decipher what it was.

Kiwanuka knew the tone because she was unleashing curses of her own, imagining what Sage was going to think when their suspected assassin got away.

"Kill them," the Cheelchan leader said, "and let's get off this planet. Let the Phrenorians have it." He drew a Gatner semiautomatic fléchette pistol from his coveralls and aimed at Kiwanuka.

At Kiwanuka's side, the Roley had gotten caught in the tangler and maybe even damaged because the wires were cutting into the armor.

Before the Cheelchan could fire his weapon, a small hole opened in his forehead and the back of his head evacuated its contents over his three companions. Spattered in blood, all of them staggered back as their companion's body hit the rough tarmac.

Kiwanuka yanked a Hokusai-made fighting knife from its sheath along her left forearm and slashed the wires around her legs. The twenty-centimeter-long carbon and molybdenum blade parted the strands with high-pitched *tings*. The other three Cheelchan were in motion now, grabbing weapons and firing.

Two of them went down under sniper fire, both hit in the head, and the third dropped with a chest wound that left him dazed and unmoving on the tarmac.

"Do *not* shoot Darrantia," Kiwanuka directed. "We want her alive." She cursed when she looked at the Roley lying there almost in pieces, and cursed again when she saw the four bodies.

Halladay was *not* going to be happy. She just hoped he had time to make his case to Whitcomb before the general heard the news.

Inside the ship's cargo area, at least two figures were in motion. Evidently other ships' crew inside were investigating the disturbance. With a metallic hiss and whine, the cargo hatch started to seal.

Drawing her Birkeland coilgun and aiming on the

fly, Kiwanuka put bolts into the hatch's safety sensor, disabling the electronic assembly. If the hatch was going to shut now, it was going to have to close manually.

"Secure the Cheelchan ship," she ordered. "Don't let any of the crew get away." It was possible, maybe only remotely, that the Cheelchans were involved in Wosesa Staumar's assassination. Kiwanuka intended to cover every base. Especially since things weren't going so well.

She rolled to her feet and swung around to face the direction Darrantia had gone. The cargo crawler roared across the tarmac, slewing wildly as the fleeing alien dodged other vehicles and pallets of cargo. The Voreus-kan leaned on the horn and cargo handlers scattered.

"I'm in pursuit, Echo Leader," Echo Two called out.

Kiwanuka tracked the soldier's direction on her faceshield. "I want her alive."

She accelerated from a standing start, redlining the suit's quickness, almost losing her stride because she hadn't quite recovered her balance from the tangler grenade and the armor pushed the wearer to the limit.

You're unstable. Do you wish to slow down?

Kiwanuka breathed out, focusing as she let her body sink into the movement, no longer fighting to control it. She smoothed out, the rhythm coming naturally. Her boots thudded against the tarmac, digging in and pushing off. "No. I've got this."

"Roger that." Echo Two and Echo Three had joined up in their pursuit. They ran like a pair of bloodhounds, dodging crawlers and leaping them when they could, flying like arrows.

Kiwanuka holstered her pistol to leave her hands free and keep her balance better. She overtook the other two soldiers, and all of them were cutting the lead Darrantia had gotten from her early jump. Despite the combat armor's micro-musculature amplifying the wearer's

speed and strength, there were differences based on
the individual. The other two soldiers were probably
stronger than Kiwanuka, but she was faster, more
coordinated.

Unable to dodge a cargo crawler that darted in front
of him from behind a suborbital ship, Echo Two went
sprawling and skidded along the tarmac like a flat stone
on a smooth pond surface. Ten meters on as he fought
for control, he smashed up against another crawler like
a cannonball.

Echo Two cursed and struggled to get to his feet.
He swayed unsteadily and put a hand to his head as if
checking that it was still there. Unfortunately, he also
stood in Kiwanuka's path.

Timing her stride and her speed, Kiwanuka leaped,
sailing over the other soldier's head by a meter. She hit
the ground, threw her arms out to her sides to regain
her balance, and tilted forward to accelerate more.

Hunched down over the crawler's controls, Darrantia
wove between the various vehicles dotting the tarmac.
Three times she had the vehicle up on one set of wheels,
leaning precariously close to tipping over, and recovered one of those times only because the crawler kissed
another vehicle in passing that thumped it back down
on the oversized tires. Rubber growled as the wheels
grabbed full traction again.

Closing in, Echo Three shouted over his PA, "Pull
over!"

In response, Darrantia turned around with a massive
pistol clenched in her fist. Echo Three tried to dodge,
but that only left him easy prey for the net that flared
from the gun. The tool had been designed to wrap
cargo quickly. The ten-meter-wide square of sticky
strands popped open wide and enveloped Echo Three.
When he crashed into the tarmac, he struggled to get

free but didn't look like he was going to be able to accomplish that on his own.

Kiwanuka raced past him and closed the distance separating her from Darrantia to ten meters. Two hundred meters ahead, a suborbital ship vented gas from the engines as it prepared for liftoff. Two men with rifles stood outside the cargo bay, fired at Kiwanuka, and missed her by centimeters.

Twisting on her seat again, Darrantia raised the net tool again, took aim, and fired.

Instead of trying to dodge to the side or leap over, which would have slowed her if not caused her to lose control completely, Kiwanuka threw herself into a headfirst dive. Hands before her, palms down, she slid across the tarmac like a hockey puck on ice. Her palms dug scars into the plascrete that ran for meters. Her armor's surface took the grinding abuse, but the friction generated a lot of heat.

Warning. Armor is under constant stress from abrasive erosion.

"Suck it up and earn your resurfacing," Kiwanuka said as the flared net passed overhead, sticking only a moment to her back and sliding away because the resistance was at an oblique angle.

I'm sorry, I do not understand suck it up. *Clarification, please?*

"Disregard. Contact HQ. Emergency connect."

Connecting HQ, Fort York. Parameter: Kiwanuka, Kjersti, Staff Sergeant Charlie Company. Emergency connect.

Kiwanuka shifted her hands, tucked her right arm under her, and came over in a bouncing roll that brought her to her feet. She found her stride immediately and added speed. She was seven meters from her quarry and closing rapidly.

A look of disbelief and fear showed in the alien's eyes and small mouth.

Kiwanuka smiled. *Got you!*

At the last minute, Darrantia locked up the crawler's brakes and pulled hard on the vehicle's controls, trying to cut to the left. Kiwanuka had expected the alien to try one direction or the other, and once she shot past out of control, the Voreuskan would plaster her with the net gun. It was what she would have done if the situation was reversed.

Instead, Kiwanuka ducked and altered her course. She ran inside Darrantia's turn and planted a shoulder into the side of the crawler. The reinforced polyplas body crumpled immediately and littered jagged shards behind it. The vehicle massed ten times as much as Kiwanuka did even with her armor on. Her velocity, though, was an undeniable factor in the collision, allowing her to drive the crawler up and over.

Rocked onto its side, the crawler balanced for just a moment, then gravity and centrifugal force caught up with it. Rolling slowly, the vehicle toppled over and landed upside down with a harsh bounce.

Lying there stunned, the breath knocked out of her, Kiwanuka worried that Darrantia had been caught under the crawler and badly injured. That would be her luck this morning, handed this mission behind Sage's back, then killing the only lead they had on the assassination.

Then the alien's hand shoved out of the debris and pressed against the tarmac. Her head and shoulders followed in a quick series of jerks as she pulled herself out. Wasting no time, Darrantia scampered out from under the overturned vehicle.

Kiwanuka pushed herself up and fired the grappling hook housed in her armor sleeve. The projectile flew true and smashed through the crawler's side with a *thwock!*

Yanking on the line, Kiwanuka pulled it taut in front of Darrantia, catching the alien just above her knees. At speed, unable to stop herself, the Voreuskan hit the line hard and toppled into a face-plant that elicited a screamed curse that ended on impact.

Before her quarry could recover, Kiwanuka was on her, gripping her by that fluffy feathery topknot and wrapping a hand around one of the alien's wrists. Mercilessly, irritated as much with her prisoner as she was with herself, Kiwanuka hooked the captured wrist up behind the Voreuskan's back just short of breaking the limb.

Darrantia shrieked in pain, a full-throated cry for relief. Maybe it was an act, but the arm was really up there and Voreuskans weren't noted for being double-jointed.

"You're breaking my arm!" she screeched.

Bullets struck the crawler with basso thuds and pieces of polyplas tore away. Evidently Darrantia's playmates hadn't given up on getting her back.

Manhandling the alien, Kiwanuka yanked them both up to cover behind the overturned crawler. Rifle rounds thudded into the vehicle but didn't penetrate. Plus, they weren't shooting at Kiwanuka now that she was covering the Voreuskan. They didn't want to accidentally hit the alien, so she wasn't someone they wanted to lose. It was something to know.

Kiwanuka swept the area with her 360-degree view, looking for other gunmen and seeing only the two at the suborbital who were slowly advancing while continuously firing. Her team had closed on the Cheelchan ship, but Echo Two was cutting Echo Three free. They would join her in another moment.

Whoever was piloting the suborbital must have realized that too, because one of the men grabbed the other by the arm and hauled him back. In the next moment, they turned and ran for the suborbital.

Her comm buzzed, letting her know that the connection linked her to the fort.

"Echo Leader, this is Charlie Company Zero Niner." The male voice at the other end sounded competent and unhurried.

Kiwanuka shoved her head above the side of the crawler and watched the cargo hatch smoothly close. The men had definitely given up on freeing their comrade. Using the helmet's vid suite, she captured an image of the ship and sent it to the fort. "Roger that, Niner. Stand by for details."

"Standing by."

The ship's name and number were clearly visible. She hoped it was registered—legally—and wasn't flying false identification. The Makaum spaceport authority had been lax in their attentiveness during their stewardship. Their records hadn't been complete and ship identification hadn't always been verified because the security officers had been thrown into their jobs with little training. The positions had been offered as a token of goodwill to allow the local populace to earn a wage and receive skills that "would be valuable if they chose to visit other planets."

Kiwanuka had read the ebrochure and recognized it as the pabulum it was. The corps had eagerly ceded the spaceport concession to the Makaum people, allowing them to make a profit on the job, while all the time taking advantage themselves of the lax security. When things went wrong, the corps made sure the Makaum understood they had no one but themselves to blame.

"I'm sending you images of a suborbital craft named

Oswald," Kiwanuka said. "I want it identified and verified, and I want to know what ship it's registered to."

"Roger that, Echo Leader. Checking manifest of *Oswald*. Gimme a minute."

Warning Klaxons blared as the suborbital lifted without clearance. Massive gouts of smoke and fire blazed from under the spacecraft as it slowly lifted into the sky. Other ships, suborbitals and dropships, ascended and descended in an orchestrated maze.

Frustrated, Kiwanuka tugged Darrantia into motion at her side.

"Why am I being arrested?" the Voreuskan demanded.

"Stolen goods, like I said. Now you can add avoiding arrest." Kiwanuka holstered her pistol and waved to Echo Two and Echo Three. "Take that cargo into custody."

Darrantia only provided token resistance to being pulled along. "There's nothing in that cargo that's illegal."

"Sure. And I bet there's nothing illegal in that package you threw the Cheelchans."

"That wasn't mine. I was just delivering a package. A favor for a friend."

Kiwanuka's comm chirped to let her know she had an incoming call from Veug. "Tell me something good, Echo Four."

"The package the target tossed to the Cheelchans was full of Snakedream and *vesgar* plants, so our op is totally legitimate."

Some of the tension in Kiwanuka's shoulders eased at that. One of the primary missions Charlie Company had been tasked with was eliminating the drug trade and biopiracy. Snakedream was a local commodity made from *vesgar* spores. The fact that there were actual plants involved made the arrest a double-offense.

She looked at Darrantia. "We found the Snakedream and the *vesgar* plants."

Darrantia shrugged her narrow shoulders.

"Records indicate this is the third felony offense in a developing planet under Terran Alliance sponsorship. You're going to get locked down for a long time."

Darrantia didn't say anything, but the seriousness of her situation bowed her head.

Kiwanuka wondered if her prisoner used drugs as well. If she did, cracking her was going to be easier as she went into withdrawal. That would be good. After last night and this morning, Kiwanuka was ready for something easier.

A shadow fell over her and she looked up, tracking the Phrenorian aircar that shot by. Even though the angle was oblique, she could still make out the armed warriors and the heavy weapons firmpoints on the vehicle.

Her shoulders tightened back up. No matter what else happened, the Phrenorians still lay in wait.

TEN

What do you do when you're not buying pretty femmes drinks and listening to them talk about themselves?"

Across the table, the Ishona woman bared her teeth—fangs, really, and a lot of them—in what Sytver Morlortai guessed she believed was a friendly smile. All the expression really did was remind Morlortai that the Ishono people were committed to their carnivorous lifestyle.

"I'm a trader." Morlortai knew the answer was innocuous enough, and he could pass for a merchant because he'd used the cover before. He knew goods, knew tradespeak in dozens of languages, and could be totally boring while discussing items he had for sale. He carried cargo on his ship as well. It was all part of his crew's cover. They did trade, and most of the time they even profited a little.

The Ishona woman made a hissing sound of disgust and waved a hand at the sprawl spread out over her shoulder. "You can't swing a dead *ightor* around here without hitting a merchant."

"There are profits to be made. Wherever there are profits to be made, you'll find traders ready to make them."

Morlortai thought her name was Xirun. She'd introduced herself when he'd offered to buy her a drink two drinks back. He hadn't planned on her sticking around, but she had and the situation was agreeable to him. She provided cover for him, a reason for him to loiter on the bar's open patio that overlooked the Phrenorian Embassy. He sat so he could watch Phrenorian warriors come and go through the main entrance.

A head taller than his own slightly less than 1.5 meters, the Ishona woman was lean and covered in corded muscle that played under her speckled golden skin. Her head was humanoid, but less so than Morlortai's own Fenipalan features. Terrans thought Fenipalans were bland in appearance. Morlortai thought the sameness of pale skin and thin bodies was good camouflage.

"Still," she said, "you could do more for yourself than cater to another's wants and needs."

"If you'd wanted someone different," Morlortai said, though he took no offense at the slight because he didn't care what she thought, only that she sat there and provided a cover for his presence—because anyone would have looked at an Ishona woman instead of him, "you could have sat at another table."

There were plenty of merchants tapping on their PADs and talking on their commlinks. Several of them, of both genders and more than a few neutrals, had looked at the Ishona woman with hopeful eyes.

Xirun, if that was her name, regarded him. "No.

Oddly, there is *something* about you that I find I am attracted to."

"Maybe it's the fact that I'm paying for the drinks," Morlortai suggested.

He removed his sunglasses and cleaned them. When he put them back on, the subcutaneous cyber connections at his temples reconnected to the lenses and stood ready to pull up whatever data he wished to watch.

"I know why you're paying for the drinks." Xirun tipped back her glass and emptied it of the violet-colored alcohol. "I can assure you, I'd have to be a lot more attracted to you for that to happen."

Morlortai smiled good-naturedly. "You are very plainspoken, femme."

"I'm told it's a trait not endearing to all."

"I'm enjoying it."

One story below the bar's open patio, several new plascrete buildings showed through the leafy boughs of the jungle, but they stopped short of the armed security fence that surrounded the Phrenorian Embassy. Over the last few years, Morlortai had become familiar with those embassies on worlds that hadn't yet become embroiled in the Phrenorian War, and none of them looked inviting. In fact, they looked like *shiashes* pustules, full of poison and ready to burst at the least provocation.

All of the buildings looked like stalagmites thrusting up from the ground. Instead of neat square or rectangular blocks, Phrenorian structures looked like they'd been excreted. They stood wide at the base and tapered to a slender spire. On the tallest of the spires, the ranking military commander was housed.

Morning light gleamed from the dark oval windows. Perched up there, the military commander was a tempting target, but Morlortai knew that was by design. Nothing less than massive gunnery would knock down the structure, and an attack would trigger an immediate response from anti-aircraft guns, satellite-based weapons (even though, by treaty, the Phrenorians weren't supposed to have them), and ground troops. A military strike or would-be assassin would guarantee the effort would be suicidal in execution. There were plenty of other ranking warriors ready to step up to a general. Phrenorian leaders weren't afraid to die on the battlefield. At least, most of them.

General Rangha had been different. The Phrenorian had been careful in his public appearances.

On the other hand, Captain Zhoh GhiCemid was fearless. But he kept himself surrounded by his best warriors and defenses.

Zhoh was proving irritatingly difficult to kill. If it hadn't been for the parameters set by Morlortai's employer, the assassin felt certain he could have killed his target before now.

Unfortunately, Zhoh's death had to appear to be at the hands of the Terran military. When he'd first arrived onplanet a little over ten days ago, Morlortai had assumed the kill would have been easily delivered. Except that Zhoh had aligned himself, however temporarily, with the Terran military for the pursuit of weapons dealers.

Strange times were occurring on Makaum.

Morlortai rotated his empty glass on the table, eyed the embassy, and wondered when Zhoh would put in an appearance. The Phrenorian captain had been inside all morning.

That was interesting, and Morlortai felt certain it boded ill for the planet. Even though it was a luxury he could ill afford, he felt sympathy for the Makaum people. They were losing their planet. He'd experienced the same thing himself years ago.

"You're ambitious," Xirun stated.

Morlortai shifted his attention to her and smiled. "Am I?"

"With the way you're watching the Phrenorian Embassy, you must think you've got a cargo the warriors there will want."

Getting caught watching bothered Morlortai. He was more professional than that. "Not really. I've just not seen that architecture before."

Xirun glanced over her shoulder at the Phrenorian spires. "I've seen similar. Have you ever visited Turoiss?"

"No."

"It's a cancerous eyesore of a planet. The sentient inhabitants there make their homes in the dung hills of the *sofoc*, the huge predators that roam the mountains." Xirun emptied her drink. "They're more an infestation of intestinal worms than a culture."

"There's an image I won't soon forget."

Xirun smiled, and the expanse of sharp teeth could have been intimidating to most of the true traders in the bar.

Morlortai gave thought to the matter of Zhoh again. The bounty offered for the Phrenorian captain's demise was an attractive one, but staying in orbit around the planet was expensive. He'd managed to put together a second contract from the (ta)Klar, but that only offset some of the expenses his ship was racking up. A captain had to be trading if he was to survive on his own.

Possibly, he could secure further employment because Makaum was a world in transition, but he didn't like working too long in the same place. If too many beings dropped dead from suspicious causes—or were outright killed—law enforcement or military asked questions.

Morlortai had succeeded by getting into and out of places quickly.

He stared at the embassy building again and thought of how hard it would be to get to Captain Zhoh GhiCemid now that the Phrenorian general was dead. Despite the credits offered for the target's death, Morlortai was leaning in favor of abandoning the contract and moving on to another star system. Wherever beings lived, there were individuals who would pay to see another individual dead.

All morning long, he had the feeling of entrapment on Makaum, and had felt he and his team had been static for too long. It was time to cut loose from his present engagement and move on.

The server brought another round of drinks. Morlortai decided he would finish that, try his luck with the Ishona woman to salve his pride, and then get his crew back aboard his ship to seek their fortunes elsewhere.

The Ishona woman's eyes appeared glassy. Morlortai felt hopeful about his chances.

Then his comm chirped inside his head for his attention.

"Pardon me for a moment," Morlortai said.

When the Ishona woman nodded, a little more slowly than she had at first, Morlortai got up and walked over to the corner of the patio that overlooked the Phrenorian Embassy. He stayed back from the rail and leaned against the side of the bar proper because he didn't want to draw attention to himself. Then he answered the call.

"We have trouble," Turit announced in the flat, unemotional voice his translator/enhancer unit gave him. The Angenen was the ship's armorer and Morlortai's spotter in the field.

"What is it?"

"Darrantia got arrested a few minutes ago."

Morlortai turned that over in his mind, not liking all

the possibilities that came with it. "Why was she arrested?"

"She was apprehended while in the possession of stolen goods."

That wasn't surprising. Although Darrantia was an excellent ship's engineer, she did like to dabble in stolen goods. Morlortai had never been able to get her to give up her side hustle.

"It shouldn't be a problem. We'll simply pay the fines. In the meantime, I want you to call the crew together. I've decided to cancel the contract here. Things have become too risky."

Morlortai shifted against the wall to his back and watched an aircar lift off from the small heliport on top of the Phrenorian Embassy. He checked the vid feed Honiban had set up through a hack into one of Silver Spin Corp's low-planet-orbit satellites. The image pixilated into view on the back of his sunglasses.

Even though facial recognition was difficult to achieve on the Phrenorians, he felt certain Honiban's programs were up to the task of identifying Zhoh. The captain was not one of the aircar's passengers, so he still remained somewhere inside the building.

"Getting Darrantia back isn't going to be as easy as you think. This isn't a matter of simply paying a fine. She was taken into custody by the Terran military."

That caught Morlortai's attention. "Why were they involved?"

"From what Ny'age has heard from contacts at the starport, the Terrans went there looking for Darrantia."

"They've discovered something about the work I did." Morlortai referred to the assassination of Wosesa Staumar.

Turit's translator/enhancer tried to emulate a sigh,

but it only sounded like a raspy squawk. "I believe so as well. Our luck has changed."

Morlortai considered his options. Leaving a crew member behind wasn't one of them. Unfortunately, the assassination had left him in a delicate place. For the first time in years, he felt the jaws of a trap closing in on him.

"Have Ny'age find out what he can." The Estadyn was a social chameleon and talented at ingratiating himself in with local populations. He served to scout out the places where Morlortai employed his lethal talents. "Surely he's got some contacts that can tell him what the Terrans want with Darrantia."

"You and I both know what they want, *syonmor.*" The Angenen term translated, more or less, into "eggling" and was meant to show affection. "The Terran military believes Darrantia was involved with that assassination the (ta)Klar wanted done."

Morlortai figured that as well. Anger boiled up in him. "Have Ny'age check into that. I wouldn't put it past the (ta)Klar to give the Terran military information about Staumar's death to trade for something they wanted."

"Having the Terran military throwing its weight around to find Staumar's assassin would muddy the water," Turit agreed. "I hate dealing with them."

"As do I, but a profit is a profit."

"Only if we get away with it."

"We'll find a way," Morlortai said. "We always do. And if it turns out the (ta)Klar betrayed us, I'll make an example of any one, or ones, who did it."

ELEVEN

Compartment 683-TMOP HQ
(Terran Military Offplanet Headquarters)
Space Station DSC-24L19
Loki 19 (Makaum)
LEO 331.9 kilometers
1218 Hours Zulu Time

You're nervous, Colonel."

Quass Leghef's announcement caught Nathan Halladay off guard. To his way of thinking, he wasn't presenting any sign of apprehension. During his career in the Terran military, especially while serving under General Howard Whitcomb, he'd learned to never betray any inner turmoil or qualm.

Or dread.

He was definitely feeling dread today, and waiting to be allowed into the general's office was wearing on him. He was Howard's XO, the man who ran Fort York on a day-to-day basis.

Beside him, dwarfed by his size, the Quass sat prim

and proper. She wore a ceremonial gown made from *kifrik* silk dyed dark green with strands of gold woven into the scheme. Silk ribbons of the same color and pattern held her black hair back from her narrow, sharp features. A little gray showed in her hair and Halladay was aware that she was old by Makaum standards even though he didn't know her exact age. Slight as she was, her presence commanded respect.

Without Pekoz, the old man who was her constant companion and bodyguard, the Quass seemed incomplete. Pekoz was on bed rest under doctor's orders and Halladay knew that only Quass Leghef's insistence that he stay there kept the man from her side today.

Pekoz was still recovering from injuries he'd suffered during the assassination at the Festival of the Beginning. The Quass had suffered from injuries as well, life-threatening ones at that, but she had bounced back surprisingly quickly.

Halladay tried to figure out how to respond to her statement. Admitting his apprehension wasn't something he wanted to do. He glanced around at the general's secretary and three other officers waiting to see Whitcomb.

"Oh, don't worry." Quass Leghef waved away his concern. "I doubt any of these other soldiers have noticed. There are no outward signs. You're very good at masking your feelings. I have simply been around you long enough to get a sense of you. That talent is part of what makes me a good politician."

Ongoing scientific studies had shown that the Makaum people had latent psi abilities. Speculation held that those abilities had been honed in the jungles, allowing them to sense the predators that filled the wilderness that comprised the planet. The Makaum weren't forthcoming about those abilities.

"Yes, Quass, I have to admit that under the circumstances I am feeling some duress." If he'd only had one battle facing him, Halladay thought he would have been fine. But there were several, and how he proceeded with them depended largely on how the general reacted to his visit.

His and the Quass's visit. He wasn't alone in this. He needed to remember that, and remember the fact that he was representing his soldiers and the people they'd sworn to protect.

Quass Leghef patted him on the arm the way his grandmothers had done when he was a boy. It felt odd, but comforting all the same. "It will be all right, Colonel. After all, it's not like General Whitcomb is waiting to devour you."

"No, I suppose not."

"Then don't feel so grim. Everything will be as it should."

Halladay wished he felt as confident as the old woman sounded. He knew that Whitcomb was no longer the man that he had been. The general once possessed a keen, incisive mind. In his younger years he had been a warrior. When Halladay was a young lieutenant and got assigned to Whitcomb, Halladay had heard the stories and taken pride in his position.

Unfortunately, by the time Halladay had become senior on the general's staff, those halcyon days were gone. These days, General Whitcomb managed planets and star systems that needed protection from the spreading Phrenorian threat. They had been planets just like Makaum. And not all of them had been saved. The general had gotten good at giving ground before the enemy.

The young lieutenant at the receptionist's desk glanced up at him. She looked tired, but she still summoned a smile. "Colonel Halladay. The general will see you and Quass Leghef now."

Halladay stood, straightened his jacket, and offered the Quass an arm to aid her in getting to her feet. "Thank you, Lieutenant."

Quass Leghef took his arm only briefly, not needing much help at all, and stood at his side. She took in a breath and let it out. Then she led the way into the general's office.

General Whitcomb rose only slightly when Halladay and Quass Leghef stepped inside his office. The effort was perfunctory, with absolutely no heart in it.

Whitcomb waved a hand toward the two seats in front of his massive polycarbonate desk. The black surface gleamed as though freshly polished. "Good afternoon, Quass. Please. Sit."

The Quass sat and left the chair to her right open for Halladay. "Thank you, General."

Halladay did not sit. He stood at attention, eyes forward, his right hand cocked to his head at a precise angle, and waited for the general's salute or acknowledgment. The last time he'd been in the general's office, Quass Leghef had read Whitcomb the riot act, defending Sage's efforts to apprehend Ellen Hodgkins. That operation had turned bloodier than Halladay had counted on, stepped on a few toes the diplomatic corps had to tend to, and involved a surprising alliance with Captain Zhoh GhiCemid.

Whitcomb resumed his own seat. "At ease, Colonel."

"Thank you, General." Halladay fell into parade rest, but still he did not sit. That required an invitation in the general's presence, and since that invitation was not given, Halladay knew the general was planning on a short meeting.

This time Whitcomb held the whip and everyone in that room knew it.

Broad and blocky, Whitcomb seemed ponderous behind the desk as he pressed his fingertips together.

His short-clipped gray hair stood at rigid attention and his cheeks gleamed from a recent shave. The scar from along his cheek was a memento from his early years, back when his battles were fought on the ground instead of over a war table, but it had faded with time. "Quass Leghef, I'm surprised to see you."

"You were invited to the Festival of the Beginning," the Quass said. "You were missed."

Whitcomb hesitated for a moment, as if caught off guard by the statement. "My apologies, Quass. My duties necessitated my presence here."

"Perhaps next year, then."

Realizing how Quass Leghef was going to guide the general to the bargaining table, Halladay had to restrain a smile.

"I don't know if that will be possible," Whitcomb said.

That reply surprised Halladay. Although Whitcomb was pretty much ROAD—retired on active duty—these days, Halladay knew the man didn't actually retire for another three years.

"Is that so?" Leghef asked.

"I don't believe I'll be here next year," Whitcomb said.

"You'll be moving on, then?"

"It looks as though that will happen." Whitcomb smiled a little then, more smug than Halladay had ever seen. "In fact, the fort will probably be closing down in the next few months."

Shocked, Halladay barely managed to keep himself in check. Whatever orders Whitcomb had received about the fort's closure should have crossed his desk. He resisted asking any of the questions that flooded his mind.

"I realize this probably comes as a surprise to Colonel Halladay," Whitcomb said. "I hadn't had the chance to talk to him about the matter. It only recently became a possibility. Major Finkley, I believe you know him?"

The corners of Quass Leghef's mouth turned down in distaste. "We have met."

"Finkley is an outstanding soldier," Whitcomb said. "His father is the congressional chairman attached to the committee overseeing the Terran military's defensive posture on Makaum." The general leaned back in his chair. "Chairman Finkley is convinced that military resources on Makaum are being wasted and can be better utilized somewhere else."

If she was surprised, and Halladay realized then that he thought the woman might not have been, Quass Leghef gave no sign of it. "Makaum has been supplying resources for your war with the Phrenorians."

"This planet has also been supplying them to the Phrenorians."

"We have a non-partisan stance, General."

"I know, and all that fence-sitting has proved troublesome to the military in the past. Now it's reached the point of diminishing returns. Chairman Finkley is on the verge of pushing the matter to a vote. Once that happens—and it will—the Terran military here will close up shop and be gone."

Halladay couldn't help himself. "If the general will allow me to speak freely."

Whitcomb looked up at him. "Permission granted, Colonel, but only to get this argument over now. You're going to be wasting your breath."

"Sir, we can't just leave these people here. The Phrenorians are pushing in toward this star system direction. We need to hold this planet. Makaum can become a stronghold for our future operations."

"That's not how Chairman Finkley sees it." Whitcomb turned and gestured to the wallscreen showing

Makaum hanging in space. "The planet had only a limited amount of time to choose who it would support when push came to shove."

"My people don't want to be involved in your war," Leghef said.

Whitcomb clasped his hands and leaned his forearms on the desk. "Your people never had a choice about that. The Phrenorians won't allow it. We tried to make that clear to you. We tried to make that transition as easy as possible, but that has been beyond our control. Instead of being supportive of my soldiers on the ground down there, your people have attacked them on more than one occasion. In fact, the last attack happened only this morning." The general punched his desktop PAD.

The image of Makaum spinning below the space station blinked out of existence and was replaced with vid of the attack against Jahup and Tanest in the sprawl.

Halladay had watched the footage on the way up to the space station.

Whitcomb tapped the PAD again and the image froze at the point where Jahup took a hit from behind with a blast of roiling fire.

"In addition to the thieves, drug dealers, weapons merchants, and all manner of other transients my soldiers have had to deal with," Whitcomb said in a voice that grew steadily louder, "they're continuing to be endangered by *your* people. The people who we're supposed to be protecting!"

Leghef met the general's gaze and held it. She spoke in a cold, clear voice. "In point of fact, General, the soldiers in that vid are *my* people. One of them is my grandson. *Both* of them are young people barely into their adulthood. I watched them grow up and now I have to sit by and hope they live through each day they serve in your ranks."

Whitcomb shot a glance at Halladay for confirmation.

The colonel nodded. "Yes sir. What the Quass says is true. Those soldiers who were attacked this morning are both Makaum volunteers."

The Quass didn't back down. "*Volunteers*, General. In *your* war. You won't find any of our young people fighting for the Phrenorians. As I understand it, the ranks of Makaum youth within your soldiers have continued to increase. We are not ready to sign on with your war, but we are not stopping those who wish to participate. Our young people have made a difference for your command."

Whitcomb worked his jaw muscles and his eyes blazed with unspoken rage. "It's too little, too late. The Makaum Oversight Committee will make its decision in the next few days, but the verdict is foregone. It's out of my hands."

Anger burned in Halladay. He knew he'd been shut out, and Whitcomb had used Major Finkley to get to his father. It wasn't the Terran Alliance leaving Makaum. It was the general.

Quass Leghef remained surprisingly calm, but Halladay could "feel" her as well and knew that she barely contained her venom. "Then, in light of your certainty that my people are to be abandoned and left for the Phrenorians, I demand relocation for them."

Whitcomb blinked in consternation, then narrowed his gaze in a silent accusation. "What?"

"My people claim asylum with the Terran Alliance. According to the terms of our agreement with the Alliance, you have to agree to that."

TWELVE

Struggling against nightmares mixed with his child-hood memories of Sombra de la Montaña and the loss of his legs on Nogdria 7, Sage blinked awake and fought the narcotic haze of the meds that tried to drag him back under. As he raised his right arm and reached across his body, it felt heavy, like it had been filled with plascrete. Ignoring the numbness in his fin-gertips making it hard to grip the IV running to his left arm, he closed a fist around the lines.

Med machinery bleeped around him, but not all of it was attached to him. There was an emergency going on somewhere else in the med center and those alarms reso-nated farther away. He took a breath, struggled at the brink of unconsciousness, and focused on the lights above him.

A uniformed nurse appeared at his bedside and tried to tug Sage's arm away from the IV. The nurse was young and determined, and he was strong enough to make getting out of the bed difficult.

"Master Sergeant! Master Sergeant! Let go of the IV!"

"Nurse." Sage's voice sounded strange to him, and his tongue felt thick and dry. "Unless you want to end up bruised, embarrassed, and regretting your present course of action, you'll let go of my arm."

Startled, the young man let go of Sage's arm but stayed close. "My orders are to keep you sedated so you can heal."

"I'm countermanding those orders."

"Captain Gilbride—"

"Isn't here right now. I am." Sage yanked the IV out of his arm and felt a sharp, fierce bite as the needle and adhesive tape tore free. "And if the captain was here, I'd be having words with him. I've got soldiers to tend to."

He swung around and put his feet on the floor. Head spinning, he paused and blinked, then clutched the bed. He wasn't sure if the dizziness was a result of the meds or injuries he'd sustained.

Gilbride, looking more disheveled than he had earlier, entered the room and stopped a few meters away. "You're not going to be helping them if you get up and fall on your face," he announced.

Sage stood. The military had taught him to do that for over twenty years. His balance swayed inside his head for just a moment, then evened out. He was tired, and fatigue was something he could deal with. "I'm fine. It's the meds. They'll pass."

Gilbride removed a penflash from his pocket and stepped forward. He peeled one of Sage's eyelids back and shone the light into his eye. "You're concussed."

"I've been concussed before. It won't kill me."

"Not yet. But you keep taking damage like this, you're going to end up with neurological problems."

"I'll be careful."

Gilbride flicked off the penflash and put it away. He sighed. "Outside of having you tranked, is there any way I can get you to stay in bed longer?"

Sage wanted to be up and moving. There was too much to do, too many things that could go wrong at any moment. "No."

Gilbride shook his head. "The colonel wants you to rest."

Sage rolled his neck, felt the dizziness slide from one side of his head to the other with that familiar twisting sickness, and maintained his standing posture through an effort of will. It wasn't the first time he'd been concussed, and this wasn't the worst. He masked his feelings as best as he could. "The colonel needs me in the field. This place is a powder keg. How long was I out?"

"A few hours. Should have been more. I'll know next time to dose you heavier."

Looking around, Sage asked, "Where is my suit? My armor? My weapon?"

Gilbride nodded to the nurse and the young man hurried from the room. "We'll have them for you in a moment." He rubbed a hand across his face. "Maybe it's good that you're up. I'm going to need the bed space."

That caught Sage's attention. "What happened?"

Gilbride made notations on his PAD. "Civil unrest in the streets, and it looks like it's going to get worse. Do me a favor before you leave, Master Sergeant."

"I'm not much in the mood for doing favors for you after this morning."

"You'll thank me later. Those few hours you slept could be all you get for a while. Things have been happening since you've been in bed."

"What things?"

The male nurse returned with a cart bearing Sage's

clothing, armor, and weapons. Sage checked everything over automatically, satisfied that his equipment
was there and in working order.

Gilbride looked grim. "Jahup's in surgery."

The news turned Sage's blood cold. He didn't want
anything to happen to the boy, and yet he'd been responsible for sticking him out there on the line where
he could be hurt. Then he pushed that out of his mind.
Jahup hadn't been a boy for a long time, not since he'd
started hunting to provide meat for his people.

"How is he?" Sage asked.

"I think he's going to be fine. He was attacked and
he got locked in his suit. The armor protected him from
the worst of it. He's got some first-degree burns that
I'm treating him for. They had to cut him out of the
suit. By the time they opened it up, he'd asphyxiated. I
don't think he was without oxygen more than a couple
minutes."

A couple minutes. Sage thought about the time,
knowing that a human brain could hold its own for four
minutes without oxygen. Under most conditions. But
he'd seen soldiers die in less time too.

"He hasn't come around yet," Gilbride said. "He's in a
coma. I'm not trying to bring him out of that until we've
finished with him and he gets some recovery time."

Sage shook his head. "What do you want me to do?
You know more about his situation than I do."

"His girlfriend is out there, waiting to see what happens. She's alone and I don't think she needs to be.
She had to kill one of the locals to save Jahup. From
what I've heard, she knew the man. I thought maybe
you could give her a few minutes."

Sage pulled his uniform on, not even thinking about
his nudity in the small space. His mind focused on
Jahup and Noojin. Then another thought struck him.

"Okay. Has anyone told Jahup's grandmother? She could be there for the girl."

Gilbride hesitated. "Quass Leghef is visiting General Whitcomb."

"Why?"

"I'm not privy to that."

Sage cinched his pants and reached for his armor. "Does the colonel know?"

"Colonel Halladay went with her."

Sage ran his hands along the bottom of the hardsuit and locked everything into place around him. Someone had taken the time to clean the armor, but it still showed wear and tear from last night's battle. He'd have to see to that soon.

He pulled his thoughts away from whatever it was Halladay and Leghef were doing. There wasn't anything he could do with that at the moment.

Finished dressing, he magnetically adhered his helmet to his hip and logged back on to the active board. He checked Kiwanuka's status and discovered she was at the fort, no longer patrolling the street. He pinged her comm but a communications tech picked up.

"Sergeant Kiwanuka is engaged and can't be interrupted at the moment," a polite male voice said.

"This is Sage."

"Can I help you, Master Sergeant?"

"What's Sergeant Kiwanuka doing?"

"Interrogating a prisoner."

There was nothing posted about a prisoner. "What prisoner?"

"A smuggler she picked up at the Styx Spaceport a few minutes ago."

"Roger that."

"I can interrupt her if you need her, Master Sergeant Sage."

"No. I'll leave a message on her comm." Sage broke the connection and turned his attention to Gilbride. "Thanks, Doc."

Gilbride nodded. "My pleasure. But seriously, Master Sergeant, if you notice anything out of line, anything that's bothering you, let me know the minute you do. The med suite on your suit can't do everything."

"I will." With the suit's assistance, Sage walked easier, but he was more aware of that assistance than he was normally.

At the end of the hallway outside surgery, Noojin sat alone in a chair. She had her arms wrapped around herself and her elbows rested on her knees so that she was partially doubled over.

For a moment, Sage stood there and stared at her, thinking how young she was, how young Jahup was. And both of them were caught up in the Phrenorian War threatening Makaum. Even though Jahup had been injured by a local, that violence had spun out of the Terran-Phrenorian aggression.

Everybody in the middle got squeezed. That was something Sage's father had mentioned on more than one occasion, and he'd been talking about life on the mountain as well as the war against the Phrenorians.

But this time, these people got squeezed because of what I started. Guilt stung Sage and he struggled to put it aside.

As if she sensed him there, Noojin looked up and locked eyes with Sage. Tears tracked her cheeks and she looked haunted. She brushed away her tears and straightened her face.

Feeling inadequate, wishing Kiwanuka was there instead of him because she would probably better know the things to say and do, Sage went forward. He was used to dealing with soldiers, not teenage girls. Some of the female soldiers he'd trained hadn't been much older than Noojin when they'd arrived at boot camp, but even a couple years' difference was huge.

And the female soldiers had chosen to become military personnel. They'd had training. Noojin had had the situation thrust upon her.

Sage gazed at the chair beside Noojin.

"Would you mind some company?" he asked.

She shrugged. "You can sit if you'd like."

It wasn't exactly a gracious invitation, but Sage sat. He held himself straight, not wanting to lean forward and chance the dizziness returning.

Noojin glared at him, as if she were upset he wasn't more damaged. "I thought you were hurt."

"The doc was being extra careful with me," Sage said. "Gilbride likes to make sure things turn out all right." He paused uncertainly. "I'm fine. In case you were asking."

"That's good." Noojin rubbed at her eyes. "You've heard about Jahup?"

"I have. He's in good hands."

"He got burned and locked in his suit. He wasn't breathing."

"He's breathing now, and he's going to be fine."

Noojin searched his face. "You believe that?"

"I do. And Gilbride promised me Jahup will be good as new." Sage paused, hoping he hadn't just lied to the girl. "The report says you saved him."

She shook her head. "Do you know what saving Jahup meant?"

"It means he lived."

"It means I had to kill an old man who was not even truly himself anymore." Noojin's voice grew tense and cracked. She stared at the floor between her scuffed boots. "Oeldo's mind was going. Old age was taking him away, and he was destroying what was left with offworlder drink."

"He doesn't sound like the kind of guy who would attack Jahup and Tanest on his own."

"No, Oeldo was put up to the attack by Throzath."

Sage thought the name sounded familiar but couldn't place it. None of that had been in the reports he'd seen so far.

"Throzath is Quass Tholak's oldest son," Noojin added. "Tholak is against all offworlder presence on Makaum."

Sage remembered the man from his and Halladay's talk with Quass Leghef regarding the attack on Fort York. Tholak had struck Sage as a grim and hard man who wouldn't dissuade easily. "You think this came from Tholak?"

For a moment, Noojin made no reply. Nurses hurried by in both directions, all of them looking exhausted, and a maintenance robot zipped noisily by and left a freshly scrubbed floor in its wake.

"I don't know," Noojin answered. "Things . . . things have gotten confusing." She took a breath. "I quit the Makaum corps among your soldiers because I thought Jahup was wrong thinking siding with your people is the only way we're going to get out of this safely."

Sage wanted to be brutally honest with her. "At this point, Noojin, there is no 'safely.' This situation that exists here, it's going to cost lives all the way around. And some of them will be your people's."

Noojin looked up at him. "You know that because you've been in similar circumstances on your planet when you were a boy."

Sage didn't know what to say. He hadn't discussed his life on Sombra de la Montaña with Noojin or Jahup. He wasn't prepared to discuss that life now.

"The Quass told me what you said about your time

on the mountain on your world." Noojin pressed her lips together. "I wanted to hate you for taking Jahup away from me. She wanted me to understand you."

"I didn't take Jahup away."

"I know, but I wanted to blame you. Jahup never really knew his father. His father was a good man, but he was gone too early. Jahup has always missed him." Accusation blazed in the girl's eyes. "Jahup had made his peace with that. Then you came here and he saw you fighting people he despised, winning against them and the odds. In no time at all, he wanted to be like you."

"That wasn't my choice."

She laughed at him, but tears still fell. "Of course it wasn't your choice. It couldn't be. If you'd tried to influence Jahup, he would have made fun of you and gone back to hunting. That was where he should have been. Hunting. With me. Not in the street where he could get hurt."

Sage looked at her steadily. "You were in the street this morning too."

Wiping tears away, Noojin nodded. "I made a mistake. I let myself be weak when I heard that he was in the sprawl. I only got back this morning, and the stories about Jahup and your team taking down the weapons suppliers was all anyone would talk of. I had to see him."

"If you hadn't been there, Jahup might have gotten killed." Sage paused, letting that sink in. "From what I saw on the vid, a lot of people might have gotten killed. Maybe you don't believe it right now, but you did the right thing."

She took a shuddering breath. "I just want Jahup to be okay. I want him healthy and strong and—" Her voice broke and she couldn't talk anymore. Slowly, she leaned into Sage's shoulder. He dropped an arm across her back and held her.

THIRTEEN

Compartment 683-TMOP HQ
(Terran Military Offplanet Headquarters)
Space Station DSC-24L19
Loki 19 (Makaum)
LEO 331.9 kilometers
1243 Hours Zulu Time

Whitcomb blanched as Quass Leghef's words registered. "You want *asylum*?"

Caught at first by surprise, Halladay could only watch as the general turned apoplectic. Then Halladay had to stifle a smile. The Quass was nothing less than spectacular as a politician.

Leghef sat calmly in her chair. "Yes. I want asylum. For my people. As is provided in the Articles we signed with the Alliance when permission was given to build your fort. Your government agreed to that, and I'm going to hold them to that."

Still trying to catch up to the surprise, Whitcomb

swiveled his gaze toward Halladay. "Did you know about this?"

Halladay was as stunned as the general looked, but he was recovering quickly. As usual, Quass played things close to her vest. He would never have thought she would make the request. Many of the Makaum people had already taken to space, but most of them wanted to stay onplanet. "No sir. I didn't know about the oversight committee's decision to pull out of Makaum either."

"The colonel did not know I was going to invoke that right, General."

Whitcomb regarded Leghef under thick brows. "That 'right,' Quass Leghef. I don't know of any such—"

"If I may, General," Halladay interrupted smoothly as he pulled it up on his PAD, "the right she's referring to is located within the Articles written for the arrangement the Terran military has with the Makaum people, through its governing body. It was one of the codicils in the contract the Alliance signed to establish the fort here. I can read you the exact wording—"

"That will be all, Colonel," Whitcomb growled.

Halladay quieted. "Yes sir."

"I can't read the codicil to you," Leghef said, "but it's something to the effect that if events should come to a head on the planet and the Makaum people should find themselves in an untenable position due to an upgrade in Phrenorian hostilities, the Terran Alliance would guarantee safe passage off this planet."

Halladay almost chuckled. It wasn't verbatim, but it was close.

Whitcomb's eyes narrowed and he shifted in his seat. "We can't undertake something like that overnight."

"I would hope not, General."

"Do you know how long moving your people off-planet will take?"

Quass Leghef stood. "No. This will be my first time to abandon a planet, General. I'm sure you're quite practiced in those procedures. Perhaps you can give me an estimate."

Whitcomb didn't reply.

"Either way," the Quass said, "I want my people removed if the Terran military is going to leave. As per terms of our agreement. Your presence here has left my people in a more precarious position than we were in before your arrival. And until you're ready to take us somewhere else, you have to protect us." She paused to let the moment hang. "As your government bound you to do."

Whitcomb was speechless, one of the few times Halladay had seen that occur.

The Quass turned and walked toward the door. "Colonel, I suspect you'll need to talk to the general. I'll wait for you, but don't be overly long. I have a population to move and I'll require assistance from a military officer who's on the ground."

"Yes, Quass."

Whitcomb looked at Halladay but didn't speak till after the door had closed behind the Quass.

"You put her up to this, Colonel," he accused.

Halladay faced the general and didn't back down. If that old woman could beard Whitcomb in his lair, Halladay had to rise to the occasion. "No sir. I did not. If I had thought of it, I would have. As you'll recall, General, I didn't know plans to abandon the planet were in the pipeline. If we pull out—"

"It's going to happen, Colonel. You have my word on that."

"—we'll be leaving these people in a difficult situation. That's not what I signed on to do."

Whitcomb stared at him. "You signed on to follow orders. It seems having Master Sergeant Sage around has had an adverse effect on you."

Halladay held his reply for a moment, just long enough to make sure it was the one he wanted on record. "Sir, Master Sergeant Sage is the kind of soldier I thought I was. A man who makes a difference. I want to make a difference." He didn't point out that he'd thought the general was that kind of soldier as well.

"Sergeant Sage has only made things worse since he arrived."

"That's not true, sir."

Whitcomb blinked in astonishment. "You're . . . *arguing* with me?"

Halladay was aware that the general was recording the encounter. He was as well. "I'm not arguing, sir. I'm stating the facts. If you'll refer to the after-action reports I've sent up to you, you'll see Sage has shut down a major part of the drug trafficking that was going on here."

"Under your orders, I'm told."

Finkley *had* been talking. The drug takedowns had gone on under the radar. Halladay cursed the major. "Sage has also shut down a number of arms dealers, including the Zukimther black market last night. And he's managed to pull in locals to act as scouts for our units operating out in the jungle."

"He wasn't authorized to do that."

"I authorized it, sir, and those people have prepared us a lot better for action out in the wilderness."

"You weren't given orders to allow such conscription."

"As XO on the ground, the employment of local people comes under my purview, General."

"To work the service industry, yes. But—"

"Those young Makaum soldiers work as scouts and help train our people. Almost every time a military unit has been assigned to a sector, orders were cut to take on locals to help with scouting and human intelligence gathering."

Whitcomb blew out an angry breath. "I'm not going to debate the matter with you. I will tell you this, though. Once we quit Makaum, you're going to seek reassignment somewhere else. You won't be in Charlie Company anymore. Is that understood?"

Halladay held back all the sharp retorts that came to mind, including the one that if anyone shouldn't be in Charlie Company it was the general. "Yes sir. Crystal."

"Dismissed, Colonel."

Halladay saluted, didn't bother to wait for Whitcomb's response because one wouldn't be coming, and executed a perfect heel-and-toe 180. He walked toward the door.

"One other thing," Whitcomb said.

Halladay faced his superior. "Sir."

"Tell Sage that I hope he enjoyed his time here. It's as close to the war as he's going to get as long as he wears a Terran military uniform. Of course, that may not be for much longer once I've finished my report regarding his rebellious service here."

"Yes sir." Halladay let himself out, wondering how the encounter could have gone so badly.

Leghef waited for him near the exit. They walked together toward the elevator.

"That didn't go as expected," Leghef said.

Halladay saluted the two guards at the elevator and stood while one of them summoned the cage. When it arrived, he waited till Leghef entered and followed her. "No."

"I know we were going to tell the general about the

Phrenorian base," Leghef said, "but I don't think it would have mattered."

"If anything, it would have made him push up our departure date."

"How long do you think it will take him to arrange closing the fort?"

"A few days to get it through the committees and Command, assuming he's already laid the groundwork, which it sounds like he has. Then everything will be packed up and loaded in a few weeks, a couple months at the most. Terran military's got moving down to a science. The fort will be abandoned and we'll extrude another one wherever we're assigned." Halladay grimaced. "Wherever *they're* assigned."

"They?"

"The general will be putting in reassignment orders for me as well."

"You can do better, Colonel."

Halladay grinned sardonically. "If you'd told me that a few months ago, I would have argued. After this morning . . . I'm sure you're right." He looked down at her. "That's not going to do you or your people any good, though."

"We'll see. Not all of the cards are on the table yet."

"I didn't know you played cards."

Leghef shrugged. "There are games on the PADs that can be played while waiting on conference calls and information to arrive. I quite like a game called Texas Hold'em." She smiled at him. "We've still got a few cards coming."

"You surprised me back there."

She smiled brightly. "Did I?"

"Calling for asylum. I didn't think you'd do that."

"That was just a ploy, Colonel. I was born on this planet, buried my husband and son on this planet. One way or another, I'll be buried here too. But . . . I'm not buried just yet. Demanding the general make allowances for our asylum should slow down everything he and this oversight committee are doing. During such time, things can . . . *develop*."

Halladay smiled. He liked her a lot. "Yes, ma'am. That's guaranteed."

"In the meantime," the Quass said, "I think it's time to draw another card. I know that Master Sergeant Sage has been working on a plan to get into that secret Phrenorian stronghold."

"One of these days, you're going to have to tell me how you know so much."

"People talk to me, Colonel. After all, I am Quass."

"Yes, ma'am. You are."

"I think we need to see if the sergeant is ready to implement what he's been planning."

"Taking out that base?"

"Yes."

Halladay took a breath and considered all the ramifications. Things could go south quickly. "An action like that may make things worse."

Leghef shook her head. "For whom? We're about to be abandoned by our protectors and left vulnerable for predators. I should think exposing the Phrenorians' disregard of the treaties with my people and with the Terran Alliance might change things."

"Are your people ready to enter into the war on the side of the Alliance?"

Leghef hesitated. "Not yet. So many of them hold on to the belief that they can escape this violence. Or play both ends against the middle. Having the Phrenorian base exposed will push them as well." She frowned. "Unfortunately, I think the Phrenorians are going to be pushed too. After this, if Master Sergeant Sage is successful in his endeavors, there will be no comfort zone left for anyone."

Halladay totally agreed. It was going to be interesting to see what happened next. So much would depend on what Sage could manage in a short amount of time.

FOURTEEN

A-Pakeb Node
Biolab
Makaum
29118 Akej (Phrenorian Prime)

Alone in his private quarters, Zhoh sat dressed in lightweight armor instead of full battle armor as he awaited the time for the duel. Plates of *daravgane* covered his thorax and groin and left the rest of his body exposed. Even those, though, wouldn't stand up to the nano-edged *patimongs* that would be used. Only the *arhwat* on his left primary would do that. The small shield was thick enough to withstand sword blows, but it wasn't big enough to hide behind.

He wasn't going to hide, though. Today, for the first time since Sxia had tarnished him with their defective offspring, he would get the chance to fight for his honor. He could no longer live without it.

A chime announced someone at his door.

"Come," Zhoh called.

The door slid to the side and Mato entered in full battle armor. For a moment, he stared at Zhoh.

"What?" Zhoh demanded. "You look as though you've never seen a Phrenorian warrior before. Well, here is one now."

"*Triarr*, I don't wish to question your choice about this fight—"

Zhoh stood. "Then don't. Watch today and learn how a true Phrenorian warrior fights his battles and gains honor."

Mato bowed his head. "Of course, *triarr*. I only wanted to inquire if there was anything else you would need."

Zhoh relaxed a little. Mato didn't deserve his wrath. "No. I have everything I need. Thank you." He looked at the other warrior. "Do you still wish to be my second in the matter?"

"It will be my honor, *triarr*."

The comm on Zhoh's personal workspace buzzed for attention. Since he had been on Makaum, it had never buzzed. That comm linked to the wormwave, meant for encrypted tightbeam communications with the home planet. Zhoh could not guess who might be calling him.

"Give me a moment," Zhoh told Mato.

"As you wish." Mato left the room.

The comm buzzed again.

"On," Zhoh commanded.

Immediately, a holo image blossomed into being and filled the room with the caller.

General Belnale, his cybernetic primary wrapped in his cloak, gazed around the room.

Zhoh snapped to attention. Anger flared through him as he guessed that the warrior had only shown up to ridicule him in some fashion. "General Belnale."

"Relax, Captain. I am here on unofficial business.

In fact, the record of this communication will be expunged as soon as we are through."

"If you're here only to descry my honor, then—"

"Perhaps," Belnale interrupted in a tone that brooked no interruption, "you would like to hear what I have to say before you commit offense, Captain."

Zhoh controlled himself with effort. "Of course."

Belnale regarded him silently for a moment. "That was quite the speech you delivered earlier. Quite impressive."

Confusion rattled through Zhoh as he stood there. He hadn't experienced any nod to his competence since the birth of Sxia's abominations.

"I could not show my true thoughts in front of the War Board because not everyone there agrees with my view of things," Belnale continued. "I know you were treated badly. Thrown out like dung after Blaold Oldawe chose to protect his family's honor instead of owning up to a weakening bloodline. He is in an untenable position, but his family has chosen their path, choosing to stay with what they perceived as safe measures. In the end, he will only save himself and perhaps his daughter. His name will wither and die, and his bloodline will disappear from the annals of our empire within a generation."

That admission surprised Zhoh. Bloodline among Phrenorians was sacred.

"I fear our battles with weaker races, those more interested in material concerns, have brought some of our people down to their level," Belnale said. "We have watered the blood, and the only way to strengthen it again is with new blood. The old blood, that which is growing stale and tepid, must be drained." The general looked at Zhoh. "You are part of that new blood, Zhoh Ghi-Cemid, and it is time others recognized that in you."

Despite his pride in hearing those words, Zhoh still suspected some trick. What he wanted could not be so easily given. Or it would, but only if it would be taken away again the moment he reached for it.

"The way to your restoration will be difficult," Belnale said, "and you will set the first stone on your new path by becoming the new general of these troops on this world. I knew Rangha would not do well here, but he was placed here—as were you—in an attempt to put him in a situation where he could do the least harm. However, where I fought against Rangha's assignment, I championed yours. I wanted the strength of a primary to supplement the weakness of a secondary. Rangha . . . lacked." He put his arms behind his back, a defenseless move that warriors did not often present. "I also know Rangha was dealing in black market enterprises and that you put a stop to that."

If Zhoh had thought he had been surprised before, he was truly astounded now. Still, he said nothing, showed no reaction, and controlled the release of pheromones as his body threatened to subvert his control.

"Rangha had powerful friends looking over him," Belnale went on. "Such things change slowly among our people. Too slowly. Tradition has become more important than honor to some, and it is meant to provide a layer of protection to warriors who are no longer good enough to follow—or serve, which is intolerable. I intend to excise the weakness from our culture once again. To do that, I will need honorable warriors. I want you to be one of those warriors."

Zhoh's surprise gave way to pride. "Of course, General."

"You see why there must be no record of my visit here. My plan will take time to develop strength and hone its edge. If I step forward too soon, if I am premature, my goals will not be recognized and will go unmet."

"Yes, General. Tell me what I must do."

Belnale's *chelicerae* rippled in excitement. "Do what you were born to do, Captain. Destroy your enemies and protect the Empire. Kill Colonel Echcha, and the others if necessary, and take your rightful place as the leader of these warriors. Then deliver this world to the War Board."

"I will, General."

"I wish you strength and cunning." Belnale faded from view as the comm disconnected.

Excitement coursed through Zhoh as he looked around his quarters. The *krayari* beetles, kept there to clean his suite, scuttled to the corner, angry and starving because he hadn't fed them. He had been stoking their hunger for Echcha's dead flesh. A meter in length, the carnivorous insects reared on their back legs threateningly, but they didn't approach him.

Soon he would have the general's quarters. He would kill whomever he needed to, and he would enslave Makaum for the Empire. All that he had lost would return to him.

Med Center
Fort York
1409 Hours Zulu Time

Sage felt someone's eyes on him and woke instantly, not moving because he felt a weight against him. Noojin slept propped up against his shoulder. Not believing he had slept as well, chalking it up to the drugs still floating in his system, he looked up.

Gilbride approached from down the hallway with a PAD in hand.

Stomach tight, dreading what was to come, Sage looked the question at the doctor.

"He's out of surgery," Gilbride said with a weary smile.

"What surgery? I thought he was okay except for a few burns."

"There was a brain bleed that showed up later. I've got that taken care of. He's got a couple bad burns, but we can regrow skin for that in the next eight hours. I'm going to try to keep him in bed, but he can be as bad a patient as you are."

"I'll make sure he understands he's supposed to do what you say," Sage said.

Gilbride shook his head. "Yeah, like you'd be the one to tell him."

Noojin sat up then, and looked embarrassed to find herself asleep against Sage. Then she saw Gilbride. "Jahup?"

Gilbride smiled at her. "Jahup is going to be fine. He's out of surgery and breathing on his own."

"What about the coma?"

"We brought him around and he's responding well. He came out of it on his own."

"Can I see him?"

"He's sedated," Gilbride warned. "We're going to keep him under for a few more hours and let the medical nanobots do the necessary repair work."

"It doesn't matter if he's asleep."

"He won't know you're there."

"*I'll* know I'm there."

"Yes, I suppose you will." Gilbride spoke briefly into his comm and asked for a medtech. In less than a minute, one joined them and took Noojin away. Gilbride turned back to Sage. "I was surprised to see you sitting with her this long."

"She needed someone. She doesn't have family."

Gilbride scowled. "I know. That also means she's not going to have anyone looking out for her when she's back in the sprawl. You know she shot somebody else besides the guy who nearly killed Jahup and the other soldier, right?"

Sage nodded. "A local named Throzath. Somebody else." That was in the report.

"Well, *Throzath* isn't happy about being shot. If you watch those vids, and I have, Noojin shot Throzath without real reason."

"That man was interfering in a med recovery op," Sage said with more venom than he'd intended.

Gilbride held up his hands in surrender. "I'm not the enemy here, Master Sergeant. You don't have to convince me. But Noojin's actions are going to cause problems because not a lot of public sympathy has been generated for her."

"She did the right thing in my book."

Gilbride lowered his hands. "You're not the only one keeping score. When you're a medical person on a world like this, where kids get sick or hurt and you're willing to treat them, you make friends among the local populace. I have. I've had more than a couple grateful parents tell me that Throzath plans to get revenge on Noojin once she's away from the fort."

"That was another reason you wanted me to be with her."

Gilbride nodded. "I knew she'd be safe with you." He sighed. "But she's not going to be safe out there."

"I can't touch Throzath. Civil disobedience doesn't fall under our charter. I can't shove a Roley in somebody's face and make them like the Terran military."

"No," Gilbride agreed, "but I'm pretty sure a murder attempt against a Terran military soldier does fall under our agreement with the Quass."

"Throzath didn't pull the trigger on Jahup and Tanest. Noojin killed the man who did that."

"Yes, she did, but the man who did pull that trigger came by that plasma burster by other means than his own."

Sage shook his head. "Weapons have been scattered all over the sprawl. We can't stay ahead of the black market supplying them."

Gilbride smiled. "I know, but what if I can put that weapon in Throzath's hands?"

"You can do that?"

"Yeah."

"That would change things."

"I thought it might," Gilbride said. "Do you have time to look at what I've found?"

"I do."

Room 1146
Med Center
Fort York
1422 Hours Zulu Time

Noojin sat on the hard bench outside the hospital room where Jahup lay unconscious in bed. A tube ran into his mouth, and much of his body was wrapped in something that a nurse had told Noojin was some kind of cyber-assisted skin graft bandage. Around him, machines beeped and clicked and gave digital readouts.

Despite the fear and sadness that had muted inside her only through exhaustion, Noojin still had to work to keep herself from crying. She felt so helpless.

And so alone.

Truthfully, though, she'd felt so alone she almost hadn't been able to stand it since the day she'd stopped speaking to Jahup. Now she couldn't even think why she would do something so absurd.

She just wanted him back so he could tell her how stupid she was being.

The door to the small room opened and Telilu peeked inside. She was Jahup's younger sister, only eight years old and still so innocent in so many ways despite everything that had happened lately on Makaum. Her hair was green-tinted, but it would get darker as she got older. She wore shorts and a pullover top with some cartoon character that was popular on the sims imported by the offworld merchants.

"Noojin?" the little girl asked.

Immediately, Noojin straightened herself up. Telilu couldn't see her like this.

"Yeah, Twig?" Noojin responded.

Telilu frowned. "Don't call me that."

"Okay."

Wide-eyed, Telilu gazed through the transplas that separated them from Jahup.

"I was at home with Kelcero's mom when I heard Jahup was hurt," Telilu said softly. "She was watching me because the Quass asked."

"I'm sorry you had to cut your visit short," Noojin said. "You should have stayed. I know how much you like spending time with Kelcero."

"Nobody knew if Jahup was going to be okay," Telilu said, "and the Quass went into space to speak to a growly-faced man."

Evidently Telilu had been spying on her grandmother again. It was almost humorous enough to make Noojin laugh.

"I wanted to come see Jahup and make sure he is going to be all right."

"He's going to be all right," Noojin assured her.

"Are you sure?"

"I'm sure." Noojin held her arms out. "Come over here and sit with me."

Slowly, Telilu came to Noojin and allowed herself to be placed on Noojin's lap. "So we can watch him sleep?"

"Yes," Noojin said. "So we can watch him sleep."

She held the little girl and they listened to the machines work. At least now, whatever happened, she wouldn't have to face it alone, and with Telilu there, she felt more hopeful.

FIFTEEN

Gilbride placed his palm against a reader and a door at the end of the narrow hallway *whooshed* open, letting Sage know the room beyond was airtight as well. They stopped in a small airlock as the door behind them shut. Immediately, a fine sterilization mist drifted over them, creating a momentary flash of colors.

On the other side of the transplas door, a gleaming array of med equipment sat around a long stainless steel table. The naked body of an old man lay on the table. The dead man's skin was sallow, covered in small sores and old scars. Sage almost didn't recognize the body as Oeldo, the man who'd attacked Jahup.

Around Sage, the room hummed, then a green light flashed and the second transplas door opened with another *whoosh*. Gilbride entered the room and Sage followed. His boots clacked against the stainless steel floor. Med equipment powered up as Gilbride swept his PAD over the room.

Sage stood to the side of the table and peered down at the dead man.

Oeldo was old, used up by the excesses he'd been addicted to. His flesh hung in greasy clumps, already separating muscle and fat, striations showing the weakening connective tissue.

Shoving a hand over the corpse, Gilbride gestured and swept his hand the length of the dead man's body. Instantly, a transparent holo of the corpse popped up above the table. "This is your shooter. He'd been killing himself slowly. Alcohol poisoning, mostly. The man's liver was a cesspool of toxins."

"He was in bad shape," Sage said. "I don't see how that helps."

"He was a time bomb waiting to go off." Gilbride waved his hand again and all the holo disappeared.

"Did he know?"

"Yeah, he knew." Gilbride took a breath. "He had a local doctor who was treating him. Trying to treat him. Quass Leghef cleared the red tape so I could talk to the woman. This guy"—he pointed angrily at the dead man—"chose to ignore what he was being told and kept drinking."

"He was sober enough to use a blaster."

"If Noojin hadn't killed him, he'd have been dead in another couple of hours anyway from a drug overdose." Gilbride waved his hand again. "You've heard of *vesgar*."

Sage nodded. He and Jahup had come across a drug lab that had made it. "Locals call it Snakedream."

"This guy was loaded with it. This drug is expensive. Whoever gave the drug to this man wanted to make certain the attack on our people wouldn't come back on him. I took a closer look to see how all the *vesgar* ended up in this guy. That's when I found this." Gilbride pointed to the inside of the dead man's right elbow.

Sage peered closely, looking at the mottled skin. "I don't see anything."

Gilbride gestured and a green thread ran up the dead man's right arm, through his heart, and up the right carotid in his neck to join the cloud in his skull.

"What am I looking at?" Sage asked. "More Snake-dream?"

"Yeah. Definitely more. Somebody used a hypospray to inject liquid *vesgar* into him."

"Did he know what he was doing when he attacked Jahup and Tanest?"

"He was in command of his faculties enough to know what he was doing. But he had been primed, Master Sergeant. With drugs and with a mission."

"You said you could tell me who did point him at Jahup?"

Gilbride gestured again. An orange oval appeared on the inside of Oeldo's elbow. When the doctor gestured again, the oval lifted and floated in midair.

Peering closer, Sage recognized what it was. "A fingerprint?"

"A thumbprint, actually." Gilbride smiled. "I have four fingerprints on the other side of that arm." He signaled again, and four more smaller ovals appeared and floated up. "Did you know that anyone who ships cargo offline has to register with ports that we control?"

Understanding fell into place for Sage. "You know who these prints belong to."

"I do." Gilbride touched his PAD and opened a window in the holo above the dead body.

An image unfolded there and showed the smug face of a young Makaum man that Sage recognized from the vid of the attack. "Throzath."

"Exactly." Gilbride waved at the table again and a complex, twisted triple chain blinked into being.

"What's that?" Sage asked.

"That," Gilbride said, "is Makaum DNA. It matches what's on file for Throzath, and it matches DNA from one of the epithelial cells I recovered from the plasma burster Oeldo used in his attack."

"Throzath's prints are on the blaster too?"

"Not his prints, but he left some skin cells behind. In addition, I found some from a Zukimther female, so I think we know where the plasma came from." Gilbride tapped his PAD again and three more sets of DNA, all of them triple chains, manifested as well. "I also have three more DNA samples, but no hits on identification. I'll bet you breakfast that Throzath knows who they belong to."

Sage was already thinking about what he could do with the information. "I'll buy you breakfast anyway. I think I'm going to go find out who Throzath's accomplices are."

Gilbride held up his PAD. "Would you like to know where he is?"

Sage grinned. "You're full of surprises today, Doc."

"I figured it would take some of the sting out of having you laid up for a few hours."

"Jury's out on that."

"I'll take what I can get. I'm sending you Throzath's coordinates."

"Where did you get them?"

"From Mr. Huang. He heard about what happened in the sprawl today and assigned one of his 'nephews' to keep an eye on Throzath. Then he told me once he heard you were in the med unit."

"Man's got a lot of family here."

"That he does."

"Thanks, Doc."

"Should I tell anyone where you are?" Gilbride asked innocently. "In case they ask?"

"You think I can send this up the pipe to the general? Get the okay to arrest Throzath for the attack?"

"Nope. That's why I wanted to tell you this off the record. Be safe out there, Master Sergeant. I don't want to see you on one of my tables again soon."

"Roger that." Sage pulled his helmet on and walked through the airlock. He thought about contacting Kiwanuka, but she was busy doing whatever it was she was doing, and he didn't want to distract her.

SIXTEEN

Standing with folded arms, Kiwanuka stared through the observation window into the room where Rakche Darrantia sat with her hands cuffed behind her. Watching the alien female leaning in her chair with her eyes closed and looking unconcerned, Kiwanuka's irritation grew.

"I think she's sleeping," Corporal Tom Culpepper stated.

Even without the AKTIVsuit, the man was massive, tall and broad. In combat gear, he looked big enough to be a monolith, and he was barely able to stand without banging his head against the ceiling. He held his helmet in one fist at his hip. His face was moon-shaped and innocent, pasty skin covered in freckles despite exposure to the elements. His blond hair was shaved almost to his scalp.

"Maybe you hit her harder than you think you did, Staff Sergeant Kiwanuka," Corporal Owen Pingasa suggested.

Like Culpepper, Pingasa stood at the window with his helmet at his hip, and like Culpepper, Pingasa was young. He was one of the fort's cyber experts, a specialist in drones and automated systems. His dark skin set him apart from Culpepper, as did the singsong Malawi accent that he refused to give up. "I saw the vid of the takedown. You face-planted her pretty good."

"You're gonna call that a face?" Culpepper asked. "I'll bet toilet seats have seen better features."

"You should tell her that," Pingasa said, tapping his temple. "Plant that seed of doubt in her. Let her know that her looks aren't going to get her out of the trouble that she's in."

Studying the alien female stretched out in the straight-backed chair, looking almost comfortable, Kiwanuka had to admit that Darrantia looked asleep. Or dead.

"Maybe she committed suicide so she wouldn't have to talk," Pingasa said.

"How would she do that with her hands cuffed?" Culpepper asked.

"Poison pill in a fake tooth."

Culpepper shook his big head. "Pretty sure Voreusks don't have teeth, and I think the medtechs would have caught a fake tooth in that beak. You've been reading too many spy novels."

"She could have killed herself another way." Pingasa leaned forward to peer more closely at the prisoner. His breath fogged the surface.

"Held her breath until she suffocated?"

"No. I had a cousin who used to do that when she tried to get her way. She only held her breath till she passed out. Then she started breathing again. She stopped trying that when she turned seven." Pingasa pointed to the prisoner on the other side of the one-way transplas. "But this one, she could have swallowed her own tongue."

"Have you ever met someone who swallowed his or her own tongue?" Culpepper asked.

"Of course not. They would be dead. How could I meet a dead person?"

"I meant *before* he or she swallowed his or her tongue."

Kiwanuka breathed out. "Do you two want to knock off the chatter?"

"Sure thing, Staff Sergeant," Pingasa agreed.

Culpepper grunted.

"We were just thinking out loud," Pingasa went on.

"Maybe you could think in a more productive manner," Kiwanuka suggested.

"Knowing whether or not the prisoner is dead is important," Culpepper said.

"She's alive. Check your HUD. Gilbride's got her bio info streaming from the bracelet on her arm."

Pingasa lifted his helmet and glanced at it, then he smiled. "She's *alive*!"

Culpepper cracked up and the two high-fived.

"Seriously?" Kiwanuka asked, only mildly irritated. She'd seen the two soldiers in action during the raid on Cheapdock for the weapons that had been stashed there. Based on what she'd seen, she'd assigned them to the present operation.

Pingasa shrugged. "Waiting gets boring. If we had something to do, it might not be so bad."

"You've got plenty to do," Kiwanuka said. "If this op goes badly, you're going to be assigned to the mess hall for a month."

"It won't go badly," Culpepper said nonchalantly. "The drone link and the crawler are prepped and ready to go. We're just waiting on you."

"We've done this before," Pingasa added.

"Normally it ends with us dropping some really incendiary packages on a target."

Pingasa yawned. "And we didn't have to wait too long to do that. Not like this."

"If this goes wrong and we lose tech support," Kiwanuka said, "I want the two of you to have eyes on her. So you can find her again."

"We won't lose her," Culpepper said. "I mean, how could you lose a Voreusk? There aren't that many of them on Makaum. Matter of fact, I think this is the only one I've seen."

"If you thought you'd seen another one," Pingasa agreed, "how would you know? I mean, there are those feathers, but they all have those."

"We could ask one of the Lemylians," Culpepper said. "I hear they go for Voreusks."

Pingasa smiled at his reflection in the transplas. "That's because once the romance is over, they eat them. One of them told me they taste like chicken."

Culpepper snorted. "Puts a new spin on dinner and vid."

"I think I liked the two of you better when you were blowing things up and breaking into security systems," Kiwanuka said.

"That's where we shine," Culpepper agreed.

"This is not a problem," Pingasa said.

Kiwanuka unfolded her arms and handed her weapons to Culpepper. Going in unarmed to a hostile interrogation was standard procedure. "It better not be. I'm going in."

Pingasa handed over a small computer chip that

looked like the head of a pin. "Just plant this on her the first chance you get."

Kiwanuka took the small device. "She's supposed to be tech savvy. She's going to find it."

"That does not matter," Pingasa told her seriously. "By the time she does find it, the damage will have been done." He gave her a thumbs-up and a confident smile.

Once she entered the interrogation room, Kiwanuka heard soft snoring and realized that Darrantia was asleep. According to the intel she had on the criminal, Darrantia wasn't going to be easy to impress.

Approaching the table, Kiwanuka kicked one of the legs. Since it was welded to the floor, the table didn't budge, but the ringing thud was loud enough to awaken the prisoner. Darrantia opened one eye and gazed at Kiwanuka. Judging from the cloudy, confused look, she had really been asleep.

"You again," Darrantia complained. "I still have that headache I told you about. You can't just hold me here without treating me. I've got rights. Get me a cell and an analgesic and send me away. I can sleep more comfortably there."

Without a word, Kiwanuka sat in the chair across from the criminal and took out a small vial of analgesics Gilbride had given her. She plopped the vial down on the table between them.

Darrantia flexed her arms. "How am I supposed to take those?"

Picking up the vial, Kiwanuka unsealed it and shook out the oblong green tabs. "I'm not freeing your hands. How many?"

Darrantia cocked her narrow head and peered closely at the pills with one eye. "Prescription or over-the-counter stuff?"

"I got them from the med center." That was the truth. One of Gilbride's techs had supplied her with the pills, including the one that now housed Pingasa's microchip. The tracker would pass through the alien's system, but there would be enough time for what they wanted to do. "They're not max strength, but they should get the job done."

Darrantia sat up straight. "You did a job on my head. You got any water? I don't do so good with dry pills."

Kiwanuka took a water bulb from her belt and held it in one hand, the vial of pills in the other. "I'm still not freeing your hands."

Darrantia cursed. At least, that's what Kiwanuka thought her prisoner did. The tone was right but the words were unfamiliar to her. "Gimme four."

The Voreusk opened her beak and turned her head so she could keep one eye on Kiwanuka. After her captor rolled the pills into her beak, she swallowed, then gulped water from the bulb.

Leaning back, Darrantia belched contentedly. "Do I get my jail cell now?"

Kiwanuka put the water bulb away and turned her attention to her PAD, pulling up the questions she'd already asked and starting in on them again. "No."

Darrantia closed her eyes and went back to sleep. Or feigned it. Kiwanuka wasn't certain.

Pingasa contacted her over the comm. "All good here, Staff Sergeant. Reading the chip five by five."

Feeling a little better about things, Kiwanuka kicked one of Darrantia's thin legs.

The Voreusk protested with another curse, this time in one of the trade languages and easily understandable. Kiwanuka chose not to be offended, though if Darrantia hadn't been handcuffed, she would have knocked the female on her feathered derrière.

"I'm not going to talk to you," Darrantia said.

Kiwanuka stared at her. "That's fine. I'm required by my commanding officer to go over these questions, so we're going to do that. And while I do, *both* of us are going to be awake."

Sighing in displeasure, Darrantia adjusted herself in the chair. "Sure. It's your party."

Kiwanuka asked her first question. Darrantia ignored it. Kiwanuka kicked her in the shin.

Darrantia tried to fold her legs under her chair and couldn't. "I'm not going to answer questions. I told you that."

Kiwanuka smiled sweetly. "That's fine. All I need is a verbal response to let the colonel know I'm trying."

"You're a—*owwwww!*" Darrantia folded her injured leg in and tried to protect it with the other one.

"You're going to remain polite, or you're going to have to be carried to the holding center."

"I hate you."

Kiwanuka nodded. "Hating's allowed." She moved on to the next question without missing a beat. She wanted to spend enough time to make everything believable.

Otherwise Darrantia wouldn't buy into the escape Kiwanuka had planned.

SEVENTEEN

A-Pakeb Node
Interstellar Communications
Makaum
27435 Akej (Phrenorian Prime)

P ride swelled inside Zhoh as he surveyed the death arena that had been marked off by a floating array of spinning *dynint* crystals in the center of one of the domes in the research center. When activated, the crystals would circle the *Ale'ory*, the field of honor where the *Hutamah* challenge would be decided, and any combatant who stepped outside of the ring would be hit with an electrical charge.

Only a short time ago, the large room had held research equipment for investigating Makaum's flora and fauna. During their tenure onplanet, the research division had unearthed several substances that could be rendered into bioweapons.

Such research was illegal, as was stockpiling munitions made from them, but Zhoh had done exactly that.

His storehouse wasn't nearly the size of the one Rangha had put together in his Yeraf River stronghold.

Zhoh had plans for that stronghold's inventory, and it would spell doom for any resistance on Makaum.

Colonel Echcha Ler'eti stepped onto the *Ale'ory* first, as was his right as the ranking officer. He carried a *braest* in his right primary and had an *arhwat* strapped to his left. Throwing daggers hung in a sash over one of his shoulders; the sash was secured to a belt at his waist that supported a *patimong*.

Echcha bowed to the *Seraugh*, and they responded in kind. Then the colonel turned to Zhoh and beat the *braest* against his *arhwat*. The sharp *clack!* of challenge rang throughout the chamber.

"Come, then, *kalque!*" Echcha roared. "Come and let your dishonor at least die a dignified death!"

Zhoh stepped onto the *Ale'ory* and the *dynint* crystals fired with purple electric pulses and whirled into eye-blurring motion. The static charge built up in the air around Zhoh and his blood felt energized.

Like his opponent, he carried a *patimong* and *arhwat*, but instead of the *braest*, he carried a *weduha*, a net woven from the sinew of *tanck* lizards on Phrenoria. Although small, the *tanck* were venomous and hunted in packs. They were prized for their thick carapaces and dense bones.

Not many on Phrenoria chose the *weduha* as a weapon because it took a lot of skill to use. Zhoh had chosen it because it represented the old ways of battling the primordial creatures that still hunted in the seas of his world.

Zhoh bowed to the War Board, then turned to Echcha. "I stand before you, and, because I respect you as a warrior of our people, I offer you this last chance to stand aside so that I may step into the destiny that calls me."

"That will not happen!" Echcha shouted. "If you want that destiny, you will have to walk in your own blood to get it!"

Silence filled the chamber for a moment, then a chime rang, signaling the start of the match.

Echcha ran forward, leaped into the air, and drove the *braest* toward Zhoh's face. The colonel was faster than Zhoh had expected, and his attack was far more aggressive.

Zhoh stepped back and batted the three blades to the side with his *arhwat*. His opponent's momentum and power drove him back another step and left him off balance. He tried to set himself to counterstrike, but Echcha spun on one foot and kicked out with the other. At the same time his foot battered Zhoh's chest, Echcha's tail flicked forward like a dart.

Twisting at the last moment, Zhoh pulled his head away from the barbed tail. The sharp edges slashed the side of Zhoh's face. Burning pain from the poison crawled under his damaged hardened outer skin and ate into the flesh beneath.

He welcomed the pain. Scar tissue was another form of *lannig*, a way for his body to become harder and stronger. Agony burned out the weaknesses in a warrior.

Echcha came at him again, more fiercely this time, and Zhoh knew his adversary was afraid he would not have the stamina to last through a prolonged battle. The knowledge made Zhoh more confident.

Echcha *feared* him.

Zhoh reveled in that and let the warrior spirit within him soar. He batted Echcha's *braest* to the side with his *patimong* and turned as it shot past him. He bent his primary and rammed the articulated joint, where his carapace was thickest, into Echcha's head.

Dazed and disoriented, Echcha stumbled to the side

in an effort to get away. Zhoh pursued his opponent and hammered Echcha's *arhwat* with his *patimong*. The ringing blows echoed in staccato punctuations in the chamber. As Echcha set himself for a third such blow, Zhoh feinted, then shifted and slid the *patimong* under Echcha's upraised primary, and sank the point into his adversary's lower mesosoma.

Black blood spilled from the wound, but Zhoh knew the blow hadn't been a fatal one. He yanked on the *patimong* to free it, but the blade was trapped in his opponent's exoskeleton. Echcha snared the blade with two of his secondaries and wrapped them around the weapon.

Echcha drove the *braest* at Zhoh's prosoma in an effort to bury the three blades between Zhoh's six anterior eyes. Abandoning his hold on his *patimong*, Zhoh threw himself backward and rolled to escape the thrust. One of the sharp blades dug a furrow along his mesosoma and nicked the bottom of his face.

He landed badly on the metal floor and tried to get to his feet, but Echcha was on him too quickly. Holding the *braest* in both primaries, the colonel thrust again. Zhoh rolled to get out of the way, but one of the blades ripped into his mesosoma, then tore a large gash in his side as it cut itself free.

Zhoh screamed in rage and pain as his black blood pumped out of him and ran down his side and leg. But he'd gotten clear and he rolled to his feet.

Attempting to make the most of his advantage, Echcha turned and thrust again and the *patimong* in his side wiggled and cut a wider wound. Echcha yelled as agony flared through him, but it didn't weaken his attack.

Zhoh ducked under the three blades and let them slide over his *arhwat* with a hiss. Stepping in at the same time Echcha came at him, Zhoh slammed the *arhwat* into his adversary's face. Echcha rocked back on his heels.

Moving quickly, Zhoh grabbed the hilt of his *patimong*, tore it free from the colonel, and opened the wound to at least twenty centimeters. Echcha was bleeding out standing on his feet.

Zhoh knew he had to win before Echcha died of the wound because he needed to show the *Seraugh* a decisive victory, not something fortune had granted him. He whipped the *weduha* forward and snared his opponent's *braest* in the tangles.

Concerned that he would lose his main weapon, Echcha yanked the *braest* back toward him in an effort to free it. Zhoh charged forward and whipped the *braest's* folds again, causing them to wrap over Echcha's prosoma and trap the weapon against the colonel's upper body. Both primaries were caught in the folds as well.

Setting himself, Zhoh pulled his adversary to the side and kicked out to knock Echcha's feet from under him. The colonel fell hard to the floor and struggled to get free. Before he could, Zhoh dropped on top of him and shoved his face into that of his opponent. His *chelicerae* darted out and caught Echcha's face.

The sudden realization of what was about to befall him triggered a pheromones release from Echcha. His fear smelled invigorating.

Zhoh's pedipalps, his smaller mandibles, flicked out and caught hold of those of his opponent and he envenomed the colonel like he would lesser prey or a female he wished to mate with.

Echcha screamed hoarsely until the poison robbed him of his voice. He shivered and shook and fought, but the venom took over his central nervous system and left him paralyzed.

Zhoh stood and faced the *Seraugh*. He was still bleeding from his wounds and his blood pooled over his conquered challenger, but he remained standing.

"This is my *Hutamah*!" Zhoh roared. "My honor was challenged! My right to lead warriors into battle was questioned! No more!" He turned his gaze to the other two colonels.

Nalit Ch'achsam and Warar Tindard stood outside the whirling lines of the crystals as they continued to circle the arena. Even from the distance, Zhoh smelled the fear and horror radiating off them.

"This is my war to fight!" Zhoh shouted. "I will take Makaum and present it to the Empire!" He pointed his *patimong* at the two colonels. "If you choose to stand in my way, I will end you as well!"

Silence hung over the arena, but Zhoh knew that everyone there could smell Echcha's terror.

The circling *dynint* crystals stopped but spun in their singular orbits on their own axes.

"Fight me or obey me!" Zhoh said. "If you betray me, I will see you dead and honor stripped from your families!"

The lieutenant colonels bowed their heads and showed their empty primaries at their sides.

"General Zhoh," Nalit and Warar acknowledged in the formal answer. "We live to serve the Phrenorian Empire, and you, who are its weapon."

The response was traditional when accepting a new leader, and it sounded like music.

Feeling a surge of ecstasy at his victory, Zhoh sheathed his *patimong* and knelt. Carefully, he removed the *weduha* and cracked Echcha's exoskeleton with his secondaries. He ripped the scales aside and carved the flesh beneath. Echcha still pulsed with life and the fear stink on him grew stronger.

Then Zhoh knelt and feasted.

Belnale and the other members of the *Seraugh* looked on with approval.

EIGHTEEN

Phrenorian Trade Sector
North Makaum Sprawl
1718 Hours Zulu Time

Sage drove the crawler deeper into the no-man's-land that existed in the uneasy ceasefire between the Phrenorian Empire and the Terran Alliance. Fort York's soldiers provided policing for eighty percent of the sprawl. Fifty percent of that was where Makaum citizens lived, and an additional thirty percent of the area was where the large corps had set up shops and warehouses. Those corps had leaned on the Terran Alliance for protection and supplemented it with their own squads who guarded corp execs and assets.

The other twenty percent had been deeded, by contract with the Quass, to the Phrenorians for development. It was an attempt to keep the Phrenorian Empire appeased.

Sage had given orders that no soldier at Fort York was to step foot into the area because it was one of the most crime-ridden regions in the Makaum sprawl. Before his arrival onplanet, occasionally Terran soldiers who wanted to tempt fate or try exotic contraband went missing or turned up dead.

Although the plascrete buildings that had been extruded to house offworld businesses weren't old, they were already falling into states of decay and disrepair. Most of those businesses were just fronts for the true profit centers of vice and black marketeering.

The only building in the area that stood against the encroaching jungle was the Phrenorian Embassy, and that edifice towered over its neighbors.

"These areas are much different than the parts of the sprawl where your soldiers police businesses, Master Sergeant." Jason Fachang sat in the crawler's passenger seat and watched the pedestrian traffic and the storefronts. His armor was protective only, with no built-in servos to boost his strength and speed.

With his augmented reflexes and muscle reinforcement, he was a weapon all by himself. Still, he was strapped with a top-of-the-line Birkeland coilgun on his right hip and Gatner fléchette pistol under his left arm. "You were right not to bring your soldiers into this."

Fachang was one of Mr. Huang's "nephews" somewhere along that particular family tree. Or maybe he'd been grafted on at some point. According to Mr. Huang, whom Sage had reached out to for this assignment, Fachang was one of his best people when it came to sec work in potentially hostile zones.

Once Sage had decided on a course of action, he hadn't wanted to bring his soldiers into the area. All of them were too green to know how to be low-key when bracing a potential enemy among unfriendlies. That kind of experience came at a cost and required a soldier who could de-escalate a situation that didn't have to go volatile.

So he'd notified Huang and subcontracted the necessary muscle. Huang had a number of trained combatants. Kiwanuka had made Sage aware of that.

"With everything the soldiers have been going through," Sage said, "they'd go guns hot at the first sign of trouble." He glanced at Fachang. "I don't want to do that here."

"Because that would make too many of these people think you were encroaching on their territory. The balance here must be maintained. Otherwise you'll aggravate more potential saboteurs against the fort. And the Phrenorians might choose to make more of it than what it is."

"Exactly. I'm glad you understand."

"The sudden death of General Rangha has left a void in the command infrastructure."

That interested Sage because none of the fort's cyber-intel groups had picked up any chatter. The Makaum soldiers hadn't mentioned it either.

"What do you know?"

"Uncle Huang believes that Captain Zhoh is preparing to exercise his ambitions."

Sage thought about that and didn't like it. Of all the Phrenorian command officers located on Makaum, Zhoh was the most experienced and most aggressive.

Terran military intelligence still hadn't sniffed out why he'd been demoted.

Sage turned his thoughts to the task at hand. He'd left his AKTIVsuit at the fort and opted for generic armor because he didn't want to announce the Terran military was coming for Throzath. He wanted a simple, quick takedown without a lot of violence.

"This may go sideways," Sage said as he checked the

crawler's GPS. Like his present armor, the crawler was unmarked, a castoff one of the larger corps had decided to abandon or had forgotten about. Mr. Huang had provided the crawler and the armor.

"I expect it to." Fachang rolled his head on his shoulders and the movement was smooth as silk. "Mr. Huang told me that. We"—he gestured to the two other security "consultants" in the crawler's rear seat—"hope to contain any negative reaction."

Sage flicked a glance at the other two sec warriors. One was a woman. Both were watchful and quiet, seemingly at ease with their assignment and not artificially relaxed with chems. That was reassuring.

Colonel Halladay wouldn't be happy with Sage's decision, but the man would accept it.

Provided they got in and out without creating a large mess. Taking Throzath was going to cause complications, but he hoped Quass Leghef would be able to put a damper on that.

The fact that Throzath was currently encamped in the sector overseen by the Phrenorians underscored the need to shut down the rebellious Makaum factions. Otherwise there would be more attacks like the one on Jahup and his unit.

"This close to the Phrenorian Embassy," Sage said as he took a right turn onto the street where the GPS told him his destination was, "people don't always worry about the law."

Fachang looked at Sage and smiled. His head was encased in an anti-ballistic and beam-resistant helmet. At the moment his faceshield was recessed. Wraparound dark glasses with ruby lenses hid his eyes.

"Mr. Huang knows that," Fachang said. "He has . . . *business* interests in this district too."

In order to be as good as he was in the spy business,

Mr. Huang had to break a lot of laws. Of course, there were also those who said it the other way around. In order to break a lot of laws, Mr. Huang had to be good at the spy business and sell information for "indulgences."

Mostly, Mr. Huang worked with the Terran Alliance and showed a special interest in developing worlds new to interstellar trade who were caught up in the war.

"What do you know about this place we're going to?" Sage asked.

There hadn't been much in the fort's intelligence files on Xurase.

"It's a mercenary bar," Fachang said. "Straight-up military special forces who have worked on several worlds, and bashhounds from the corp space stations. Some of the people the corps employ for wetwork and assassinations come down here to play and not have to worry about finding a place to drop a body. Or two. Their excesses are unlimited. People here quickly separate into predator and prey. *Xurase* is a Cheelchan word that means 'death art.' Because the people that go there are killers."

Sage couldn't help thinking that was a reflection promoted by the proximity of the Phrenorian Embassy. He knew that was skewed thinking, though, because every world he'd been to had a zone just like this one.

"Do you know the guy we're going after?" Sage asked.

Fachang nodded and frowned. "I know him. Mr. Huang doesn't do business with him or his father. Throzath isn't a merc or an assassin. My uncle is aware."

"I'm not exactly off the reservation with this," Sage said, "because Throzath is wanted, but I didn't hang around for a blessing from my CO."

"Mr. Huang told me. I am fine with this, Master

Sergeant. I know that Throzath is responsible for the attack on your soldiers this morning." Fachang pursed his lips. "That is one bit of information Mr. Huang missed that he especially regrets."

"It's not his fault," Sage said.

"No, but it has made Uncle, and us, more aware that control is slipping away on this planet. Helping you will aid Uncle's efforts to find better intelligence streams."

"Is Huang thinking now might be the best time to get offplanet? With his assets intact and ahead of the rush? A few of the smaller corps are doing that."

"On the contrary, the smaller corps aren't pulling out. They're selling out. In every case such as Makaum, where there is a discovery of a new planet and profits are to be made quickly before the trade balance swings to something more equal or the resources dry up, everyone who can rushes in. Then, when the war begins, they hang on to what they own—materials, land, contracts, resources—so they can sell it to the highest bidder when the time comes. This is an old technique. The transitory corps make a quick profit, seed money for their next enterprise, and go to find their next strike."

"You make war sound like a stock market."

"Profits are always available in wars, Master Sergeant. You just have to figure out where your bottom line is. Uncle teaches all of us this." Fachang paused. "When Uncle asked me to help you with this, he told me that you once saved his life."

That surprised Sage. "I've never met your uncle." Even now, he had used the commlink number Kiwanuka had given him when she'd first told him about the man to make contact. There had been no face-to-face.

"Uncle said he saw you on Nogdria 7 when the (ta)-Klar betrayed the Terran Alliance to the Phrenorian Empire and caused that world to fall to the Phrenorians. He told me you and your men saved a lot of people that day by holding the Phrenorians at bay till they could ship offworld."

For a moment, memory of that old police action rose up in Sage's thoughts. Those recollections had been in his mind when Gilbride had put him under too. He could still remember losing his legs there, thinking that he was going to die.

But he hadn't.

"Nogdria 7 was a bad situation," Sage said.

"It is the reason that Uncle no longer does business with the (ta)Klar," Fachang said.

"I didn't know he didn't do business with them."

"Mutual trade proximity elicits talk, and talk becomes information, but there is no serious trade with the (ta)Klar." Fachang nodded ahead. "There's Xurase."

The mercenary bar stood between a cyber-enhanced pleasure palace and a casino. Like the two businesses it shared space with, the bar had once been a sophisticated establishment. But now it was just one more seedy-looking dive among many.

It was plain and unadorned, gun-metal gray and three stories tall. Foot traffic weaved and stumbled across the street in both directions. A crowd had gathered around an overturned crawler and several of the onlookers held weapons.

That's not your problem, Sage told himself as he pulled the crawler to a stop in the alley down the block from Xurase. He didn't have jurisdiction here, and seizing Throzath was going to be complicated enough.

Still, part of him was relieved to see two Phrenorian warriors stride out of the casino and break out weapons. The crowd around the crawler thinned immediately. If someone there needed help, they would get it. Or if they were a problem, they wouldn't be for much longer.

The Phrenorian "protective" services believed in instant justice.

Sage got out of the crawler and pulled at his armored jacket to make sure it covered his weapons. The jacket hung to his thighs and covered the Smith and Wesson .500 Magnum on his hip and the twin Kalrak plasma pistols in shoulder holsters he'd liberated from the Zukimther weapons his team had brought in last night. Tangler grenades, lethal and nonlethal, were concealed in the jacket's pockets. And, in case Throzath resisted the coming arrest, he had a Rakan tranq pistol in his boot.

The arsenal didn't compare to having a Roley and an AKTIVsuit, so he was going to have to make do. He also didn't have the 360-degree view of his surroundings, and he missed that most of all.

Old school, Sage thought, and even though the danger was high, part of him welcomed it.

Two Lemylian warriors, both tall and broad-shouldered with blue crystal eyes and covered with ridged muscle, guarded the featureless plasteel door. Unlike the Lemylians that had protected Zorg's Weeping Onion the night Sage had captured the Makaum men who'd attacked the fort, these guards wore lethal weapons instead of shoktons.

Sage motioned to himself, Fachang, and the two other sec operators as he held out a credstick. "Me and my friends."

The Lemylian holding the wand reader studied Sage for a moment, then wanded the credstick and waved him through.

Sage pushed through the door and went inside.

NINETEEN

"ETA is two minutes twenty-seven seconds to impact point."

Kiwanuka stared at the vid showing the crawler trundling through the narrow streets packed with other vehicles. Most of those other vehicles were *dafeerorg*-drawn carts, but there were a few corps crawlers and pedestrians. All of those avoided the beasts and native wagons.

The crawler had Terran Army markings, which made it a target for rebels and enemies alike. That alone made Kiwanuka's gut clench. She would have preferred the vehicle be anonymous, but she needed the advertisement for her catch-and-release plan to work. It wasn't exactly something she felt Halladay would have approved of, but she thought Sage would have supported the subterfuge.

The image was streamed by overlapping gel cameras that had been fired onto buildings by an aerial drone less than an hour ago. The gel cameras had a short life span once they were implanted. They'd dry out and flake away within three hours. Nothing would be left behind.

"Roger that, Lima Two," Pingasa replied. He sat in front of the small computer he was using to run the op over an encrypted MilNet frequency. The unit used a tightbeam connect that made it hard to detect, much less crack, and provided instantaneous communication. "Reading you five by five."

In addition to the expandable main screen that was 1 meter by 1.5 meters, six other screens sat in two rows of three on either side. All of the screens showed part of the target neighborhood.

Culpepper sat in the corner and watched the main door of the small room they'd set up as op base for the current mission. The big man ate fried *ysecki* with a pair of chopsticks like he was on a day trip. The carton advertised Uncle Huang's Noodle Shop. Huang had a lot of pushcarts in the area today, and Kiwanuka had wondered if that was merely a coincidence.

Five other armored soldiers sat in the room too, but they were young and tense. Their inexperience showed in their attentiveness and rapid heart rates, which presented on her suit's sensors.

Kiwanuka preferred Culpepper's lackadaisical approach to the mission. He was relaxed, but he would shift into full-on mode in the space of a breath. Pingasa was totally locked into his element. This was all a game to him.

"Let me see the crawler's holding area," Kiwanuka requested.

Pingasa tapped the keyboard and an inset window opened on the screen.

Darrantia still wore the orange coverall she'd been outfitted with in the holding cell. She looked totally bored.

Three other prisoners, all of them soldiers, wore
orange coveralls. They talked quietly among themselves and ignored Darrantia like they'd been told to.

"Okay," Kiwanuka said.

"She's pretty relaxed," Pingasa said. "She should be
spazzing over the prospect of being shot offworld and
Gated to a prison colony. I know I would be."

"Why?" Culpepper used the chopsticks to dredge up
another bite of *ysecki*. "What's so bad about a prison
colony? You get fed. You get a bed. You even get
entertainment piped in. All you have to do all day is
whatever piecework the prison is contracted out to do.
Manufacturing. Packing goods. Hydroponics. Mining.
You ask me, it sounds a lot like the Terran military."

"Yeah, but look at all the undesirables you get at a
prison colony." Pingasa shook his head.

"Have you taken a look at some of the people in
our barracks?" Culpepper asked. "Nah. You ask me,
prison colony is easy. You even get your own bed and
don't have to hot bunk the way we do here. If you don't
change the sheets, you're sleeping in somebody else's
sweat here."

"Then why did you enlist?" Pingasa asked.

Culpepper grinned. "Like I told you before, they put
you in prison for blowing stuff up, but when you're in
the military, they pay you to do it and give you plenty
of explosives to do it with."

Pingasa laughed and reached back over his shoulder
to bump fists with the other corporal. "Terran military
all the way!"

"ETA is fifty-nine seconds, Lima One," the crawler
driver said, and those numbers took shape on the upper

left corner of the computer screen. They counted down too quickly. "Are we good?"

Pingasa flicked to another camera view. This one showed an unmarked crawler loitering in an alley. The vehicle was only a short distance from the jail transport crawler.

"Roger that, Lima Two," Pingasa said. "Lima Three, get moving in three . . . two . . . one . . . go."

The second crawler pulled smoothly into motion onto the street. At the same time, a cart driver slapped the reins across his *dafeeorg's* back and the big lizard lumbered into motion in front of the crawler.

Lima Three's driver cursed. "Do you see what happened?"

"I see it," Pingasa said calmly. He tapped keys and mathematical equations ran in a transparent stream across the screen. "I'm working on it. Be ready to break left and go around it on my mark."

"Roger that."

Pingasa tapped more keys and a red dot formed on the screen.

"What's that?" Kiwanuka asked.

"That," Pingasa said, "is a *SchmeltzerPress* media drone I just hijacked."

"You hacked it that fast?"

Pingasa hesitated.

"No," Culpepper said. "He hacked it right after we got here. He's been using it to track women in the bar across the street when you aren't in the room. What's the name of that place again? The Carmine Belelt-Cha? Something like that?"

Kiwanuka watched the numbers. They'd reached twenty-two seconds and continued dropping. The red dot swooped toward the cart.

"Man, Culpepper," Pingasa said, "do you think before you speak?"

"I do. I thought, if you let the staff sergeant think you can hijack an encrypted media drone in the blink of an eye, she's going to expect you to do it again in the future."

Pingasa's scowl turned into a grin. "True. It was me that wasn't thinking."

Culpepper grinned and returned to his meal. "Count on me to always have your back, brother."

The red dot flew past the *dafeerorg's* head. The lizard reared fearfully, bolted to the right, and burst through a collection of tables outside a small restaurant. Luckily only a few diners were there and they escaped harm.

Lima Three accelerated around the cart and sped toward the prearranged interception.

"Ultrasonics," Pingasa said. "Those big geckos hear things most humanoids can't. Thankfully, those media drones come with a full aud package of splendiferous sonic suites."

"Good job with the drone," Kiwanuka said, meaning it.

"Thanks, Staff Sergeant."

"But if you'd gotten discovered by the reporter piloting that drone while you were people-watching, you'd still be working latrine detail with the sewage treatment corps."

"Understood, Staff Sergeant, but in my defense, I would like to point out that I needed hands-on experience with the drone appropriation."

Despite her tension over the coming sequence of events, Kiwanuka had to repress a smile.

"Lima Two and Three, collision is in . . . three . . . two . . . one . . . *now!*"

On the screen, the second crawler bolted through

the intersection and T-boned the prisoner transport crawler. Instantly, the concealed gel-based explosive packs under the transport vehicle exploded along the right side. The shaped charges had been positioned to knock the crawler over.

Panels blew loose along both crawlers, torn free by fingernail-sized charges designed to make the damage look much worse. In reality, the crawler tipped over onto its side, rolled onto its top, and was driven four meters forward because Lima Three hadn't been at speed during the moment of impact.

Smoke and sparks spewed from the crawler's under-carriage.

As prearranged, several of Mr. Huang's noodle carts blew up as well. The old spymaster had volunteered his services, and never mentioned how he knew what Kiwanuka planned to do.

Kiwanuka looked at Culpepper. "Was the crawler supposed to end up upside down?"

The explosives ordnance operator was grinning happily. He leaned forward in his seat and stared at the computer screen. "Yes, Staff Sergeant. We found out the transport's rear door didn't always open when it was on its side. Getting it upside down was tricky, but there you go."

Kiwanuka eyed the thickening gray-white clouds around the tangled vehicles. "It looks like it's on fire."

Culpepper grinned bigger. "All blue smoke and mirrors, Staff Sergeant. Cosmetic effect only. It'll last a few minutes, then disperse on its own. And those fire extinguishers people are carrying out now? They're only going to make it worse."

A crowd of people gathered at the crash site. Most of those assembled outside the shops unconsciously formed a perimeter. Media drones swooped in to record the event. Only a handful of brave onlookers charged toward the overturned crawler. They unleashed streams of fire retardant foam and most of them actually hit the target.

Instead of suppressing the sparks, the foam made the pyrotechnics worse. An instant later, two geysers of flames shot up two meters. The onlookers darted back inside the shops.

A third geyser shot up, this one hitting at least four meters in height.

One of the crawler drivers swore. "Did you guys screw this up? If not for the armor, we'd be baking in here."

"Negative, Lima Three," Pingasa said. "Everything is going according to plan. Sit tight and let things develop."

"You're not sitting here, Pingasa."

"Stop the chatter," Kiwanuka ordered. "Maintain comm silence." She shot a glance at Culpepper, who had returned to his carton of *ysecki*.

Culpepper shrugged. "Artistic license. I felt it would help sell the wreck. Nothing's gonna burn down." He pointed the chopsticks at the screen. "And that smoke? It's laced with pepper spray, so anybody who thinks about playing hero will take one whiff and decide it's not worth it. That perimeter will be maintained."

Kiwanuka looked back at the screen. "I'm going to hold you to that, Corporal."

The transport crawler's rear doors shoved outward and more smoke roiled. For a moment it looked like flames filled the cargo compartment.

"Dry ice," Culpepper said. "Heated by a plasma charge to vaporize immediately. Also seeded with pepper spray. Your prisoner will come out of there struggling to breathe and not seeing well. She'll buy the accident, and the threat of an imminent explosion will hurry her on her way."

"You enjoyed this way too much, Corporal."

Culpepper's image was reflected in the computer vid and he was smiling wider than ever. "Did I ever tell you I was a concert stage manager in my teens before I signed up in the Terran military?"

"No, and we'll save those particular stories for over a beer later," Kiwanuka said. "Provided we get what we want."

Pingasa tapped the keyboard and the view flipped to a camera facing the back of the transport crawler as Darrantia stumbled into view. Coughing and rubbing her eyes with her cuffed hands, the Voreuskan peered out uncertainly.

"C'mon," Pingasa muttered, "you know you want to run. Buy this, buy this. You got lucky. It happens. And you know you don't want to go to a prison colony. Run!"

Darrantia threw herself from the overturned crawler and sprinted for the nearest alley.

Triggered by the computer chip within the alien, the camera angles on the monitors changed quickly to pick up her escape.

Kiwanuka knew their fugitive would elude their vid net in seconds.

Pingasa played the keyboard in quick syncopation. "I'm plotting projected flight lines now and looping in the hacks I've set up on local sec cams, but we're gonna run out of those quick because there aren't a lot of people down here who believe in passive defense systems."

That meant there were a lot of trade merchants and shoppers who carried weapons. Kiwanuka tensed. That facet of the op was beyond their control.

Somewhat.

Pingasa had installed a neural inhibitor in the tracking chip as well. If they needed to, they could shut Darrantia down with a signal. Before they had to do that, though, she wanted the Voreuskan to make contact with her team.

She intended to give Halladay the assassins of Wosesa Staumar. If they could prove the political leader wasn't killed by Terran military, it might help tip the balance of power in the sprawl.

"Is that tracker online?" Kiwanuka asked.

A grid overlay of the neighborhood flared to life on one of the screens. Darrantia's tracking chip showed up as a blue dot racing through an alley.

"Confirmed, Staff Sergeant," Pingasa said. "Reading tracking signal five by five."

Kiwanuka relaxed a little, but she still hated being a spectator. *C'mon,* she thought. *Reach out to your team. You're still handcuffed. You need help.*

For a moment, Darrantia disappeared from the vid streamers and became only a dot on the mapping grid.

"Does that store have vid?" Kiwanuka asked. "Do you have—"

Pingasa hunched over the keyboard. "I got this, Staff Sergeant."

Almost immediately, a vid view from inside the store came online.

Darrantia dodged into the electronics shop from the alley and barreled over a man walking through the exit. The tracking chip picked up the curses that followed Darrantia's arrival. The shopper, a Terran standard humanoid who spoke with a Mytntrod accent, reached for a concealed weapon on his hip.

Without hesitation, the Voreuskan slammed into the shopper with enough force to knock them both to the ground. The weapon slid free of the man's hands and skidded across the plascrete flooring tiles.

"What kind of weapon is that?" Kiwanuka demanded.

Pingasa locked on to the weapon and opened a magnified view of it on another screen. It was short and stubby, with an abbreviated stump of a barrel.

Don't let it be lethal, Kiwanuka thought.

"That's a Shednal neuropulse pistol," Culpepper said. "Short-range, non-lethal. Designed to incapacitate a target, not kill."

"You're sure?" Kiwanuka asked.

"I am."

Kiwanuka nodded. The assessment agreed with her own weapon recognition. "Leave her operational."

"Roger that," Pingasa said.

On-screen, Darrantia elbowed the man in the face as he struggled to get up. Then she head-butted him and grabbed his hair to slam his face against the floor.

Kiwanuka cursed. The Voreuskan could kill with her bare hands.

Darrantia threw herself after the stun gun as the shopkeeper broke out of his daze and reached behind the counter. Wrapping her hands around the pulse pistol, Darrantia rolled onto her side and pointed the weapon at the counter. The shopkeeper rose up behind the counter with a Kerch shrapnel burster in both hands.

The shopkeeper fired prematurely and Kiwanuka steeled herself, expecting her bait to be reduced to bloody rags on the shop floor. Instead, the shrapnel cluster vaporized a display containing Net-driven media earwigs into a spray of colorful plastic confetti less than a meter from the Voreuskan. The weapon's basso *boom* temporarily deafened the tracker as the aud compensator kicked in.

As the shopkeeper racked the Kerch's action, Darrantia fired. Although the beam didn't show up on vid, the Voreuskan's accuracy showed when the shopkeeper fell back limply.

Scrambling to her feet, Darrantia ran to the other side of the counter. Pingasa changed vid angles and pulled back behind the counter. Darrantia dropped to one knee and robbed the unconscious shopkeeper, taking a few loose cred notes, a credstick, and a handcomm.

When the Voreuskan juiced the handcomm, the screen flared to life.

"That's not password protected," Pingasa observed. "That's stupid."

"But it works for us," Kiwanuka said. "Can you access that comm unit through the store's Net array?"

Pingasa tapped the keyboard. "Actually, I'm booting off the tracking chip. Gimme a minute."

Darrantia clipped the comm to the front of the jumpsuit and turned her attention to the store's cred reader.

"Is she robbing that guy while she's using his comm to call for help?" Culpepper sounded impressed.

"That she is," Pingasa replied.

"I bet there are some unhappy old boyfriends in her past."

"Your kind of girl?" Pingasa asked.

"I don't know if I could work around the feathers."

Kiwanuka ignored the duo. If they weren't running their mouths, they weren't at their best.

The comm connected at the same time the cred reader spilled its profits onto Darrantia's borrowed credstick.

"She is good," Culpepper said.

"This is Darrantia," the Voreuskan said as she picked up the Kerch for a moment, then put it down and grabbed the pulse pistol again. She headed for the door.

"Trace that comm," Kiwanuka said, but she knew

she was speaking too late. Pingasa was already hitting keys.

"I've been compromised," Darrantia said, "but I'm loose. I need an exfil if you can manage it. Comm me back."

Once she stepped outside of the shop, the vid ceased and Darrantia was once more a blue dot on a grid map.

Silently, hoping they got lucky, Kiwanuka pulled on her helmet, slid her Roley into a ready position, and ran for the door. Pingasa, Culpepper, and the five other soldiers followed at her heels.

TWENTY

Sage swept the bar with his gaze as he led his group into the soft darkness that filled the large space. Xurase occupied the whole lower floor of the building. The second floor surrounded an open area that looked down on the first floor. Plasteel rails decorated with weapons framed the opening. Doors led to private rooms on the second floor.

In his estimation, only a few actual mercenaries occupied tables in the bar. There were a lot of posers. Some of them were Makaum youths who stood out with their humanoid features and slightly green skin tint. Male and female, they dressed in cheap armor and wore cheap weapons that would have been against martial law in the sectors patrolled by Charlie Company.

A lot of the hangers-on were offworlders, so the wannabe syndrome wasn't confined to just the locals. The collection of clientele came from at least a dozen different planets that Sage could pick out. They wore the same style of armor and weapons, and some of them had stylized Xurase logos featuring a flaming reticule. Nothing was low-key about the bar.

Alcohol and drugs were in use at the tables. Multicolored smoke drifted in layers against the high ceiling and along the partial ceiling that ran under the second floor. The dim lighting softened the appearance of the bar as well as the hard, blank features of the pleasure girls trolling the guests. It was early and the long night was coming, so there was no hard-sell push going on yet.

Along the wall to the right, four fighting rings held combatants who used different weapons and fought while referees managed the action and scored points. The one-on-one matches drew a lot of attention from the crowd and were also displayed on holos around the bar. Cheering burst out at irregular but short intervals. From the way credits changed hands at the table, gambling was encouraged.

Throzath and his friends sat at a back table near a pole where twin Caszom femmes used their tentacles to seductively hide their modesty while working through martial arts katas.

Like most of the clientele in the bar, Throzath wore offworld mercenary armor and carried a large plasma burster on his hip and a Nemkcha two-handed sword sheathed over his shoulder. A white medcover wrapped his left thigh.

Sage knew the young man intended the medcover to be a badge of honor. The story about the shooting that morning was still being broadcast on various media channels Sage had seen. He doubted the wound was still there. Throzath's father, Tholak, had been one of the big lottery winners among the Makaum when the worlds came to trade. Top-of-the-line med treatment would have been available to Throzath.

"Love the sword," Fachang said quietly. "Nemkcha steel, if I'm right."

"You are," Sage said. "And you rarely see those blades in anybody's hands who aren't Nemkchand."

"Do you think Throzath knows how to use it?"

"No."

Fachang chuckled. "Neither do I. It's a showpiece. He'll never get it out of that rig in time to do anything with it. He's fortunate there isn't a Nemkchand warrior in the bar to take it from him. They usually take the head of the offending party as well."

Sage silently agreed. His anti-ballistic wraparound combat specs had quickly changed to allow enhanced vision that swept away the shadows trapped in the bar. Curved and reinforced, the lenses would take a direct hit from a low-powered projectile weapon and turn it away.

Even so, getting shot in the eyes would incur a lot of hydrostatic shock. Sage intended to prevent anyone from shooting him in the face, but the lenses worked to keep fingers and knives at bay as well. Once he'd activated the glasses, they'd adhered to his face through static electricity generated through batteries in his armor.

"Good evening," a Shaqis femme said as she met them at the door. "Welcome to Xurase."

The hostess was petite with flawless light-blue skin and pink hair that swept her bare shoulders. Her antennae stood out from her forehead and wiggled slightly as she imprinted Sage's scent. If they had met before, she would know and remember where and when. And she would not easily forget him. The chances were good that she'd know him if they met again.

"Will you be sitting at the bar?" she asked. "Or would you like a table?"

"A table," Sage said.

A number of people sat at the bar, and it was twenty meters from Throzath and his group. All the variables between the bar and Throzath's table would be problematic when they had to move because Sage wanted to act quickly along the path of least resistance.

"Of course. You are in luck. This evening we have several tables available."

Sage nodded to a table. "That one."

Smiling, the hostess guided them to a table only three down from Throzath.

The young Makaum man was drinking and playing a game of *Ytasi*. On the holo projection floating only a few centimeters above the table surface, an army of men armed with spears and shields battled a flock of birds that were capable of launching feathers and dung at their opponents. Snow capped the mountainous landscape in places and offered treacherous footing.

A server in semitransparent orange synthwrap approached them and took their drink orders.

Throzath cheered loudly at the end of the turn as the game computer tallied both sides' losses. Most of the seventeen hangers-on cheered Throzath's step toward victory, but the congratulations might as well have been a canned response because the excitement was feigned. Even the losing player congratulated Throzath.

"He's a pampered one, isn't he?" Fachang asked.

"Yeah," Sage said, "but he also almost got some of Charlie Company killed this morning, and he's got a connection to weapons that are contraband under martial law. If they're in our sector, I want to know about it. And I want to send a message to anyone else who thinks attacking Terran Army personnel is a smart thing to do."

"Uncle is happy to help with that, Master Sergeant."

While the server went for the drinks, Sage took stock of Throzath's company. The three Terrans, two men and one woman, looked like corp muscle. All of them moved smoothly, like they were wired. Two others were Zukimther warriors and they towered over the rest of the group.

A sixth was also female, but she was Ishona, all corded muscle and fangs. The tips of her elongated ears poked through her black tresses. Her pelt was golden and glowed in the light-enhancing glasses. Her protective armor sheathed her full body like a second skin. She wore a Kimer beam weapon at her hip, but Sage knew she'd have several edged weapons concealed on her body. Ishona loved their claws and anything that was sharp and personal.

"I make six of them as bodyguards," Sage told Fachang.

Fachang nodded. "Agreed. I would assume they were added after the incident involving the soldiers this morning. How do you want to do this?"

"With as little blowback in the bar as possible," Sage replied. "I want Throzath's arrest to send a statement, but I want everyone alive. The head is close to the entrance." He pointed at the bathroom area. "The way it looks like Throzath's been drinking, he'll have to go soon enough."

"Unless he's had kidney filters put in," the woman said. Fachang had introduced her as Mei. The male was Min. Sage didn't believe for a moment those names actually belonged to them.

"When Throzath goes in that direction," Sage said, "we fall in behind him, take out the bodyguards as quickly and quietly as possible, then take him into custody."

"The same if he decides to leave?" Fachang asked.

"It doesn't look like he has plans to leave anytime soon, but if he does, we take him out on the street."

"Have you fought an Ishona?"

"No," Sage said.

"Let me give you some advice, if I may."

Sage nodded.

"Don't try to fight her face-to-face if you can avoid it. Stay out of her reach. She will be incredibly quick and totally vicious. Use whatever you can to keep the fight from being up close. Otherwise she'll kill you."

"I'll keep that in mind," Sage said.

The server arrived with the beers all around and set them down. Sage paid with a credstick and added a tip. They sipped the native brew slowly and watched Throzath play.

Only ten minutes after their arrival, Throzath got up and walked toward the bathroom. Two bodyguards led the way. The other four, including the two women, trailed after him.

Sage waited a beat, then pushed away from the table and followed. Fachang moved an instant behind him and fell into position behind and two steps to his right like they'd been doing this for years.

The women didn't hesitate to follow the men into the bathroom.

Sage pulled the Kalrak pistols from his shoulder holsters. The human woman trailing the group turned and set herself. Sage put one of the Kalraks against her midriff and pulsed a stun blast that traveled through her anti-ballistic armor and rendered her unconscious.

The woman dropped like a stone. Fachang caught her in mid-fall and dragged her through the door.

Striding up behind the Zukimther standing next in line, Sage put both pistols to the base of his target's neck, thumbed the power up to almost max, and shoved the muzzles against the base of the mercenary's skull. At the same time, Sage was aware of his reflection in the long mirror that ran down the side of the wall over the sinks.

In the mirror, the Ishona woman turned and locked eyes with his reflection.

"Look out!" she shouted. Long claws popped from her fingertips. She brushed Throzath aside and stepped toward Sage and his team as they entered the room.

Sage pulled the triggers and the Zukimther groaned loudly and collapsed to his hands and knees.

Sage passed the mercenary, knowing he wasn't out, only dazed for a moment, but the rest of the group had become aware of them and he had to clear a path for his team to enter the room.

Thrusting his pistols forward, Sage blasted the second Zukimther warrior as he spun and backhanded him. Airborne now, Sage sailed across the bathroom and slammed into the plascrete tiles covering the wall. The plascrete shattered and broken tiles dropped to the floor. The body armor he wore wasn't nearly as protective as an AKTIVsuit and his breath rushed from his lungs.

Immediately, the Zukimther warrior strode toward him and drew an oversized pistol that Sage didn't recognize. Willing himself into motion despite the spinning in his head, Sage rolled to the side as his opponent fired his weapon at the wall where he'd been.

TWENTY-ONE

Kiwanuka ran down the alley after Darrantia. She controlled her breathing and made her breaths come slow even though excitement tingled through her. The escape ploy was risky and she knew it. She was embellishing on Halladay's orders and it could all blow up in her face.

She pushed that thought out of her mind and glanced at the grid overlay on her HUD. With the images of the street map and the overlapping vid views that popped up as the fleeing Voreuskan ran into range of sec cams Pingasa had appropriated for their "network," as well as keeping track of people and vehicles around her, her attention was maxed.

Her boots slapped against the uneven plascrete surface where tree roots had broken through. Overflowing trash cans lined the alleys. Lizards and carnivorous spiders dug through the trash. A small *kifrik* emboldened by territorial aggression leaped at her and wrapped its legs around her helmet. Its fat body obscured her view and its fangs struck her faceshield repeatedly.

Cursing, Kiwanuka grabbed the spider and burst its body in her glove as she threw it away. Gray and white pulp stuck to her faceshield and only smeared as she tried to wipe it clean.

"Initiate helmet cleanse," Kiwanuka said.

Cycle initiated, the AI responded.

Pressurized cleaning fluid sluiced from the top of her helmet and washed the smears and remaining pulp away.

"Darrantia." The voice that came over the Voreuskan's stolen comm, relayed by the tracking chip, sounded mechanical. "I am here."

"Turit." Darrantia sounded pathetic over the tracking chip. "Can you track me?"

"Tracking you now." The person at the other end of the connection remained calm. The mechanical voice didn't give away the gender of the speaker.

"Can you get me out of here? I'm pretty sure I've got Terran soldiers following me."

"They are. Six or more."

Kiwanuka cursed and tried to decide whether she should increase her speed and settle for keeping Darrantia as a prisoner or give the scheme a little more time.

Of course, it was possible that Darrantia's mercenary team would write her off.

Or kill her.

There were too many variables in play that Kiwanuka had no control over. She ran out of the alley onto the next street and cut to the left. She almost met the oncoming crawler face-first at the same time the vid footage revealed the obstacle. There was no time to stop.

"Traffic," Kiwanuka warned as she leaped at the last moment.

She wasn't able to get the clearance she needed to vault over the crawler, but she got enough height to swing around feetfirst and slide over the vehicle. Metal screeched and her boots left long scars in the crawler's paint.

Across the street, Darrantia ducked into another alley and went off-vid again, but the tracker still pulsed on the street grid.

Darrantia cursed, gasped, and still somehow ran, as fleet of foot as an ostrich. Kiwanuka had seen the ungainly birds when she was a girl back in her native country.

"It's going to be okay," the mechanical voice said. Whatever reassurance the speaker had intended was lost due to the artificial nature of the device. "We have a plan."

"Did you copy that, Pingasa?" Kiwanuka asked.

"Yes, Staff Sergeant."

"Keep your head on a swivel."

"Roger that."

Kiwanuka gave a brief glance back at her team. They effortlessly avoided the traffic now miring the narrow road because of Huang's exploding carts. She couldn't help wondering what the "plan" was and how Darrantia's people had put something together so quickly.

Then she realized there was only one possibility.

They were already in the area. And if Huang's information was correct and they were chasing a phantom assassin, that meant they already had another target in their sights.

Kiwanuka knew she had to roll the dice. She only hoped Darrantia reached her team in time for Kiwanuka to prevent the coming assassination.

The Carmine Belelt-Cha
North Makaum Sprawl
1741 Hours Zulu Time

Breathing easily in spite of the knowledge that the
Terran military was even now in pursuit of Darrantia, Morlortai stood near a tree that grew through one
corner of the patio three stories above street level. The
threat of capture sweetened the experience of going
for the kill on his target. His blood cycled smoothly
through his body and he knew his heart rate had actually slowed.

The Phrenorian Embassy was a hotbed of activity.
Aircars flitted about and he was hopeful that Zhoh
would show up soon. Honiban still hadn't succeeded
in hacking into the Phrenorian network, but he was at
least able to monitor the traffic taking place.

Something big had happened in the embassy. During
his afternoon's surveillance, he'd noted the arrival of
the three officers to the structure. Normally Phrenorians
kept their command members compartmentalized so
they couldn't all be taken down at once.

General Rangha's death had left a void. Morlortai
had known that it would. And he'd guessed that Zhoh
would attempt to usurp command of the Phrenorian
forces onplanet.

"If Terran soldiers are pursuing Darrantia into this
part of the sprawl," Morlortai said, "they'll soon have
air support as well."

"They do," Turit confirmed. "Two jumpcopters are
now inbound from Fort York."

Morlortai slid his comm-assisted glasses into place.
"Good."

"How is that good?" Turit asked.

"Because things are already confused due to the exploding pushcarts and the crawler Darrantia escaped from."

"She didn't escape," Turit said. "That incident was carefully orchestrated. We've used such subterfuge ourselves."

Morlortai smiled at a passing hostess as he walked to the more distant corner from the Phrenorian Embassy. "I know."

He was also aware the angle to the aircar docks was still good. A few trailing branches from the trees offered some potential for disaster, but he didn't believe it was anything he couldn't manage.

"Imagine the chaos on this planet when I'm successful in taking out our target," Morlortai said, "when Zhoh goes down and a Terran Army contingent is on hand. The Phrenorians won't search for an independent contractor like us. They'll think the Terrans killed Zhoh."

"You haven't killed him yet," Turit reminded.

"I will. What's the ETA on the jumpcopters?"

"Two minutes and thirteen seconds."

Morlortai worked out the variable in his mind. "Direct Darrantia to me."

"There?"

"Yes."

"The Terran soldiers are snapping at her heels."

"That's where we want them." Morlortai pressed a finger against the magnification stud on his sunglasses.

Instantly, the image grew larger and his view of the Phrenorians milling around the aircar dock became clearer.

"One way or another, I'm taking a shot at the Phrenorian Embassy that will increase the tensions between these two armies."

"That's not going to help us acquire our target."

"Our target," Morlortai said, "is either going to be dead on his own account or he will have taken his place as general of the Phrenorians."

They had planned for that possible eventuality after seeing all the inner fighting taking place among the Phrenorians.

"Once Zhoh is general," Morlortai said, "he'll insist on leading his troops into battle. He'll become an easier target then."

On the airship dock, the doors parted and Captain Zhoh GhiCemid walked through them. The Phrenorian marched to the waiting aircar and boarded.

"How far away is Darrantia?" Morlortai asked.

"She's on the first floor and headed your way."

"ETA?"

"At her present speed, forty-seven seconds."

"That will work," Morlortai said. "Have our extraction route prepped and ready." He looked over at a multi-armed, matte-black Phrenorian drone that floated thirty meters away over another building.

The drone was three meters tall and half a meter thick. It hovered in a preselected grid and looked harmless. Over the time of the Phrenorian occupation at that end of the sprawl, people had gotten used to it.

Morlortai clicked buttons on the small pad he had in his pocket. A scarlet reticule popped up on his lenses, followed by wind speed and distance from the bar to the aircar dock. "Honiban, give me control of the drone."

"The drone is coming online," Honiban said in his cultured voice. The faint tinkle of piano keys in a jazz riff carried along the connection. "Did I mention to you that hacking a Phrenorian drone is almost impossible?"

"You did," Morlortai said.

The reticule on his sunglasses faded for a moment,

then came back an even deeper red color. Out over the street, the hacked drone stopped moving along its grid.

For a moment, Morlortai expected the other drones in the area to turn swiftly and fire on the hacked drone. That didn't happen. Instead, all of them except the one he now had control of kept churning through their preprogrammed flight routines.

Morlortai clicked more buttons and made certain he had complete control of the drone. He'd practiced what he was about to do several times on board *Kequaem's Needle*. His ship had a top-of-the-line holo suite that they used to run ops through at times. As part of the ship's cover, the holo suite was listed as an entertainment complement for passengers they sometimes carried.

"Darrantia's ETA is eighteen seconds," Turit said in his calm, synthesized voice.

Morlortai was focused now, only existing in the moment. Nothing else mattered but taking the shot. He pressed the arming button. "Understood."

Out above the street, the drone's upper hull split into halves and a Kimer 20mm mini-gun folded out of it on an articulated stand till it looked like a one-legged bird of prey had nestled on the floating platform.

Morlortai only had a tangential sense of the drone. Through his sunglasses lenses, he was a gunsight. He placed the reticule on Zhoh, cursed the fact that the Phrenorian was behind the bulk of the aircar, made the windage adjustment, and fired. The mini-gun spun into action and unleashed a stream of 20mm projectiles.

TWENTY-TWO

A-Pakeb Node
Aircar Docks
Makaum
27632 Akej (Phrenorian Prime)

There was no warning before the explosive rounds hit the embassy's aircar docks.

The plascrete railing framing the aircar dock ripped into shards and became deadly missiles in their own right. A handful of jagged pieces skidded across the aircar's reinforced top, tore into Zhoh, and staggered him. All of the shards but two shattered against his armor and exoskeleton, but two of them penetrated his mesoma and created knots of blinding agony.

He blocked out the sudden pain easily because he still had anesthesia in his system from having his combat wounds treated. He resisted the impulse to pull the shards from his body because he would only unleash torrents of blood. For the moment, the things that caused the damage also prevented his wounds and his condition from worsening.

"Protect your general!" Mato roared. He lifted a ballistic shield from a fallen guardsman who had been ripped apart and set the barrier in front of Zhoh and himself. The fusillade of 20mm rounds continued slamming into the aircar dock with decaying accuracy.

Other Phrenorian warriors surrounded Zhoh and set up their ballistic shields as well.

Dazed and in pain, forcing himself to think above it, Zhoh crouched behind the aircar as more rounds slammed into the vehicle and rocked it.

Mato studied Zhoh with the eyes in the back of his head. *"Triarr."*

Zhoh peered through the aircar's windscreen as another wave of destruction hammered the vehicle back a few centimeters. "I'm all right."

The aircar dock area shivered beneath his feet and seemed on the brink of separating from the main building. The long fall promised death if he went down with the platform and vehicles.

A half dozen warriors knelt at the wreckage with their rifles over their shoulders as they searched for the sniper.

Zhoh peered cautiously over the top of the aircar and spotted the drone that was firing on them. Recognizing it for what it was shocked him. "That's one of our drones."

"Yes," Mato said. His pistol lay on the ground in front of where he crouched. He held a PAD in his secondaries and typed. "Someone has hacked it."

"Is it the Terrans?" Zhoh's anger grew larger than his pain. He took a fresh grip on the Kimer pistols as the drone kept laying down suppressive fire. To have the Terrans attack him on the day he was promoted to general was intolerable.

"I don't know. Right now I'm trying to shut down that drone."

As a fresh wave of rounds hammered the dock, one of the Phrenorian warriors staggered back. His head and primaries had been separated from the rest of his body. Death claimed him and he fell. The rifle the colonel had carried lay only two meters away. A rocket launcher was mounted under the long barrel.

Zhoh threw himself from behind the aircar, hit the plascrete on his shoulder, and grabbed the rifle as he rolled. With the aid of his tail, he came up on his feet and shouldered the rifle. He pulled the weapon in and activated the targeting magnifier. He settled the reticule on the drone and flipped open the secondary trigger for the rocket launcher.

He squeezed the trigger and rode out the weapon's recoil as the dock area trembled under him once again. The rocket sped true and left a smoking contrail twisting in its wake. An instant later, the depleted uranium round carrying an explosive payload struck the drone and turned it into a smoking fireball.

For a moment, the drone's anti-grav drive core maintained integrity and it stayed aloft, but that quickly ended as the damage continued tearing through the sec machine. Screaming through the air, the stricken drone smashed into a small shop. A secondary explosion from the craft's power drive ripped the shop apart and spread blazes in all direction. A human ran from the shop with flames trailing him. He didn't make it far and became an incendiary pile of tissue in the street.

Movement to the right at one of the local bars drew Zhoh's attention. He was the only one standing on the aircar dock. His warriors remained hunkered down, ready to return fire.

Through the rifle's telescopic sights, Zhoh watched as armored Terran military soldiers spread out through the bar on the upper patio level. Most of the bar's patrons had hit the floor when the shooting started. A few had made a try for the stairs leading down.

Others shot at the Terran military.

Zhoh sighted in on one of the soldiers but held his fire for a moment. "Was the hack committed by the Terrans?" he demanded.

"I can't answer that," Mato replied. His attention was still on his computer.

"Find out."

Mato used all four of his secondaries to tap the keyboard. "I'm trying, General."

The Terran soldiers became embroiled in a skirmish on the patio as several of the bar's patrons drew weapons and opened fire. An explosion ripped through the bar and one of the armored soldiers flew out over the railing and fell.

As Zhoh watched and tried to figure out what he should do, a large-caliber bullet struck him in the chest and rocked him back. The trajectory of the shot told him it had come from the bar.

He aimed at the closest armored figure and fired. "Kill the Terrans," he ordered.

He had no doubt that they intended to assassinate him. He would not back down from the fight. He sighted at one of the Terran soldiers and fired again.

This time the soldier was knocked back and disappeared in the flash of another explosion.

The Carmine Belelt-Cha
North Makaum Sprawl
1742 Hours Zulu Time

Morlortai cursed as he watched the hacked drone hit
one of the shops across the street and explode. A glance
at the aircar dock at the Phrenorian Embassy showed
him that Zhoh still lived. Even worse, it had been Zhoh
who foiled his plan.

The assassin made himself breathe out. At best, the
drone had been a solid hope, but it hadn't been a sure
thing. He hated working without a true plan, and this
had been put together on the fly.

The gunshots and beam discharges behind him let
him know he had other concerns, as well as his own
safety to consider.

"Sytver!"

Hearing his name over the deafening thunder of
weapons fire and the detonation of a grenade, Morlortai wheeled to face Darrantia as she ran toward him.
Behind her, several of the bar's patrons had opened fire
on the arriving Terran soldiers. Evidently the civilians
blamed the military for the attack. A section of the bar
was in flames and was showered with debris from a
high explosive.

Doubtless several of those people thought the Terran
military was conducting a raid because the soldiers
were raising their security levels across the sprawl. If
the patrons hadn't been drunk or stoned or paranoid of
getting caught, they might have realized the Terrans
didn't have jurisdiction here. However, those were armored soldiers and they were sporting weapons. So,
jurisdiction or not, the Terran military had arrived.

"I have her, Turit," Morlortai said over the comm.

"They're tracking her, *syonmor*," Turit said in his coldly efficient voice. "There's no other way they could be on to her so quickly."

"I know. I've got a workaround." Morlortai pulled a degausser from his kit and flicked it to operational mode. It was a little wider than his palm, a little thicker than his finger, and held a one-time charge that would knock all electronics within a meter of activation off-line.

Unfortunately, there were also physical side effects on a being, too, because everything organic carried an electromagnetic field. Darrantia's eyes widened when she spotted the degausser.

"No!" she squawked.

Morlortai didn't give her a chance to protest any further. If she hadn't been valuable as crew and there was no personal relationship with her, he would have killed her outright to prevent her giving up any of their secrets.

But she was valuable, and he did like her.

So he slapped the degausser into the center of her chest and activated it. The dampening field discharged immediately and dropped Darrantia in her tracks.

Morlortai picked her up and slung her over his shoulder. He ran in the opposite direction of the arriving Terran soldiers. They'd gotten slowed down by the hostile guns among the bar crowd.

A Lemylian warrior emerged from a doorway that led into the private rooms in the bar's central hub. He was big and brawny and half dressed. He looked at Morlortai and held a Yqueu sniper rifle in both hands.

"What's happening?" the Lemylian demanded. His words were slurred and his reddened eyes couldn't quite focus. "Are we under attack? Is it the Phrenorians? I knew they—"

Morlortai swung his free arm up into the Lemylian's throat and dropped him to his knees. As the Lemylian struggled to regain his breath and panicked that his paralyzed throat might be smashed beyond repair, Morlortai bent and scooped up the sniper rifle. He turned to the railing and stared at the Phrenorian Embassy.

Zhoh stood there with his rifle to his shoulder. Like any good tactician, the Phrenorian was surveying the battlefield before committing.

"Get moving!" Turit admonished.

"A moment," Morlortai said. He dropped to his knees at the railing, leveled the Yqueu rifle on it, and sighted on Zhoh. Calmly, he squeezed the trigger and felt it buck against his shoulder.

The .50-caliber round struck Zhoh in the chest and knocked him back. Evidently the sights were off. Morlortai had been trying for a headshot where the heavy round might have a chance of penetrating the Phrenorian's exoskeleton.

Before he could fire again, a plasma charge slagged the railing only a meter away. The intense heat drove Morlortai from his position. He dropped the sniper rifle, grabbed Darrantia, and ran.

That shot hadn't killed Zhoh, but it had escalated the street battle into an all-out war zone.

Morlortai threw himself into the nearest door, found the closest stairway, and joined a dozen other beings in fleeing the bar. By the time they reached street level, he was just one among many trying to leave the area.

TWENTY-THREE

Kiwanuka's faceshield lit up and revealed fields of fire inside the bar. She overturned a nearby table and took cover behind it. Darrantia wasn't anywhere to be seen. Thankfully the tracker inside the Voreuskan was still operational. The blue dot held steady on her HUD and was only 22.3 meters away.

"Stun setting!" Kiwanuka ordered as she made the change to her Roley. "We've got civilians here!"

"You don't normally see civilians this heavily armed, Staff Sergeant," Pingasa said.

"I don't want to see them dead by our hands." They were already so far off the parameters of the mission Kiwanuka knew the fallout from it was going to be toxic. She didn't doubt that Halladay would stand with her to weather it, though.

"Copy that," Pingasa said.

"I don't think they're civilians," Culpepper said.

Private Zhu got to his feet and scrambled forward, obviously intending to secure the people trapped in the snare, but a plasma blast caught him in mid-stride and knocked him over the railing. The aud dampers in Kiwanuka's helmet quieted his screams as he plummeted.

They ended quickly.

"Status report on Private Zhu," Kiwanuka said.

Private Zhu isn't responding, the AI said.

"Is he alive?"

Private Zhu still lives but is nonresponsive. His vitals are low.

Zhu's readings flashed over Kiwanuka's faceshield. At least he was still alive.

Kiwanuka popped up and targeted two people with weapons and knocked them both down with stun rounds. Six more "civilians" with weapons took their place. Kiwanuka wasn't surprised. Makaum had started out as a powder keg, and the events of the last few weeks had only ratcheted up tensions.

The whole planet had slid into survival mode and the resulting factions had marginalized everyone.

"Lima Leader, this is Lima Control."

"Roger, Control," Kiwanuka answered. "Lima Leader reads you."

"Be advised that someone has attacked the Phrenorian Embassy."

Kiwanuka peered over the table as heavy rounds smashed into it. From her position, she could just see the Phrenorian Embassy and the aircar dock that listed dangerously, barely clinging to the structure. As she watched, the dock toppled in slow freefall.

For a moment, Kiwanuka was mesmerized, watching the plascrete chunks and boulders come down in a rush, tangled with aircars. Almost at ground level,

three aircars took flight with several Phrenorians huddled aboard.

When the mass of plascrete hit the ground, several
explosions detonated from the vehicles. Flames lashed
out, splashed across the thoroughfare, and reached
nearby shops.

Kiwanuka dragged her attention away and she
yanked a tangler grenade from her combat harness. She
pulled the pin and lobbed the grenade toward a knot of
men firing at her team.

The tangler strands exploded out, then contracted in,
snaring several of the gunmen into a knot.

"Pingasa, Culpepper," Kiwanuka said as she got to
her feet and ran forward, "on me."

The two corporals formed up on her at once and
matched her stride.

Kiwanuka ran across the bar, vaulted overturned
furniture, and stunned anyone who had a weapon and
looked like he or she was ready to put up a fight.

She focused on the blue dot on her faceshield till it
winked out of existence.

"Pingasa," she said as she rounded the curved bar
area where the dot had last been.

"I know," Pingasa said. "The tracker's toast, Staff
Sergeant. They must have realized she was chipped
and burned it."

Kiwanuka cursed as she reached the spot where the
dot had vanished. All she saw was a dazed Lemylian
getting to his feet and reaching for an Yqueu sniper
rifle a short distance away. She dropped him with a
stun round.

As she turned to search the area, a gel-grenade
plopped against the nearby wall and pulsed.

"Get down!" Culpepper roared.

Kiwanuka threw herself down, but the concussive

blast hammered her hard enough that she teetered on the brink of consciousness.

Stim suite online, the AI said. *Combat readiness required, Staff Sergeant Kiwanuka. You are under attack. Administering stims package.*

The chems raced through her body before she had a chance to refuse them. Her synapses fired on pure adrenaline and her head cleared, but there was already a dull headache lodged in the back of her skull.

Four orange warning vectors flashed onto her faceshield.

Pushing herself up, she looked in the direction of the attack and spotted four Phrenorians firing from the back of an aircar only a few meters from the bar's railing. Autofire from a machine gun that had popped up from a recessed area in the aircar sprayed rounds through the railing, chopping it to pieces. The rounds hammered Kiwanuka and her team and drove them back.

"Sting-Tails!" Culpepper roared.

Kiwanuka hesitated only a second. Terran soldiers and Phrenorian warriors currently operated onplanet under a truce that put them outside the Phrenorian War. That détente was violated now, and there would be repercussions later.

But first Kiwanuka intended to get her team to safety. They were outnumbered and the odds were growing longer.

She brought the Roley to bear, activated the grenade launcher, and put three gel-grenades into the air. One landed on the machine gun mounted on the front of the aircar, the second missed, and the third landed in the aircar's passenger compartment.

The machine gun blew into shrapnel and the heavy fire went away. Below, the second gel-grenade blew out the roof of a shop, and the third explosive munition punched a hole in the aircar. As the vehicle sank, the Phrenorian warriors abandoned the aircar and leaped onto the open area of the bar.

Tactical Command Center
Fort York
1744 Hours Zulu Time

Halladay stared in disbelief at the screens depicting the street battle around the Phrenorian Embassy. He hadn't been back to the fort more than three minutes before everything had hit the fan.

Views from the different soldiers' suits, as well as street cams they had access to, spread across the monitors at individual desks and on the big wall ahead of him. For the moment, he was staying with Kiwanuka's armor, watching as she and her team battled four Phrenorian warriors.

It was something he hadn't been expecting to see on Makaum, and it brought back memories of when he'd fought the Sting-Tails himself. That had been a long time ago. General Whitcomb had kept himself and his people out of the hotspots for the last few years.

Halladay knew the general was going to call for him at any second and demand to know what was happening. But the colonel also longed for the chance to strike back at the Phrenorians because he was certain they had no intention of letting the Makaum people off-planet. The Sting-Tails didn't want only the planet's resources. They wanted the labor force as well.

"What's happening?" Leghef asked. She stood beside him.

"Sergeant Kiwanuka was working an op for me that I'd hoped would clear up the confusion about who killed Wosesa Staumar."

"Do you know who did that?"

Halladay tensed as he watched the soldiers—*his* soldiers—locked in battle. "We think so, but we can't prove it."

"Proving it would be helpful."

Halladay swung to one of the comm officers near him. "Where are those jumpcopters?"

"Twenty-seven seconds out, Colonel."

"Show me."

The comm tech's screen cleared and revealed a sat view of the area around the Phrenorian Embassy. As usual, interference showed around the embassy building itself due to electronic cloaking devices. The two jumpcopters sped through the sky toward the target zone. Fires had broken out all along the street where Kiwanuka and her team were.

Halladay regretted sending so few people. If the Phrenorians had decided to go to war they could field a lot of warriors in seconds. Those soldiers he'd sent there would be dead in minutes.

"Scramble another four jumpcopters," Halladay ordered.

"Yes sir." The comm tech spoke rapidly into his headset.

"Colonel Halladay," another comm tech called. "I've got General Whitcomb online."

"Patch him directly through to me." Halladay flipped his monocle down in front of his left eye and blinked as Whitcomb's image flared into being.

"What is going on down there, Colonel?" the general demanded. His face was red. "I gave you strict orders not to engage the Phrenorians."

"We didn't engage them, sir," Halladay said. "They engaged us."

"Why?"

"I don't know, sir."

"I'm getting reports that *we* attacked them."

"Reports from whom, sir?" Anger tightened Halladay's voice, but he pushed it away because losing control now wouldn't do any of them any good.

"It's all over the Zaysem Network."

Halladay covered the headset mouthpiece and caught the attention of another comm tech. "ZNet. Now."

The comm tech tapped keys and his screen flickered and displayed real-time vid of the battle taking place in the northern end of the sprawl around the Phrenorian Embassy. Like the sat view juicing through the Terran military feeds, the embassy building was blurred and out of focus.

Block text on the screen read: TERRAN MILITARY DECLARES WAR AGAINST PHRENORIANS ON MAKAUM?

The question mark was subtle.

"Colonel?" Whitcomb said.

"Sir, ZNet is owned by the (ta)Klar. It's always in their best interests to keep us and the Phrenorians at each other's throats with false reports and fake news."

"Did the (ta)Klar initiate the attack on the Phrenorian Embassy?"

"No, sir." *Not that I'm aware of.*

"Disengage from that battle."

"Sir, we've got people in that area under fire."

"What are they doing there?"

Halladay swallowed hard. "I sent them."

"That's no-man's-land, Colonel. You knew that and you sent those people anyway?"

"They were following up on a lead that would take them to the assassin who killed Wosesa Staumar, sir."

Silence sounded for a moment, long enough that Halladay realized Whitcomb didn't know who Staumar was. He barely kept himself in check. Only years of observing the chain of command helped him do that.

"It doesn't matter," Whitcomb finally said. "Disengage."

"Yes sir." Halladay had no intention of following the order. Not immediately. He wasn't going to leave Kiwanuka and her team stranded to die.

Whitcomb broke the connection.

"Sir," the comm tech handling the jumpcopters called.

"Yes?" Halladay responded.

"We just lost the jumpcopters arriving on scene."

Halladay stared at the sat view and saw flaming wreckage tumbling from the sky where the two jumpcopters had been. "What happened?"

"Surface-to-air missiles mounted on rooftops took them out," the comm tech replied in a hoarse voice. "Their screens lit up in warning, but they were hit before they could react."

Halladay cursed.

"Those people were fired on from rooftops?" Leghef asked.

"Yes," the comm tech answered. "From civilian shops, Makaum dwellings, and apartment buildings."

Leghef looked at Halladay with pain in her eyes. "My people are more divided than I'd thought, Colonel. I'm sorry."

"It's not your fault," Halladay said. "This is how war goes, and the lines that separate opposing forces and combatant and noncombatant shift every day." He glanced at the comm tech commanding the jumpcopters. "Pull those jumpcopters back."

"Yes sir."

Not knowing how many pro-Phrenorian forces were in the area made sending in reinforcements impossible. Halladay scrambled to think of some way to salvage Kiwanuka and her team.

Lieutenant Murad stood nearby watching.

"Where is Master Sergeant Sage?" Halladay asked.

"I don't know, sir," Murad answered. "The last I'd heard, he was in the med center."

Halladay opened a channel to the med center. "Captain Gilbride, this is Colonel Halladay."

"I'm busy, Colonel," Gilbride responded. "From what I hear, we're going to have fresh casualties coming in."

Halladay watched the vid of Kiwanuka and her team battling the Phrenorians in a building of some kind. "I'll be brief. Do you know where Master Sergeant Sage is?"

Gilbride hesitated.

"Captain?" Halladay prompted.

"Yes sir. Sage is in the northern part of the sprawl too."

"What is—" Halladay stopped himself. There was no time to get into what Sage was doing there now. Soldiers needed help. "How do I reach him?"

"He and I had a special project, sir. He needed to be off grid for a couple hours. I've got a comm channel you can reach him on."

"Give it to me."

TWENTY-FOUR

Although the Zukimther merc's beam missed Sage, the plascrete tile vaporized and left a meter-wide impact area at least ten centimeters deep in the wall where he'd been standing. Twisted and torn pipes gushed water onto the floor.

Roaring, the Zukimther merc swung a big fist at Sage's head. Sage ducked and slid forward. He pressed one of the pulse pistols to the Zukimther's groin and the other to the mercenary's knee, then fired both weapons.

The huge mercenary howled in pain, his leg went out from under him, and he spilled onto the floor, but he immediately made an effort to get back up.

Mei stepped in behind him while holding a med-delivery spike. She swung the spike into the Zukimther's ear and the device shrilled as it delivered its tranquilizer payload.

The Zukimther's eyes widened in surprise and his efforts to get to his feet turned sluggish and awkward. Sage grabbed the mercenary's head by looping his wrist and the pistol behind his neck and bringing the bodyguard's face into contact with his reinforced knee armor.

Although he'd been roaring in pain, the Zukimther ceased moving once contact was made. He spilled bonelessly to the floor.

Fachang squared off against the Ishona woman and slid two small batons from under the back of his jacket. He flicked them and the weapons telescoped. Once extended, the batons were less than a half meter in length and colored black with gold trim.

The Ishona woman slashed at Fachang, and Sage hoped she wasn't about to hand him his head. Cuts opened along Fachang's neck as he ducked back and gave ground. Crimson threads trickled down immediately.

"Come get me," the Ishona spat, and smiled. "After I kill you, I'll stretch your hide for boots."

Fachang said nothing, but the batons flashed. He used his size and skill to beat her back into the other bodyguards and crowded them up so they couldn't easily use their weapons.

Mei and Min flowed behind him and took out the remaining two bodyguards with the tranqs. They moved efficiently, shifting only slightly to avoid blows and to administer the chems.

Throzath ran through the alley they'd intentionally left open for this exact reason, but Sage cut him off and blocked the way to the door.

"Sage!" Throzath gazed at him wildly. "What are you doing here? You can't do this! You're not allowed—"

Sage holstered one of the Kalraks, shot Throzath

with the other, and scooped up the unconscious man with his free hand. With Throzath over his shoulder, Sage stepped into position to try to take down the Ishona woman with the pistol. She was the only one left fighting.

Shooting her was impossible because she and Fachang were locked in such tight combat and moving too quickly. Even Mei and Min stood back and watched as they established a perimeter to shut the woman down.

The woman's savage cries reverberated in the room. Her claws flashed again and again, but nearly every time they were turned away by the batons. Fachang's armor was sliced in several places, but there was no blood except for scratches on his face, arms, and neck.

Three men wearing sec armor crowded the door.

Sage pointed his Kalrak at the nearest one, fired, and dropped the man in his tracks. Mei threw tranqs and the other two managed only a couple steps each before succumbing to the chem cocktail.

When Sage turned back around, Fachang swiveled almost too quickly to see and planted an elbow in the middle of the Ishona woman's chest that drove her back against the wall. She bounced off awkwardly, but was already slashing. Disoriented from the impact and committing solely to offense, she couldn't block Fachang's straight baton blow to her forehead. Her eyes rolled white and she fell.

Fachang didn't try to catch her. He turned and looked at Sage.

"Let's go," Sage said.

Batons in hand, Fachang took the lead, followed by Sage. Mei and Min walked slack behind them.

The bar's patrons were out of their seats now, trying to see what was going on. None of the professionals showed any interest in the confrontation. Three

Makaum men threw beer bulbs and invective, but kept their distance.

Once Sage passed through the door, he held the Kalrak close to his side so it wouldn't be as noticeable. Carrying someone out of a bar wouldn't attract more than a passing glance.

He put Throzath in the crawler's cargo compartment and snapped restraints on the man's wrists and ankles as the comm in his pocket chirped for attention. He pressed the comm to his temple and it adhered.

He headed for the driver's seat. "Sage," he answered.

"This is Halladay," the colonel said. "The comm signal shows you're still in the north section of the sprawl."

Sage didn't bother to deny it as he slid behind the crawler's wheel. "I am."

"We'll talk about why later. Right now I'm going to send you some coordinates. Staff Sergeant Kiwanuka and her group have stepped into a hornet's nest and they need help not far from your twenty. I'm sending support, but it's going to take a few minutes. You can get there first."

The coordinates pinged into Sage's comm and he saw Kiwanuka was only a couple klicks away. "Roger that."

In the distance, the *boom* of heavy weps fire was unmistakable. And it was coming from the direction Kiwanuka was.

Sage put his foot down hard on the accelerator and the crawler jumped into motion. "What's Kiwanuka doing there? She knows that section is provisionally listed as under Phrenorian control."

"Like you know grabbing up Makaum citizens in broad daylight will be frowned on. Both of you are off the reservation today." Halladay sounded tired and tense. "At least she's there on my orders."

Sage steered around carts and other crawlers, drawing curses in dozens of languages. "I'm on my way, Colonel."

"Understood. Be advised that you've got a contingent of enraged Phrenorians defending what they see as their turf. Things are . . . confusing there, and you're out on the pointy end, Master Sergeant."

"Connect me to her frequency."

"Will do."

Sage looked at Fachang as another series of explosions rolled over the area. Black smoke plumed into the blue sky between the plascrete buildings and tall trees.

"We're headed into that," Sage told his passengers. "I can put you out along the way."

Fachang shook his head. "No, Master Sergeant. We're here to help. Uncle is weighing into the conflict. Let's go."

Sage nodded and concentrated on his driving. He swung out around another corner and spotted a section of a jumpcopter lying in the middle of the street. Flames chewed at the twisted wreckage and nothing lived inside it. Black smoke trailed into the air. Two bodies of soldiers lay in the street.

Scavengers were already at work taking what they could from the downed aircraft. Makaum men and women and other beings wrestled gear free as he watched.

Fachang leaned outside the crawler with his Birkeland coilgun in one hand. He fired a few rounds into the air and the weapon's bullfiddle moan drove the scavengers into hiding.

Sage roared past the downed aircraft. "Colonel Halladay says we've engaged with the Phrenorians."

Fachang nodded as he reloaded his weapon. "That is going to make things difficult."

"I can still put you out."

"No. We're in this now." Fachang touched his comm and brought it online, then talked so rapidly in Mandarin that Sage couldn't keep up.

Sage drove and closed on the area as Kiwanuka's frequency showed up on his comm. "Kiwanuka, this is Sage. Be advised that I'm on my way to you in civilian armor."

"Copy that," Kiwanuka said.

Heavy weapons fire rattled in the background and Sage hated the fact that he wasn't in an AKTIVsuit. He wouldn't be as much help in the armor he had on now, and he didn't have HUD access to the soldiers.

He made the final turn onto the street where Kiwanuka and her team were holed up. He stared up at the arboreal bar and wondered what Kiwanuka was doing there.

"I'm here, Kiwanuka," Sage said. "When is our exfil coming?"

"There's no exfil," Kiwanuka said. "Two jumpcopters got taken out by unknown agents. Not Phrenorians. The colonel can't send in other aircraft because they don't know who the enemy is. We're on our own."

Sage stepped out of the crawler, thought furiously, and tried to remember what he knew of the area. It wasn't much. He'd stayed away from that part of the sprawl because of the rules of engagement agreements in place to negate a potential conflict between Terran soldiers and Phrenorian warriors. All he really knew was what he'd learned to pick up Throzath.

Fachang got out of the crawler. "Uncle has a way out, Master Sergeant. Not far from here, there is a well. That well is one of four in this sprawl that opens onto one of the many underground rivers that thread through this area. I am told that river is sometimes used to transport contraband."

Sage couldn't believe he hadn't known about the rivers, but it made sense. Makaum was a jungle world not unlike South America where he'd grown up. The land tended to be porous and caves formed there naturally. He and his parents had visited cenotes in the Yucatán Peninsula one summer when he was a boy. Those ceremonial wells had been connected by an underground river.

"Where's the well?" Sage asked.

"Three hundred sixty-two meters southeast of our present position. We'll need oxygen to make it through. Nearly all of the channel is filled with water."

"That's not a problem for the soldiers," Sage said. "AKTIVsuits carry oxygen on board."

"We will need oxygen, then."

"AKTIVsuits come with buddy breathers. All we have to do is pair up and we can go." Sage tagged his comm. "Kiwanuka, we have an exfil route. Can you get clear?"

"Not easily. The Phrenorians have got us pinned."

"Then I'm coming to you." Sage looked at Fachang. "I'll meet you there. Drop a pin in my comm to locate the well."

Almost immediately, a pin location appeared on Sage's comm.

Fachang turned to his companions and spoke to them. Mei and Min took Throzath and quickly carried him to the nearest alley.

"I'm coming with you," Fachang said.

Sage didn't have time to argue, and he'd seen the younger man in action. Together, they ran for Kiwanuka's location while Sage filled in Kiwanuka and Halladay on the exfil point.

TWENTY-FIVE

During his approach, Sage spotted the fallen Terran soldier lying in the shattered remains of a small shop at the foot of a large tree. The man's faceshield was dark and he couldn't see through it.

He ran over to the soldier and knelt by the man, then punched in an override command into the side of the soldier's helmet. Data pulsed across the faceshield and let Sage know the man inside the AKTIVsuit— Private Michael Zhu—was badly hurt and unconscious. Fully sedated, the soldier wouldn't be moving under his own power till after he received medical treatment.

Fachang took cover amid the debris and exchanged shots with a handful of locals who had chosen sides in the battle. Badly wounded, two of those locals reeled back to cover and the others halted their approach.

Return fire was immediate. Bullets and plasma bursts struck the shop and knocked plascrete chunks away.

Sage initiated the suit's major med suite, validated the nanobot recovery procedures, and made certain the onboard AI kept the young soldier alive.

"We can't hold this position," Fachang said. "We're going to be overrun."

"No, we're not," Sage said. "I can gear up."

Kiwanuka had told him she and her team were fighting clear of their location.

Sage stripped the soldier's external combat harness from the armor and slid it on. Hunkered down to take advantage of the remaining cover, Sage pulled the pins from two flash-bang/tear-gas grenades and heaved them toward the buildings where their closest attackers had taken up positions.

The first grenade fell short, but the detonation quieted the opposing weapons for a moment. Bilious yellow gas clouds welled into the street. Some of the nearby hostiles backed off immediately. Evidently they'd had prior experience with similar crowd control efforts.

The second grenade fell through a broken window and an instant later the concussive wave blew out the remaining windows. More smoke rolled out into the street from there as well.

Sage reached into the combat harness and removed a thin gas filter membrane soldiers handed out to civilians caught in a battle zone. The filter covered his face and adhered to his features with a tingling static charge that he'd never gotten used to. He hated the masks. They kept most of the gas from his lungs and sinus membranes, including his eyes, but they reduced his visual acuity and gave a false sense of protection.

He handed a second membrane to Fachang, only to

discover the young man was already equipped with a built-in mask he'd pulled up from his collar.

Fachang's voice was only slightly muffled. "Uncle likes us to be prepared."

Sage nodded, put the membrane mask away, and picked up the Roley. A quick inspection let him know the rifle had survived whatever punishment had landed the young soldier in the shop, but the weapon was inert. He punched an access cipher into the rifle's butt and spoke his name and passcode.

Immediately, the rifle came online and linked with the armor.

A half dozen street people advanced on the shop in ragged hops from cover to cover.

Sage didn't know what drove those people to attack, but he'd seen it before. Sometimes it was just a crowd mentality, an old, hardwired instinct that knitted individuals into a group that attacked a perceived threat.

Right now they perceived Terran soldiers as a threat.

Or they were scavengers hoping to pick up credits for stealing Terran military hardware the same as the other people had been doing to the jumpcopter.

This part of the sprawl only masqueraded as civilized. With the Phrenorians providing a barrier from legal repercussions and peacekeeping efforts made by the Terran military, Makaum's outliers and offplanet rogues had gathered here and preyed on those who ventured into the district.

Sage pulled the Roley to his shoulder, set it to stun, and opened fire. His first two shots dropped attackers in their tracks. He switched to the grenade launcher and fired a gel-grenade at an overturned cart. When the grenade exploded, it blasted pieces from the cart and turned the rest of it into a battering ram that took out three combatants.

"Sage!" Fachang warned. "Above!"

Glancing up, Sage spotted the Phrenorian aircar dropping altitude in front of them and swooping at them. Dual laser cannons mounted on the front of the vehicle strafed the street and came up behind the people closing in on the shop. The blasts left liquid pools that cooled into glass behind them. The high-pitched squeals of the laser cannons cut through the other gunfire.

Sage curled into a ball and covered his head with his armored arms. The face membrane filtered out the choking effects of the smoke from the fires that burst into being around him, but the scent and the heat still came through. Soot dusted the membrane and further blurred his vision.

As soon as the line of fire passed him, Sage rolled onto his back and pointed the Roley skyward, waiting for the aircar to fly by. When it did, he emptied the grenade launcher's last four rounds at the vehicle. All of the gel packs slapped onto the aircar's undercarriage.

Without access to the AKTIVsuit's munitions reservoir because he needed personal access to the armor, Sage couldn't load the launcher with fresh rounds. He switched the Roley over to lethal munitions and saw that he had forty-seven rounds of depleted uranium in the magazine and a full laser charge left. Moving quickly, he shoved himself to his feet.

All four gel-grenades exploded in a blistering string of detonations as he closed on the aircar just now coming around in a tight turn. Sage put an armored hand in front of his face as he slung the Roley over his shoulder. Shrapnel from the aircar thudded into his armor and knocked him off balance for a second, and another piece sliced through the face membrane above his right eye, disrupting the seal over his eye.

Tear gas floated into the gap left by the cut, but the

toxicity had somewhat thinned. Still, the chem brought tears to his eyes and hot blood flooded his vision in the next instant.

Ahead, the aircar shuddered and came around. The handling was wonky and it dropped to within eight meters of the street. At the rear, a Phrenorian struggled to swing a mounted 20mm cannon around.

"Stay with my soldier, Fachang," Sage ordered as he pushed himself into a sprint. "Keep him safe."

The enhanced body armor wasn't as good as the AKTIVsuit. The servos pumped up muscle effort and speed, but not to the parameters Sage was used to. Still, he willed it to serve because he knew the aircar warriors would kill them if he couldn't stop them.

As he neared the aircar, he timed his moves, first leaping up onto an overturned crawler, then launching himself at the rear of the aircar. He caught hold of the vehicle's rear armor, hauled himself up, and kept his head below the edge because he knew the Phrenorian warrior might have seen him.

His additional weight caused the aircar to wobble and Sage knew all of the Phrenorian warriors aboard must have known they had an unwanted passenger. Clinging to the aircar with one hand, he drew the .500 Magnum with the other and shoved his arm and shoulder above the edge.

The Phrenorian warrior had released his hold on the 20mm cannon and pulled his rifle up. A plasma blast just missed Sage's head and the heat melted the face membrane to his skin. Although he didn't care for the AKTIVsuit's chem suite or the way the onboard AI doled out treatment so easily at times, Sage missed the pain relievers it could have pumped into his system. The side of his face was a mass of writhing agony.

He shouted in pain and rage but remained focused as

he dropped the Magnum's sights over the Phrenorian's thorax. He squeezed off two rounds and the frangible bullets blew holes through the armor, driving shrapnel into the warrior.

Already dead, the Phrenorian toppled from the aircar as the pilot continued bringing the vehicle around.

Ignoring the pain in his face and his eye, Sage shifted his attention to the gunner. The warrior hung limply in the seat harness. From the amount of blood staining the inside of the windscreen, Sage guessed that one of the gel-grenades had blown the undercarriage up through the seat.

Sage pulled himself up and sprawled on the rear deck of the aircar. He took a fresh grip on the 20mm cannon's gimbal support shaft and aimed the Magnum at the Phrenorian pilot.

"Put us down now!" Sage ordered. He expected the Phrenorian to try for a weapon, and he was prepared to leap from the aircar if he had to.

He didn't expect the Phrenorian to push the aircar into a nosedive and scramble back toward him. He used the pistol to block his attacker's primary claw from his face, then swung around the gimbal shaft to plant both feet into the Phrenorian's chest. At the same time, the barbed tail sank into the aircar's body with a hollow *boom*.

Propelled by Sage's kick and unable to compensate for the tilted surface of the aircar, the Phrenorian fell away and dangled by his tail. He flailed all six arms while trying to gain purchase. The aircar continued on, out of control. Its engines screamed as they struggled against gravity that would no longer be ignored.

Instinctively, Sage clung to the shaft as the vehicle tilted to a forty-five-degree angle and crashed into the second floor of a three-story building. He threw his free hand over his head and hung on as the aircar plowed through the wall.

Plascrete chunks rained down on him and the 20mm cannon snapped off. Blackness rushed up to meet him.

The Carmine Belelt-Cha
North Makaum Sprawl
1751 Hours Zulu Time

Kiwanuka led her team down the winding stairs that had taken them up to the Carmine Belelt-Cha bar. She kept the Roley pointed ahead of her and stunned two gunmen who'd lain in wait at the bottom of the steps.

"Sage?" she called over her comm as she reached the street. She swept her gaze through the rolling yellow clouds of tear gas and tracked her fallen soldier.

An armored Asian man sat with Private Zhu in the scattered and burning debris of what had been a shop.

"I'm Fachang," the man said. He held his hands and his weapons up. "I'm with Sage."

Kiwanuka logged Fachang as a "friendly" on her HUD's IFF system and his color status changed from questionable yellow to blue. "I'm Sergeant Kiwanuka. Where's Sage?"

Fachang pointed to a building two blocks away. A huge hole gaped in the side on the second story. An instant later, an explosive mix of flames and debris vomited out of the hole.

"Sage!" Kiwanuka covered her face as falling debris thudded against her armor.

No response came over the comm.

A plasma charge blasted Kiwanuka between the

shoulder blades and staggered her. As she turned, Pingasa
stunned the plasma rifle wielder and the Lemylian warrior
dropped unconscious into the street.

"Staff Sergeant Kiwanuka," Halladay called over the
comm.

"Sir," Kiwanuka responded as she took cover behind
a low wall that now held back a burning section of the
jungle that had invaded the sprawl.

"Get your team out of there. Sage said he had an exfil
route. Use it."

Kiwanuka pushed away the confused knot of feelings that swirled within her. "Sage isn't here."

"Huang's nephew is," Halladay said. "Get your team
out of there, Staff Sergeant."

"Sage may need help."

Halladay was silent for a split second. "Sage is either
dead or will find his own way, Staff Sergeant. You need
to get your people out of there now or we'll lose all of
you. That area is being overrun by the Phrenorians. Is
that clear, soldier?"

Kiwanuka took a breath. "Yes sir."

She knew Halladay was right, and she owed it to her
troops to bring them home. So far she hadn't lost any
of them.

She turned to Fachang. "Show me the exfil point."

Fachang nodded. "Someone will have to carry this
man. He's alive but unconscious. I can't carry that suit
with this armor."

"Understood," Kiwanuka said. "Culpepper."

"I've got this, Staff Sergeant." Culpepper stepped
forward and shoved debris off Zhu, then leaned down
and picked up the wounded soldier. He settled him over
his shoulders in a fireman's carry.

Fachang got to his feet. "This way, Staff Sergeant."

He ran toward an alley in the direction of the pin showing on Kiwanuka's HUD.

Kiwanuka hesitated only a moment and stared at the building where Sage was supposed to be. Then, because she was responsible for her team, she sprinted after them and sprayed suppressive fire behind her, chopping down any who were foolish enough to attack their group.

TWENTY-SIX

Standing on the rear dock of the aircar, Zhoh manned the 20mm cannon and strafed the retreating Terran soldiers. They were too quick, though, and all of them managed to duck safely into an alley. The 20mm rounds collapsed the side of a building and felled two trees, setting all of it on fire when the secondary incendiaries cooked off.

Zhoh ignored the ball of pain that currently resided in his thorax. He told himself that he wasn't dead, wasn't dying, and would heal. *Lannig* would see to that. "Mato."

"Yes," Mato responded.

"Where are the Terrans fleeing to? They are not headed in the direction of their fort."

Mato was silent for a moment and Zhoh knew the warrior was checking his tablet, scouting through maps of the sprawl.

"I don't know, General. I don't see any reprieve in the direction they've gone."

Zhoh seethed and started to give the aircar pilot orders to pursue the fleeing Terran soldiers. However, following them might only lead to a trap. The Terrans were crafty and were content to fight from hiding and to spring ambushes rather than meet on battlefields where strength and skill decided the victor.

Still, it was a risk he was willing to take.

"But I do have something for you," Mato said. "I monitored some of the comm traffic that was going on. Master Sergeant Sage is among the Terrans there."

"Then I will pursue him."

"He's not with the group, *triarr*. He got separated. I am marking his position on your visuals."

Almost immediately, a blue dot formed on Zhoh's HUD. According to it, Sage was less than eighty meters away, on the opposite side of the street from the fleeing Terran soldiers.

"What is he doing there?" Zhoh asked, thinking perhaps his enemy was laying a trap.

"Sage attacked an aircar, General," Mato said. "He successfully brought it down but did not escape it when it crashed into that building."

"He is still inside?"

"Yes."

"Is he alive?"

"I do not know," Mato admitted. "I have assigned warriors to that area, but there is resistance in the street. The local populace is confused as to who started this battle and is attacking indiscriminately out of fear."

Shifting on the aircar, Zhoh looked back toward the embassy. A group of warriors with fire suppression equipment battled the blaze left in the hollow where the aircar dock had been. Drones, now with their weapons

revealed, zipped through the air and protected the
embassy's perimeters.

"They will be delayed reaching you," Mato said.

"Assign one of the drones to me," Zhoh said. "I'll
find out if Sage yet lives."

"Are you ready?"

Zhoh brought up his drone interface and took over
piloting the drone as Mato linked it to him. "Yes."

Occasionally, shots were fired at the aircar, but the
vehicle's defenses held and the two Phrenorian warriors returned fire, driving away or killing anyone who
dared shoot at them.

Zhoh reveled in the feeling of being in command as
he stood on the aircar's fighting deck. He had missed
the sense of being in control of his destiny, of his *lannig*,
but now that he was once more in battle, no longer held
back by a cowardly commander, he intended to make
the most of his new position.

Makaum would fall. He would break it and bend it
into another resource planet for the Phrenorian Empire.
Then, once he'd handed the planet over, he would be
recognized and would be given other commands that
would bring further glory.

His mate and her father would be made to pay for
their cowardly actions against him.

In control of the drone, not as smooth with piloting as
he would have liked, Zhoh used his secondaries on the
touch pad to send the craft skimming toward the building where Mato had said Sage still was. Zhoh wanted
control of the drone. He hoped the Master Sergeant
was not yet dead. He wanted to kill the human himself.
Sage had proved himself an honorable opponent.

If Sage had been Phrenorian, they might have been
fellow warriors. They would have conquered all.

The drone slowed as it approached the gaping hole

in the side of the building and Zhoh peered through its vid feed. Smoke trailing from the crash site blinded the drone for a moment, but momentary glimpses gave an indication of the area.

The aircar remained mostly intact and the fighting deck jutted through the hole. Hung by his own tail, an injured Phrenorian warrior dangled below the aircar's rear defensive plates. The warrior was dying or lapsing into unconsciousness and his limbs worked pathetically to pull him up or seek his release.

Zhoh didn't care. Either way the warrior would have died gloriously in battle. Only a little time separated when. He flew the drone past the wrecked aircar and moved slowly now because the opening was narrow. The hull bumped against the sides of the opening.

The aircar guards continued returning fire at ground-based snipers. Zhoh decided then that the embassy's defensive perimeters would be expanded. They had held back from doing that at Rangha's command. Knowing everything he did now, Zhoh felt certain it was so the dead general could maintain his illegal arms trade more easily.

A moment later, the drone slid inside the building. Zhoh switched the powerful lights on and illuminated the room. The warrior in the front passenger seat lay still in death, half buried under rubble that had spilled from the building's ceiling and surrounding walls.

Turning gently in the tight space, Zhoh maneuvered the drone around and scanned the area more thoroughly. Then he made out a human boot standing at the rear of the aircar. As he tracked up the armored leg, he spotted Sage behind the 20mm cannon on the aircar's fighting deck just behind the overhanging debris that covered the back section of the vehicle.

Blood and some kind of torn material covered one side

of Sage's face. One eye was bloodshot and filled with pain, but the human swung the 20mm cannon around.

Not at the drone as Zhoh would have expected, but at the aircar hovering just on the other side of the wall.

"Get back!" Zhoh shouted.

Operating on instinct, he forgot about the drone and pulled his rifle up. He almost had it level when the wall blew out. He shouted his command again, but the roar of the cannon buried his words.

Chunks of plascrete blew out of the building and hammered the aircar. Dents covered the side facing the attack and only fragments of the windscreen remained. Dust and smoke boiled out of the room.

Zhoh fired repeatedly into the side of the structure and blew out sections of the wall as he hunted Sage.

Taoldir Street
North Makaum Sprawl
1754 Hours Zulu Time

Return fire from the Phrenorian aircar chopped into the building and drove Sage to cover. He leaped forward toward the front of the wrecked aircar, dropped behind it, and took shelter as he unlimbered the Roley.

"Sage!" The voice broadcasted over a public address system from a Phrenorian system. "I know you're in there!"

Sage didn't reply. He knew his chance of knocking down Zhoh and his aircar was small, but he'd had to take it.

"You could have asked me for personal combat!" Zhoh shouted.

Falling debris had trapped the drone against one of the surviving walls. The unit jerked and shuddered as it tried to get free. At least the damage had snapped the 20mm cannon from it, reducing it to a large vid cam.

"I would have honored such a request," Zhoh said. "Instead, you tried to assassinate me."

Sage looked around the room desperately. "It wasn't me. It wasn't any of my people."

The room had housed people before it had become collateral damage. An arm lay visible at the back of the room, through the shattered remains of a wall. Sage couldn't tell if the limb was still attached to the victim now buried under the debris, but the onboard limited AI of his present armor detected no life signs.

"You lie!" Zhoh thundered. His amplified, artificial voice ricocheted inside the space.

Another wave of depleted uranium rounds splintered the debris. Sage kept his head low and tried to block out all the pain coming from the side of his face.

Sage turned over, rose to a crouch, and tried to peer through the makeshift plascrete curtain formed by buckyball strands woven through the material. "I'm not lying."

The buckyball strands hung in chunks and deflected rounds and beams alike.

"The Terran military didn't pick this fight today," Sage said. "It was the work of someone else. Probably the same people who killed Wosesa Staumar and General Rangha. Someone is pulling your strings, Zhoh. They want us to fight."

"I want to fight," Zhoh said. "You want to fight."

Sage knew that was true and didn't argue. He felt alive now, in this battle, and he knew he should have felt remorse at all the death.

"There will never be peace between our worlds,

Sage," Zhoh continued. "There can only be one victor in this war, and it will be the Phrenorians. It will be *me*. I am now the general in charge of the Phrenorian forces on Makaum. Things will be done differently here."

General? The thought left Sage chilled. Zhoh was a battlefield officer. He lived for war, unlike General Rangha. This current action was only a preview of the hell that would come.

More rounds chipped away at the hanging plascrete.

The drone shifted in the debris and succeeded in knocking some of it off. It rose higher, gaining a few centimeters in altitude. The weapons gimbal rotated at the top a few times.

"Your robot viper has had its fang yanked," Sage said. "You're not going to be able to use it." He laid his rifle on the aircar for support and considered his situation.

No help was coming.

There was no way out except the way he'd come in because the debris formed barriers all around him.

The drone suddenly reversed and smashed against the barrier, rocking it and knocking free a few chunks of plascrete. When its backward momentum ground to a halt, the drone shot forward again and powered toward Sage.

He ducked behind the aircar and the drone bounced from the vehicle's body and smashed against the pile of debris. Plascrete scree skidded down and a small dust cloud blossomed.

Then the drone reversed and smashed against the outer barrier, almost tearing free. Sage realized that Zhoh was trying to destroy the barrier. Once it was gone, Sage would be trapped.

TWENTY-SEVEN

Sweating, bleeding, and hurting, Sage ran his hands over his borrowed combat harness and searched for the explosives ordnance every soldier was supposed to carry into the field. Shaped charges were used to take down doors and walls for search and rescue missions, and they were employed against enemy vehicles and munitions stores.

He located both bricks of Beryllium+8 and attached thermal triggers that could be detonated by remote control and turn the material into a highly explosive bomb. After a quick application of sticky foam from the abbreviated med kit to the explosives, he ducked again as the drone smashed against the debris pile. This time, when he was as certain as he could be that he couldn't be seen by the drone's vid cam, he slapped both B+8 bricks onto the weapon's carbonized skin.

The sticky foam instantly bonded with the drone's body, and when it sped toward the barrier this time, the B+8 bricks went with it. More debris rained down when it hit, but the bricks stayed in place.

Sage stood and made a show of firing at the drone, but he deliberately missed most of his shots. He wanted Zhoh to think he was frightened and frantic.

The drone ground to a halt once more, but there were holes in the barrier now. Daylight showed through those openings and afforded glimpses of the Phrenorian vehicle poised outside like a predatory avian. Sage shifted his aim through the hanging pieces and hit the aircar's pilot at least once because black blood sprayed up from his shoulder.

The pilot ducked and flailed and managed to jockey the aircar back.

Zhoh returned fire and, for a minute, Sage was afraid the Phrenorian warrior had forgotten about the drone. Then the drone rocketed forward again and drove Sage to cover.

Metal screeched as the thing grinded against the aircar wreckage. It pounded against the aircar violently four times, moving up, then pancaking down again, like it was hoping to flatten the aircar and Sage with it.

He realized almost too late that the tactic was intended as a distraction. Glancing back up at the barrier, which had more daylight than ever spilling through it, he spotted the two Phrenorian warriors who had climbed the side of the building to get at him.

He recharged the uranium rounds from the ammo rack on his combat harness and brought the weapon to bear. On full-auto, he fired into the facemask of the Phrenorian on the left, cored through the lighter armor, and blasted apart the alien's cephalothorax. He switched to the other Phrenorian and opened fire just as

a round caught him in the chest and rocked him back
on his heels.

The drone swung at him again and he barely escaped
the impact. By the time he got in a protected position
to fire, the second Phrenorian was on him. The warrior
pointed his rifle at Sage point-blank and opened fire.
Rounds tattooed Sage's armor and he knew the integrity
was thinning as the anti-kinetic plates fractured under
the barrage.

Lunging up, Sage knocked the rifle barrel aside with
his own weapon and hit the Phrenorian just as the drone
came down again. This time the Phrenorian caught the
brunt of the impact. His exoskeleton split and burst,
and the warrior's insides evacuated the smashed shell.

Sage didn't know if the alien was dead or dying. Nor
could he guess at how much pain the Phrenorian was
in. Terran PsyOps had a lot of unanswered questions
because Phrenorians almost never survived capture.
They died fighting, or they killed themselves once
taken prisoner.

He drew the Magnum and put a mercy round through
the Phrenorian's brain. Even after he was certain his opponent was dead, the Phrenorian twitched and moved.

The drone hammered the corpse twice more, then
shot backward toward the barrier. As Sage shoved
the Magnum into his thigh holster, he reached for the
remote detonator attached to the combat harness.

This time the drone ripped through the hanging plascrete and shot out into the open. Before the drone pilot
thought to stop the aircraft, it collided with the hovering aircar. The impact didn't do much to either one of
the vehicles, but when Sage triggered the detonators, a
massive fireball dawned on the drone.

With the explosion still ringing in his ears despite
the aud dampers in his helmet, Sage sprinted forward.

When he reached the wrecked wall, he climbed the pile of debris, thought he could span the distance to Zhoh's aircar, and threw himself forward.

For a moment, his fingers caught the aircar's edge, but it tipped slightly as it took on his weight. The shift was just enough to cause him to lose what little purchase he'd managed.

He fell four meters to the ground and instinctively bent his knees to absorb the impact. Although the armor he now wore wasn't as heavy as an AKTIVsuit, the impact shattered the plascrete boardwalk when he hit. He rolled, shed more of the force of the drop, and pushed himself to his feet.

Knowing he didn't have a chance of going toe-to-toe with the aircar crew and Zhoh, Sage focused on the pin Fachang had dropped onto his HUD map and sprinted toward the well. His heart hammered and he resisted the impulse to comm Kiwanuka and tell her he was coming.

He wouldn't hold his soldiers up. If he got there too late to accompany a soldier in an AKTIVsuit that had an air supply, he'd try to make the distance himself without it.

Staying out on the street was just going to get him killed.

Sprawl Provisional Protectorate
Makaum
27843 Akcj (Phrenorian Prime)

Zhoh blinked his forward eyes but couldn't clear them from the brightness of the explosion. His suit's faceshield had reacted too late. He turned his back and used his rear eyes, scanning the area for Sage. He'd expected to see the Terran master sergeant lying on the ground helpless.

Sage wasn't there. The large cracked crater showed where the human had hit, but he was gone.

The aircar struggled to maintain a hovering position. The pilot was wounded, barely able to maintain control of the aircraft.

"Mato!" Zhoh shouted.

"Yes, General?" Mato responded.

"Where is Sage?"

"I'm looking."

"Why weren't you tracking him?"

"There are other points of conflict that have to be managed. Looters have taken to the streets and are attacking our warriors. Some have even dared to attack the embassy."

"Give the order to kill anyone who stands in our way," Zhoh said.

"I have."

"And look for Sage."

Zhoh scanned the streets and only then registered the presence of hot metal burning against his carapace. He brushed the shrapnel away with his secondaries but had to stop when the more vulnerable limbs threatened to take more damage than he currently was.

"I'm playing back recordings of the drone cams now," Mato said. "I will have Sage in a moment."

Zhoh leaned toward the pilot. "Put us down, Corporal."

"Yes, General," the warrior responded weakly.

A moment later, his forward eyes now clear, Zhoh leaped from the aircar as it sat on the ground. Bullets and beams struck the vehicle. Reaching back into the aircar, Zhoh pulled the pilot free and laid him on the ground next to the vehicle.

Instead of a rescue as he'd intended, Zhoh only succeeded in pulling a corpse from the aircar. Immediately, Zhoh plucked a grenade from the dead warrior's
gear, pulled the pin with one of his secondaries,
and wedged it under the pilot. He marked the booby
trap on the battlefield so his warriors would know to
search carefully before taking the pilot's body back to
the embassy.

If someone else reached the body first and didn't
notice the grenade, the pilot would manage a kill even
while dead. It was the best a warrior could hope for on
the battlefield.

"I have Sage," Mato said.

"Where is he?" Zhoh stood and pulled a grenade
from his harness. He lobbed it toward a tumbled-down
store where hostile guns fired at him. The resulting explosion brought down what remained of the building
and crushed or buried the gunners hiding within.

"Sage took the same path as the other Terrans."

Zhoh looked at the alley where he'd seen the soldiers
fleeing earlier. He ran across the street. "Send warriors
to me."

"Twelve are already on the way, *triarr.*"

Zhoh spotted the warriors through the eyes in the
back of his head. They came on the double, hurried
through the smoke and flames and debris, and fired at
targets in the street and in nearby buildings. Zhoh's
heart swelled with pride, and he smelled his own pheromones issuing a challenge to all around him.

"Where have the Terrans gone?" Zhoh asked.

He waved a scout into position and the warrior leaped
forward and entered the narrow passageway. Zhoh ran
after him.

"I don't know, General," Mato said. "None of the sec
cams we have access to have them in view."

"They're not running toward the fort. What can they hope to reach?"

"I don't know."

Zhoh flicked through the map on his HUD and searched through the streets and businesses listed there. He wasn't certain the list of shops and outlets were up to date because new businesses took over for old businesses that had pulled out of Makaum at a rapid pace.

Some of the buildings in this sector had become homes for homeless beings from a dozen worlds. The economic downsizing after the assassination at the Festival of the Beginning had stranded several beings who now didn't have passage offplanet. Zhoh had seen the same thing happen on several other planets the Empire had enslaved.

Once Makaum was broken, then would come the culling. Those beings unable to work would be executed.

For now, Zhoh wanted to find Sage and kill the master sergeant. The Terrans would pay for their attack on him.

Nainir's Well
North Makaum Sprawl
1757 Hours Zulu Time

Bullets and beams pursued Sage as he ran through the alleys toward the location Fachang had marked for him. As far as he could tell, none of them were fired by Phrenorians. Looters and opportunists raided the local shops. The fact that he couldn't do anything to stop the thievery or protect the people inside the shops chafed at Sage. But this wasn't the place or the time to try to do anything.

He knew he was being pursued. Zhoh wasn't the type to just give up and go away.

Especially not if he thought the Terran military was behind the assassination attempt on his life.

Thankfully, as Sage sprinted around buildings, crawlers, and carts that were on fire, there appeared to be no innocents on the streets. Several dead people and a few *dafeerorgs* lay where they'd fallen.

Nainir's Well 72.8 meters flashed across the map. As Sage glanced at it, the numbers rapidly dropped. He looked for the well and still couldn't see it.

A Phrenorian aircar flew overhead as he ran across a street. Almost immediately, the vehicle slowed and the 20mm cannon on the fighting deck swung around. Rounds crashed in Sage's wake, caught up rapidly, and left small craters punched into the street. As he sprinted into the alley, more rounds blew out the side of a building.

A wooden fence blocked the end of the alley. Without slowing, Sage barreled toward it, tore through like a bullet, and left shattered boards behind him.

The well stood before him in a large, open area. Rectangular and low-walled, the well was six meters long on the shorter sides and nine meters in length on the longer sides. Bodies lay around the well, torn and bleeding and in pieces, but none of them were Terran soldiers.

Breath ragged despite the armor's augmented musculature, Sage reached the well's side and peered down five meters at the dark water. Ripples covered the surface and he knew it came from the cannonade chasing him.

There was no sign of the tunnel that Fachang had

said was there, but Sage knew the man had told the truth. Kiwanuka and the other soldiers were gone, and Sage hoped they were safe.

The aircar rose above the building and fired at Sage again. Knowing he had no choice, he threw himself over the wall and dropped. He hit the surface and sank deeply. The chill of the water soothed his torn and blistered skin almost immediately, but the rest of his face felt frozen because his current helmet didn't self-seal.

He held his breath, wished he had a helmet light or infrared or even an idea of which way he needed to head. Knowing how deep he needed to go would have helped. His best guess was that he'd dropped at least six meters, and perhaps ten. The well was deeper than he'd thought it would be.

He was still sinking.

TWENTY-EIGHT

Nainir's Well
North Makaum Sprawl
1801 Hours Zulu Time

Panic rose in Sage as his lungs tightened, but it was nothing he wasn't familiar with. He pushed it away and concentrated on survival. He almost drove his armored fingers into the stone wall and climbed, then he realized that any kind of underground waterway would have to be deep. He continued to descend into the darkness.

The pressure on his chest increased. Sage wanted to surface but the body armor was too heavy to climb quickly enough and he couldn't get out of it easily. Maybe not even in time to keep from drowning. If he succeeded in getting free of the armor and swimming up, he knew the Phrenorians would close on him and he'd have no chance at all.

Even as he was thinking that, something hit the top of the well and blew it to pieces. Large stones and broken mortar rained down into the water. The depth he was at prevented the debris from smashing into him, but the light went away and he knew the opening was sealed.

With no choice but to go on, Sage continued to drop. Even though his instinct was to leave the mask in place because of his injuries and the water, he peeled the filter from his face. Cold needles flared into both his eyes.

He didn't have voice control over the HUD, but the map software kept him oriented. His feet finally struck bottom but he had no idea how far down he was. His lungs burned, desperate for oxygen. Falling debris continued streaming over him and a large stone struck him hard enough to knock him down.

Operating on stubbornness and his own will to survive, Sage pushed up to his feet and reached out to find the nearest wall. The current pulled at him, but he realized he didn't know if he was supposed to go with it or against it. Fachang hadn't said. Or maybe Sage hadn't been listening.

The pressure on his body let him know he'd gone deep, and the need to breathe grew stronger. Locating the wall, he turned and dragged his fingers across the rough surface. When he felt the edge of an opening, he drove himself forward. There was no time for second-guessing.

Ramming his stiffened fingers forward, he dug a handhold in the side of the underground river. Natural stone, not mortised, lined the channel. He continued driving his fingers into the wall and climbing up as his lungs threatened to explode.

Black spots swam in his vision and he knew he couldn't remain conscious much longer. He didn't know if he would black out first or draw in a breath. If either one of those things happened, he was dead.

Two more pulls with his arms and he reached the

top of the river. It was at least eight meters deep and the current was strong and steady. Unable to hold back, he shoved his face toward the ceiling, unable to see in the darkness if there was any air space.

His helmet butted into the stone ceiling and he knew the river was flush, filled to the top.

There was no air.

Strength drained from him and the current took him. He sank and his armored body dragged across the stone bottom worn smooth by years of erosion. He tried to move and couldn't.

A bright light suddenly flared before him and he guessed that his struggle was over. He was going to die on Makaum, lost and alone, and no one would know what happened to him. The war that he had longed to return to would be fought and won or lost without him.

Arms closed around his chest and he automatically tried to fight them off because the only instinct he had was to battle whoever came upon him. Then an armored hand tore away his faceshield and fitted a breather across his lips.

He opened his mouth and bit down on the rubber guard. When he breathed, his lungs filled with air, not river water. The swirling black spots cleared slowly from his vision.

Weakly, working to recover his strength, Sage wrapped an arm around the armored soldier who had him. His eyes adjusted to the light and he saw Kiwanuka's face on the other side of her shield.

She pressed her helmet against his, linking their comms through direct contact.

"Sage?" Kiwanuka said.

He flailed a hand and managed to tap her shoulder in an acknowledgment.

"I've got you. Okay?"

Sage tapped her again. His helmet comm was exposed and he couldn't talk with the breather in his mouth.

"We've got to turn around. Just hang on to me."

Still weak, Sage managed to get both arms around her as she maneuvered around and headed back the way she'd come. Like he'd done, she clawed her way along the river wall. Sage tried to turn because he wanted to help.

"No," Kiwanuka told him. "Streamline yourself. Let the armor do the work. I got this."

Sage tapped her shoulder once more and held on as she carried them away.

A-Pakeb Node
General's Personal Quarters
Makaum
28534 Akej (Phrenorian Prime)

"Are you in pain, General Zhoh?"

Lying on the hospital table, Zhoh was disgusted by the question. His pheromones radiated his displeasure and the female Phrenorian medtech attending to him drew in her secondary limbs and *chelicerae* in response. For a moment he thought his sharp annoyance would drive her away.

She was tall and lean, an attractive female with mostly blue coloration, and threads of green swirled through her exoskeleton. Among Phrenorians, she would be sought after and fought over for breeding rights. Her lack of political connections would lessen her appeal, but she would birth strong children.

Not like Sxia's abominations that had been ended as soon as they'd been born.

If Zhoh had not lacked for political affiliations himself, he might have mated with someone like the female before him. But he'd wanted glory, and that desire had left him *kalque*.

Now, though, glory was once more possible. He longed for it, and he knew he would not let it slip away again.

"I am fine, Geneticist Nhez," Zhoh told her calmly in spite of the pain that radiated from his wounds. "Continue."

Cautiously, Nhez unfurled her secondaries and took up the surgical tools she was using to remove the plascrete shards from his thorax. As she pulled and prodded with the forceps, she also used a laser to cauterize blood vessels and sprayed artificial chitin over the wound once cleared.

"I can shut down the pain, General," Nhez said.

Zhoh stared at the ceiling and the floor. "Pain is what makes us strong. I will grow from this."

He separated himself from the burning ache that was rooted in his thorax by thinking of the Terran soldiers he would kill and eat in the near future. He would harvest a mountain of their skulls.

Nhez continued working. She was the only one in the room with him. Mato was overseeing the defensive efforts and reconstruction of the embassy. Zhoh watched the progress of those labors on a dozen different screens set up around the hospital room.

"How much longer will this take?" Zhoh asked.

"Only a short time, General. I'm working as fast as I dare. I am being thorough."

"Good, because I am needed."

"Are we going to war with the Terrans?" Nhez asked.

"Yes. They attacked me. They attacked us. That cannot be tolerated. We cannot show weakness. Otherwise there will be others who rise up to challenge our authority on other planets. We will break this show of force now."

"I heard there were beings in the streets other than the Terrans who attacked Phrenorian warriors."

"There were." Zhoh took in oxygen and let it out. "The Empire has conquered several worlds. We have enemies everywhere. We will keep those enemies forever, either as slaves or as enemies we have not yet killed. They will fear us, and they will stop daring to fight us. They will accept their subjugation and learn to live in it. We've seen this on a hundred worlds."

Nhez continued prying at the second of the plascrete shards. "I know. I have never before been this close to the front line."

Zhoh took in the air and tasted her pheromones. She smelled of excitement and bordered on a mating frenzy and fear. The fear was insufferable, but he didn't know if she was apprehensive of the situation on Makaum or of her work healing him.

"Everything is as it should be," Zhoh told her.

"You came close to death today."

Zhoh smelled his own courage and bravery and he noted that her secondaries worked more steadily when she took in his pheromones. "I have been closer."

"What will you do?" Nhez asked.

"Heal. And await word from the *Seraugh*." Zhoh had already contacted the War Board and let them know the situation on the planet. "Once I am told that I may attack the Terrans, we will destroy them."

He had plans for the secret base General Rangha had set up in Stronghold RuSasara to the southwest of the sprawl. Once the *Seraugh* gave its permission for those weapons to be brought out into the open, the only two choices the Terrans would have would be to go to war or submit.

But once those weapons were unleashed, it would be too late. The Terran soldiers didn't have that kind of firepower. They would die rapidly and the Phrenorian victory would be assured.

The *Seraugh* awarded special medals to generals who delivered planets to the Empire. Zhoh had seen them, had coveted them, and he had known he would achieve one or die trying. He just hadn't known it would come this soon.

A warrior wearing such a medal was given instant respect wherever he went in the Empire.

Zhoh watched one of the screens as repair drones floated across holes in the embassy walls and laid down layers of plascrete. They swam together like *cridelrad*, the small fishes that lived in the shallows of the Phrenorian oceans. All of them mimicked the same movements and flowed smoothly. As they passed, the embassy walls reformed.

Another screen swept out to view a sec drone shooting down another being in the street. Zhoh saw no weapon on the creature and suspected that it only ventured out to rescue the body of a loved one or perhaps to loot the dead. The execution was a reminder of how worthless emotions like love and greed were. Blood would only be shed to achieve a goal worth accomplishing. Rescuing a dead body or gathering hardware for resale was not a worthy objective to spend a life on.

A warrior's life was spent killing his enemies.

Zhoh's comm blared for attention and he acknowledged it.

"General," Mato said, "I have an incoming message from General Belnale, senior among the *Seraugh*."

Nhez extracted the final plascrete shard and laid it in a surgical pan to the side of the table with a small clink. She worked quickly to cauterize and cover the wound.

Zhoh waved her back and sat up on the bed. Dizziness swam through his senses and he waited just a moment till it passed. "Put the general through, Mato."

The screen shimmered and Belnale's countenance filled the main section while Mato's image shrank to a corner.

"General Zhoh," Belnale greeted.

The title swelled Zhoh with pride and he was glad that the other warrior was not in the room to taste the self-satisfied pheromones he secreted in that moment. There was no excuse for his excitement and it would appear unseemly.

"General Belnale," Zhoh replied.

"I have been apprised of your recent troubles," Belnale said.

"They're only momentary, I assure you."

"They are insufferable. We negotiated with the Terrans in good faith, and yet one of them tried to assassinate you."

"The man paid the price for his transgressions," Zhoh said.

"You have identified him?"

"There was not enough left of him to do so." That wasn't necessarily true, but no one would know any different.

"You know he was a Terran soldier?"

"Yes." Zhoh had no reservations about lying. He believed what he was saying even though a body had not turned up and there had been no confirmation on the assassin's identity. He would not be denied his prize. Makaum would be his. The *Kabilak* medal would be his.

Then he would have his revenge on his wife and father-in-law. Their deaths would be true horrors.

"Good," Belnale said. "Then we will attack without mercy."

"I've already planned for that," Zhoh said. "Our first attack is only hours away."

"Hold off on that for a time."

Zhoh couldn't believe what he was hearing. "General, why would I delay?"

"Because the Empire is even now negotiating with the Terrans regarding the attack."

"Why would we negotiate?"

"The Empire wants to put on a good face for the other worlds," Belnale said. "Our war with Terra must be won first before we move into other sectors. The Empire doesn't want any more star systems aligning against us. Makaum has been chosen as a turning point in the war. Once we take that planet, others will more easily follow."

"Then let me proceed."

"Wait, General. At present, you are outnumbered and outgunned on that planet."

"It doesn't matter. We are Phrenorians."

"I know that. But the Empire wants to assist in your victory."

"How?"

"Your superiority on land is without question, but there still remains the issue of the orbiting space stations."

"The battle won't take place in those areas." Zhoh felt confident he could get enough warriors into orbit to take the offworld holdings when the time came.

"The space stations can't easily leave orbit, so they will take sides in the war. And they will challenge us too. They can wreak a lot of damage onto the sprawl in their efforts to destroy you. They can provide intelligence that the Terrans at Fort York won't have without them. The Empire doesn't want to lose those resources so readily. Captured space stations can be used as staging platforms for the recovery of that planet's raw materials. So we propose to help you capture them. Some of them. The others will be destroyed."

"What is the Empire going to do?"

"In due time, General. We must each play our parts. Until we are ready, stand down."

Zhoh bristled at the command. As general of the Phrenorian forces on Makaum, the decision of whether to attack or not attack should have been his. But he answered the way he knew he had to. "Of course."

Belnale looked at him. "Congratulations again on winning your command there, General Zhoh, and on surviving the assassination attempt. You have come a long way toward glory. I would see you finish the journey you have begun today. Heal from your wounds. The next step is ours. We will be in touch soon."

The comm cut and Belnale's image disappeared.

Zhoh seethed and it took him a moment to see that his pheromones were eroding Nhez's professional behavior. He calmed himself and slid from the table to stand on his peds. "You may leave, Geneticist Nhez. Thank you for your ministrations."

Nhez folded her secondaries and backed out of the room.

"Mato," Zhoh said.

"Yes, General?"

"Notify Stronghold RuSusara to ready the armored units there."

"I will."

"And send in a full complement of seasoned pilots for those units. Once we are given permission, I want them to lead the attack against Fort York."

"At once, General."

Thinking of the victory that lay ahead of him lessened Zhoh's pain from his wounds. He would have to wait even though his blood boiled to strike now, but he told himself that would be fine. The Terrans didn't know about the stronghold, the existence of which was also a breach of the treaty, but it wouldn't matter.

Makaum was going to fall in days, if not hours.

TWENTY-NINE

Med Center
Fort York
2341 Hours Zulu Time

Sage blinked his eyes open and felt the numbness that spread across his face on both sides. He reached up, touched his jawline, and trailed his fingers across a metallic surface that ran along his left cheek to the underside of his jaw. Another metal surface covered the right side of his face over his eye to his temple.

"It's nanite membrane. Dr. Gilbride didn't have time to grow clone skin or harvest skin from your back and thighs to cover the burns."

Sage turned his head slightly to the right and saw Kiwanuka sitting on a chair beside the bed. She held a water bulb out for him to drink.

Not trusting his dry throat to speak, Sage drank.

"Slowly," Kiwanuka admonished. She took back the water bulb.

Sage looked at her and thought of how she had saved him, and how much she had covered his six since he'd been on the planet. "I have to admit, Kjersti, I didn't think I was going to make it out of that well. I thought I was lost."

For a moment, he thought her eyes misted a little, and maybe his did too.

She shook her head. "I can't allow you to get lost, Master Sergeant. You're not going to leave me with all this mess you made and expect me to clean it up."

"No," Sage said. He reached out for her hand and she let him take it. For a moment they sat in silence, then Sage smiled at her. "When we get this mess on this planet sorted, I owe you a drink."

She smiled. "You owe me more than that. Dinner at least." She looked at him. "I'm curious what Frank Sage is like when he's not in a war zone."

"Not much different," Sage said.

"We'll see."

They released hands and Sage hated letting go, but he knew they both had things they had to do. The coming war wasn't going to wait while they figured out what was going on between them.

"Don't you have somewhere you're supposed to be?" Sage asked.

Kiwanuka leaned back a little and became all business again, something that Sage appreciated. "Not according to Colonel Halladay. I'm supposed to watch over you and sleep as I can. His orders."

"How long have I been out?"

"A little over five hours."

"What are the Phrenorians doing?" Sage rolled to his side and sat up. Kiwanuka didn't try to stop him and Gilbride was nowhere around.

The med center was packed with wounded people,

most of them civilians, but there were four soldiers in beds that Sage could see.

"The Phrenorians are shoring up their defensive perimeter," Kiwanuka replied. "They're rebuilding the embassy and adding military fortifications."

Sage closed his eyes against the bright lights and shook his head slightly to try to clear the fog from his thoughts. Part of it was from the anesthesia and part of it was from the physical damage he'd taken. "I figured they would have attacked by now."

"The Alliance is talking to the Empire," Kiwanuka said.

"Is that doing any good?"

"No. The Phrenorians claim that a Terran soldier attacked their embassy. We say we didn't. Nobody has any proof one way or the other."

"What happened out there?"

Kiwanuka shook her head. "I think the assassin we were looking for tried to kill Zhoh to create more confusion onplanet. The colonel and I have reviewed the vid footage and that's the best we can come up with."

"Do you know who the assassin is?"

"We think it's a Fenipalan male named Sytver Morlortai."

"Fenipal?" Sage considered that. "They weren't attacked by the Phrenorians. Some corp sucked them dry."

Kiwanuka nodded. "The Black Opal Corp. Years ago."

"Then what's Morlortai doing here?"

"According to Huang's network, Sytver Morlortai is a professional assassin. Huang doesn't know for certain, but there are rumors that someone back in the Phrenorian Empire took out a contract on Zhoh."

Sage shook his head. "I've never heard of that happening. The Phrenorians usually stand together on the battlefield."

"My guess is that this is a personal matter. Not a military one."

"Usually they work that out in combat."

"Hutamah," Kiwanuka agreed. "I've heard that too."

The assassin's location was a small piece of everything that was now going on, but Sage needed to know everything he could. Especially since Morlortai, and whoever had hired the man, was responsible for pushing Makaum to the brink of war. "Where is Morlortai?"

"I was trying to find out when everything went off the rails in the north sector."

Sage listened and drank water slowly as Kiwanuka brought him up to date on her operations of the day.

"This is my fault," Kiwanuka finished. "If I hadn't tried to get cute with Darrantia, things might not have gone so sideways."

"I would have done the same thing," Sage said. "Finding Morlortai and exposing him as Wosesa Staumar's murderer would have helped shut down some of the anti-Terran feelings among the Makaum."

"Maybe. We won't know now."

"Morlortai's got a ship in orbit?"

"Yes."

"Get the colonel to clear you and go after him."

Kiwanuka smiled at him. "Already done. Huang identified the ship for us. I'll have a ride in the next couple hours."

"Good. Do we still have Throzath?"

"He's locked up."

"Then I'll have a word with him."

"No. That's being handled. Colonel Halladay wanted you to report to Command as soon as you woke up."

Sage pushed himself to his feet and was surprised at how fit he felt.

"Feel better than you thought you would?" Kiwa-nuka asked.

"Yeah."

Kiwanuka showed Sage a small smile. "That's Captain Gilbride's doing, and the reason you were out so long. Doc said that if you were to get cut open now, you'd bleed nanobots, but he guaranteed you at a hundred percent. Colonel Halladay wouldn't accept anything less."

"Good to know."

"The thing is, Sage, you're running at the edge of what medtech can do. You may feel great, but if you take a lot of damage, you may not recover."

"It's been my experience that if a soldier gets vaporized or shot full of holes, chances of recovery are pretty slim too." Sage looked for his armor and found it at the foot of the bed. "I'll keep that in mind, but I'm not going to lie in bed while this tenuous peace ramps up into a full-blown war."

"Do you think that's where we're headed?" Kiwanuka asked.

Sage pulled his armor on, locking in tight and taking comfort in the AKTIVsuit. "That's exactly where we're headed now that Zhoh has been made general on Makaum. And he'll make that move as soon as he can. We've got to get out ahead of him."

Tactical Command Center
Fort York
2352 Hours Zulu Time

"The colonel's waiting for you in his ready room, Master Sergeant." The corporal heading up the security detail was young and stood tensely at the entrance to the command center. Her eyes were bloodshot and she looked pale. Too many of the soldiers at Fort York looked the same way these days. They weren't ready to be under siege.

Sage knew his view of them was tainted by the knowledge that they were on the precipice of war. He'd felt the same way about the young soldiers he'd trained in boot camp before he'd gotten back in the war. They had gone on, not as complete as he would have hoped.

Sage nodded at the woman and walked to Halladay's ready room. "Thank you, Corporal."

Two privates guarded the ready room door. One of them pressed a button and announced Sage and Kiwanuka. The door unlocked and slid to one side.

A holo table occupied the center of the room. At present, the space was blank, but as soon as the door locked behind Sage and Kiwanuka, the image came up again, unveiling a scene of rushing water and towering green trees.

Sage recognized the section of river and jungle immediately as the area where the Phrenorians had hidden their base containing rolling stock and aerial vehicles. He stopped at the table with Kiwanuka beside him. Both of them saluted sharply.

Halladay stood on the other side of the table and wore a grim expression. He looked tired too, but a fire burned inside him. "Feeling better, Master Sergeant?"

"Tip-top, sir." Sage swept the room's other occupants with his gaze. The roll call was pretty much as he'd expected, consisting of Leghef and Lieutenant Murad. Jahup was a surprise addition.

Leghef sat in a chair and surveyed Sage, taking measure of him. She looked fatigued but her eyes glittered.

"I would say good evening, Master Sergeant, but we're way past that. It's late, and there's not going to be anything good about it, I'm afraid." A small smile quirked her lips.

"Ma'am," Sage replied.

At her side, Jahup looked much better than Sage had last seen him, although he, too, wore silver nanite reconstructive membrane on the left side of his face and down his neck. The young man wore his armor with the scarlet *ypheynte* emblazoned on it.

He also sported sergeant's chevrons on his shoulders.

When Jahup saw that Sage had noted the change in rank, he looked embarrassed, but he squared his shoulders.

"Congratulations, Sergeant," Sage said.

"Thank you, Master Sergeant," Jahup replied. He seemed to stand a little taller.

"You're squared away with the med center?"

Unconsciously, Jahup touched his face and neck, then caught himself and put his hand down. "Captain Gilbride cleared me for duty."

Sage nodded and shifted his attention to Halladay.

"Field promotion," Halladay said, and nodded to Jahup. "I pushed through the paperwork on your new buck sergeant a few hours ago because you're going to need him in the field with you."

"Sir," Sage said, "no disrespect intended, but if you're going to send me where I think you are"—he nodded at the holo of the river area—"that's not a place Jahup needs to be."

Halladay opened his mouth to say something, and Jahup did the same, but Leghef beat them both.

"Master Sergeant Sage," the Quass stated, "my grandson has already visited this location on the Yeraf River with you."

"I understand that, ma'am, but things have changed. With Zhoh in as general of the Phrenorians here on Makaum—"

"It is even more imperative that we do something to destroy the arsenal that lies in wait there," Leghef said. "I do understand the dangers, Master Sergeant, and I admit that I am loath to risk my grandson on such an expedition."

"Then keep him here," Sage suggested.

"I can't," Leghef said. "He would only follow you."

Sage glanced at Jahup. "Not if he wants to keep those new stripes, he won't."

The boy's eyes narrowed, but he said nothing. Sage had almost expected him to strip off the chevrons and offer them to him.

"His new rank isn't going to buy his loyalty," the Quass said. "You already have that. If I were to order him to remain behind, he wouldn't." She paused. "The colonel and I talked about this before Jahup's promotion, and before you walked into this room. My grandson is going with you because it's the best place for him to be. You need him in this endeavor, Master Sergeant. Only the two of you have seen this place, and if something happens to you—well, we need redundancy for the operation."

"Ma'am—" Sage remembered the last time he and Jahup had gone out to that part of the jungle. They'd barely escaped with their lives, and they hadn't been trying to take down a Phrenorian stronghold at the time.

"In fact," Leghef said, raising her voice, "I made the argument to Colonel Halladay that he keep you at the fort rather than send you off to attack that weapons depot because I felt you would be better assigned here attending to the troops. No one else has the experience you do with what we're going to face in the next few hours." She grimaced. "I certainly don't think Zhoh will wait any longer than that."

Sage barely kept himself silent. The assignment to stay at the fort wouldn't have sat well with him, and all of them in the room knew it. Going out into the jungle was dangerous. So far Zhoh hadn't made a move against the fort or the sprawl.

Leghef nodded. "So you can appreciate our dilemma."

"Yes, ma'am," Sage replied, and he could see her point as clearly as he could see she wasn't about to give up on it.

"The bottom line," Halladay said, "is that you and Jahup have both been there." He leaned in, touched the holo, and lit up the hidden access hatch that opened into the underground complex.

Several bright dots manifested on both sides of the jungle.

"This is from the latest satellite imagery," Halladay said. "Those bright dots are Phrenorian troops and sec drones." He tapped the holo image and stats blinked to life. "There are thirty Phrenorians and ten assault drones on either side of the river on patrol. Getting past them will be difficult."

Drawn into the situation, Sage studied the troop placement. "How did we get this sat intel? The Phrenorians have been more or less invisible to us with the cloaking they've put into place over that area."

"We have Huang to thank for that," Halladay said.

"Huang's crossing the line," Sage said.

"As I understand it, he crossed it earlier when he sent people in with you to get Throzath. I talked to him. He's all in on this. The way he looks at it, his people are at risk even if they try to sit this one out. I agree with him."

Sage did too, but he didn't say that. If Zhoh and the Phrenorian Empire did make their bid to take control of Makaum, they wouldn't settle for anything less than everything.

Fort York and its personnel had to find a way to prevent that from happening.

THIRTY

Halladay looked at Sage. "We've got some ideas regarding how best to destroy the complex but we wanted to run everything by you. See if you see something we haven't."

Sage stuck his hands into the holo and blew up the image. "We don't know how big the stronghold is inside."

"Big enough to house a lot of munitions and vehicles," Halladay said. "Otherwise there's no reason to put it there. Once you get in place at that stronghold, you can set up ground-penetrating radar beacons that will give us a better idea of what you're up against. You'll also need to carry in a mobile netlink to give us access to the GPR units."

Sage nodded, turning it over in his head as he scanned the image.

"The location, below the water level, is going to work

for us. The radar beacons will enable us to find pressure points where we can use the location against that base."

"To flood the stronghold. Let the water do the damage."

"Blowing a hole in the riverbank is a start," Halladay agreed. "Drain the river water into that area and take out whatever war machines they've got hiding there. That might not take out the amphibious vehicles, but it will knock down what they have on hand. If you can find ordnance to put into play, so much the better." He looked at the image. "They made a mistake locating their stronghold there."

"Not if we never managed to find this place," Sage pointed out. "It was well hidden, and we got lucky finding it."

"We did, and we're going to make the most of it."

"Any overland approach we make is going to be spotted," Sage pointed out. "The Phrenorians will button that place up fast."

"Or boil out of there like ants," Kiwanuka said. "Getting away won't be easy for a small unit."

"We won't be able to take in many troops," Murad said. "This is going to have to be a surgical strike." He frowned. "Most of the soldiers we take with us probably won't be coming back. Those sacrifices will give the soldiers who remain behind a chance against the Phrenorians. That's not going to be easy either."

Sage rubbed his chin, and stopped when his fingers encountered the nanite membrane. "We're going to bring back all of the men that we can, Lieutenant. We're not planning on throwing lives away."

"I didn't mean that we were, Master Sergeant. I'm going with you, so I'm not inclined to act foolishly."

"We get in if we can, and we get it done," Sage said. "Then we return to the fort. We're going to have plenty of fighting to do here."

"Not here," Leghef said.

Sage glanced at her.

"Colonel Halladay and I have agreed that trying to hold the fort might not be possible. It's too big a target, and we can't know how badly compromised it is."

Sage knew that was true. They'd already seen evidence of Makaum civilians tasked in support roles who were anti-Terran.

"We're working on getting people organized," Leghef said, "those that will listen, and have them regroup in bands out in the jungle."

"Once you start moving people," Sage said, "you're going to push the Phrenorians into action. There'll be no hiding."

"We need to get civilians out of harm's way," Halladay said. "The Quass has already been getting word out to people that will listen to her."

"Unfortunately, even after today's events," Leghef said, "not all of them will believe the Phrenorians are our enemies."

"Or they'll throw in with the Phrenorians in the expectation of mercy." Jahup sounded bitter. "The people are already divided over this war."

"After today," Leghef said, "some of them will see things differently. The attack in the north sector has shown them that. The Phrenorians showed no mercy to anyone caught in the streets there."

"Throzath got his weapons from someone among the Phrenorians," Sage said. "I brought him in because I wanted to expose that network. Having that knowledge will help show that."

"We will get the information from Throzath," the Quass said. "I have someone seeing to that now. Once she has the story, and she will get it, we can let more people know how the Phrenorians have been working against us. And how some of our own people have betrayed the majority of us."

"Understood. Getting that story from Throzath isn't going to stop the Phrenorians."

"No," Leghef agreed, "it won't, but it will sway some of my people, and it will make more real the threat the Phrenorians pose." She glanced at Kiwanuka. "In much the same respect Sergeant Kiwanuka's success in finding the assassin who killed Wosesa Staumar will aid our efforts to appeal for more help from the Alliance. Both of those endeavors will enable us to open multiple fronts in the discussions that are being made now regarding what is to happen between the Phrenorian warriors and Terran soldiers here on Makaum." She returned her gaze to the holo. "That's why your mission tonight is so critical. We have to take away whatever advantage that stronghold poses."

Halladay nodded. "Agreed. So we have a little time and luck on our side."

"Zhoh will move quickly," Sage said.

"He already is," Leghef said. "According to some of the people I've had watching the Phrenorians, General Zhoh has already sent a contingent of warriors out there."

"Probably pilots and drivers," Halladay said. "They'll be gearing up to bring those vehicles online as soon as they're given the command."

"Why hasn't that command already been given?" Sage asked.

"The Phrenorian Empire is working through diplomatic channels," Halladay answered. "You and I both know that 'Phrenorian diplomats' are as rare as unicorns. In the end, the Phrenorian Empire is going to do what they want to, meaning they will attempt to take Makaum, but the Alliance is negotiating with them."

He paused. "The decision has been made to withdraw our troops from the planet."

Anger ignited in Sage and he barely kept himself under control. "We can't just leave these people here, sir."

"That's not what I want either, Master Sergeant." Halladay's command tone kicked in a little. "What I'm telling you is that the Makaum Oversight Committee under Chairman Finkley is negotiating terms of Terran military withdrawal as we speak. That's the only thing holding the Phrenorians back. They want to put a good face on this if they can. The Quass has asked for asylum for the Makaum people."

"They're not going to get it," Sage said. "The Phrenorian Empire won't let that happen."

"It's not just about the planet and its resources," Kiwanuka said. "The Phrenorians are going to want slave labor as well."

"I know," Halladay said. "That's why we're going to act. I signed on here to protect these people. We're going to do that. The oversight committee and General Whitcomb aren't going to like that."

"Best-case scenario," Sage said, "the Phrenorians agree to let us pull out and leave a skeleton crew of Terran soldiers behind to facilitate the asylum. They'll make us take most of our soldiers and our weapons offplanet first, then allow a few Makaum people to transport out also. But at some point, they'll shut down the removal efforts and keep most of the people here as slaves to procure the resources they want. They've done that before."

"I'm well aware of that, Master Sergeant," Halladay said. "Which is why we're going to drown that munitions encampment. If we are allowed to provide asylum for the Makaum people, which I don't think we'll get to do,

we're going to level the playing field as much as we can."
He took a breath. "After that, we'll just have to see."

"We are, as I believe your people put it," Leghef said,
"between a rock and a hard place."

"Yes, ma'am," Sage agreed. "You are. But you're not
there alone." He looked at Halladay. "Have you passed
this mission on up the line, Colonel?"

"I have not," Halladay said. "This is being written
up as an expeditionary recon acting on rumors we've
recently gotten from in-country intel. When things go
badly at the stronghold, which I assume they will since
that's what we're planning on, you're simply doing your
best to rout Phrenorian troops who have broken the
treaty we have regarding this world."

"Command will see through that," Kiwanuka said.

"I think, in the end, what we do at that stronghold
is going to be a pittance when weighed in with everything else that's going wrong tonight," Halladay said.
"If Command discovers that I knew about the Phrenorian stronghold longer than I claim to have known in
the parameters of this mission, they could just as well
applaud me for waiting as long as I could. In the end,
we didn't choose this war. The Phrenorians did. We're
just making the best of it that we can."

"Yes sir." Sage turned his attention back to the holo
and concentrated on the problem at hand. "We could
take four fireteams overland into the area. Heavy weps
teams. Sniper teams. And we'd have to have at least one
demo team to blow the river wall along the stronghold."

"Take Corporal Culpepper," Kiwanuka suggested.
"He's the man you want when you want something
obliterated."

Sage nodded. He remembered Culpepper from the
assault on Cheapdock. The soldier also had an impressive amount of battlefield experience.

"Sixteen soldiers aren't many," Halladay said.

"We can't have many, sir." Sage stood and folded his arms across his chest. "Even sixteen might be pressing our luck to stay undiscovered out there, but I can't see doing it with any less. Not if we want to succeed at this."

"We want you to succeed," Halladay said. "Getting close to the stronghold is going to be problematic."

"When Jahup and I were there," Sage said, "Zhoh arrived at the stronghold in a submersible. That's how the Phrenorians are ferrying supplies and materials into that compound."

"I know," Halladay said. "After you told me about that, I asked Huang if he knew anything concerning those operations." The colonel smiled. "I wasn't surprised to learn that he did. As it turns out, Huang has worked his way into supplementing some of the Phrenorians' larders there. His people are providing offworld delicacies that are hard to come by on Makaum even in the bazaars."

"Something called *yerendy* was a favorite of General Rangha's, I believe," Leghef said. "I don't know for certain what that is, but Uncle Huang told me it was served while alive."

"*Yerendy* is contraband on several worlds," Kiwanuka said. "The Alliance still isn't sure whether they need to be flagged as sentient and recognized as a culture because some of them have passed the mirror self-recognition test. Some behaviorists think the MSR doesn't work uniformly because *yerendy* aren't vain enough to care to see themselves."

Leghef grimaced.

"Huang has a meeting place for the submersible?" Sage asked.

Halladay reached into the holo and shifted the image. A digital readout kept track of the distance. "Here." He stopped the image 34.8 klicks from the stronghold.

"This is where Huang's people have delivered cargo."

The site showed a wide spot in the river. Trees lined the banks on both sides and the current was so smooth it looked like glass.

"That's Ackurna," Jahup said.

"You know this place?" Sage asked.

The young man nodded and his brow furrowed in thought. The nanite membrane gleamed and Sage made a mental note that the sheen on Jahup's coverings and his own would have to be reduced so it wouldn't reflect. It wouldn't show behind a faceshield, but he didn't want to take chances.

"We've hunted at Ackurna in the past," Jahup said. "It's a levee, built up over the years by the passage of the Yeraf River. It is dangerous there. The *jasulild* spawn in that place, and when they do, they're constantly aggressive and have even left the waters in pursuit of prey."

Sage was familiar with the creatures after seeing one close up during the trek to Cheapdock. The one he'd seen had been over seven meters in length and three meters in diameter. They grew larger than that.

"We've taken meat there during desperate times," Jahup said. "In the end, hunters gave up on the area. The *jasulild* are too numerous there. When they can't find enough prey, they eat each other. We haven't hunted in that area in over two years."

"Huang's intel indicated the same thing," Halladay said.

"That's why the Phrenorians picked that spot," Sage said. "The location provides natural barriers, the local hunter groups no longer go there, and it appeals to their sense of a dangerous environment. How do the shipments work?"

Halladay flicked another spot on the holo and a smaller image sparked to life. This one showed two rounded submersibles, both of Phrenorian design with articulated arms attached fore and aft and along the sides.

"The larger submersible is a *Kinob*-class, I'm told," Halladay said. "Fifty meters long, it's a troop transport the Phrenorians had designed by Tianysen weapons engineers after they took over the planet. You'd think with Phrenoria being a water planet and inhabited by undersea giants the Phrenorians would have already had submersibles. They didn't. Now they have these."

"So we'll need some people familiar with Tianysen weapons systems, including submersibles," Sage said.

"I already have them for us," Murad stated. "One of the fireteam squads can double as a crew aboard the submersibles."

"The troop transport is being used as a ferry for the cargo," Sage said. "What's the second one? A gunboat?"

"Exactly," Halladay said. "*Oringu*-class. Twenty-seven meters long and zips through water like a fish. Designed to be support and defense, and it's armed to the teeth. Getting one of the submersibles will be hard. Taking over both of them is going to be next to impossible."

"That river is deep enough to allow both of those vessels to navigate?" Sage asked.

"The Yeraf River is over two hundred meters deep in that area," Jahup said. "In other places, it is even deeper."

"The Zaire River in Africa is over two hundred meters deep," Kiwanuka said. "Makaum is a slightly larger planet, and it has more surface land mass than Terra."

All of it filled with things that want to kill you and eat you. Sage glanced at the two submersibles. "How many crewmen are on the boats?"

"The *Kinob* will be stripped down," Halladay said. "Huang's best guess was seven, including captain, pilot, navigator, and quartermaster. It will have three or four grunts to handle cargo. The *Oringu* is harder to access. Terran mil intel lists crews of up to twenty aboard. Captain, pilot, navigator, quartermaster, weps, and the rest are warriors who specialize in asset recovery and boarding crews."

"Boarding crews?" Sage asked. "Like pirates?"

"Like naval crews used by Lord Nelson's British Navy," Halladay said. "They'll be experienced warriors used to fighting in close quarters."

"Then we'll fill our complement with special forces people," Sage said. "We've got a few men who fought the Phrenorians at Cidra. They had to dig the Phrenorians out of the tunnels at Samoq. And we've been training for urban terrain tactics. We can make do with those people."

Halladay nodded. "I've already got most of them on your list, Master Sergeant. You've got a thirty-minute window to review it, then you've got to join Huang's caravan. They're already en route to that destination."

"Copy that." Sage looked at Jahup. "You and I will review those lists, Sergeant. I want some of your people among them. People who know the area and how to fight in a tight environment. Can do?"

Jahup nodded and didn't look excited, for which Sage was grateful. "Can do."

Sage glanced at Halladay. "Anything else, sir?"

"No. I'll just wish you luck."

"Roger that." Sage saluted and performed an about-face that was textbook perfect.

At his side, Jahup did the same, but he relented his stoic demeanor when his grandmother reached out to hug him and speak privately to him for a moment.

By the time Sage reached the door, Jahup and Kiwanuka had fallen in behind him.

THIRTY-ONE

"Master Sergeant," Jahup called after the sec door shushed closed behind them.

"Yeah?" Sage responded.

Jahup hesitated, then hurried through his request. "Can I have five minutes? I'll meet you at the helipad."

Sage was pretty sure he knew what the younger man was going to do, so he nodded. "You have your five minutes, Sergeant, but if you're late, I'm leaving without you."

"You won't be leaving without me," Jahup promised. He turned and hurried back down the corridor.

Kiwanuka walked at Sage's side as they continued their trek. "Those two needed to have more time together. It's hard enough figuring out you're in love at that age without a war going on around you."

"Knowing you're in someone's crosshairs allows you

to live life more honestly, too. You know it could be over at any minute, so you follow your instincts. If this situation hadn't turned worse, they might not have figured it out at all."

"I know they've been divided over the situation here," Kiwanuka said. "Do you think they've truly figured out where they are with each other?"

"For the moment, sure."

"Noojin's rejoined the military. She's one of us again."

Sage nodded. He'd had the feeling earlier after their talk that was where Noojin was headed.

"When are you leaving?" Sage asked Kiwanuka as they walked through the corridor leading away from the tactical command center.

"I've got to leave the fort in nine minutes if I'm going to make the shuttle at North Star Spaceport," Kiwanuka replied.

"The assassin and his team are going to expect company after today's events. Us or the Phrenorians. Those people are used to being hunted."

"Copy that," Kiwanuka replied.

"Do you know where to find their ship?"

"I do. Corporal Pingasa tracked Morlortai's shuttle burning off from the planet when it left. Further investigative efforts on my team's part turned up a snitch inside Wosesa Staumar's staff that sold information to a man named Ny'age. Ny'age is part of Morlortai's crew who usually acts as a go-between."

"The Phrenorians could have found the same guy."

"I'll let you know if they beat me there."

"You can't hide in open space," Sage pointed out.

"Neither can Morlortai or his crew. Maybe he'll see me coming, but once I have eyes on him, he can't get away."

Sage brooded for a moment over all the fronts that

were popping up around them. "I don't like the fact that we're getting spread thin on this."

"Neither do I," Kiwanuka admitted. "So you be sure you make it back, Master Sergeant. As I recall, I saved your life earlier and you owe me dinner."

"I do. You make sure you show up. I don't like drinking alone."

"Copy that."

They stopped at a juncture in the hallway and Sage realized they were heading in different directions. He turned to her and looked into her eyes.

"I'll see you on the other side," Sage said.

Kiwanuka nodded. "You will." She turned and went, and—for a short time—he watched her go. She didn't look back. He'd known she wouldn't.

0015 Hours Zulu Time

Noojin sat at a table in the mess hall where Jahup's near-AI had located her. For a moment, he stood in the doorway and watched her sitting there.

She was alert and ready, but her mind was somewhere else. Her armor gleamed and showed her attention to its readiness. Her short-cropped dark hair framed her face and made her look younger than her years, almost child-like. But the bleakness in her eyes almost broke his heart.

When they'd hunted together, when they'd lost hunters who were their mentors and younger hunters they themselves were training, they'd grieved together. But those losses hadn't dragged them down—or apart—the way the war had. The hunts had been everything, a way to prove they could take care of themselves against everything the jungle and the planet could throw at them.

But the arrival of the Phrenorians and the Terrans had changed that. Jahup hadn't realized how innocent he had been until he'd almost lost Noojin to the corp drug traffickers, and then again when she had stepped away from him and chosen to go her own path.

He'd been a fool thinking nothing would ever come between them.

As if sensing she was being stared at, a skill learned out in the jungle, Noojin looked at him. For a moment, her expression didn't change and he thought she was still mad at him for almost getting killed earlier.

He quashed the immediate impulse to feel frustrated and instead walked over to her.

"Are you feeling better?" she asked.

"Yeah." He gestured to the bench across from her. She nodded.

He sat. "I got called in to the colonel's office."

"The Quass told me."

"I'm going on a mission with Sage."

"I was told that too."

For a moment, Jahup was silent and tried to figure out what he wanted to say. "You weren't there when I woke up."

"I had to rest. Your grandmother ordered me to. I didn't have the strength to argue with her. I was asleep when you were released from the med center. Then I had to go get my equipment ready."

"This is really what you want to do?"

"We don't have a choice. The Phrenorians are coming now. There will be no stopping them."

"You do have a choice. You can get offplanet."

"And go where?"

"Anywhere."

She shook her head. "No. This morning when I thought I'd lost you proved that to me. I could live without you, anywhere else but Makaum, but that's not what I would ever choose to do. Not as long as there's a chance we can be together."

"I feel the same way, but if letting you go meant you would be safe, I'd do that."

Noojin showed him a small smile. "This is what I have to do. I tried sitting out of the war. I tried not to worry about you." She shook her head. "None of that worked. I worried about you during the hunts too, but at least during those there were breaks in between. With this . . . it's all the time. There are no breaks."

"I know." Jahup pulled off one of his gauntlets and took her hand in his. Her fingers felt strong and alive, and he hoped she stayed that way. He couldn't imagine life without her. "I don't want us to be apart, Noojin."

"Neither do I."

Her helmet buzzed for attention.

"I've got to go," she said. "I'm meeting up with Sergeant Kiwanuka."

Surprise spiked through him. "You're going after the assassin?"

Noojin nodded. "I'm a hunter. Like you. I'm better trained in close quarters combat than most of the soldiers she has available to her."

Jahup suppressed the immediate anxiety that threaded through him, and he knew Noojin was dealing with the same fears. "Make sure you come back."

"I will. You do the same."

They stood and were awkward for a moment. Then Jahup leaned in and kissed her. Maybe she was surprised because he'd never done that before, or maybe it was because they were in a public place and she didn't like showing emotions like that, but she didn't respond.

Not at first.

Then she kissed him back and his head spun.

Her helmet buzzed again, and his did the same, letting him know the five minutes he'd asked for had elapsed.

With a final kiss, they separated and went their own ways. Jahup turned his thoughts to the mission with Sage, and his resolve to accomplish whatever he had to do in order to return to Noojin burned within him.

THIRTY-TWO

Zhoh shifted through screens of information on the computer, flicking from one to another with quick deliberation. Sat vid from recon units they had hidden and paid for among corp support arrays in near-planet orbits played in other screens.

Several of those screens showed a steady line of beings creeping out of the sprawl through shadowy alleys and flowing into the solid dark of the waiting jungle. To Zhoh, it didn't make sense. The beings worked hard to maintain their urban area, fighting back the creeping vegetation that would not give up, and cohabitating with it when they couldn't fight it. They had spent generations building the area into a habitable environment. Even a few days away from it would see large tracts of land lost to them. The jungle would reclaim everything.

"The Makaum people are withdrawing from the sprawl?" he asked.

"Yes, *triarr*," Mato replied. He had brought the news to Zhoh only minutes ago.

"What is the purpose?"

"Our analysts believe the beings are abandoning the sprawl."

"Because of today's violence?"

"Yes."

That didn't make sense to Zhoh either. The battle in the streets had been nothing compared to areas where total war had broken out. But he remembered these beings weren't fighters. They were barely civilized, and they hadn't had any enemies except the planet's natural predators. An opposing army would be a frightening thing to them. "Where will they go?"

"Into the jungle."

"There's no place for them to gather out there."

"None that we have ever seen."

Zhoh considered that. Such a retreat meant that there would be less combat necessary in the streets as the Phrenorian army seized the assets there, but rounding up the populace as slave labor would become more tedious. It would still be done, but it would be accomplished more slowly.

And then effort would be required to rebuild the sprawl. This development was infuriating.

"For what purpose?" Zhoh demanded. "If the Terran military was going to give these beings asylum, they would use shuttles to take them into space. And they wouldn't do that until they had proper transport in place. Supporting hundreds of extra beings on a space station will stress its resources and make it more indefensible for a blockade. Once we cut off their food and water, they'll have no choice but to capitulate."

"Agreed," Mato said. "Our analysts also believe this retreat is being done to get the Makaum beings out of the path of the coming military engagement."

Zhoh sat up straighter in his chair. His primaries clicked irritably and his pheromones were thick and threatening. He quickly checked himself and forced himself to be calmer.

"The Terrans are planning on fighting." The thought excited Zhoh even though his warriors were outnumbered. His warriors were also blooded combatants. Many of the Terran soldiers lacked such experience.

"They know we will give them no choice."

"This is a delaying tactic," Zhoh said.

"I think so too, General."

"They wish to avoid a confrontation. Or maybe they hope to hide and live in the shadows while we take what we want. Then, after we've taken our fill, they'll live on the dregs of this planet and be forgotten."

"That is a possibility."

"I don't like the idea of having to dig those beings out of that jungle," Zhoh said. "It will be too costly and too slow."

On top of that, he didn't like being in the jungle. There were too many dangerous things out there. He wasn't afraid of combat, but there were creatures and plants out in the wilderness that would kill a warrior before he even recognized the threat.

"Still, *triarr*, they can do nothing to stop us from doing exactly that."

Zhoh thought of the jungle and the times he'd been out in it. Everything on the planet seemed determined to kill anything that was foreign to it. The Makaum beings had managed to live within it, even to build a city where they could live together, but they hadn't truly thrived in the ecosphere. Their number had slowly grown over the years after the generation ship had crash-landed four hundred years ago.

"Have you been out in the jungle, Mato?"

"Not often."

"I've been on thirty different planets during my career," Zhoh said. "I've fought Terrans and other beings on all of them. I've had to wear radiation suits to protect me from fallout in nuked sprawls while salvaging technology and scientists, lived through the ravages of disease in internment camps that could have killed me, and fought every hellish monster and being that lived on those planets. But I have never before faced something as vile as this world."

"Nor have I."

Zhoh watched the vids of beings streaming from the sprawl. They went in groups, transporting only what they could by carts pulled by *dafeerorg* and anti-grav "mules," flat cargo platforms they'd bought from corp-sponsored shops. Most of the beings only carried what they could pack out under their own power.

"Do we have an estimate of how many beings are leaving the sprawl?" Zhoh asked.

"Our best estimate is seventy-two percent."

The number was intolerable. The after-conquest stats were in and the success of the follow-up mission was dependent on the labor force they intended to enslave.

"And the other twenty-eight percent?"

"Most are staying where they are. Others have taken shuttles to the space stations."

"They can't remain as a large group out in the jungle," Zhoh said. "They would become easy prey for predators, and they wouldn't be able to find a sustainable food source. That is the problem with trying to become urbanized without resources. Water out there will be no problem, but living off the land is hard. They will exterminate their food supply, meat and vegetable. And if too many of them try to congregate in the same area, even with an abundant supply of fresh water, they will be living in their own filth in short order."

There had been worlds where Zhoh had been forced to do that with troops for a time so he knew the hardships those beings faced. Having to live off the land had defeated armies in the past. Large groups of forces were only viable if they had supply lines. If a unit could not be fed, it could not be fielded.

Then there was the matter of sanitation and sickness.

The Makaum beings were only delaying the inevitable.

"This makes no sense to me," Zhoh said. "They will have to fragment, divide their numbers into smaller groups, and become prey for the predators that dwell outside the sprawl. I wouldn't do this. I would rather fight to the death and die free."

Mato nodded. "As would I, *triarr*. But we are not these beings. Their ways are not our ways. We are warriors. These beings have been agriculturally based and have had no wars."

"The generation ship crashed on this planet four hundred years ago," Zhoh said. "How long have the Makaum lived in the sprawl?"

"I know only a little of their history. Perhaps two hundred and fifty years? Not more than that. They feared living in groups for a time. Earlier efforts to build a sprawl ended in defeat until they learned to fight off the larger predators like the *kifrik* and others that immediately hunted them as a prey source."

"Do we know who is behind this withdrawal?"

"According to our sources, word was sent out from Quass Leghef."

Zhoh knew of the woman, though he'd never met her. "She is a puppet of the Terran Alliance."

"Not exactly," Mato said. "She has been a strong leader of the Makaum."

The answer surprised Zhoh.

"Who was it General Rangha was working through?" Zhoh knew the general loved playing at spy games. Rangha was not a true champion of the Phrenorian Empire, only a warrior resting on the accomplishments of his ancestors.

"Tholak. He is also a member of the Quass."

"Where is he?"

"Currently, Tholak is trying to get his son Throzath from the holding cells in Fort York."

"Why do they have him?"

"Throzath instigated the attack on Quass Leghef's grandson this morning. Master Sergeant Sage took him into custody."

Zhoh barely remembered the report he'd looked at earlier. Since assuming command of the Phrenorian forces, he'd had access to a lot more details of the Makaum campaign. Most of them he'd known from other avenues of intelligence, but he preferred the reports because they were concise and pertinent.

"Tholak is still accessible to us?" Zhoh asked.

"Tholak still hopes to negotiate a position in the Phrenorian occupation of this planet."

"Have him dig into Quass Leghef's plans. See if he can find out more about what's going on."

"I will."

"This information about the abandonment of the sprawl is surprising," Zhoh said, "and it is frustrating, but in the end it will give these beings small solace. After a few days of hardship out in that jungle, they will choose the comfort of servitude over whatever illusions of freedom they are currently harboring. We can let those hardships provide the convincing. Rebels are only a minor problem because they will only rebel until their path becomes too difficult. It's the patriots that are dangerous. They won't give up until they are dead." He looked at Mato. "Where is Sage?"

The fact that the Terran master sergeant had survived the attack in the north sector had been astounding. Zhoh had learned too late that the well had been an opening to an underground river. By the time they had found the other end of it, Sage was gone.

Still, Sage's continued existence offered Zhoh a chance to defeat the Terran in combat at some later date. Sage would not quit, the Phrenorian general knew, until he was dead.

"Sage is at Fort York, *triarr*."

"Do you have eyes on him?"

"No. We have been trying to achieve that, but getting into the Terrans' inner command circle has gotten much harder."

"Find him. Whatever the Terrans are planning, Sage will be at the eye of it."

Mato hesitated. "I will."

"What?" Zhoh asked.

"There is one other thing. Something I thought you might enjoy."

"Now I'm intrigued."

Mato's pheromones indicated that he was pleased with himself. He tapped the computer keyboard. A moment later, a media story spun onto the screen.

The image focused on Zhoh standing on the aircar with his rifle in his secondaries, bleeding from his chest wounds, and looking formidable.

"What is this?" Zhoh asked.

"This is from a media vidcast on a channel owned by the (ta)Klar," Mato answered. "They are hailing you as a hero, the newly minted general of Makaum, who is fighting against cowardly Terran forces who tried to assassinate you."

"The (ta)Klar are only presenting this to incite the Terrans." Zhoh didn't buy into the propaganda. "They've done this before on planets they gave up on acquiring. Before they pull out, they make sure the Empire and the Alliance are at each other's throats. The more we pour into war efforts, the less we have to chase the (ta)Klar away from their predations on other planets. They are like *krayari* beetles feeding on offal."

Zhoh tapped keys and went back to his reports. The pilots would arrive at the stronghold within a few hours. He awaited confirmation of that.

And he still wanted to know what the Phrenorian Empire planned to do to support his efforts on Makaum.

THIRTY-THREE

Master Sergeant."

The jumpcopter copilot's voice came over Sage's helmet comm and woke him from the light slumber he'd managed to ease into only minutes after departing Fort York. He blinked and pulled up the local map on his HUD. Sitting up a little on the bench seat that ran along the jumpcopter's cargo area, he ran his hands over his combat harness and checked his gear.

"Yes sir, Lieutenant," Sage replied. He studied the map in detailed relief. All he saw was jungle except for the wide swath created by the Yeraf River cutting through it 10.8 klicks to the southwest. The blue X that marked the rendezvous point pulsed slowly.

"We're coming up on your drop point," the young lieutenant said. "Three minutes out and closing."

Sage couldn't remember the woman's name and had to pull it up on his screen.

Dundee, Alice, First Lieutenant.

"Copy that, sir." Sage glanced back at the jumpcopter's cargo area.

Murad, Jahup, and the other thirteen soldiers of his mission op sat armored up and wearing hang glider descent equipment. They were going to join Huang's caravan en route approximately seven klicks out from the river.

Like Sage, Jahup had taken the time to sleep while sitting in the safety netting on the bench across the cargo hold. All of the other experienced Makaum hunters in the group had slept as well during the hour-long hop at treetop level.

Swaying with the jumpcopter's movement, Sage stood and nudged one of Jahup's feet with his own.

Jahup's helmet rolled from his shoulder to face Sage.

"Time to rise and shine, Sergeant," Sage said. "Get your teams ready."

"Copy that, Master Sergeant." Lithely, giving no indication of yesterday's injuries or the fact that he'd just awakened, Jahup stood and swayed with the jumpcopter's movement.

Sage, Murad, Jahup, and Culpepper headed up the four fireteams, each having their own squads, which were further broken down in command. Culpepper was leading the demolitions team, Murad had the snipers, and Sage and Jahup had split the heavy weps teams that would do most of the close-in fighting.

"Two minutes," the lieutenant called back.

"Roger that," Sage said.

He went through checking his team's readiness. All of them packed a grenade-launcher-equipped Roley for lead weapons. They also carried monofilament-edged boarding axes for when they were hand-to-hand inside the vessels if it came to that. Projectile weapons would be dangerous inside the Phrenorian submersibles. The final check was on the glide-assist pack. Without it, surviving the drop to the jungle floor would be next to impossible. The canopy crowned at two hundred meters.

"One minute," the pilot called back.

Sage stood at the jumpcopter's rear section and waited as the lift assembly dropped the boarding ramp. Wind rushed by him and moonlight filtered into the dark cargo area but didn't highlight the armor with the camo function absorbing ambient light.

A sea of trees blew by beneath the jumpcopter, and they would be the most dangerous aspect of the descent. Even with the light-amplifying feature of the armor and the fast reaction provided by the artificial musculature, running into a tree could result in injury or death.

"Thirty seconds and counting," Lieutenant Dundee said. "Good luck on the ground. Fifteen, fourteen . . ."

At zero, Sage hurled himself out of the jumpcopter and spread his arms. "Deploy glide assist."

Deploying glide assist, the near-AI announced.

Immediately, the glide-assist pack unfurled along the backs of Sage's arms and down his legs, becoming a four-pointed wing that gave him some control over his descent. Once it was in place, the wing caught the wind and slowed his descent hard enough to shake him. It wasn't as efficient as the no-see glidesuit, but with the current setup he didn't have to shed his armor. They were jumping off in the middle of the jungle. Stealth wasn't an issue tonight.

The line of soldiers deployed behind Sage quickly. He marked the Makaum soldiers in his HUD and watched to make sure they were on task. Most of them had only worked with the glide-assist packs on computers and never physically deployed. The suits' near-AIs would help with navigation.

As long as they trusted them and didn't fight them.

"Zhulong," Sage broadcasted over the frequency they were using for the op. "Zhulong, this is Fox Leader. Do you copy?"

"Fox Leader," a calm female voice responded. "We read you. We see you. We're switching on the beacon now. Confirm sighting."

Zhulong, according to what Sage had been told, was a Chinese dragon of legend. He was also called the torch dragon because he created the day and night by opening and closing his eyes.

A heartbeat later, a reddish-orange beam sparked up from the jungle floor 288.8 meters to the south/ southwest.

"Fox Leader confirms beacon, Zhulong," Sage said. "We'll be there in seconds."

"Be safe, Fox Leader. And be careful. We've had trouble with *kifrik* over the last couple days. We think we hit on a spawn cycle."

"Copy that." Sage relayed the warning to his teams and adjusted his glide pattern to take him in the direction of the beacon. He watched the shadows spread across the tree canopy, but it was hard to discern details even with the light amplification ability of the HUD.

Kifrik didn't have a way of controlling their body temperatures, so their internal heat dropped with the arrival of night and they blended in with their surroundings. Still, motion-activated sensors picked up some of them nearby as they scuttled across the trees.

"Webs!" one of the soldiers behind Sage called out. "I'm burning through!"

Fifty meters behind, laser beams torched a wide-spread web in two horizontal spots. Another laser beam burned through a large *kifrik* and set it on fire. The arachnid screamed and tried to scuttle away, but the flames quickly overcame it. Burning, it plunged through the trees and hit branches on its way to the jungle floor. Embers scattered, but no trees or brush caught on fire.

Lasers burned through a few more close calls, but the soldiers stayed on track and slid out of line only a few meters.

Within seventy meters of his destination, Sage headed down and tried to avoid the large trees during his descent. Twigs and branches cracked around him, and broken limbs tore at the glider-assist pack. He was still ten meters above the ground when the glider assembly took so much damage it finally shredded and gave up the losing battle.

Sage dropped like a rock and managed to land on his feet. He quickly rolled to shed velocity and got to his feet once more with the Roley at the ready. Instinctively, he took cover behind the thick bole of a tree.

Behind him, the other soldiers fell to the jungle floor as well. The noise they made crashing through the branches and thudding against the ground carried through the jungle.

Sage ticked off the arrivals, flicking through their injury stats to make sure all of the soldiers arrived unhurt. When they were all down, they ditched the remnants of the glide-assist packs and dumped them in the jungle. There was no need to hide them because after tonight the Phrenorians would know they'd been there.

Sage noted the three blips on the HUD's radar approaching from the south/southwest. He turned to face them with the Roley at his shoulder. He sighted on the lead figure.

"On your marks," Sage ordered.

The three other members of his fireteam posted up around him and took cover where they could find it.

"No one fires till I say so," Sage said.

The three figures stopped advancing twenty meters out.

"Lieutenant Murad," a woman said loudly enough for her voice to carry to the fireteams. She spoke English like a native and her voice held a singsong cadence. "I am Zhulong."

"Approach, Zhulong," Murad ordered. "Keep your hands where I can see them."

"I have two people with me."

"We know. Bring them too."

The three figures moved forward again and came into view. The lead woman was lean and tall, outfitted in combat armor with her helmet hanging at her hip. Her hair was short-cropped and framed her face. From her features and skin tone, Sage guessed that she was biracial, Chinese and European.

"Master Sergeant," Murad said, "let's say hello."

Sage dropped his rifle into a carry position and stepped out from cover to join the lieutenant in his approach to the group.

"My name is Qiao," the woman said. "Uncle Huang told me you would be joining the caravan. I am to be your guide."

Sage glanced at the other woman, a younger version of Qiao, and moved on to the man that accompanied them. He recognized Fachang immediately.

Reaching out to shake the man's hand, Sage said, "You get around."

Fachang bowed his head. "As I have told you, Uncle is fully invested in Charlie Company's efforts to save the Makaum people, Master Sergeant. He felt I would be most helpful in this endeavor. I agreed. If you will allow, I have a group of warriors who will be able to assist with your operation."

"We're not taking anybody inside with us," Sage said. "That would be too confusing."

Fachang looked like he wanted to put up an argument, but he bowed his head in acceptance. "Then we can cover your retreat should that become necessary."

"That we'll take," Murad said before Sage could say anything.

"Then get your men sorted and let's get moving," Qiao said. "You're going to have to cover a lot of ground quickly if you hope to catch up with the caravan."

"Yes, ma'am," Sage said. "Just lead the way."

Qiao waited till the soldiers were organized, then set off at a rapid trot, moving through the jungle like she'd lived there all her life. Fachang and the other woman fell in on both sides, running slightly ahead and on either side.

Sage ran with Fachang out on the right and his team followed as they crashed through the brush and frightened away nocturnal animals. Jahup and his team ran on the left side of the trail and followed the other woman. Murad and his snipers and Culpepper's demo team ran the main route.

Sage hand-signaled Fachang to go to an independent channel so they could speak.

Fachang nodded.

"How far to the caravan?" Sage asked.

"Seven klicks," Fachang answered.

Sage estimated the distance based on their current rate of speed. They'd make it just before daybreak and with less than twenty minutes before the appointed meeting time.

"Why so far away?" he asked.

"Qiao's idea," Fachang said. "She thought the run might calm your soldiers, get them loosened up, and have them focused on the battle ahead of them instead of lying around waiting for it."

As he thought about that, Sage realized he would have done the same thing had he considered it.

THIRTY-FOUR

Despite the unfamiliar and rough terrain, Sage knew the soldiers made good time and arrived twenty-two minutes ahead of the arranged delivery time. He crested a tall hill with Fachang at his side and gazed down at the Yeraf River gurgling contentedly in the valley a hundred and twenty meters in front of him at the bottom of the thirty-four-degree grade.

With the moonlight reflecting on the dark green water, the river gleamed blackly in the darkness. The thick stands of trees on the riverbanks looked dense and impenetrable, but narrow alleys ran through them that allowed Sage to scan the small clearing where the caravan had gathered.

Twenty-three vehicles, some motorized and some pulled by *dafeerorgs*, waited on the riverbank beneath the broad, leafy branches of the tall trees around them.

With all the foliage, the caravan personnel would be hard to see from overhead. It would take a low-flying jumpcopter or a drone to spot them, and even then the pilots of either would have to know what was being searched for.

"Qiao cleared out the brush so her sniper teams would have clear fields of fire to the loading area," Fachang said. "In case they were ever found out by a crew of hijackers. Before you arrived and started hitting the criminal organizations, getting attacked was sometimes a problem."

"She did a good job," Sage commented. "If I didn't know what I was looking at, if we weren't standing here, I wouldn't even see these areas. And the fields of fire for snipers are good." He glanced around at the men and women Qiao had stationed in hiding places as overwatch.

"Uncle holds Caravan Master Qiao in the highest regard," Fachang said. "She has worked with him on other worlds and she is very good at what she does."

"She also knows that once we've initiated contact she's to pull her people out and get somewhere safe?"

Fachang nodded. "On that, you can rest assured. To be honest, she is not a willing participant of this ruse. She wanted her team clear of any potential harm and did not wish to be here. Uncle had to bargain hard with her to get her assistance in your subterfuge."

"If she'll get them out of the way," Sage said, "we'll keep them safe."

"True, but in either case, her work here as a caravan master will be over."

"It's over anyway," Sage stated. "The Phrenorians aren't going to hold back now. They'll go public with all the munitions they've got hidden. That attempt on Zhoh provided the Empire all it needs to go to war." He glanced at Fachang and spoke again in a neutral tone. "And if I'd found out about this operation, I would have shut it down anyway."

Fachang smiled. "Qiao knows, Master Sergeant. As she's gone about her business, the threat you have posed has been uppermost in her mind. Other than a betrayal on the part of the Phrenorians, you have been her greatest concern." He paused. "She has never said that to me, but Uncle mentioned it in confidence."

The fact that Qiao had successfully managed her operation under Sage's nose bothered him. Still, he'd known there were various illegal endeavors that had continued inside the sprawl and deep in the jungle. Some of them he'd allowed to remain in play because the intel coming through them had been valuable.

He couldn't say for certain that he wouldn't have left the caravan traffic in play if he'd discovered it after he'd found out about the Phrenorian secret base. He would probably have let it operate so he could use it as bait just as he was planning to use it this morning.

The caravan workers had hunkered down to await the morning. Cargo was strapped to flatbed anti-grav mules, carts pulled by *dafeerorgs*, and battered crawlers that had been outfitted for the harsh terrain. All of the transport equipment was hard-used and had debris in the wheels from the trek through the jungle.

Once Qiao was back among her people, they got up and looked sharp. They cleaned their vehicles, cared for their animals, and checked over the cargo without being told.

Charlie Company stayed out of the caravan guards' sightline and hung back. A hundred meters away, Pingasa released three micro-drones into the air and they fluttered away on rapidly spinning wings. One of the drones went upstream, another went downstream, and the third hovered in a hiding spot on the other side of the river.

Sage was only able to track them because he was keyed into the command architecture for their programming. Their matte green coloring rendered them invisible against the foliage and the river.

The Phrenorian vessels were supposed to come from the stronghold downstream. They would be submerged and be unseen until they surfaced. Pingasa hoped to pinpoint the submersibles before they arrived.

Sage checked the time and saw that it was 0501 hours. According to the intel he had, the pickups had been no later than 0515. Sunrise was supposed to happen at 0538. The cargo exchange was scheduled to be finished by then and the submersibles once more beneath the river's surface on their return leg.

He wanted that twenty-three minutes of full dark before the sky brightened.

"Master Sergeant," Pingasa called over the comm. He headed up the three-person cyber-attack team. The fourth soldier in the squad was providing protection for them.

"What have you got, Pingasa?" Sage asked.

"The two vessels. Putting them up on your screen and the lieutenant's now."

An instant later, a transparent view of the river overlaid Sage's HUD. The water was rendered in green and turned a deeper green according to depth. The smaller submersible led the way and the larger cargo vessel trailed by a hundred meters. Both were submerged to a depth of 50.3 meters.

The first vessel was 34.6 meters long and the smaller one measured only 21.8 meters. The larger submersible was the cargo transport while the second was the more heavily armed escort.

"Lieutenant," Sage said, "do you copy?"

"Roger that." Murad sounded tense but ready.

"This is going to go fast, sir. We've got to get the situation in hand quickly."

"I understand. We've got this, Master Sergeant."

"Yes sir." Sage waved his two squads forward and they crept through the jungle, careful to stay out of sight of the caravan handlers as well as the Phrenorians.

Jahup brought his fireteam down parallel to Sage and fifty meters out. That way if one or both was spotted, they couldn't be taken out in one burst of fire.

Both submersibles slowed as they came even with the caravan. Small red squares floated free of the vessels and broke the river surface. Switching back to night-vision, Sage spotted four drones shooting up into the air.

"Pingasa?" Sage paused. "What are we looking at?"

"Those drones have vid and aud capabilities," Pingasa said. "No comm interceptors. They won't be able to hear our encrypted comms, but they may register the transmissions. They can't immediately identify us, but they may be suspicious."

"We'll have to hope they're more interested in acquiring their cargo. How well can they see?"

"Like hawks. And they've got a full suite of motion-detecting software."

"Can you do anything about that?" Sage held his position.

"I'm hacking into their systems now. Luckily those things aren't true spy drones. Their firewalls would be more sophisticated. Not to say that they aren't. But I'm good at what I do."

"Roger that, Corporal."

Sage watched two minutes tick by. The Phrenorians weren't in any hurry to surface. He didn't know if the boat captains were being extracautious because of yesterday's attack or if they normally took time to come up. Qiao might have known, and Sage was frustrated because he hadn't thought to ask.

Slowly, the Phrenorian vessels blew their ballast tanks and floated up. Their depth numbers smoothly counted down as they reached the surface.

"Okay!" Pingasa called out. "I've got the drones temporarily blinded by looping their programming, but it's not going to last long. When they breach, I've got to shut down the onboard comms or they can warn the stronghold."

"Get it done," Sage said.

"I've got this."

"Let's go." Sage rose up to a half-crouch and sped down the incline. The soldiers in his fireteam followed immediately.

Sage slid around trees, trying not to disturb the brush and draw attention to his position, but the ground was soft and tore away beneath his boots in places. Seconds later, he was in the water and, within two steps, he was submerged because the drop-off was steep. The AKTIVsuit's diving bladders filled with water and kept him on the river bottom.

The subs were still nine meters below the river's surface.

Sage stayed on the bottom and didn't give in to the momentary panic of the river closing in over him. For an instant, he flashed back to his near-drowning in the well and made himself take a deep breath to relax. He had oxygen. He could breathe.

He trudged forward. Even though he was prepared for the steep drop-off of the river bottom, he was still surprised at how quickly the ground fell away. Over the centuries of its existence, the current had eroded a deep channel.

Even though he couldn't see the members of his team, the HUD clocked them as they followed him. He also wasn't able to see the Phrenorian sub, but the suit's near-AI told him it was there.

Six meters out from the smaller vessel, Sage blew out the suit's bladders in a gentle rush and floated up slowly. "Pingasa, we're about to make contact. Are the subs going to register physical touch?"

"Negative," Pingasa said. "I'm in their computers now, but the auto-sweepers are checking the software. I won't be able to stay concealed inside their systems for long."

"Roger that." Sage checked the HUD and shifted to Jahup's feeds. Jahup and his team were also closing on their objective. "Remember that we need these vessels mostly operational if we're going to make this work."

His armored fingertips grazed the sub's skin. He expected to feel a buzz of contact, something, but the vessel remained huge and unaware that he was there.

Continuing his ascent, Sage followed the sub's curvature and the blueprint revealed on his HUD. He kicked his feet and stroked with his arms to maintain the contact while he swam up. As the submersible breached, he heaved himself on top of it and trusted that it wouldn't register the weight displacement he caused due to the vessel's sheer tonnage.

Kneeling, Sage pulled his Roley into his arms.

Corrigan, a slim soldier on his team, slid the equipment backpack from her shoulders and opened it. She removed a heavy-duty Kimer industrial-strength laser from the bag and powered it up as she pulled it onto her shoulder.

The other soldiers took up positions in a half-circle across the submersible. The second squad duplicated the entry attempt at the front of the vessel.

Corrigan leaned into the task. The laser bit into the vessel's composite hide and chewed through the centimeters-thick hull. Deep-sea boats had two hulls, an outer and an inner, to provide a more stable environment for crews. As the submersible went down and the pressure increased, the outer hull compressed slightly, but the inner hull remained unmoved.

Sparks and flecks of burning metal and carbonite material flew from the white laser beam as it sliced through the outer hull. The composite hull turned cherry-red and smoked from the heat. As the river current swept over the area, the water hissed and burned off in thin clouds of steam.

Forty meters away, Jahup and his team worked on the cargo vessel at both ends. The lasers there burned fiercely.

Sage's stomach knotted as he grew grimly aware of the passage of time. All it would take was a glance around by a Phrenorian sailor, a momentary lapse of the computer hack, and the operation would be blown.

Zhoh would button down there and protect the stronghold.

"It's okay," Pingasa stated calmly. "I got this. The only thing we have to worry about is the first Sting-Tail who sticks his head out of the boat. Once that happens, the cat's out of the bag."

An oval section of the outer hull dropped into the sub and Corrigan followed it. The laser fired up again immediately.

Toward the forward end of the submersible, a conning tower telescoped up from the vessel. Gleaming composite stood tall against the slow rush of the river.

Sage made himself remain silent even though he wanted to ask Corrigan how the entry was coming. He watched the conning tower. It had more vid slits. Not all of those were linked to the boat's computer systems.

"Clear!" Corrigan called up.

Stepping over, Sage peered down into the hole.

Corrigan sat hunkered down in the small space between hulls. She pushed the laser aside and pressed a palm against the second composite oval she'd cut from the vessel. The material contained enough metal to allow her glove's magnetic field to hold it. She added her other hand, powered up the magnetic field to adhere to the oval, and shifted the section to the side.

Sage dropped through both openings and into the compartment below. Darkness filled the compartment and his infrared vision clicked on as he pulled the Roley against his shoulder.

THIRTY-FIVE

Cargo Ship *Iggulden*
Makaum Space
0508 Hours Zulu Time

How are you holding up?" Kiwanuka asked Noojin.

"I'm good," Noojin answered.

The young woman's reply sounded brittle, though, and Kiwanuka knew the rapid trip up from the planet aboard a cargo ship wasn't agreeing with her. Especially after they'd broken free of Makaum's gravity well. Like Kiwanuka, Noojin stood in the ship's hold and held onto the wide nylon straps used to secure materials during shipping.

The ship wasn't so much launched from the planet's surface as it was fired. Cargo vessels only had amenities in the pilot's and navigator's section. They were bare-bones projectiles designed only to deliver materials, not passengers. The holds didn't have oxygen or gravity field emulators.

Almost weightless in the microgravity after the pilot

broke free of the gravity well and cut the main engines, Kiwanuka bumped gently against the composite wall where she was held in place by cargo straps as the pilot made small course corrections with thrusters to bring her into the correct approach apogee. She looked over the rest of her team and scanned their biometrics.

Everyone but Noojin was more or less calm and relaxed. The girl's heart rate and respiration were elevated, but that could have been caused as much by her concern over Jahup as her present situation. Kiwanuka was worried about Sage as well, and her own vitals were slightly up from norm. Thankfully, no one else could see them.

For a moment, Kiwanuka thought maybe she should have left the young woman behind. Then she reconsidered that. After everything Noojin had been through in the last two days, not to mention the stress of figuring out where she stood in the whole shifting political paradigm of Makaum, she needed to be part of a team. More than that, she needed to be part of *this* team.

And there was the fact that Noojin was better trained for close-in fighting than most of the other soldiers. The experience she had in the jungle would translate, more or less, into the close quarters of a spaceship. Most of the men and women from Fort York were trained, but not blooded. Living on Makaum and hunting in its jungles, Noojin had been fighting practically since the day she'd been born. No matter the mess that was going on inside her head, she would be clear about survival.

Her decision to kill to save Jahup the previous morning was proof of that. Noojin hadn't hesitated before acting.

When they closed on *Kequaem's Needle* and confronted Sytver Morlortai and his crew, Kiwanuka needed people who didn't flinch or overthink, people who would just get the job done.

"Staff Sergeant." The pilot's voice carried clearly

through the ship's comm. She was calm and collected, not sounding like she was even aware of the fact the ship she piloted now wasn't hardened against ship-to-ship lasers or low-yield nuclear torpedoes.

"Yes, Captain," Kiwanuka replied.

"Five minutes, thirteen seconds out from your target on my mark . . . now."

Kiwanuka set a timer on her HUD and passed it along to her troops. "Roger that."

Automatically, she counted them again, noting all sixteen members of the four fireteams by sight instead of just accepting the HUD's report. She tried not to acknowledge that some of the soldiers with her might not return to the fort. Morlortai and his crew had a reputation for violence and resisting arrest.

She took a deep breath and let it out, allowing the suit's carbon dioxide scrubbers to clear the air. She opened a closed comm to Noojin. "Are you ready for this?"

"Yes." Her response was strained and her voice was on the verge of breaking.

"Those people on that ship won't hesitate about shooting."

Noojin returned Kiwanuka's gaze. "Neither will I. I'm not going to die up here. I'm going back home."

Kiwanuka nodded. "You and I will follow close behind Goldberg."

Goldberg was the point of Kiwanuka's team. She'd seen action on two different worlds against the Phrenorian Empire and was currently on Makaum cycling through a rehab sequence that had finished eleven days ago. She had been just awaiting orders to report back to her unit.

Kiwanuka went back to the team comm. "Corporal Goldberg."

The woman was average-sized and relaxed. "Yes, Staff Sergeant."

"That'll be me on your six, soldier."

"Looking forward to it, Staff Sergeant. I won't worry so much about what's behind me." Her humor echoed in her words.

In spite of the situation, Kiwanuka grinned. Regardless of the danger, or maybe because of it, she was more excited than afraid. Fear was in there, but it was a low and steady burn, and she was going to use it as fuel to stay alive.

"Target is in sight," the captain said.

"Copy that, sir." Kiwanuka pulled the ship's vid imaging up on her HUD and spotted *Kequaem's Needle* ahead and to the side of them.

The ship was long and slender, resembling its name, and studded with detachable cargo containers that could easily be shifted to cargo ships. A few of the dozen docking rings telescoped around the vessel held cargo ships like the Charlie Company squad currently occupied as well as rectangular cargo storage units. In space, shape and weight didn't matter. There was no air resistance and no gravity to affect them. In fact, most of the containers were sheathed in solar panels that were connected to the ship and helped power the onboard electronics.

The ship's operational quarters were divided into two areas, fore and aft. Crew quarters were housed in the stern along with a medical bay and fabrication shop. The bridge towered thirty meters above the flat "deck" formed by the bilateral cargo containers running the length of the ship's spine.

Kiwanuka had looked over the ship's manifests. *Kequaem's Needle*'s cover story was heavily backgrounded and ran deep. If Kiwanuka and her team hadn't identified Darrantia, Kiwanuka wouldn't have been able to trace Morlortai's ship. As a cargo trader, *Kequaem's Needle* stayed just enough in the black to appear legit as a struggling merchant. Not an overly profitable enterprise, but enough to justify her presence in Makaum's orbit.

As a hauler, she had contracts with DawnStar and some of the other smaller corps that had set up shop in orbit around Makaum. Those contracts came with a history that would now work against her when she was exposed.

Kiwanuka was betting Morlortai and his people would ditch the ship's history and bang down a new one once they cleared the system. In fact, they probably already had one in the pipeline. More than likely, they would have a few. By the time they transited through the Gate, they'd be another crew on another ship.

Kequaem's Needle's profile and that of the cargo ships swapping out goods revolved on a gentle access and blocked out stars as they rotated.

"Decelerating," the cargo ship pilot warned. "Standby."

Kiwanuka gripped the cargo straps. "Copy that. Count us down."

"Three," the cargo pilot said, "two, one . . . thrusters coming online."

The cargo ship jerked as the reverse thrust slowed its approach toward its target. Like *Kequaem's Needle*, the cargo ship's manifests were in order too. She was listed as carrying frozen produce from Makaum to trade out for farm tools and seed stock.

Even though she'd braced herself as well as she could, Kiwanuka thudded against the cargo hull a handful of times before she was able to lock down.

"Docking," the ship captain said.

Linked to the ship's vid system through her HUD, Kiwanuka watched the cargo ship nudge gently into the *Kequaem's Needle*'s forward port dock. She passed the information on to her troops.

"Everybody copy the twenty?" Kiwanuka asked.

"Roger that," Goldberg answered, and her assent was quickly followed by the other troops.

"Goldberg," Kiwanuka said, "head to the prow. We're taking the bridge."

The crew's quarters were in that direction, back behind the ship's drive engines. Kiwanuka expected Morlortai and his crew to hold up back there to allow transport bots to handle the cargo transfer. Humans didn't have to do the grunt work.

"Copy that," Goldberg said.

"Cipriano, your team is responsible for the engine rooms."

"We got this, Staff Sergeant."

"Remember: nobody dies, them or us, if we can help it, because we need the truth from them. But if you have to choose, they die. When you're inside, stay on suit atmosphere in case these people get clever with their air supplies."

Kiwanuka had heard stories of pirate freighter crews who stayed on suit atmosphere and flooded their decks with carbon monoxide or something equally as lethal to keep intruders at bay.

A half dozen dulled *thunks* echoed through the cargo hold as the ship bellied up to the larger vessel and locked on magnetically. Minutes passed as the two systems linked up and shook hands to acknowledge each other.

Kiwanuka wasn't happy with the point of egress, but aside from blowing a hole in the *Kequaem's Needle*, being allowed onto the ship through a subterfuge was the only way inside.

She just hoped it worked.

"We're being hailed," the cargo captain said.

"Answer back and stall them as long as you can," Kiwanuka ordered.

"Roger that. Whoever I'm talking to says they're not prepared to transfer goods for at least another twenty-two minutes."

Kiwanuka hoped the boarding effort was over by then. And she hoped that her troops were all still alive. "Copy that." She cut back to the op comm. "Veug, we're waiting on you."

"Roger that, Staff Sergeant. Working on it. I'm waiting for their boarding protocols to engage." The electronics intelligence specialist sounded calm and steady. "As soon as they reach out to shake hands, I'll own them."

Kiwanuka stared at Veug, who was the eighth soldier in line. His Roley hung from his shoulder while his gloved fingers twitched, operating the virtual keyboard open to him in his HUD.

"Get ready," Veug said. "I'm knocking through their sec firewalls . . . *now*."

The oval hatch that had extended the docking tube to the *Kequaem's Needle* irised open. Only a small puff of air sucked out into the vacuum of the sectional transplas docking tube. The tube was three meters in diameter and fourteen meters in length. The transplas was cloudy, but the thick material was clear enough that Kiwanuka could see the open space on the other side of it.

Kequaem's Needle rolled over slowly as it orbited the green and blue planet far below. With all the verdant jungle covering it, Makaum looked more emerald from space than sapphire. Several space stations, including DawnStar's huge, multilayered construction, orbited the world, endlessly tumbling to provide artificial gravity.

Goldberg sprinted across the tube with Kiwanuka at her heels. Kiwanuka held the Roley across her chest with one hand while she carried an electronic pry bar in her other hand. When she reached *Kequaem's Needle*'s hatch, she slapped the pry bar into place against the vertical hatch track. She pressed the activation button and the pry bar's telescopic arms extended and locked against the hatch frame. It was strong enough to prevent the hatch closing if anyone inside tried to block their entry.

Without hesitation, Goldberg pointed her weapon at the two sec cams in the storage hold and fired quick three-round bursts. The ceramic bullets shattered on impact and took out the transplas-covered cams too.

Kiwanuka tapped the back of Goldberg's helmet even though the soldier could see her in the 360-view provided by the HUD. The tactile presence was how they were all trained. The tech was handy, helpful in most cases, but PsyOps said nothing beat physical presence that told a soldier another soldier was nearby.

Goldberg reached the compartment hatch, hit the access panel, and cursed. The panel light flared ruby. "Locked."

Veug let his rifle hang from its strap and tapped his virtual keyboard. "I got it, I got it!"

Time crawled and Kiwanuka felt like someone was running liquid sandpaper through her veins. She wanted to scream in frustration. They didn't know for certain how many crew *Kequaem's Needle* carried. The ship's manifests claimed ten, but that number couldn't be verified.

The ruby light winked out and turned green. The hatch jerked to the side and disappeared into the wall.

Goldberg ran into the hallway and Kiwanuka followed. Behind her, Noojin slammed her pry bar against that hatch as well, in case whatever Veug had done didn't hold. Kiwanuka didn't want the team separated, and she wanted a clear retreat.

Most of the team poured into the hallway in seconds.

Kiwanuka tapped Goldberg on the helmet again and her team went forward, moving rapidly down the hallway now.

An instant later, the cargo ship they'd come up on got hit with an explosive packet. With no atmosphere, there was no sound, but the impact shuddered through *Kequaem's Needle*. Light flooded the hallway behind Kiwanuka.

Still moving, she accessed Private Niemczyk's HUD view. He was walking slack, covering their flank, and was still in the cargo compartment. Through his HUD, Kiwanuka watched as their ship exploded and went to pieces. With so little atmosphere loose in the vessel, flames only flickered for a moment before they exhausted all the freed oxygen.

The transplas transfer tube shattered.

Miraculously, the pilot and copilot managed to eject from *Iggulden* in full armor. They headed toward the ship, thrown by the blast.

There was no way off *Kequaem's Needle*. They had to take the ship or die.

"Niemczyk," Kiwanuka called over the comm. "Tether them if you can."

"Copy that." Niemczyk raced toward the hatch and raised an arm to fire the suit's built-in grappling hook toward one of the pilots. The pilot grabbed the line as it went by, then fired one of her own toward her companion.

When both pilots were safely tethered, Kiwanuka turned her full attention back to the assault on the ship.

Morlortai and his crew knew they were coming.

THIRTY-SIX

Sage swept the Roley around the empty cargo compartment and tracked the confines through infrared vision. Small lizards no longer than his fingers scattered across the compartment walls and skittered across the surfaces all around him. No one else was in the room.

Sage strode toward the compartment hatch and hit the release control. "Clear."

With heavy clanks, the hatch's locks cycled and disengaged. Sage gripped the oblong plate and pulled it open. He swept the Roley across the next compartment and discovered it was empty as well.

The three soldiers in his squad followed him.

As soon as he released the locks on the next compartment hatch, orange-tinted crystal fléchettes sliced through the air and cut into his armor.

Caution! the near-AI advised. *Sustained bursts of crystal ammo can cut through your armor.*

Sage had already recognized the danger from past experience with the crystal projectiles. They were manufactured from native reefs on Phrenoria, although the reefs were also grown in large hydroponic tanks everywhere the Sting-Tails served. They were used on Phrenorian starships and naval vessels to prevent damage to those craft.

The staccato pings of the fléchettes shattering against the walls, the compartment hatch, and Sage's armor filled the room.

Sage fell into profile against the compartment hatch, taking as much shelter as he could, and returned fire. Instead of unleashing a stream of ceramic rounds, Sage fired an incendiary gel-grenade into the chest of the lead Phrenorian warrior of the two in the compartment.

With a quiet *whump*, the gel-grenade ignited and a mass of flames wreathed the Phrenorian and quickly spread to the second warrior as well. Shifting a little, Sage fired again and put a gel-grenade onto the second warrior.

Their armor and thick chitin might have prevented the warriors' skins from burning, but those things didn't keep the flames from invading breathing membranes and sinus pockets. The Phrenorians cooked with hisses and popping cracks.

Frantic with fear and pain and determined to kill their attackers, the Phrenorians were torn between trying to return fire and putting out the flames with their secondary hands. The smaller hands picked up spatters of the gel combustible and caught fire as well.

"Keep the armor buttoned up tight," Sage ordered as he rounded the heavy compartment hatch. As he pushed the first Phrenorian back into the second and knocked both of them down, he reloaded the Roley's grenade supply. "Pingasa."

"Here, Master Sergeant," Pingasa replied.

Sage drew a long combat knife from his hip and thrust it into one of the eyes atop the downed Phrenorian's cephalothorax to hasten the warrior's death and release him from his pain. There was no way he would survive his injuries. "The crew of this ship knows we're on board."

Smoke from the burned bodies and armor roiled through the compartment.

"Roger that. I don't know that I can block the ship-to-ship comms like I have the sat relay."

Sage yanked his knife free just as Corrigan delivered a mercy killing of her own to the second warrior. He kept moving forward, stepping over the twitching body. "Understood. Make sure Jahup knows."

The next compartment hatch opened before he reached it. A Phrenorian warrior took shelter beside the hatch frame and opened fire. Orange fléchettes screamed from the weapon's muzzle and shattered against Sage's faceshield. The AKTIVsuit flaked away in fingernail-sized chips and left pits in their wake. The hammering impacts rocked Sage back for a moment.

Caution!

Sage ignored the suit's warning and returned fire. The incendiary gel-grenade slammed into the hatch frame and splashed over the Phrenorian warrior. In seconds, flames licked over the warrior's upper body as well as the composite bulkhead. The composite would burn free of the chems and the flames would extinguish. The Phrenorian warrior wasn't as fortunate. The warrior tried to hold his position, but the agony of his burning flesh broke his concentration and he stepped away.

Moving more quickly now, knowing he had to shut

down the crew before they had a chance to lock up the boat or perhaps trigger a self-destruct sequence, Sage drew even with the warrior and drove him backward with a shoulder. Even as he fell, the warrior swiped at Sage with his tail. The barbed end streaked toward Sage's faceshield and he knew it probably had enough velocity and strength to penetrate the armor.

Reacting instinctively, Sage grabbed the tail in his fist and directed it to his helmet's side. Even with the suit's added muscle, Sage couldn't stop the warrior's attack, but he was able to avoid it. The barbed end slammed into the bulkhead behind him. He wrapped his hand around the tail to shorten it up, and then yanked. The Phrenorian struggled to stand his ground despite his wounds.

Sage kicked the Phrenorian's forward leg and broke the chitin plating. With the exterior fractured and the musculature beneath torn free, the limb gave way and bent backward. The Phrenorian fell sideways and Sage shoved the Roley point-blank into his opponent's face and squeezed the trigger. A burst of ceramic rounds shredded the warrior's cephalothorax.

He dropped the tail and kept moving farther along the hallway.

Murad's HUD showed Sage an image of the caravan's people fleeing the immediate vicinity as two Phrenorian warriors reached the conning tower. The lieutenant and his snipers chopped the Phrenorians down with depleted uranium rounds as a deck gun popped up. A third Phrenorian manned the deck gun only briefly. A salvo of 40mm rounds turned a copse of trees along the riverbank into kindling before one of the snipers took the Phrenorian down.

"Jahup and his group have made contact with the enemy," Pingasa stated calmly.

Sage flicked to an overview of Jahup's fireteam just as one of the soldier's biometrics blanked out.

For a moment, Sage pulled up Jahup's HUD feed, glimpsed the frantic battle going on there, and swore softly. Then his attention was forced back to his own situation as a Phrenorian stepped from behind a wall of equipment and attacked him with one of the crystalline swords they favored as personal weapons.

Unable to avoid the attack or deflect it, Sage braced himself and brought the Roley around. The sword slammed into his faceshield and knocked him back. Momentarily stunned as the tempered faceshield suddenly starred, Sage tried to center his rifle on his attacker. Before he could, the Phrenorian knocked the Roley away.

Partially blinded by the cracked faceshield, which was also spotty with confusing colors and effects because the HUD display was shorting out, Sage got an arm up in time to block the warrior's efforts to skewer him with the sword.

Warning! the near-AI said calmly. *Faceshield is damaged. Vision is compromised. Take evasive—*

Unable to bring his rifle up, Sage used it instead to block the Phrenorian warrior's follow-up swing. The crystal sword battered the Roley but didn't shatter. Instead, the keen-edged blade bit into the rifle's composite barrel.

Warning! the near-AI stated. *Rifle compromised. Grenade launcher still viable.*

Powering forward while keeping the sword trapped, Sage drove the Phrenorian into the bulkhead behind him. The impact staggered the Sting-Tail for a moment, then he lashed out with his tail, driving it at Sage's face. At the last instant, Sage rolled his head to the side and the barbed end of the Phrenorian's tail embedded in his helmet.

Sharp pain bit into the left side of Sage's head behind his ear. The burning rush of venom followed. He felt woozy at once as the neurotoxins spread from the wound.

"Inject Phrenorian anti-venom now," Sage growled.

The command was automatic and he knew the near-AI was probably already aware of the wound, but he didn't want to take chances. Phrenorian venom acted notoriously fast.

Anti-venom—

Inside the helmet, the side of Sage's face immediately swelled. A sudden headache beat at his temples. His vision turned even more blurry and his eyes watered. He rammed the rifle under the Phrenorian's head. The warrior's *chelicerae* fastened on to Sage's forearm and tried to tear through the armor covering his hand and forearm. Leaning his left shoulder into his opponent and shooting boot spikes into the deck flooring, Sage held his ground.

—cycling now, Master Sergeant Sage. Monitoring biometrics. If your system starts crashing—

Sage fisted the .500 Magnum and hauled it up. Weakness traveled through his body and the big pistol suddenly felt like it weighed a hundred kilos. He shoved the barrel into the center of the *chelicerae*, which tried to wrap around the weapon, and pulled the trigger three times in quick succession. The ceramic hollowpoints tore through his opponent's flesh and spewed gore onto the bulkhead behind him.

The hollow *booms* of the shots rolled through the control room.

—you will be taken off-line and held in stasis till proper medical care arrives.

"Negative," Sage told the near-AI. "You will take me off-line only if I pass out."

Your heart rate is elevated. The venom is entering your system more quickly.

"So is the anti-venom." Sage knew it was stupid to argue with the suit, but with the narcotic effect of the Phrenorian venom in his system, he also knew he wasn't in full control of his thoughts.

But he was in control of his body. Training took over when a soldier was wounded or didn't have time to think.

Supporting the dead Phrenorian, Sage wheeled to face the remaining warrior in the command center. The Phrenorian had been trying to get through on the comms. Now he picked up a rifle and took aim. A burst of orange-tinted fléchettes smashed through the dead Phrenorian's body and embedded in Sage's chest armor.

He fired the revolver by instinct and blasted through the final two rounds. Both struck the Phrenorian warrior and staggered him. One impacted against armor and did nothing, but the second ripped the warrior's right primary to pieces and the rifle fell.

The Phrenorian ignored the wound and reached for his Kimer pistols with his secondaries.

The cool flush of the anti-venom spread through Sage's head as he dropped the corpse he'd held on to. The embedded end of the Phrenorian's tail refused to let go and he jerked forward as the dead warrior fell.

Off balance and head spinning, Sage dropped to his knees before he could stop himself. He yanked at the Phrenorian's tail with his free hand and still couldn't free the appendage. At the same time, he holstered the .500 Magnum and pulled the Birkeland coilgun from his shoulder holster. Before he could aim, Corrigan stepped into the command center and fired a gel-grenade at the Phrenorian.

The warrior slapped at the flames for only a moment before succumbing and dropping to the deck.

Using his combat blade, Sage cut through the Phreno-rian's tail to free himself. He tried to stand, slipped in the gore left by the Phrenorian he'd killed, and growled, "Put that fire out."

Smoke quickly obscured the room and further eroded Sage's flickering vision. He stood, mostly leaning against the wall, and tried not to be sick.

In order to rid your system of the venom/anti-venom, the near-AI said, *you will have to purge.*

Sage knew that. He'd been envenomed a few years back. The experience was one of those he never cared to relive. He barely got his faceshield up before the first torrent of bile came up so hard and so fast he thought he was going to pass out.

Corrigan paused in sweeping the fire with the mini-tank of fire-suppressant foam she carried in her kit. "Master Sergeant?"

Sage raked his armored forearm across his mouth. "I'm all right. Make sure that fire's out." He fumbled at his combat harness and found his own foam. When Corrigan's tank ran dry, Sage passed his over to her.

Then he threw up again and wondered if the suit had managed to deliver enough anti-venom to counteract the poison he'd gotten injected with. He forced himself to think more clearly.

Getting the submersibles was only part of the plan.

The easy part.

THIRTY-SEVEN

Kequaem's Needle
Makaum Space
0515 Hours Zulu Time

The evacuation of air in the hallway triggered the emergency systems on board *Kequaem's Needle*. Rectangular airtight hatches slammed shut between the compartments and slowed the advance of Kiwanuka and her team.

Hacking each locking mechanism took time, and even though Veug managed to get through them in seconds, the obstacles allowed the ship's crew more time to prepare themselves to repel boarders.

Or set traps.

During other missions that had ended up on board space vessels, Kiwanuka had set traps herself. Her mind filled with the mayhem she could cause in the time they were allowing Morlortai and his people to work.

Red alarm lights flashed in the hallway but were

silent in the vacuum that filled the space because Kiwanuka's HUD filtered out the shrill screeches.

Goldberg kept a steady pace as she moved forward. She kept her Roley pointed forward and the stock was collapsed against her shoulder so she could easily peer around corners. The ship only had one corridor that ran from prow to stern, but several hatches branched off it to cargo access shafts where the crew could access the containers. Each of them flared yellow on Kiwanuka's HUD to alert her of the possibility of an ambush point.

Goldberg slammed a fist against the access hatch controls on the wall at her side, stepped back with the Roley ready, and watched as the barrier recessed into the wall with a hiss. With the airlock sealed and the ship's atmosphere protected, the automated lockdown of the cargo hatches hadn't occurred.

"Clear," Goldberg said. She pressed a hand against the control again and the hatch slid back into position. "Sealed and armed." She moved forward again.

Kiwanuka's HUD logged the sec wafer Goldberg's armor had extruded onto the entrance. The wafer was low-key tech and would alert them if the hatch was used. It also carried a flash-bang charge that would disorient anyone who wasn't armored. The sudden concussive wave, sound effects, and light show would alert the boarding team and give them a small edge.

Goldberg continued forward, checked the hatches quickly, and placed more sec wafers.

Four hatches farther on, Goldberg reached for the opening only to get knocked back by the burly figure rushing from within. The scout banged up against the bulkhead on the opposite side of the corridor.

Kiwanuka pulled the Roley to her shoulder. Just as her sights settled over the interloper's head and shoulders, he shifted and flung Goldberg at Kiwanuka. The sudden impact bowled Kiwanuka over and drove her backward. She and Goldberg went down in a tangle of limbs.

The red warning lights lifted the Lemylian from the shadows as he pulled the large-caliber Hin'ath slug-thrower pistol from his hip. He brought it up and his brutish face lit with a grim smile.

"Gonna die, Terran," he promised.

Kiwanuka threw her left arm up and managed to lever Goldberg to the side.

"Open right glove," Kiwanuka ordered the suit's near-AI.

Instantly, the armor peeled back from her bionic hand. She willed the arm to conform into the shotgun configuration hidden within it, but even as her bionics shifted, she knew she was going to be too late. She hoped the armor would withstand the Hin'ath's projectiles and that the shotgun's double-aught buckshot would at least knock the Lemylian from his feet.

Noojin vaulted over Kiwanuka and Goldberg. Her left hand and both boots adhered against the bulkhead and held her there for an instant, then she ran upside down over Kiwanuka. The Lemylian shifted aim and fired, but the large-caliber round only smeared and fragmented against the bulkhead with a large muzzle flash.

In mid-stride, Noojin fired her grappling hook. The small, hooked head pierced the Lemylian's right shoulder in a burst of flesh and blood. The Lemylian dropped his weapon, grimaced, and wrapped his hand in the buckyball strand that trailed the grappling hook. He set himself and pulled. The move caught Noojin in mid-stride. She peeled from the corridor roof and thudded against the floor.

The Lemylian grabbed a fresh hold on the grappling line and pulled again hard enough that Noojin skipped across the floor.

Before Kiwanuka could fire, a second Lemylian stepped from the cargo hatch with a Kerch shrapnel burster in her arms. Mercilessly, she took aim at Noojin's back.

Still struggling to get to her feet, realizing that Goldberg had been left dazed by the unexpected attack, Kiwanuka shifted her aim to the second Lemylian and fired. Even with the enhanced supports wired into her reinforced spine, the shotgun blast felt like it was going to tear Kiwanuka's shoulder free like it had felt every time she'd used it before.

The double-aught burst struck the female Lemylian in the chest and face as she fired her weapon. The flaming shrapnel load smashed against the corridor floor only centimeters from where Noojin had been. The girl was already running up the side of the corridor and heading for the male Lemylian.

Kiwanuka flexed her bionic arm and cycled another round into the chamber in her forearm and watched in disbelief as the female Lemylian stirred back to life. Shredded flesh hung from her head and shoulders as she sat up and turned her attention to Kiwanuka. The Lemylian roared, her mouth dripping gore, pushed herself to one knee, and leveled her weapon.

Goldberg got to her feet, still listing to the side. Kiwanuka fired again and rode out the recoil as she dove for her Roley. She slid on her stomach across the corridor floor, grabbed the weapon, changed her bionic arm back to its normal mode, and brought the Roley to her shoulder as she pushed herself to her feet in front of Goldberg.

The female Lemylian's face hung in tatters. One of

her eyes was gone. The other was cyber and stood out in sharp, gleaming relief and still tracked her target with manic speed.

Behind the female Lemylian, the male drew a short sword and reached for Noojin as the girl pushed herself to her feet.

Kiwanuka squeezed the grenade launcher's trigger and fired a grenade into the Lemylian's open, broken-fanged maw. The gel explosive glowed an instant before it detonated.

Hammered by the concussive wave, Kiwanuka slid backward a few meters before she placed her gloved hand on the corridor floor and activated the magnet-ics. Fire-suppression systems kicked on and a blizzard of white foam filled the corridor. The metal surface turned slick.

Kiwanuka screeched to a halt and rolled over imme-diately. She peered through the smoke that almost filled the corridor to see what had happened to Noojin. The fire-suppression systems kicked off, their charges ex-pended in seconds. The foam, looking like new fallen snow, covered the lower section of the corridor.

The female Lemylian lay headless and still only a few meters away. A few meters farther on, covered in foam, Noojin lay facedown with one arm twisted up behind her. The male Lemylian's big hand clasped Noojin's forearm and held it behind her, but he was gasping and clutching at the hunting knife that jutted from his throat.

As Kiwanuka got to her feet, the Lemylian shud-dered and relaxed in death. She hurt all over and her vision doubled in frantic bursts.

Would you like something from the pain manage-ment suite, Staff Sergeant? the near-AI asked.

"No," Kiwanuka answered as she took stock of the corridor.

Goldberg righted herself carefully. Nothing else in the corridor moved.

Kiwanuka's HUD showed that Noojin was still alive, but that didn't mean she'd escaped brain damage or a bad concussion. Kiwanuka strode forward, aware that the AKTIVsuit aided her in keeping her balance.

The hatch the Lemylians had come through hung by its hinges. A narrow passageway filled with darkness stretched out behind it. Blast scarring scored the bulkhead, visible behind the detritus of the female Lemylian.

Kiwanuka held the Roley at the ready as she sto over Noojin. Grimly, Kiwanuka reached down to t. girl's shoulder and gently shifted her. Noojin flexed and rolled to her feet a meter away. She drew her hunting knives in a blur of movement and crouched in a ready stance.

"Noojin," Kiwanuka said softly. "Are you with me?"

For a moment Noojin's stance held, then she relaxed and stood a little straighter.

"Yes," Noojin said. "That was you with the grenade?"

"Didn't have a choice at the moment."

Noojin nodded. "I'm surprised the ship held together."

"These things are made more resilient than they look. You ready to go on?"

Noojin recovered her rifle and knelt beside the fallen Lemylian. "I am. This one's still alive." She drew one of her knives.

"Keep him that way."

Noojin hesitated. "When you're in hunting territory, leaving a wounded predator behind you isn't a good idea."

The statement surprised Kiwanuka because Noojin had broken from the Terran military. Kiwanuka had thought that was because the girl hadn't wanted to kill people. Evidently that wasn't the case, and her hunter's instincts were at the forefront now.

Kiwanuka captured a picture of the unconscious Lemylian. "We don't kill helpless combatants."

She rolled the alien over and pulled his hands together behind his back. A burst of restraining foam pumped through her armor's reservoir bound the Lemylian's hands together. Another secured his feet.

Kiwanuka stood and sent the captured image off to Veug with instructions to find out who the Lemylian was from Tactical Ops and perhaps have more information about how many ship's crew they were dealing with.

Kiwanuka turned her attention to Goldberg. "Corporal?"

Goldberg straightened herself. "Ready, Staff Sergeant."

"Move out."

Goldberg headed forward and Kiwanuka fell into step behind her. Hatch after hatch opened, but no one else stepped through one of them.

"Staff Sergeant," Veug called.

"Go," Kiwanuka replied.

"Your hostile is in the criminal database on Makaum and other planets," the computer specialist said. "His name's Taidend. At least, that's the way it translates. He's got a history of smuggling, robbery, and murder. There are warrants out on him in eight systems. He usually runs with a female Lemylian named Issor, so you may want to watch for her."

"She's accounted for," Kiwanuka said. "He's not part of the crew."

"Roger that. Probably local talent our targets picked up to handle grunt work and to better fit in with the established crews and businesses."

Kequaem's Needle had a small crew. Uncle Huang's spies had confirmed only six to ten crewmembers, and was only able to identify five of them. Morlortai, the assassin. Darrantia, the ship's mechanic. An Angenen named Turit who served as the ship's armorer. Daus, an ex-Silver Spin Corp R&D scientist. And the pilot, Wiyntan, a Turoissan.

All of them had records in the system.

Ahead, Goldberg crouched at one of the hatch openings running along the ship's spine and held up a fist. She brought her assault weapon to the ready position and peered over the sights.

"Bridge is dead ahead, Staff Sergeant," Goldberg said. "But there are two Gatner heavy machine gun fléchette firmpoints by the hatch."

Kiwanuka took cover on the other side of the hatch opening and peered at the gun emplacements. Their specs rolled up on her HUD at the same time the guns came online and spewed streams of fléchette rounds that studded and scarred the bulkheads, floor, ceiling, and hatch frame.

Kiwanuka lifted her weapon and took quick aim. "Gel-grenades, Corporal."

Sharp-edged fléchettes ricocheted from the Roley and from the combat suit's arm. Some of the rounds jutted out from her weapon and her armor.

She squeezed the trigger and launched a tri-burst that splatted onto and around the Gatner machine gun on the right of the hatch leading to the bridge access lift. She ducked back and counted down even though the HUD flashed the sequence on her faceshield.

THIRTY-EIGHT

S age stood out of the way in the submersible's command center. Since the space was so small, even built to Phrenorian dimensions, the task was difficult.

From his position, the monitors that showed the submersible's progress ten meters beneath the surface of the Yeraf River were visible. Two of the monitors offered digital displays of the boat and its place in relation to the river bottom. All of that was rendered in red on black. Numbers around the submersible flickered and changed constantly. Sage had watched long enough to realize those numbers reflected relative distance from the surface, the river bottom, and the banks on either side.

Other monitors tracked the proximity of large objects, like the *jasulild* that trailed in the submersible's wake and occasionally swam up to "challenge" what they must have thought was an invader in their water by ramming them. The attacks only happened randomly, enough to create a barrage of noise throughout the boat and knock it slightly off-course each time, but Sage knew they could have been much worse. Jahup had told him stories of how *jasulild* had destroyed early boats and ships. That was one of the reasons the Makaum people hadn't used the rivers as transport, or lived too close to them. *Jasulild* could, for a time, live outside the rivers because they had limited amphibious abilities.

"Brace yourselves," a young private at the workstation to Pingasa's left warned. "Snaggletooth is making another run at us."

Pingasa had nicknamed the *jasulild* after the first few attempts the behemoth had made on the submersible. One of the underwater drones slaved to the Phrenorian boat had captured an image of the *jasulild* when it swam for them. Scars covered the *jasulild's* face, turning the cold features into something that looked positively malevolent. That declaration had come from Corrigan. The thing was also missing several of its fangs, but that made it no less lethal.

"The creature is getting more antagonistic," Pingasa said. "It's been less than two minutes since its last attack." He held on to his seat as the *jasulild* closed in. The thing definitely wasn't going to settle for a threat this time.

The impact sent shivers through the submersible and the hollow *bong* of contact echoed through the boat's compartments.

"Have you figured out the weapons console yet, Private Escobedo?" Sage asked.

Private Remedios Escobedo, still a little worse for the wear from the attack on the Zukimther mercenaries only a day ago, sat at the weps station. She was one of

the few soldiers at the fort who was certified to recover
and reverse-engineer alien technology the Terran military encountered in their postings. She specialized in
weapons systems.

"I've got most of it, Master Sergeant," she replied.

"Do you have something that might encourage that
thing to go somewhere else? I don't want it dead. That
might alert the Phrenorians, or bring the rest of the
pack down on us."

"The submersible's equipped with a passive resistance
suite," Escobedo said. "I'm confident that I can trigger
an electric grid around the boat if the creature returns."

"Do that, then," Sage said. He was in command of
the operation while Lieutenant Murad sorted through
the Phrenorian log files. Communicating with the
Sting-Tail base was going to be a problem. Pingasa had
come up with a suggestion to work around that.

Sage hated feeling useless in the submarine's bridge.
With everything going to pieces, with Makaum's people
in jeopardy, and with his fellow soldiers putting their
lives on the line, he needed to be doing something.

Piloting one of those vessels was beyond his paygrade.
The AKTIVsuit carried some schematics and instructions regarding the boat that might have helped him stay
alive, but it wasn't enough to pass any observation made
by Phrenorian warriors watching the vessel's arrival at
their secret base.

Pingasa, on the other hand, handled the boat like
he'd been born to it. He sat at the controls and worked
smoothly. In the beginning there had been a learning
curve that had included a small collision with the riverbank and a few minutes spent repairing a leak. There
had been some good-natured taunting, with an undercurrent of nervousness, but everyone had settled in.

A repair crew had also patched the hole Sage had

made when he'd gained entrance. The bodies of the
Phrenorians had been jettisoned into the river. Although
the river current flowed toward the hidden base established by General Rangha, the submersible would
arrive there well before the dead enemy had been
scheduled to.

Lieutenant Murad stood at the CIC. "It says here that
the boat is called the *Dramorper*."

The red glow of the instruments before him and
around the Command Information Center made his
features look eerie and his voice sounded strange to
Sage, but maybe that was caused by the close confines
of the submersible's command center.

Even in his AKTIVsuit, which was underwater capable, Sage didn't like the idea of being trapped in the
submersible while in the depths of the river. The experience with the well might have been weighing on him,
but he'd never liked water. The danger of open space
bothered him a lot less.

Murad ran a decryption device over the computer
terminal he had accessed with Pingasa's help. "At
least, that's the nearest I can come to managing the
syllabic translation." He looked around. "Does anyone
know what a *dramorper* is?"

"It's probably not something edible," Pingasa offered
from the helm.

"Nope," Culpepper agreed over the suit comms.
He was busy with another crew setting up explosives
throughout the submersible. The plan was to use the
boat as a weapon against the fortress in a surprise
attack. "It's probably some evil, nasty thing as big as
a jumpcopter that lives in the Phrenorian oceans and
only wants to eat your face."

"Shouldn't this decryption device tell me?" Murad
asked.

"The translator's more like a broad spectrum unit, Lieutenant," Pingasa said. "The software will get you close to the actual words, but it's not going to convert everything. Think of it as a hand grenade, not a sniper rifle."

The mention of explosive ordnance reminded Sage of the task he'd assigned to Corporal Culpepper. He opened a private channel to Culpepper. "How is it coming, Corporal?"

"We'll make the deadline with time to spare, Master Sergeant," Culpepper replied.

The demolitions expert sounded distracted, but totally at ease, lost in his element. That was how Sage wanted an explosives professional to sound while performing his job.

"At first I was worried we might not have packed in enough B+8," Culpepper continued, "but with all the firepower this tub is carrying, we're going to be fine." He chuckled. "The trick is to not be anywhere around this thing when this load goes off."

"I'll keep that in mind," Sage replied dryly.

"You know the problem with what I do, Master Sergeant?" Culpepper asked. "Nobody gets to see my finest work. They don't see all the math, all the wiring, all the placements I have to figure out. The blast ratios, explosion versus implosion, shaped charges. People just don't take any of that into consideration. All they see is the collapsed buildings, broken bridges, and smoking craters I leave behind."

"I'll be happy with those," Sage said. "Stay with it."

"Looking forward to it. Even if I have to say so, and no one else is gonna ever see it, I gotta say this is gonna be some of my finest work. I'm recording it, though, so if we survive this, maybe I can show it while we drink beer."

Sage grinned. "After we pull this off, the first round is on me."

"I'm gonna hold you to that, Master Sergeant."

Sage cut comm.

Despite Culpepper's calm, if not jubilant, response, the closer the submersible got to the hidden fortress, the less Sage believed the subterfuge was going to work. There were too many variables in play. They had to get the boat in close to the shoreline in order for the munitions to do the most good, and do that without being discovered.

Otherwise they were going to face a much larger and better-equipped enemy group on what was home territory for them. There were far too many things that could go wrong.

He thought maybe his doubts were fed by the lingering effects of the venom and anti-venom still cycling out of his system. The suit's internal transfusion system had insisted on kicking in and washing all of it out of his body to get him back up to prime. The lieutenant, after he'd learned what had happened, had also insisted.

He stood hooked up to a saline bag and the coldness of the fluids flushed through his forearm, elbow, and shoulder. The nanobots Gilbride had infused in his blood carried the residual toxins from his system and pumped him full of antibiotics and anti-inflammatories. He felt better than he suspected he had any right to.

"Okay, Master Sergeant," the young medtech beside Sage said. "You're good to go." He disconnected the saline bag from the suit's medport under Sage's left arm and buttoned the armor up tight.

"Thank you," Sage said.

The medtech gathered his kit and called up the next soldier that needed attention.

"I think I've found the communications log," Murad announced.

"Splendid," Pingasa congratulated. "Send the information to my suit and I will see if there's something in there we can use to convince the Phrenorian guards that we are who we hope they think we are."

"On its way," Murad said.

Communications was one of the big problems. So far there had been no contact with the Phrenorian base, but Sage knew that wouldn't last long. Whoever monitored the supply run for the Phrenorians would reach out soon enough.

If they weren't ready for that, they wouldn't get any closer without running into resistance.

A thought occurred to Sage and he opened the comm channel to Culpepper again. "If I was in charge of the supply run, I'd consider the possibility that someone would think about doing exactly what we're doing."

"Taking the boat?"

"Yeah."

"And you'd want to make sure that didn't happen, right?"

"Yeah."

"So you'd probably wire the submersibles with explosives you could set off from a distance."

Culpepper's relaxed tone told Sage all he needed to know. "You've already found them."

"I have," Culpepper replied. "And I've repurposed them. Those explosives, kinda primitive and not sexy at all, but definitely packing enough *boom* to get the job done, are now ours. When we light this thing up, there's not gonna be much of it left."

"And there's going to be a big hole into that base?"

"Oh, yeah. I'm looking forward to that. Like I said, this is some of my best work."

"I found the blueprints of the fortress," Murad announced.

The lieutenant waved his hand over the CIC table and the holo software came online with a flicker that formed what Sage assumed was a three-dimensional model of the secret Phrenorian fortress.

Sage stepped over to join Murad at the table. Some of his anxiousness settled down. Figuring out how best to attack the Phrenorians there was something he could do. "Good job, sir."

"This thing is bigger than what we thought." Murad spoke softly over the private comm he shared with Sage. He dragged his hand through the holo and flipped it around to examine it from different angles.

"How big?" Sage asked. He couldn't find any point of reference.

Murad spread his hands inside the holo and blew up the image. He pointed to two parallel sections that looked small in comparison to the rest of the structure.

"This is quarters for the troops," Murad said.

Sage gazed at the rooms but didn't know how large they were. Phrenorian warriors tended to cluster in large groups until they made rank. "Do you know how many troops?"

"Over a hundred from what it says here," Murad told him. "Closer to two hundred. At least a company. Maybe more." He wiped a nervous hand over his face. "We're seriously outnumbered."

The number of Phrenorian warriors surprised Sage. He'd thought his soldiers would be outnumbered three or four to one. If Murad's numbers were correct, they were closer to being outnumbered ten to one.

"We didn't account for this many Phrenorians," Murad said.

"We're not here to go toe-to-toe with the enemy, sir,"

Sage reminded. "We're just here to take away their toys and cut down on the odds against us somewhat. Any idea what General Rangha has hidden there?"

Murad tapped the holo and brought up another list. "I don't know if this file has everything. Like you discovered at the storage facilities in Cheapdock, Rangha had his hands on a lot of mil-spec weaponry. There are Yqueu tracked assault vehicles that range from squad-based fast-attack craft to thirty-meter-tall rolling strongholds equipped with batteries of laser and solid-projectile cannons that can level a city and transport several dozen warriors."

Images of the Phrenorian TAVs flipped by on the holo.

"Powersuits," Murad continued. "Manned and un-manned aerial fighting ships." He shook his head and stared at the images. "This is bigger than we thought."

"How long has that base been there?" Sage asked.

"For years from the looks of the data in this file. Way before Fort York's first cornerstone was laid."

"The only explanation is that Rangha was running his side business a lot longer than anyone knew," Sage said. "Makaum was a fringe world for generations, a place the Alliance didn't have any interest in."

"Not until resources for the Phrenorian War in this sector became an issue a few years ago and Command negotiated a treaty to build the fort," Murad agreed. "Rangha probably chose this planet to do business under the radar because it was away from Alliance and Empire interests. Only that didn't last. It was just Rangha's bad luck that we came in. Until then, he could buy, sell, and trade black market weapons without any problems. Makaum was a trade planet for independents for years. After Fort York was constructed and manned, Rangha got himself assigned here to protect his black market profits."

"It could have been our bad luck too," Sage said. "If we hadn't found out about this place, Rangha would have run roughshod over Makaum. Now, if we don't shut this place down and destroy those materials, Zhoh could still do exactly that. I'm surprised he hasn't already rolled the heavy armor out into the streets and filled the skies with his aircraft."

"The Phrenorian Empire won't field these units until they can put a face on them," Murad said. "PsyOps says the Phrenorians have elaborate layers of honor they have to negotiate. The weapons here would have benefited them, but until they can legitimize what Rangha was doing with them here, they won't use them."

"That doesn't make any sense."

Murad faced Sage. "Does walking away from this planet make any sense to you?"

"No." Sage was convinced of that. "If we do that, if we leave these people to be run over by the Phrenorians, history will look back and say it's one of the worst things we've ever done."

"That will be later generations, then," Murad said. "Not the commanders who are telling us what to do. The policymakers in the Alliance are thinking the military has embarrassed itself on Makaum because we haven't been able to contain the situation."

Sage spoke softly and held back the anger that threatened to explode within him. "We haven't been given the chance. We were understaffed, loaded with green soldiers who hadn't seen much more than basic training, and told to keep a hands-off protocol with the Phrenorians. We should have been on firmer footing and sent the Phrenorians packing."

"I agree," Murad said. "But to do that, we'd have had to ignore what the Makaum people said they wanted. Even Quass Leghef felt that way initially." He paused.

"The colonel has told me you think a lot of her, and that she feels a closeness to you. Would you have been willing to go against her wishes?"

Sage thought of Quass Leghef and remembered the *draorm* the woman had given him not so long ago. The purple and white wood band had been carved from a single piece of wood. Before she had given it to Sage, it had belonged to her dead husband. The term translated into "seed of my seed." Fathers made them for their children.

"No," Sage said. "I would not."

"Not even if it were for her own good?"

That was a harder question, but Sage knew the answer. "No, not even then. She's an adult. She's paid the price to make her own decisions, whatever they are."

Murad let out a breath. "You realize the Phrenorians probably think we're pretty stupid letting go of a military asset that we could have easily taken."

Sage nodded. "We have rules of engagement."

"So do the Phrenorians," Murad said. "Be glad this one has worked out, mostly, in our favor."

In that moment, Sage understood that Murad operated on a different level than he did. Murad looked at all the politically motivated pressures behind the war where Sage only wanted to deal with the human side of things. He knew he wasn't officer material. He'd known that for a long time. He didn't have the patience or temperament for it. He was glad people like Halladay and Murad—and even Kiwanuka, because she was better at those things than he was—existed.

Thinking of Kiwanuka reminded him of where she was, and he couldn't help but think of what she might be facing even now. Or—if things had gone badly—*had* faced. He put the thought out of his mind because it had no place there now. Not with the fortress looming only minutes away.

Morlortai wouldn't be easy to catch. Even if the assassin ended up in military custody, Sage didn't think it would much matter. The Alliance was pulling off Makaum.

"Lieutenant," Pingasa called from the pilot seat.

Murad blanked the holo. "Yes, Corporal."

"We're getting hailed by the Phrenorians, sir. We need to respond."

THIRTY-NINE

Kequaem's Needle
Makaum Space
0526 Hours Zulu Time

The explosion threw smoke and flames into the corridor. Fire-suppression systems kicked into operation immediately afterward and added a frantic flurry to the confusion.

Kiwanuka stepped through the opening and sprinted for the lift hatch. The firmpoints had been reduced to scrap. Wiring and chunks of protective armor hung on the wall on either side of the hatch. More lay on the corridor floor.

Kiwanuka slammed into place against the bulkhead next to the electronic lock on the lift hatch. She tapped the controls but nothing happened.

She opened a channel to Veug, the elint specialist. He had gone with Cipriano's team to secure the ship's engines in the stern compartments. "Veug, I need assistance."

Goldberg and Noojin joined Kiwanuka, but she raised a hand and held the rest of the team back. She signaled for them to maintain their positions in case she and the others had to retreat.

"Copy that, Staff Sergeant." Hoarse breathing punctuated Veug's words. "We're securing the engine room now. What do you need?"

Kiwanuka checked the stats on Cipriano's team. Two of them were wounded, one of them in a medically induced coma instigated by his armor, but they were alive.

Kiwanuka placed a wafer over the electronic lock. She tapped the activation sequence. "I need a hatch opened. Standing by for a handshake."

"Copy that," Veug responded. "Handshake on its way."

Kiwanuka brought up Sergeant Cipriano's vid display and looked over the large engine room. The computer systems all appeared to be online and operating smoothly. Two of Cipriano's squad members had some experience working in backup capacities in engineering on Terran military ships.

Kiwanuka hoped that would be enough.

"Sergeant Cipriano," Kiwanuka said. "Do you have control of the engines?"

"Roger that," Cipriano replied. "We have all four drives locked down tight. This ship isn't going anywhere except on thrusters, and it won't get far on those."

"Good."

"Mostly good," Cipriano said. "Corporal Dewan tells me she's discovered circuitry and programming that suggests this ship's bridge was designed to break away from the main body and navigate on its own."

Kiwanuka cursed and pulled her attention back to the waver on the lift hatch's locking mechanism. "Can you stop it from there if they try that?"

"Negative. But we have some leverage. While taking the engine room, we captured two of the ship's main crew from the list we were given. Maybe our target won't be so quick to leave without them. We've got Darrantia, the Voreusk that managed to escape from us, and Daus, the lab rat. And I do mean rat. Have you ever seen a Nidakian up close?"

"No." Kiwanuka pulled up the images from Cipriano's files and looked at Darrantia and Daus, who did indeed look like an oversized rodent.

"They smell worse than you think," Cipriano said.

"I'll take your word for it, Sergeant." Kiwanuka cleared her HUD and watched the wafer. "Veug?"

"Almost, almost," Veug replied in a distracted tone. "There. Got it."

The wafer pulsed green.

Canting her Roley at her side, Kiwanuka tapped the release mechanism.

The hatch released with a hiss, and a bilious cloud of heavy gas spilled out of the lift. The gas was colorless, but it looked cloudy against the ship's atmosphere.

Warning, the near-AI said. *Immediate atmosphere is toxic. Analyzing vapor, but it appears to be—*

Kiwanuka let the suit talk to itself while she stepped onto the circular lift platform. It didn't matter what the gas was as long as she could avoid it. As the gas's viscosity grew, the harsh light struggled to penetrate the roiling vapor that continued to spew from jets above and below the lift. Goldberg and Noojin followed her into the lift.

Suit integrity intact and maintaining, the near-AI said.

Kiwanuka pressed the controls to go up to the bridge. The lift remained dormant.

"Veug," she called.

"I'm working on it, Staff Sergeant," the computer specialist responded. "Lots of layers in the programming, but I got this."

The lift door closed abruptly. Kiwanuka pressed the button to reopen the door, but it didn't move.

"Veug?" Kiwanuka looked at the lift and spotted the vid cams tucked in behind sec transplas.

"Not me," Veug said. "Somebody else has control over the lift."

Smooth, interlocking plasteel plates created the lift walls. The lift jerked into motion and spun rapidly, gathering speed. Centrifugal forces shoved Kiwanuka against the plates. Lethal voltage juiced through the plasteel and only the AKTIVsuits kept Kiwanuka and her charges alive. She ignored the suit's warning because the lift's top or bottom lowered or rose. Maybe it was both, because the space available inside the lift quickly grew inexorably smaller.

"Veug," Kiwanuka said.

"I see it, I see it!" Veug replied. "On it!"

The comm connection crackled and spat, and Kiwanuka guessed the lift chamber was juicing interference as well. Whoever had constructed the trap had done a thorough job of it.

Senses whirling despite the anti-nausea meds automatically administered by the suit, Kiwanuka took a degaussing grenade from her armor rack, pulled the pin, and heaved the ordnance at the blank space on the other side of the lift. The grenade struck the wall and stayed there, trapped by the centrifugal force.

An instant later, the grenade exploded and released an electromagnetic pulse that flared out twenty meters. The lights flickered and went out. The lift ceased spinning suddenly enough that Kiwanuka almost couldn't recover and only just remained standing.

Noojin leaned against the wall section where she'd been trapped only a moment before. Goldberg spilled to the floor and threw up in her helmet. The suit broadcasted her cursing and the gurgling of the helmet suctioning her stomach contents clear before she could shut the comm down.

"Veug," Kiwanuka called.

"Something happened, Staff Sergeant," the computer specialist said. The comm connection was only slightly improved. "I got locked out."

Kiwanuka studied the lift cage. "That was me. I hit the lift with a degauss grenade."

"Well, that explains that. The lift system is fried. I can't help you with access to the bridge anymore."

"We'll make our own way from here," Kiwanuka said. "Sergeant Cipriano, hold your position there. Under no circumstances are those drives to be used."

"Roger that," Cipriano said. "Can you get free?"

"Working on it."

One of the vents that had spewed the poison gas into the lift opened and dropped a half dozen micro-drones about the size of golf balls into the cage. Three of them hit the plasteel floor, bounced up, sprouted wings, and buzzed in an evasive manner toward Kiwanuka, Noojin, and Goldberg. The other three rolled across the floor.

Kiwanuka drew her Birkeland coilgun and shot the lead flying drone. It exploded and the force drove Kiwanuka into the wall behind her. Noojin yanked a degaussing grenade from her ammo rack and threw it into the center of the room. Kiwanuka relaxed her finger on the coilgun's trigger.

When the degaussing grenade went off, the three drones on the ground stopped in their tracks and the two flying ones dropped and bounced on the floor.

"Good thinking, Noojin," Kiwanuka said.

"I hoped those things weren't hardened against an EMP blast. I didn't know how many of those explosions our armor could handle." Noojin held another grenade in one hand and her rifle in the other.

Kiwanuka studied the lift cage's ceiling, which was much closer than it had been. She tiptoed and found she could easily touch it.

"Cipriano said the bridge can separate from the rest of the ship," Goldberg said. "Do you think if it does, maybe this lift gets jettisoned?"

"So we'd be thrown into space?" Noojin sounded horrified.

Kiwanuka knew she was because the girl hadn't ever spacewalked. She hadn't even visited one of the space stations when the opportunity presented itself. She was used to being planetside.

"I don't want to wait to see." Kiwanuka aimed her rifle at the ceiling, switched over to laser, and fired concentrated blasts.

The plasteel plating turned cherry-red and silver-gray droplets, along with a frantic cloud of sparks, splashed against her armored arms and the lift floor. Gradually, though, a hole opened up. As soon as the lift cage's integrity was breached, the bilious fog still in the compartment sucked through the hole.

"There's no atmosphere on the other side," Kiwanuka said.

"Does it open to space?" Noojin asked in a flat voice.

"The gas and air in here didn't evacuate quickly enough to indicate that it leaked out into open space," Kiwanuka said. "I'm betting we're still inside the lift shaft."

When the opening was a little more than three centimeters wide, Kiwanuka stopped firing, lowered her weapon, and stepped back. She tiptoed and pressed her fist against the hole.

"Run a vid line," she told the armor.

Immediately, the armor extruded a thin fiberoptic cable that snaked through the opening. Vid relayed back to Kiwanuka's faceshield and showed only the empty shaft above the cage. Satisfied, she retracted the cable.

"We're good," Kiwanuka told the others. "We're still inside the shaft."

She resumed firing the Roley until she'd cut a crescent a meter in diameter at the ends. She slung the Roley and reached up for the glowing plasteel smile. Hooking her fingers over the edges, she pulled on the ceiling section. The cage roof held and she raised herself up from the floor. She lowered herself to the floor, kicked in the magnetic fields in her boots, and pulled again.

The muffled screech of the plasteel as it bent told her the cage and shaft still held atmosphere. When the opening was wide enough, she pulled herself up and squirmed through. The armor made it a tight fit. Outside the cage, she hunkered down on the lift and held the Roley at the ready.

"Okay," she told the others. "Let's go."

Goldberg and Noojin quickly scrambled through the opening and took up positions as well.

The shaft ran another thirty meters to the bridge. Kiwanuka suspected there would be other sec measures in place.

"We go slowly," Kiwanuka said. She created magnetic fields in her boots and left glove, then leaned into the shaft wall and climbed toward the bridge.

She'd only covered ten meters of the distance when a massive impact rocked *Kequaem's Needle*. She slammed herself against the shaft wall and held on to ride out the resulting shudders.

Goldberg cursed as she fell from the wall toward the lift roof below. Her descent slowed abruptly and she lightly bounced against the lift before she flailed out with her empty hand to magnetically secure a hold in the now-weightless environment.

Noojin clung to the wall and her heart rate spiked. "We lost gravity."

Kiwanuka knew that because her suit was already telling her that. For a moment she thought maybe *Kequaem's Needle*'s bridge section had torn free from the rest of the ship, but there had been no flare of explosions to blow it free.

"Cipriano," she called over the comm.

"We're good, Staff Sergeant," Cipriano replied.

"Where did the gravity go?" Kiwanuka asked.

"No idea. It felt like we got hit by something."

Before the man's words faded away, a large plasteel shard ripped through the shaft. The atmosphere vented out into space in a rush. Kiwanuka stared at the eight-meter-long shard and struggled to fathom where it had come from.

With all the space stations and orbital traffic passing through Makaum's gravity well, *Kequaem's Needle* shook repeatedly as she was struck several more times. Then the shaft spun in a lazy circle and shuddered again as it was struck by another wave.

Kiwanuka clung to the wall and rode out the impacts. Debris was something to be expected. Accidents happened. The corps didn't always report them.

Especially if they were one of the corp-sponsored smuggling runs.

"Staff Sergeant Kiwanuka," a man said over the comm. He had a definite accent, one that Kiwanuka wasn't immediately familiar with, but it was soft and carried intensity. "I am Sytver Morlortai, captain of this ship. At this point, I have two choices: strand you and your people here in space while I separate the bridge from the rest of my ship, or negotiate an accord. I would rather not leave my two crewmen in your hands, and I feel certain you would want to ensure the survival of your own people."

"I've got one mission," Kiwanuka said, "and that's to bring you back to Fort York. I'd like to do that with you still alive and breathing so you can admit to your crimes, but that's your call."

Another onslaught hammered the ship. Tremors quivered through the wall Kiwanuka held on to.

"If you want to live, Staff Sergeant," Morlortai said, "we need to agree to put our individual goals aside for a time."

"Not acceptable. We didn't come here to lose this fight."

"I didn't come here to lose my ship or my crew. If we had more time, I think I could win this skirmish. However, we don't."

Another wave of impacts shook the ship.

Kiwanuka considered the possibility that the events taking place around her, even the shard, though that was a stretch, was purely theater. That didn't seem logical, and Morlortai's history, what there was of it, suggested he was more direct in his actions.

Still, she had a job to do. She slung her rifle and used both hands to climb the wall. She wasn't sure what she was going to do when she reached the bridge hatch, but she still carried shaped B+8 charges that would open just about anything Morlortai's ship had to offer.

Noojin and Goldberg climbed slowly after her.

"I have time," Kiwanuka said.

"The Phrenorian Empire has launched a surprise attack on every space station and ship orbiting Makaum," Morlortai said flatly. "Those people weren't prepared for that. All those impacts you're feeling are from debris from those space stations and vessels."

A chill twisted sharply in Kiwanuka's stomach. "The Phrenorians wouldn't do that." She placed a hand farther up the wall and continued climbing.

"There was no one here to stop them," Morlortai said. "Let me connect you to our external drones."

"He doesn't need to do that, Staff Sergeant," Veug said. "I'm in those systems. I can—" The computer specialist cursed immediately. "Staff Sergeant—"

Whatever Veug said was lost as Kiwanuka stared at the images that played against her faceshield.

FORTY

dentify . . . respond . . ."

The transmission coming through the translator unit wired into the Phrenorian communications system sounded jerky and distant. Sage assumed that was because the software struggled to make sense of the Phrenorian clicks, whistles, and hisses that carried over the broadcast as well as to keep everything in real time.

"Man, that language sucks." Escobedo wrapped her arms around herself and shivered even though she still had blood and tissue on her armor and hadn't batted an eye. "I've never heard anything like it. Puts me on edge every time."

"Good for you that you're not gonna be part of a diplomatic mission," Culpepper said. "All you have to do out here is shoot the Phrenorians you meet. Keeps it simple."

"I heard the Sting-Tails didn't even have an audible language until a trade ship landed on their planet a thousand years ago and introduced them to the idea that they weren't alone in the universe," Corrigan said. "Once they had that, they captured some of the traders, tortured them, and figured out how to build starships. They realized they had to create this language to talk to each other over comm, so these clicks, whistles, and hisses are all a secondary language."

"How did they talk to each other before that?" Escobedo asked.

"I heard they exuded pheromones and just smelled each other," Corrigan answered.

"Like dogs?

"Maybe."

"Ick."

Sage didn't know if the story was true, and he didn't care. Who the Phrenorians had been in the beginning weren't who he was dealing with now.

"Pipe down," Sage ordered.

He'd allowed the soldiers to let off steam because they'd needed the brief downtime and they told stories when they were together. But the submersible was only minutes away from the mission's primary transition point. They were back to business.

The soldiers fell silent at once and checked their gear and weapons again. That was another thing they did automatically after it had been drilled into them.

Pingasa tapped a small keyboard beside him. "I'm sending the Phrenorians a return message that states we had engine trouble. To explain any possible lateness on our part. I told them one of the small *jasulild* went through an engine and damaged our communications array."

"You learned that in the time it took to get here?" Corrigan looked impressed.

"No," Pingasa said. "I searched through the log entries Lieutenant Murad located for mention of something similar that was in an aud file. Seven months ago, a similar event occurred. I copied and pasted that to send."

He waved a hand at the monitors above him that showed nearly a dozen *jasulild* pacing the submersible on all sides. Escobedo's shock treatments had kept Snaggletooth at bay, but the other sea monsters insisted on accompanying the Phrenorian boats.

"Those *jasulild* should help sell that story," Pingasa said. "But I predict those things are going to be problems as well."

"I don't," Culpepper said. "When this boat blows, the concussive waves coming off it will scramble their brains for a time. If it doesn't outright kill them on the spot." He looked around the group and grinned ghoulishly. "Gives you more reason to swim quickly, boys and girls. You don't want to be around Snaggletooth or any of the others that come through those explosions. They'll feel like they're coming off a three-day bender."

Sage hoped Culpepper was right about the window regarding the *jasulild*. Tension built within him as time passed.

"Why haven't the Phrenorians responded?" Escobedo asked.

"It takes a moment for the translation software to do its job," Pingasa said. Sweat trickled down his forehead despite the climate-controlled atmosphere. "Should be any second now."

"Or maybe they've already put a torpedo in the river with our names on it," Culpepper suggested.

The comm crackled again.

"—understood—problems—waiting—repairs—combat now—"

"Combat *now*?" Escobedo repeated. She hovered, poised over her weapons board.

Sage watched the radar and sonar monitors as the red lines swept *Dramorper*'s vicinity out to a half-klick. The distance would give Escobedo an instant to trigger a defensive response.

Everyone waited a beat, then Murad said, "Since we're not being fired upon, I'm going to take that as us passing muster."

"Why don't they just check with the other boat?" Corrigan asked.

The other soldiers in her immediate vicinity glared at her like she was on the edge of jinxing the luck they were having.

No, Sage reminded himself. *Not luck. We've got a lot of skilled people on this mission.* He didn't want to forget that, and he wanted to bring them all home.

He also knew that a post like the fortress, a place with no real duties, would bring out the worst in a soldier. When a soldier had nothing to do, that soldier usually worked really hard to do nothing. Comm checks became perfunctory so whoever was on duty could get back to whatever diversion the soldier was doing before the interruption.

Phrenorian warriors had the same weaknesses when it came to downtime.

"They won't contact the other boat," Pingasa said. "This is the lead submersible. Therefore we are the only ones they will talk to. They expect us to keep the second boat in line like a mother hen with a chick."

He trimmed the planes, charged and depleted the ballast tanks, and adjusted their approach to the base. Sage had picked up enough of the boat steering to know that. He'd watched Pingasa and learned from the tutorial his

HUD had walked him through. Redundancy helped keep a unit moving forward even at the worst of times.

The distance to their chosen delivery point was less than a thousand meters and falling rapidly.

Murad linked Sage in on a commlink to Command.

Colonel Halladay answered the call immediately.

"We're coming up on the three-minute mark, Colonel," Murad said. "Is this op still a go?"

"You're still a go, Lieutenant," Halladay said. "The jumpcopters are standing by for your fallback once you're clear. Be advised that we're tracking four Phrenorian aerial troopships that are closing in on your location. My guess is Zhoh is making his move to retrieve those war machines. You know what we're up against. If they get their hands on them, things will go a lot harder for us."

Sage knew that Charlie Company couldn't hold against the firepower inside the fortress. If they failed here, there would be nothing to keep the Phrenorians from rolling over the Terran military and taking the planet in a matter of hours.

They needed to move.

Now.

"Copy that." Murad cleared comm and looked up at Sage. "Get them out of here, Master Sergeant. Hopefully I'll see you soon."

"Roger that, sir."

Murad smiled and it almost looked genuine and fearless. "We'll see if Corporal Culpepper lives up to his reputation."

"I've got it on Sergeant Kiwanuka's authority," Sage replied, and shook the man's hand. He turned and called the soldiers to him as the time counted down inside his HUD.

They double-timed to the middle of the submersible and used the airlocks on either side of the corridor to evacuate the vessel.

Sage's armor shifted to neutral buoyancy immediately when he floated into the river. The sluggish current carried him along slowly.

Suit integrity optimum, the near-AI told him.

"Copy that," Sage said to himself as he swam away from *Dramorper.* The armor's speed and strength allowed him to navigate the current easily and he swam toward the other submersible. He got caught for a moment in the turbulence created by the boat's plasma propulsion engines, then broke free of it.

The HUD showed the other soldiers swimming with him, all of them vectoring in on the ping from the second submersible they had captured. There was enough light streaming through the river for him to see the boat powering nearer, but he tracked it primarily by the sonic signal it was giving off.

"Sergeant Jahup," Sage called over the comm. "Knock, knock."

"We have you, Master Sergeant." Jahup's voice was flat and dry.

"Copy that." Sage reached an interception point with the submersible and hung motionless as it approached. He amplified his vision and his HUD reduced everything to green. Since the human eye could more easily make out different shades of green, the details became sharper.

Prior to setting sail, Jahup's crew had spot-welded plasteel cargo nets onto the boat's port side. He and his soldiers were already in place, holding on to the nets as the submersible glided through the water.

Sage pinged Jahup's suit, locked on it, and swam over to join the younger man clinging to the net.

Jahup lay flat against the submersible so he streamlined through the water. Sage did the same, but he turned so he could face Jahup. He switched to a private frequency.

"Are you ready for this?" Sage asked.

"Yes." His voice was strong. "The worst thing has been the trip underwater."

"Worse than the trip we took along the bottom of the Tekyl River to get to Cheapdock?" Sage asked.

"It's been longer. I don't care for being underwater. Too many things can happen, and I need air."

Memory of the well echoed in Sage's thoughts and tightened his stomach. "I agree. But we're almost to the end of this. A lot of things will happen, and they'll happen fast."

"I'll be ready for them, Master Sergeant."

"See that you are," Sage said.

The submersible powered forward.

Sage tracked *Dramorper* on the HUD. The other submersible was pulling ahead, putting distance between itself and the following vessel as it closed on the Phrenorian fortress.

"Have you heard anything about Noojin or Sergeant Kiwanuka?" Jahup asked.

Sage thought about trying to reassure Jahup, but he didn't want to do that. The younger man was smart enough to know he would just be patronizing him. "No."

"They have their job and we have ours," Jahup said.

"Yeah. Let's concentrate on ours and stay alive."

Sage pinged Murad's and Pingasa's armor and discovered were still inside *Dramorper*. The window on their evacuation had almost closed.

Tensing up a little, Sage opened a comm link to Murad. "Lieutenant, it's time to get out of there."

"On our way, Master Sergeant," Murad replied. "We got another hail from the base that Pingasa had to attend to."

"Problem?"

"They haven't fired on us, so I'm thinking not. Pingasa was of the opinion whoever was at the other end was asking about some item that was supposed to be on the shipment. The corporal just copied and pasted the manifest. That should keep whoever contacted us busy for a little while."

Sage breathed a little easier when the two dots that were Murad and Pingasa showed up outside the submersible. They were closer to ground zero than they'd planned.

Murad and Pingasa swam away quickly, but one of the *jasulild* turned away from the others of its kind and pursued them.

"Look out," Sage warned.

"I see him," Murad said.

Sixty seconds and counting, the near-AI announced.

Culpepper had armed the *Dramorper.* It was now a traveling bomb.

The numeral *59* showed up on the HUD in transparent red letters and counted down. *58. 57. 56 . . .*

The submersible Sage clung to heeled in the water and came around to present its starboard side to the fortress. The Phrenorians would take notice now, but it was almost too late. A counteroffensive should be impossible at this point.

At twenty-four seconds and counting, the *jasulild* overtook Pingasa and gulped him down. The corporal never made a sound.

Sage kept his hold on the cargo netting and watched in numb horror as the sea monster swam away. Pingasa had become an integral member of his team, and Sage

could barely believe he had just lost one of his own to
that creature.

Focus, Sage commanded himself. He concentrated
on his breathing, pushed Pingasa's loss from his mind
the way he had countless others before, and concentrated on his job. He'd had to do the same thing when
he was training soldiers in boot camp and knew that
most of them would only survive minutes after hitting
groundside on whatever planet they ended up on. Staying focused now would save other lives.

Pingasa, Owen, Corporal—signal lost flashed
across the HUD. Sage dismissed it.

When the timer hit zero, Murad was 13.7 meters out
and on the wrong side of the second submersible with
three *jasulild* closing in on him. Culpepper's timing
and Pingasa's navigator skills were textbook perfect.
Dramorper struck the riverbank and exploded. The
barely seen stone underwater edifice disappeared in a
roily cloud of silt and debris that spread outward.

Clinging to the cargo netting, Sage made himself
stay where he was, told himself the armor would protect the lieutenant, and kept tracking Murad's ping,
then lost it in all the interference caused by the displacement of the bank and river floor.

The concussive wave from the detonation hammered
the submersible and set off a series of shivers that ran
the length and breadth of the vessel. When he was satisfied the worst of the explosion was over, Sage propelled
himself down and swam under the submersible.

"Close in," he ordered.

Jahup swam at Sage's side and the rest of the soldiers
fanned out around them. Sage pinged Murad's armor
and spotted the man hanging limp in the water, slowly
floating away from the submersible.

The urge to check on the lieutenant's condition

surged within Sage, but he put it aside. His whole team
was vulnerable now. They had to stick to the plan, and
he had to lead them.

"Corrigan," Sage called as he swam for the riverbank
and hoped the opening they had planned on would be
there.

"Yes, Master Sergeant?" Corrigan responded.

"Take care of the lieutenant."

"Copy that."

Most of the *jasulild* that had accompanied them
downriver floated limply and were carried away by the
current. A few of them moved weakly.

Sage swam toward the GPS pin he'd dropped on the
blast site. If that opening wasn't there, they were going
to be trapped in the river without a defensive position
or an exfil route.

And if the opening was there, they were going to
be in the fight of their lives with Phrenorian transport
ships about to deliver fresh troops.

FORTY-ONE

Operation Anthill
Yeraf River
Southwest of Makaum City
0536 Hours Zulu Time

A dead, dying, or unconscious *jasulild* lay across the
20.8-meter-diameter hole in the riverbank's side.
The creature partially blocked the rush of water filling the cavernous hardsite on the other side of the wall.

Sage swam beneath the behemoth and entered the
dark cavern. "Culpepper."

"Yes, Master Sergeant," Culpepper replied.

"Take two soldiers and clear this debris."

"Copy that."

Sage factored the manpower available to him. Pingasa was gone. Murad was out of action, with Corrigan
attending. Culpepper and his demolitions team took
out four more. That left nine soldiers including himself
taking part in the raid.

Against impossible odds.

The suit switched on the sonar system and the thermographic display, which was only a slight upgrade from guesswork as Sage followed the river flooding the riverbank's interior. The constant, almost soundless *blipping* of the sonar array mapping the enclosed space gave Sage an immediate headache that throbbed at his temples and created flickering blindspots in his right eye. Most soldiers had no complaints with the sonar, but Sage had never been able to tune out the noise.

Judging from what he could make out of his surroundings, the fortress was mostly a natural cave system that had remained watertight. The Phrenorians had just taken what they'd found and enlarged it, then made it their own.

The amount of profits General Rangha made from his side business must have been staggering. After the attack on Cheapdock, Uncle Huang had ferreted out rumors that some of the Phrenorian general's weapons had gotten destroyed by a mysterious blast. That had been when Sage realized what Zhoh and his team had been doing at the spaceport that night: destroying the evidence of Rangha's crimes.

The black market dealings would have embarrassed the Phrenorian Empire and Zhoh, since it had been taking place around him. More than that, proof of black market dealings might have drawn in other systems' coalitions that had so far stayed above the Alliance war with the Phrenorians.

If Zhoh had been left to his own devices, he might have destroyed the fortress on his own. Now, having chosen to go into battle, Zhoh was going to use all the arms contained within the caverns to annihilate Charlie Company and anyone else who stood in his way.

Sage took all of that in and realized the general would have put in systems to protect his ill-gotten black market goods. He hoped the river flooding into the chambers would partially clear the way.

The current swirled around him as it hit the end of the cavern and started to rise. The fortress had been constructed mostly underground. The people who had backgrounded the mission based on what they'd learned from Sage's and Jahup's observations, guesswork, and data retrieval believed the complex would fill from seventy-three to eighty-four percent capacity.

They hoped most of the war machines were below the level of the river.

The blast shattered nine meters of stone wall where the fortress abutted the river. Smaller rocks and silt ran with the high-velocity current rushing in from outside. Even the sonar was obscured and muddied by the constant motion and debris swirling around Sage.

Jahup, Escobedo, and Robinson swam with Sage.

"Corporal Palchuk," Sage called.

"Here, Master Sergeant," Palchuk replied instantly.

The HUD showed the corporal swimming eight meters behind Sage's group with the remaining soldiers. Culpepper and his team would follow as soon as the blast opening was cleared.

Sage had chosen Palchuk as the second team leader inside the fortress because he was one of the few, like Sage, who had been inside a Phrenorian fortress. He would have a clearer idea of the base layout.

If Rangha followed standard layouts, Sage reminded himself. Rangha had proved he wasn't much of a follower when it came to Phrenorian edicts. And the overall dimensions of the cave system would have presented problems as well.

"Take your team to Bravo Point," Sage said. "We'll take Alpha Point."

He brought up the sonar mapping grid and dropped

GPS pins labeled A and B onto the fortress layout. He also clearly marked the exit even though that would only mean a slow death somewhere out in the jungle if they had to run.

Retreat wasn't an option. The Phrenorian warriors would catch up to them.

Sage uploaded the map to the combat package.

"Copy that, Master Sergeant. Good luck to you and yours."

"Copy that. Same to you."

A few meters farther on, the sonar mapped the first of the war machines. Aerial drones and gunships, hulking powersuits, and tracked assault vehicles that were four and five stories tall lay knocked over and in pieces. Culpepper had designed a series of shaped blasts. The first one had evidently accounted for the wall, and the rest of them had floated into the caverns, then exploded.

Seeing the destruction left by the explosives and the river current filled Sage with pride. Even if they all died here, they'd made a difference.

But he didn't want Zhoh to get his hands on any salvage within the fortress. It had to come down too.

He swam up and had the suit jettison ballast it had taken on to render him more buoyant. The water continued to rise as the void filled, but he was overtaking it now.

The fortress generators, at least some of them, were above the waterline. Artificial light streamed down from overhead and the water got light enough to see.

Sage backed the sonar down so that it showed only as a thin overlay on the HUD. The 360-degree view with all the input was hard to manage, but he'd trained for years on the systems and it came as second nature to him.

Jahup, Escobedo, and the younger soldiers wouldn't be so lucky.

"Stay with me," Sage transmitted to the two soldiers with him.

"Copy that," Robinson responded, and Jahup echoed that a moment later.

Three limp Phrenorians lay in a sprawling cluster atop the rising water surface. Sage surfaced beside them and intended to use them as cover while he sorted out the situation. The swirl of water animated them and they bobbed on the choppy waves.

Sage put a hand on one of them and pushed. The corpse moved easily, held on top of the water because of the dead warrior's inherent buoyancy. Phrenorians were evolved water inhabitants. They hadn't completely quit marine living. Their respiratory systems could separate oxygen from water.

That was something Sage had learned about the enemy when he'd first gone into combat against the Sting-Tails, but it wasn't something he'd encountered before. It also made him realize the danger the teams were in.

"Master Sergeant!" Robinson yelled.

Sage whirled in the water, frustrated by his slowness. A couple meters away, Robinson struggled against a Phrenorian that must have been knocked unconscious by the explosions and had only just recovered consciousness.

The Phrenorian held Robinson's helmet in one primary while it brought up a sword with its secondaries. The warrior's tail struck at Robinson's faceshield again and again and scored the surface in jagged scars.

Around them, other Phrenorians stirred and returned to awareness. Some appeared to be more dead than alive, but Sage didn't trust that because they were clever enemies.

Sage drew the .500 Magnum from across his chest above the water and grabbed the tail of another Phrenorian as the new warrior lashed out at him. He took deliberate aim at one of the eyes on the back of the head of the Phrenorian attacking Robinson, reared back the pistol's hammer, and squeezed the trigger.

The Sting-Tail tried to move, but it was too late. The Magnum round missed the black eye, but it cored through the Phrenorian's cephalothorax and evacuated most of the contents over Robinson and the surrounding floodwaters. The warrior continued to fight, but the efforts were disjointed and Sage knew from experience that it was dead.

The Phrenorian whose tail Sage held used Sage's grip as an anchor and pulled himself closer. The warrior held a beam pistol in one secondary, a sword in another, and one of his primaries was open wide as he reached for Sage's neck.

Sage pulled on the tail and yanked himself around to face his opponent, shoved the .500 Magnum into the Phrenorian's maw amid the *chelicerae*, and pulled the trigger as the warrior swung his sword. The sword's edge slashed Sage's helmet, but didn't penetrate. The force of the blow knocked him back, but he hung on to the Phrenorian's tail and jerked it off balance with him.

"Stay alert," he warned over the op frequency. "The Phrenorians are water breathers. Some of them might have been killed by the concussions, but not all of them. Make sure they're dead. Don't just assume they are because they're not moving."

Thirty meters away, Palchuk and his people were embroiled in a battle of their own.

"Get out of the water!" Sage roared. "Get those explosive packs in place!"

Sage glanced overhead. The cave's roof was only twenty meters away and covered with stalactites. He released the dead Phrenorian and raised his arm. He fired his grappling line and the sharp hook bit into the craggy rock between the catwalks that overlooked the lower level of the cavern.

Jahup was already riding his grappling line up to the ceiling. He held his Roley in one hand and fired laser blasts all the way up. He crouched next to a large stalactite and continued firing.

Sage holstered the Magnum and brought his assault rifle around, then triggered the grappling line retraction. He zipped up out of the water ahead of Robinson and Escobedo, and three Phrenorians swimming in his direction.

Laser fire and projectiles struck Sage's armor repeatedly.

Warning! the near-AI stated. *Suit integrity weakening rapidly. Eighteen percent efficiency lost.*

Sage thudded against the cavern roof and switched over to the Roley's grenade launcher as he took cover behind a stalactite. He fired a half dozen grenades into the water where Phrenorian shooters floated. Some of the gel-grenades stuck to the Phrenorians and others smashed against the rising water.

The explosions ripped some of the Sting-Tails to pieces or blew off big chunks. The grenades in the water created shock waves that incapacitated other warriors.

Sage reloaded his weapon from the armor reserves and scanned the battlefield.

Palchuk and his team ascended grappling lines on their side of the caverns. They exchanged fire with the Phrenorians as they locked into place against the cavern roof.

Dozens of the Phrenorians had survived Sage's initial attack and now floated or swam among their dead comrades. Others found purchase on the sides of the cavern and scrambled up from the water, but their positions would only be dry for minutes at most. During that time they could do a lot of damage, though.

"Use the gel-grenades," Sage said. "The water conducts the concussive effect better, and any detonations against the cave walls weaken the overall structure."

The soldiers immediately switched their attacks to the grenades and thunder filled the cavern. More debris and smoke swirled through the air. And still the floodwaters rushed in.

Reloaded now, Sage aimed for two of the groups and pumped grenades at them. A beat later, the explosions ripped the Phrenorians to pieces, from their perches, and blew chunks from the wall that turned into shrapnel that tore into everything in the vicinity.

The suit's aud dampers negated most of the noise for Sage. Quivers ran through the roof of the cavern and debris rained down into the rising water. The stalactite Sage took cover behind cracked and fell into the water. It landed on a small knot of Phrenorians and took most of them down as well.

"Culpepper," Sage called.

"Coming, Master Sergeant," Culpepper replied. "Our doorway's mined and ready to blow as soon as me and my crew get inside with you."

"We're on the roof, but we can't hold that position long."

"Copy that. Get your charges in place. We'll be along with ours soon enough."

The ops map loaded back into Sage's battle computer. When he opened it up, X's marked the areas where the teams were supposed to place their designated charges. Instead of B+8, the charges contained fissionable nuclear materials that promised a much bigger bang.

They'd put together a preliminary placement package to shatter the cavern's integrity, and they'd go with that if they had to. However, Culpepper had worked out a new design based on the sonar map created by the feeds from the suits of the soldiers already in the main cavern.

More Phrenorians poured into the room from two doors. Sage marked both entrances on the combat map and sent the upgrade to his team. He readied his rifle.

FORTY-TWO

Sage raised the Roley to meet the oncoming Phreno-rians and opened fire. Depleted uranium charges smashed into the enemy warriors and the catwalks alike. When the catwalk nearest Sage held a dozen Phrenorians, he fired four grenades at the supports connecting the platform to the cavern roof.

The explosions ripped the catwalk from the roof and spilled the Phrenorians into the floodwaters just as the charges along the crack in the riverbank detonated. More water rushed into the cave and covered the Sting-Tails just as Culpepper and the two soldiers with him zipped up their grappling lines to the cavern roof.

Two other soldiers zoomed up lines as well, propelled by the armor's musculature. Sage's HUD marked them as Murad and Corrigan.

Sage switched to the command frequency. "Glad to see you're all right, sir."

"I'm late to the party," Murad said, "and my ears are still ringing, but it looks like I have a front row seat. As you were, Master Sergeant. See it through."

"Copy that, sir."

The new flooding threw whitecaps across the turbulent surface of the rising water. The Phrenorians clinging to the rock walls got washed away.

"Man, I am *so* good at what I do!" Culpepper roared.

"Get the explosives in place!" Sage yelled.

More of the Phrenorians initially stunned by the blast that had blown a hole in the riverbank were recovering, but they were struggling against the floodwaters.

Using stalactites as cover, Sage fired his grappling hook again and swung over to the designated area for his charge. Around him, the other soldiers did the same. Phrenorian laser beams and projectiles chipped away at the roof as they pursued. Some of the stalactites ripped free of the room and tumbled into the water, but oftentimes struck other Phrenorians.

After he had the charge seated, Sage spotted a cluster of Phrenorians firing on Escobedo from one of the catwalks. She was pinned down and sheltering in place as best as she could.

Sage scanned the cavern roof, selected four stalactites that looked like they were in the right position, and fired the last of his gel-grenades. The grenades stuck to the stalactites and exploded. Shorn free of the cavern roof, the stalactites dropped onto the Phrenorians, hammered the catwalk to pieces, and dropped the dead, wounded, and disoriented warriors into the water.

In quick order, the demolitions map lit up, showing that each charge was in place.

Munitions ready, the near-AI announced.

"Time to go," Sage said. "Deploying drones."

Sage released the two drones from his armor and set them to mapping. The small projectiles unfurled their rotors and sped toward the doors marked on the map. The vids of each opened on windows of his HUD and were joined by two others from Lieutenant Murad's armor.

By the time the drones blew through the doors over the heads of the Phrenorians taking cover there, Sage fired his grappling hook, pulled it secure, and got ready.

"Jahup," he called.

"Yes, Master Sergeant."

"Do you have any grenades left?" If Jahup didn't, Sage knew they would have to go at the problem another way.

"Three."

That made it a little easier. "Put them in the middle of those Sting-Tails blocking our door." Sage marked the chosen door on the map and sent it to Jahup.

Jahup fired the grenades an instant later. Two of the gel projectiles sailed true and slapped onto some of the Phrenorians on the catwalk in front of the door. The third landed against the wall behind them.

The resulting explosions threw Phrenorians in all directions.

Sage let go of his perch and swung over to the catwalk, which quivered uncertainly under him for a moment when he landed, then held, before the Phrenorians could recover. He crouched and fired depleted uranium rounds into the warriors who still lived and were lifting their weapons.

Sage turned and squeezed off bursts of suppressive fire to cover Jahup, Robinson, and Escobedo as they swung over to join him. Escobedo misjudged her approach by centimeters, but Jahup moved before anyone else could and seized her arm. He held her suspended over the water and the enemy troops for an instant till he could get his feet under him, then hauled her in as bullets and beams hammered the edge of the shaky catwalk.

Palchuk's group, accompanied by Culpepper and his team and Murad and Corrigan, made their way to the other door. Grenades cleared the way there as well and they were inside the passageway.

"Culpepper," Sage called as he sprinted through the passageway following the paths marked by his drones.

"Yes, Master Sergeant?" Culpepper responded.

"You're set?"

"Affirmative, Master Sergeant. Just waiting for when we get clear. There's enough fissionable materials in those packages to take the roof off this place."

"I'd rather they dropped it onto everything below."

Culpepper's grin sounded in his voice. "Oh, they'll do that, Master Sergeant. Or I'll go over and stomp it down myself."

Sage led the way out of the fortress. The drones let him know about the ambush waiting ahead. He sprinted faster and put some distance between himself and the others. At the corner, he threw himself down into a skid in a seated position with the Roley at the ready. When he slid into the corner with one leg tucked under him, he opened fire on full-auto.

The depleted uranium rounds chopped into chitin and Phrenorian flesh but ricocheted from the abbreviated armor over the vital organs.

Sage shoved himself to his feet and was a half-step behind Jahup as the younger man rounded the corner, ran up one side of the hallway over Sage, and flung himself onto the lead Phrenorian. Jahup's forward momentum and the armor's weight knocked his opponent down.

One of the Phrenorians was dead. A ricochet had torn through the warrior's cephalothorax.

The Phrenorian Jahup grappled with managed to get in one tail strike and fasten his *chelicerae* onto the young Makaum man's faceshield. Then Jahup drove his hunting knife into the Phrenorian's opisthosoma and ripped the blade sideways. A steaming pile of guts evacuated the wound and the warrior died.

The second Phrenorian drove a fighting spear at Jahup's back, but the warrior stumbled backward when Sage shot him repeatedly in the face. Jahup dropped his dead foe just before the last Phrenorian hit the stone floor.

"That was pretty stupid," Sage said as he reloaded his weapons. "You could have gotten killed."

"Me?" On the other side of his faceshield, Jahup looked astonished. "What about you?"

Sage replaced the two spent rounds in his pistol. "We're not talking about me."

"Do you want to talk about this now, Master Sergeant?" Jahup asked coolly. "Or do you think we can save it for the after-action report?"

In spite of himself and the situation, Sage had to work hard to keep a smile off his face. He said, "Move out, soldier."

They ran.

Minutes later, they formed up with the other group, who looked worse for the wear. Two soldiers carried Private Suvari between them.

"We ran into a group of Phrenorians," Palchuk said. "We left them lying there, but we took some damage."

Murad pointed overhead to the north where storm clouds gathered and filled the sky with the promise of rain. "There are the four Phrenorian birds the colonel told us about."

Sage glanced up and his faceshield automatically polarized against the dulled morning sunlight. The HUD classified the aircraft as Phrenorian *Crayst*-class transport ships. Those aircraft would be gunned up.

Small explosions went off inside the fortress and resonated through the surrounding jungle.

"Some little going-away presents I left," Culpepper said. "And begging the lieutenant's pardon, but those aircraft aren't the big problem. There are gonna be some mad Sting-Tails boiling out of that place here in a minute or two, in spite of the party favors I left behind us, and they still outnumber us. I suggest we use that big hammer we left hanging from the cavern roof and cut down on those odds."

"Can't you do it now?" Murad asked.

"If I do, and we're standing this close to ground zero, sir, it's more than likely we'll drop right in there with them."

"Take the lead, Corporal," Murad said. "When we reach a safe area, light it up."

"Copy that, sir." Culpepper took off at once and the other soldiers fell in as he raced downriver.

Sage and Jahup ran slack together.

The four Phrenorian aircraft arrived at the fortress and hovered.

"What are they doing?" Jahup asked.

"Waiting for orders," Sage answered.

The thick branches of the trees and brush hid the aircraft intermittently.

"I could save them some time if we had rocket launchers," Jahup said.

Two of the Phrenorian ships peeled off and swooped in pursuit of the Terran soldiers. Almost immediately, they opened fire with cannons. Explosions tore through the jungle. Smoking craters opened up and ten-meter-tall fires leaped up through the trees. Several small weaponized drones whizzed through the air and shot cannons and sniper rifles.

"Pop EMP smoke!" Sage bellowed. He pulled out three EMP-charged smoke grenades from his chest pouch, pulled the rings, and tossed them a short distance away.

Most of the other soldiers threw grenades as well.

Small detonations released the purple smoke laced with ionized particles containing electromagnetic pulses from the grenades. The EMP lacing wouldn't harm the armor because it was hardened against such a weak attack, but the Phrenorian drones would be vulnerable to it. The smoke obscured visibility.

Drones that encountered the smoke quickly fell or lost control. One of them, about a meter in diameter, smashed into a tree trunk on Sage's right and turned into scrap.

"Grab dirt!" Culpepper warned.

Sage went to ground beside Jahup. He covered his head with his arms despite wearing the helmet. Medtech could regrow anything below the neck if a soldier could stay alive long enough to reach a bio-support tank for transport.

For a moment, everything seemed normal. Then the fortress vomited into the air and the ground around Sage rolled and pitched. The Phrenorian transport became a series of explosions that punched holes in the air, the jungle, and scattered debris in all directions.

The world turned silent as the aud dampers kicked to max and took away Sage's hearing. He watched as the top of the riverbank collapsed in on itself. Then the mass of earth that had gotten thrown into the air came down like an avalanche of sudden death dropped from the heavens.

Sage was buried in an instant.

FORTY-THREE

Kequaem's Needle
Makaum Space
0550 Hours Zulu Time

At least a dozen corps space stations—Silver Spin, Tri-Cargo, and SulatetDev among them—hung in clouds of debris in space. Dozens of ferries, cargo ships, and transport haulers formed smaller pockets of debris. Still more exploded and were reduced to slag as Kiwanuka watched in growing horror.

She counted four Phrenorian dreadnought-class battlecruisers powering into the orbital paths of the civilian stations and ships. The Phrenorian vessels were constructed with two forward decks backed by a superstructure that made the battlecruiser look like a giant horseshoe. MilNet believed the design was taken from one of the large ocean predators on Phrenoria, the *garisul*. The creature was present in a lot of the Phrenorian formative mythologies, always idealized as a strong, unrelenting god.

Smaller attack ships zipped from the dreadnoughts' launch decks. They were the *Reryt*-class, and were based on venomous hive crustaceans that hunted in schools. Bright beams flashed against the darkness as the pilots attacked without mercy.

Morlortai was right in his assessment of the situation. Without a space-based defensive squad, none of the corps would stand a chance against the Phrenorians.

"Staff Sergeant Kiwanuka," Morlortai said. "If we're going to escape execution by the Phrenorians, we're going to have to act quickly. In order to escape, if we can, I need those engines."

"And we need a ship." Kiwanuka tried not to think about how their ship had gotten destroyed shortly after their arrival.

More debris slammed into *Kequaem's Needle* and rocked the ship violently.

"Then we have an agreement?" Morlortai asked.

Kiwanuka didn't hesitate. Even if the situation she and her squad were in wasn't as desperate as it was, and even if she had more time and more access to ways to escape the Phrenorian attack, taking Morlortai into custody was no longer a primary objective.

Arresting him and proving that he, or one of his people, had fired on General Zhoh was no longer a viable objective. The assassin's confession might have given the Alliance ammunition to counter the Phrenorian Empire's charges of Terran military aggression, but that no longer mattered because of the threat now imminent. The Phrenorians were making a definite bid for conquering Makaum.

"We have an agreement," Kiwanuka answered. "Sergeant Cipriano."

"Go, Staff Sergeant," Cipriano replied.

"Give the captain back his ship's engines."

"Copy that."

"Excellent," Morlortai said. "Staff Sergeant Kiwanuka, bring your people up to the bridge. I give you my word that you and they will be safe until we are out of this situation. Will you guarantee the same?"

Kiwanuka resumed climbing. "Yes."

"I look forward to meeting you."

Kiwanuka wondered how she was going to respond to that. Before she figured it out, something collided with *Kequaem's Needle*. One of her hands and both feet swung free of the plasteel plate of the shaft and she barely maintained contact with her other hand.

The lift shaft suddenly sheared away from the main body of the cargo ship. Open space, marked by the fiery flares of freighters and ferries exploding from Phrenorian cannons, yawned below her.

Noojin, evidently knocked free of the shaft wall, flailed her arms and legs wildly as she floated toward the gaping hole.

A-Pakeb Node
Strategic Intelligence Command
Makaum
30252 Akej (Phrenorian Prime)

Pride filled Zhoh as he watched the carnage unfolding on the huge monitor at the front of the room. Deafening explosions formed an undercurrent around the workstations where Phrenorian information officers tended to the constant streams of vid and aud downloading

from the seven *Garisul*-class dreadnoughts attacking
the various space stations in geosynchronous orbit
around the planet.

Since space didn't carry sound, aud was captured
from scattered space stations and spacecraft frequencies. Most of them were pleas for help in several different languages, but the emotions that drove the words
made the broadcasts easily understood. The crescendo
of explosions, screams of frightened, wounded, and
dying beings, and warning Klaxons came from the
various vessels caught up in the attack.

"—came out of nowhere—"

"—no warning—"

"Help!"

"—are we supposed to—"

"—no way of protecting—"

"—are dead right in front of my—"

"They're everywhere!"

All of the fear was music to Zhoh and he reveled in it.
He knew his pheromone secretion was high, but so was
every warrior's in the room. Mato's pheromones were
strong as he stood beside Zhoh. Only personal battle
would have heightened his sensation.

"Just think, *triarr*," Mato said, "the *Seraugh* assigned
that attack force to Makaum to support your efforts
here. This is for *you*."

"I know." Reluctantly, Zhoh turned away from the
glorious battle playing out on the huge monitor and
glanced at Mato. "What is happening at the Terran
fort?"

Mato slid into a workstation seat and tapped the keyboard with his secondaries. The monitor blinked and
filled with six different images of Fort York.

Lights marked the training fields and some of the buildings in the fort, but Zhoh knew those were deliberately

placed to allow distraction. The colonel in charge of the fort was no fool, and the being probably knew the soldiers he had involved in various pursuits there would be recognized as attempts to draw the attention of any spies away from the Terran military's main objectives.

Still, the effort had to be made. Zhoh would have done the same himself.

"They pretend to reinforce their defensive posture," Mato said, "but our spies at the fort tell us the soldiers' efforts are more directed to equipping the Makaum beings fleeing the sprawl."

Mato tapped the keyboard again. The views reconfigured and picked up vid feeds from drones monitoring the sprawl. Groups of Makaum people slipped through alleys and walked into the surrounding jungle.

"Do you have an estimate on how much of the sprawl populace has departed?" Zhoh asked.

"The numbers fluctuate between forty-two and fifty-seven percent. These figures are raw, *triarr*, not hard data. Our intelligence specialists have not yet gathered enough information to create the proper algorithms to reveal the actual numbers."

Zhoh nodded, feeling somewhat irritated.

"The attack on you," Mato said, "as well as Master Sergeant Sage's apprehension of Throzath at around the same time, polarized the Makaum populace. However"—he tapped the keyboard rapidly—"the dreadnoughts' attack on the space stations is currently playing over all the sprawl media outlets."

The screens reconfigured again. This time they opened up on street scenes where sprawl inhabitants gathered in public places and gazed up at the night sky. Huge chunks of the space stations had fallen into the planet's gravity well and streaked toward the ground, trailing fire as they burned.

"Unfortunately," Mato said, "it appears that several pieces of the debris are going to strike the sprawl and outlying regions. They will cause even more fear and unrest."

On-screen, one large section of something and several smaller ones hit the Offworlders' Bazaar. Blinking blue warning beacons left by the Terran military still marked the area as off-limits.

Explosions ripped along the impact area and left smoking craters in their wake.

A distant rumble reached even the underground complex beneath the Phrenorian Embassy. Tremors raced through the room.

Mato sat straighter and tapped the keyboard again. "I have an incoming communication from General Belnale for you."

"Put it on-screen," Zhoh ordered.

Immediately the screen filled with the general's broad features. "General Zhoh, I trust that you are monitoring the attack."

"I am," Zhoh responded. "Express my appreciation to the War Board. The space-based operations centers provided a lot of information and intelligence to the Terran military."

Belnale squared his shoulders. "They won't anymore. However, since the Phrenorian Empire has attacked while negotiations were still underway regarding the assassination attempt made on you by the Terran military, there exists the possibility that the Alliance may choose to move against us."

Zhoh glanced at the big monitor still broadcasting the space battle. The dreadnoughts continued chewing through their prey like their namesake.

"The Alliance will have to shift considerable forces through the Gates to offset the ships the War Board has fielded," Zhoh said. "Perhaps they won't be in a rush to reassign those forces for fear of weakening other positions."

"They won't have a choice," Belnale said. "Their agreement with the Makaum Quass, especially since the beings on that planet have requested asylum, will force them to invest those ships. They will come."

"Then they will die," Zhoh said.

Belnale's *chelicerae* twitched irritably around his mouth. "No. Those dreadnought-class vessels won't be in space around that planet for much longer. They will have to return to their units in short order. The board was only able to task those ships as part of a reconnaissance mission for this attack to draw Alliance forces from another sector."

Disappointment and rage warred with Zhoh. The help he'd received hadn't totally been given to him. The War Board had used him and the circumstances on the planet to further their own stratagems.

He masked his feelings but knew that his pheromone scent was now tainted, no longer as satisfied as it had been.

"I understand, sir," Zhoh said. *And I will make someone pay for this affront.*

"Understand that this was not my decision," Belnale went on. "I was only able to intercede on your behalf this much. If I'd had my way, I would have left those ships in place and let them take out as many of the Alliance ships as they could before they died glorious deaths."

Zhoh kept his voice level. "I appreciate your efforts, General. When the time comes, I'd like very much to know who the architect of this plan was."

"Perhaps that can be arranged," Belnale replied. "Until such time, however, devote yourself to delivering that planet. Once you have control of things on the ground there, you can use the Makaum populace to hold the Alliance ships in check there after they arrive."

"It will be as you say, General."

Belnale cut comm and vanished.

"Triarr," Mato said, "I know this is not what you wished—"

"What I wish doesn't matter," Zhoh said. "I will have my victory here."

He stared raptly at the large screen as the destruction continued. The attack ship pilots were thorough as they chased down single ships attempting planetfall. Several ships turned into flaming explosions on the edges of the atmosphere, either as kills to the attack ship guns or victims of shoddy construction or poor piloting skills.

"Where is Colonel Halladay?" Zhoh asked.

"Our spies confirm the colonel's still at the fort."

"What about Sage?"

"Our warriors haven't been able to ascertain the master sergeant's whereabouts."

"And the contingent of pilots on their way to the stronghold?"

Mato pulled up another screen that showed a top view of Stronghold RuSasara. The river gleamed silver as the moon reflected from the choppy current. The area looked calm and sedate, especially when juxtaposed with the falling "stars" burning across the night sky.

"Only minutes away from arrival," Mato said.

The four-ship contingent sailed into view and descended toward the riverbank. Before the first one touched down, an explosion ripped through the water and the nearby land. A huge chunk of land and a deluge of water vomited upward and shredded the lowest two aircraft. Like the space debris falling from the heavens, the aircraft crashed into the jungle and the river in flaming pieces.

"It appears," Zhoh said with cold fury, "we now know where Sage is. Contact those surviving warriors on-site. Tell them to bring me back Sage's head."

Mato swiftly relayed the orders to the surviving aircraft. When he was finished, he looked up at Zhoh. "Shall I send more air support?"

Zhoh considered that briefly. He also considered getting aboard an aircraft himself, but he knew that Sage would either be dead or gone by the time he arrived.

"No," Zhoh answered, "but tell our spies in the fort that I want Quass Leghef found. She and Sage have a relationship, correct?"

"Yes, *triarr*. They have been working together."

"Sage has weaknesses when it comes to beings around him," Zhoh said, "and I mean to exploit those weaknesses to break the backs of the Terran military's presence here on this planet. One way or another, I will make Sage come to me if he survives the coming encounter. When he does, I will have his head."

He looked forward to that confrontation.

FORTY-FOUR

Watching Noojin drifting closer to the hull hole into space, Kiwanuka set herself, took stock of her position, switched off the magnetic fields to her gloves and boots, and pushed off the plasteel plate where she'd been adhered.

A short distance away, Goldberg twisted and maintained contact with the shaft wall.

"Staff Sergeant?" Goldberg called.

"Hold your position in case I need you," Kiwanuka ordered as she floated toward Noojin.

"Copy that," Goldberg replied.

Kiwanuka kept her mind clear as she focused on Noojin. She knew that telling the girl to keep calm under the circumstances wouldn't work. Noojin would be nearly out of her mind with fear. Kiwanuka also tried not to think of what might have happened to the rest of her squad waiting on the other side of the lift door, or with Cipriano's team in the engine room.

They're alive, she told herself. They had to be alive.

More debris struck the cargo ship. There was no noise because of the vacuum and, since she wasn't in contact with any section of the lift shaft, Kiwanuka didn't feel any tremors.

However, several pieces of debris ripped through the ship's hull and, velocity diminished by the initial contact, bounced around inside the lift shaft. At least one struck Noojin and altered her course.

Five meters from Noojin and passing by the girl, Kiwanuka fired her grappling line. The hook slammed into the armor covering Noojin's leg, but the sharp projectile didn't penetrate. Even if it had, the near-AI would have sealed off the suit to save oxygen. Noojin would have lost her leg, but she would have been alive, not lost in space, and legs could be regrown.

The hook ricocheted at a sharp angle and sailed under Noojin's other leg. Kiwanuka pulled the line taut and watched in satisfaction as the buckyball strand jerked to a stop. The forward momentum translated into a parabolic spin that wrapped both of Noojin's legs.

The addition of the girl's mass altered Kiwanuka's trajectory, but she was still on course to make contact with the opposite wall she'd been aiming for.

"Easy," Kiwanuka said over a direct commlink to Noojin. "Easy. I've got you."

Noojin stopped struggling and instead reached for the grappling line. She held on with both hands.

Kiwanuka hit the wall first and slapped a magnetically charged glove against the plasteel. Noojin hit shortly thereafter and scrabbled for a hold.

Kiwanuka tugged on the grappling line to remind the girl she was there. "Use your magnetics. Take a breath. I'm not going to let you go. You're safe."

After a moment, Noojin locked on to the plasteel with all four extremities.

Kiwanuka let the girl cling to the wall and turned her attention to the rest of her team.

"Niemczyk," Kiwanuka called.

Her HUD reception was spotty and the team's stats flickered in and out. She suspected part of the weak performance was due to signal jammers the Phrenorian dreadnoughts were using, but some of it might have come from the debris. Those space station pieces might not have gone inert all at the same time.

That made her think about the people possibly trapped in those sections who would drift into Makaum's gravity well or spin endlessly through space. She forced her mind away from those possibilities.

She'd do what she could for whomever she had a chance to save, but she and her team came first. Otherwise no one got saved.

"Here, Staff Sergeant," Niemczyk responded.

"How is the rest of my team?"

"Shaken and bruised in places, but we're all here."

Some of the tension balled up in Kiwanuka's stomach uncoiled. "Sergeant Cipriano, are you there?"

"We are," Cipriano answered. The comm connection was scratchy and hollow. "But we're getting less there as we go."

"Explain."

"*Kequaem's Needle*'s broken up into five big pieces that we've seen through the external drone system. We've got the engines in our section, but we don't have a way of using them. If we light them up, there's no telling where we'll end up. I'm hoping the Sting-Tails don't decide to use what's left of the ship for target practice just so we can burn up during an uncontrolled reentry or die out here when we run out of air."

"Roger that," Kiwanuka said. "So let's not do any of that."

"You have a plan? Because I haven't ever been in a situation like this."

Neither have I. Kiwanuka kept that thought to herself. "Working on it." She paused. "Morlortai? Are you still in one piece?"

"We are," Morlortai said. "We're sending a drone down to you and your crew."

Above, the bridge hatch opened and a spacesuit-clad figure waved at her. A moment later, the figure opened a hand and released a drone that unfolded itself to nearly a meter across.

Miniature thrusters fired under the drone and propelled it toward Kiwanuka. A slender line paid out behind it. In only seconds, the drone stopped mere centimeters from Kiwanuka's helmet and hovered, revolving on its axis. She took the line, threaded it through her combat harness, then reached down and did the same for Noojin.

The girl didn't release her hold on the wall.

"You have to let go, Noojin," Kiwanuka said softly. "We can't stay out here. We've reached a truce with Morlortai and his people. They're allowing us onto the bridge. Once we're there, we'll figure out what we're going to do. Do you understand?"

Noojin was silent for a moment, then she whispered, "C-Copy that, Staff Sergeant."

"Good. Now follow me."

Keeping the magnetic fields active in her boots and gloves, Kiwanuka led the way around the lift shaft to Goldberg. Once the other soldier was tied onto the line, they climbed toward the bridge while still more shrapnel that had once been space stations, ships, and maybe even people thudded into the hull.

Kiwanuka concentrated on the climb and hoped that Morlortai had been speaking the truth.

0601 Hours Zulu Time

Remaining calm only because he'd been in worse situations—Morlortai told himself that even though he couldn't remember a single instance that even came close to where he was now—he sat in the command chair and studied his current predicament on the ship's monitor. External drones captured the complete problem from five different angles.

Kequaem's Needle floated in five pieces that spun through space and got farther from each other with each passing second.

"Can we still separate the bridge from the lift shaft?" Morlortai asked.

At the helm, Wiyntan, the ship's pilot, surveyed her systems panel. Lights flickered, glowed, went dormant, and changed colors. Her Turoissan heritage made her the largest person on the bridge. She stood almost three meters tall. Her indigo skin, the color of fresh Terran blueberries, also made her stand out. Her two lower canines parted her lips and bookended her habitual, challenging smile. For all her size, she piloted the ship effortlessly. The pilot's seat and controls were custom-fitted.

"Yes," Wiyntan replied. She sounded distracted and Morlortai took no offense. She was mapping the various interception points with pieces of wreckage that used to be space stations and other space vessels. "All I have to do is blow us clear of the hidden docking ring and we're on our own." She looked over her shoulder at Morlortai and grinned coldly. "I'd be happy to do it now."

Morlortai checked the monitor at his left that showed the Terran military soldiers' progress up the lift shaft. "No."

"Let me remind you," Wiyntan said, "taking on those Terrans isn't going to help us. They'll be using up almost half our oxygen. The carbon dioxide scrubbers on the bridge can't work quickly enough to keep the air clean. We'll only have enough air for seven or eight hours."

"We won't last out here for seven or eight hours." Turit's mechanical voice was flat. His actual growls carried more emotion. He stood beside the emergency bridge access hatch on the floor with Ny'age to one side and slightly behind him. "Once the Phrenorian pilots realize we're still alive, they'll be along to correct that."

"Trying to escape across space is impossible," Ny'age said. "We don't have the air, the fuel, or the supplies. The Oakfield Gate to this sector is well beyond our capabilities."

On the ship's monitor, two of the drone feeds showed *Reryt*-class gunships blowing up other ships and escape pods that had blasted free of other spacecraft.

"The Phrenorians consider the elimination of helpless prey as great sport," Ny'age said. "They'll eagerly search out survivors in the wreckage until their commanding officers call them off."

As the ship's social engineer and trade-face, the Estadyn knew enough lore about other races and alien worlds to fill several volumes. He was humanoid enough to pass as a Terran. His blond hair was tousled and his gray-green eyes shone warmly.

"Medals are awarded for pilots who have enough confirmed kills." Ny'age studied Turit, who held a Shednal neuropulse pistol in one scaled hand. "Might I suggest, Turit, that you not greet the Terrans with a pistol in hand?"

"I'm not comfortable with greeting them at all," the Angenen countered. "I side with Wiyntan on this. We should leave them where they are."

"And give up on Darrantia and Daus?"

"If we can't save them, we can't save them," Turit said.

Morlortai was certain Turit's words would have sounded cold even without being filtered through the translator he wore. "I'm not ready to give up on them, Turit."

Turit managed a sigh through the translator that sounded true and put-upon. Reluctantly, he returned the Shednal pistol to his boot.

"The airlock's cycled through," Wiyntan stated.

Morlortai cut his gaze to his personal screen and tapped the code for the airlock vid feed.

All three of the Terran soldiers stood in the airlock. None of them held weapons at the ready.

Morlortai opened the hailing comm in the airlock. "Welcome aboard, Staff Sergeant Kiwanuka."

"Thank you," Kiwanuka said.

Morlortai nodded to Turit. The Angenen tapped the proper sequence into the numeric pad on the wall.

Air cycled into the airlock and pressurized the compartment. Kiwanuka and her team maintained their armor integrity. Morlortai accepted that. Need was stronger than trust when it came to uniting different people.

The hatch opened. Turit and Ny'age stepped back as one of the soldiers clambered through. She stepped to one side and kept the bulkhead to her back. Her rifle was slung with the barrel pointing down.

Morlortai knew from experience that a weapon in that position was easily and quickly lifted into readiness. That was all right, though. The abbreviated Kerch shrapnel burster built into his command chair was quick to hand as well, and he had a two-shot Vorgar pistol up his sleeve that fired 20mm caseless ammunition.

The other two soldiers clambered onto the bridge and took up positions beside their leader. Their faceshields remained black and blank.

"Which of you is Staff Sergeant Kiwanuka?" Morlortai asked.

The first arrival's faceshield cleared to reveal a dark-skinned woman.

"I am," Kiwanuka said.

She was all business, and Morlortai could appreciate that.

"We meet under auspicious circumstances," Morlortai said.

"They're not ideal for me either," Kiwanuka replied.

Despite the deadly earnestness in the woman, and the fact that his ship was lost, Morlortai smiled. "Still, this is better than any other resolution than we might have reached."

Kiwanuka's gaze flicked to the large monitor at the front of the bridge. "This is your fault. All of it."

"Mine?" Anger stirred within Morlortai. He knew what she was getting at and it bothered him. He'd lost his ship and several million credits because replacing the vessel would be expensive. And when word got around about the missed assassination, he would lose

more profits. At the moment, he hated Makaum, the
Alliance, and the Phrenorian Empire.

"You failed to kill Zhoh," Kiwanuka said. "As a
result, he used your failing to launch a preemptive
strike against Makaum."

"Blame the Alliance," Morlortai said. He clamped
down on his anger. "They should have given you the
soldiers and the supplies to properly safeguard this
planet instead of playing political games with the
Phrenorians. The Empire should never have been allowed
on Makaum."

"Permission to blast free of the area, Captain?"
Wiyntan asked.

"Not yet," Morlortai said. "First the staff sergeant
and I need to agree on what we're going to do."

"Begging the captain's pardon," Wiyntan said with
a trace of sarcasm, "but the Phrenorian gunships are
coming this way."

"I know that." Morlortai focused on Kiwanuka.
"Here's the agreement: I get you and your people to
safety, and you clear the way for my crew and me with
the Terran Alliance."

"You want a free pass?" Kiwanuka shook her head. "I
can't do that, and if I said I could, I'd be lying to you."

"I just require passage out of this system," Morlortai
said. "Once I jump through the Gate, we're even."

Kiwanuka hesitated only a moment. "I can do that."

Wiyntan snorted. "None of that's going to matter if
we can't get out of our present situation. Maybe I need
to point out that this escape ship isn't built for combat
fighting or for planetfall. And once we start moving, we
become an instant target for the Phrenorian gunships."

"Then we're going to have to move fast," Kiwanuka
said.

That surprised and pleased Morlortai. He still hadn't worked out their escape from anyone other than the Terran military. Getting to the planet's surface and finding another ship was a distant hope.

"You have a plan?" Morlortai asked.

"I do." Kiwanuka sounded confident. "First we rescue our people."

Morlortai liked that she had said "our" people, grouping their objectives into a common effort. Ny'age probably appreciated it as well.

"And after that?" Wiyntan pressed.

"We do this one step at a time," Kiwanuka said.

"I would like to know more," Morlortai said.

"I would like it if we weren't gunning for each other only minutes ago."

"For what it's worth," Wiyntan put in, "I'd like it if we weren't being hunted by the Phrenorians. Maybe we could think about that."

"Noted." Morlortai swung his attention back to the monitor. "We have two groups of people in two sections of what used to be this ship. Staff Sergeant, how would you recommend we proceed?"

Kiwanuka stepped forward and surveyed the broken ship pieces in their immediate vicinity. "I left one of my teams in the corridor in front of the lift."

Wiyntan tapped a keyboard and the ship section lit up in soft blue light. "Here."

"Yes," Kiwanuka said. "We go there first. Then the engine compartment."

The pilot shifted uneasily at her station. "Once we blow free, the Phrenorians are going to see us. By the time we reach that section, some of them will be on to us. Our approach to the engine compartment will draw fire."

"Then," Kiwanuka said, "I guess we're going to find out how skilled you are."

"I'm amazing," Wiyntan said.

"Let's hope so." Kiwanuka glanced back at Morlortai. "I assume this vessel has armament."

Morlortai nodded to Turit, who was already moving. "It does."

In less than a minute, the ship's armorer unlocked the heavy-duty laser cannons from hiding and pulled out skeletal seats from the floor. Workstations reconfigured to weapon controls.

"They're not much," Turit said in his mechanical voice, "and we can't go toe-to-toe with the Phrenorians, but they'll give us fangs against the gunships."

Morlortai gestured to the available seats. *Kequaem's Needle* was set up for twelve passengers on the bridge. Holding all of the Terran military soldiers in armor would be a tight squeeze. Morlortai didn't look forward to the claustrophobic environment once they were aboard.

Kiwanuka and her team sat and strapped in.

"Ready when you are, Captain," the staff sergeant said, "and let's hope your pilot is as good as she thinks she is."

Wiyntan snorted mockingly and tapped her keyboard. "Blowing docking ring in three . . . two . . . one . . ."

The series of detonations rang throughout the ship and it shivered for a moment as it fought to free itself. The external drones showed the docking ring blowing apart.

"The Phrenorians have noticed us," Turit said.

Wiyntan fired the thrusters and heeled the ship back toward the section that held Kiwanuka's first group of soldiers. "They still have to catch us."

Outside Interview Room B
Security Building
Fort York
0604 Hours Zulu Time

"I don't want to go!" Telilu protested. She had her arms folded over her chest and glared at Leghef. "I want to stay with you! I want Jahup and Noojin to be here with us!"

Knowing the child was afraid and there was nothing she could do about that, Leghef didn't give in to her own weakness. Consoling her granddaughter when it might all prove false wasn't in her.

They stood outside the interview room where Throzath awaited interrogation.

"Telilu," Leghef stated in her flat, no-nonsense voice. "Things have gotten dangerous for us here."

"I know!" she wailed. "That's why I want all of us here!"

"We can't be here. Not for long. We won't be safe."

"We *will* be safe! That's why the soldiers are here! That's what you said! You said that if the soldiers came to live with us, we would be safe! *All* of us! Instead, Jahup nearly got killed by Oeldo because he was drinking again and Noojin had to shoot him!"

Leghef looked up at Pekoz, who stood nearby. Today he looked thinner and more withered than ever. His bony face looked tight around his small, sad eyes. His skin was so pale the gray scars on his hands and features were hard to see even in the hallway's bright light. Today he used a cane to walk.

The old man shook his head. He still wore a shiny silver bandage around his head. He held a backpack containing Telilu's things in one scarred fist. Despite

Captain Gilbride's admonishments, and her own instructions, Pekoz had refused to lie abed any longer. Not when Leghef needed him.

"She has been talking with her friends," Pekoz said. "Over those . . . *devices.*" He didn't care much for the computers the merchants had brought to Makaum. "I didn't know until it was too late."

Leghef waved that away and returned her attention to Telilu. She knelt and put both hands on the girl's shoulders. "Daughter of my son," she said in that old way so that her granddaughter would know she was serious, "times have changed."

Tears leaked from Telilu's eyes. "No," she whispered. "No, don't send me away. Please!"

Leghef smiled but showed no weakness. She could not let her granddaughter see what was truly in her heart. She brushed hair out of Telilu's face. "I must."

Telilu shook her head in denial. "I won't go."

"Then you will have to break Pekoz," Leghef said, "because I'm going to have him take you to Keladra. Once I set him to this task, he will not fail me unless you beat him senseless. Are you going to do that to him?"

Telilu glanced up at the old man. "I would never do that," she promised.

Pekoz smiled. "Thank you."

"Pekoz and Keladra will keep you safe until I can join you," Leghef said.

Telilu looked back at Leghef with more desperation. "Why aren't you coming with me?"

"Because there are things here I must do if we are to be safe."

"I don't want to go."

"And I don't want to be away from you, little one, but we each must do our part. Mine is to stay, and yours is to go. Now come. Tell me goodbye and that you will mind Keladra and Pekoz until I return to you."

Telilu's face crumpled and a wave of guilt rushed over Leghef. She made herself stay strong as she hugged her granddaughter back as fiercely as the little girl hugged her.

Then Leghef peeled herself free and stood. "Do you have your doll? The one Noojin gave you?"

The doll was special because it had a transponder in it that Telilu could use to signal for help.

Telilu sniffed and nodded. "She's in my bag."

"Good. Then you take care of her and I will see you soon."

Telilu nodded, took Pekoz's free hand, and walked away.

Leghef took a breath, put her heart back together, and faced the door to the interview room. On second thought, she put her heart away. She wasn't going to use it for this.

FORTY-FIVE

Operation Anthill
Yeraf River
Southwest of Makaum City
0607 Hours Zulu Time

Do you require more medical attention, Master Sergeant Sage?

Sage struggled back to wakefulness and finally got his eyes open. The HUD gleamed before him and scrolled stats on his team and gave his GPS location as somewhere by the Yeraf River, which rang a bell for some reason but he couldn't figure out why.

Only he couldn't see. Nothing but darkness lay beyond the faceshield. He tried to raise a hand to wipe his faceshield in case something had gotten stuck to it. Except he couldn't move.

Memory came back to him in a rush.

Realizing he had to be lying on his face, he forced his hands out beside him and pushed. Even with the suit amplifying his strength he was hard-pressed to make any headway against the sheer tonnage bearing down on him.

His head came up from the dirt and stone that covered him and he realized that the Phrenorian cavern hadn't just imploded. It had exploded. He didn't fault Culpepper for it. The fortress had been a high-tech powder keg. They had no way of knowing what Rangha had kept on hand.

Incoming! the near-AI warned.

Targeting crosshairs drew Sage's attention to a Phrenorian troop transport bearing down on his position. He remembered there were two of them. He also saw that he wasn't the first soldier to get to his feet.

Six other soldiers stood in the loose earth that had rained down on them. Four of them raised their weapons as they followed the calls to action of the near-AIs.

Sage found his Roley at the end of his arm. He hadn't let go of it even when he'd been briefly unconscious. Focusing, he brought the Roley up and sighted in on the lead airship. Somewhere around him, eight other soldiers had to be lying buried. He wasn't going to leave them unprotected.

He squeezed the trigger and a line of depleted uranium rounds danced across the transplas nose of the troop transport. Two Phrenorian pilots sat behind the controls and never blinked.

None of the rounds pierced the bulletproof transplas. Beneath the airship, a rocket pod shifted as it locked on target. Before the Phrenorian gunner could release a rocket, air-to-air missiles struck it in a sharp staccato of explosions.

In the next instant, the Phrenorian airship became a twisted cloud of flaming debris. The ammo cooked off in a series of detonations that sped shrapnel across the jungle. The largest pieces that survived the attack knocked down trees in a ragged line thirty meters from Sage.

The second troop transport airship whirled around and tried to dodge, but the two jumpcopters screaming in low over the jungle attacked mercilessly. Air-to-air ordnance leaped from firmpoints mounted on the boxy aircraft.

The Phrenorian ship never got a rocket off. Trailing smoke, coming apart, it drifted sideways and crashed into the trees only a few meters from the Yeraf River.

A commlink chirped for Sage's attention.

"Master Sergeant," a woman said. "This is Blue Jay 12."

"Acknowledged, Blue Jay 12." Some of Sage's tiredness went away. He'd met the pilot briefly after the attack on Cheapdock. She was a stand-up soldier and fearless pilot.

"The colonel sent us out here to give you a ride home," Blue Jay 12 said. "Save you a walk."

"We appreciate the assistance." Sage reached down in the loose earth, found Jahup, and pulled the younger man to his feet. His vitals looked strong and he was just now getting his bearings.

The jumpcopters hovered above the soldiers—*all* the soldiers, Sage was glad to see—and payload masters lowered baskets attached to winches to the ground.

"Jahup," Sage said.

"Yes, Master Sergeant."

"Make sure everyone gets on board."

"I will. Where are you going?"

Sage held his Roley at port arms and advanced on the stricken Phrenorian gunship. "To find out if there's anything worth salvaging. I'll be along."

Three of the Phrenorians had tried to evacuate the wreckage but hadn't gotten far. Their burned bodies lay stretched on patches of ground that still held flames.

Two of the warriors inside the troop section were still alive, but death couldn't be more than a few minutes away. Sage fired mercy rounds that put them out of their misery before wading through flames to get into the wreckage of the cockpit.

"You're going to get yourself blown up," Jahup said.

Sage glanced at the open cargo door. He'd known someone was coming and had been ready.

"You're not supposed to be here," Sage said.

"Everyone's loaded up," Jahup said. "We're waiting on you. You said you wanted me to make sure everyone got aboard. I'm here to make sure you get there."

Sage tore open the airship's console, located the on-board computer, and stripped one of the input wires. He was by no means proficient with computers, but he knew how to break into a drive. He pulled a jack from his chest armor and let it thread itself into the drive.

A screen popped up on his HUD.

Making connection, the near-AI said. *Connection made. Commencing download.*

A bar lit on the HUD and showed the progress of the download. All around Sage, the airship continued to burn, hiss, pop, snap, and crack. He hoped all of the firepower had cooked off. If it hadn't been for his armor, he would have burned alive.

Download complete.

Sage returned the jack to his chest armor and climbed out of the downed aircraft. He had no idea what he'd gotten or if it was even worth the effort.

The two jumpcopters hovered just above treetop level and the door gunners maintained watch behind 20mm cannons. Despite how welcome the sight of the airships was, Sage knew the flight back to Fort York would only provide a short respite. Zhoh would probably already be planning another attack. The newly minted Phrenorian general wouldn't lose the fortress—even if its existence would mar Phrenorian honor—without exacting his pound of flesh.

Zhoh would pursue the Makaum people, and then they would see the monsters they'd allowed to come to their planet. They would find out that the Sting-Tails wouldn't let them leave the planet, and Sage was torn because he didn't know how many of them the Terran military would be able to save in the time they had left.

A dark shape slapped the surface of the river a few meters away. The *jasulild* surfaced and rolled, then flopped over as though in pain. Its head landed on the riverbank.

Sage peered at the creature over the Roley's sights, but it continued to lie there as young *kifrik* dropped by strands to land on the *jasulild*. The *kifrik* bit into the corpse and feasted.

Just as Sage turned away, the *jasulild* blew up. Bloody flesh flew in all directions.

Weakly, Corporal Pingasa stumbled from the dead monster. His armor was worse for the wear and cracked in places, but he was alive. He cursed in at least two Terran tongues and six alien languages that Sage was familiar with.

"That was the most horrible experience of my life," Pingasa said. He walked with difficulty, either because he was injured or because his armor was damaged.

"I thought you were dead," Sage said. He couldn't hide the smile of disbelief from his voice.

"For a time, so did I," Pingasa admitted. "I have never before been eaten." He brushed dead *jasulild* from his armor and looked around. His gaze focused on the collapsed fortress and the cloud of smoke and dust that hung over it. "Was I in that thing's belly for that long? Is it over already?"

"Just this part, Corporal," Sage told him. He ran over to the man, pulled one arm over his shoulder, and guided them toward the waiting jumpcopter. "We've got plenty left to do. This fight's just gotten started."

Jahup grabbed Pingasa's other arm. Together they managed a staggering double time toward the waiting exfil aircraft.

As they clambered through the jumpcopter's doorway, several flaming objects streaked from the sky and landed in the vicinity of Makaum City and Fort York, and spread out beyond into the surrounding jungle.

The jumpcopter's engines howled and the aircraft leaped into the sky.

Sage tapped into the jumpcopter frequency. "Blue Jay 12, do you want to tell me why the sky is falling?"

"It's the Phrenorians, Master Sergeant," the pilot replied in a hushed voice. "At 0529 hours, the Sting-Tails launched a space-based attack against the corp space stations and civilian spacecraft. We have no idea what the casualties are, but Command thinks they're going to be extensive." She paused. "Those people never had a chance, Master Sergeant."

Sage watched the space debris burn through the atmosphere trailing fire and it took away the fleeting sense of victory he'd gotten after the destruction of the weapons storage and Pingasa's unexpected return. Emptiness and dread filled his stomach. Sour bile bit at the back of his throat. None of their planning involved dealing with an attack by Phrenorian spacecraft.

If the Sting-Tails succeeded in surrounding Makaum, if the spaceports were destroyed, there was no way off the planet. They were trapped.

Zhoh and his army would have free rein to ride roughshod over any survivors, especially if he was reinforced by new troops.

Sage looked at all the destruction in the jungle and knew it would be worse in the sprawl.

"Staff Sergeant Kiwanuka was up there on a mission," Sage said. "Do you know anything about her status?"

"I'm afraid not," the pilot said. "Sorry. Wish I did."

Leaning back in his seat, strapped in as the jump-copter screamed just above the treetops on the way back to Fort York, Sage watched the fire and smoke filling the sky. Light rain spattered the leaves of the trees and bushes around him. He hoped it was raining harder in Makaum City. The rain could help put out fires and it would slow the Phrenorian Empire's heavy assault vehicles.

But it was going to take more than rain to save those people.

FORTY-SIX

Who do you see when you look at me, Throzath?"
Quass Leghef sat on the other side of the plasteel
table in the small room that felt too cold to someone who had spent all her life in the fetid Makaum
jungles.

The rebellious, entitled young man seated across
from her was only a few years older than her grandson,
yet the difference between Jahup and Throzath made
them worlds apart. Throzath had given himself to the
worst parts the offworlders had brought with them,
and he had turned away from the common decency her
people showed one another because they had depended
on each other for survival for so long. Instead of em-
bracing the worst parts, Jahup had found, perhaps, the
truest calling he had ever known.

It was an eye-opening experience, and one Leghef took great pride in.

Throzath didn't answer her question and pointedly looked away from her.

No one else was in the room. Leghef had wanted it that way. Just as she'd wanted Throzath's restraints removed. She wanted him to believe he had control over himself and his current situation. To a degree.

He believed he could overpower her. Maybe he was even considering doing that. Leghef hoped so. Such aspirations would make him break even more easily.

"Do you see an old woman?" Leghef asked in a conversational tone, like they were talking about the price of *corok* melons in the marketplace. "I wouldn't be surprised if you do. That's what many people see. Especially offworlders, young people, and dullards who have no life experience."

"Are you calling me a dullard, Quass?" he asked in a mocking tone that told her he gave her words no value.

"No. You are much worse. You are a *veskin*. An otherwise insignificant parasite that sometimes manages to burrow into the heart of a *lorkelis* tree and poison all the berries." Leghef touched the rolled *taruwe* skin on the table beside her.

Old and weathered, the leather carried scars from decades of hard use. Leghef stroked it lightly, drawing Throzath's attention to it for a moment. For now it was a curiosity. Later it would be something else.

Throzath looked at her then and scowled. "My leg hurts."

Leghef smiled, but she knew, from experience, the expression was cold and distant and had no warmth. She had practiced that smile to show unsuspecting prey. "Good."

"I have no interest in talking to you," Throzath

replied. "I want to be returned to the detention center to await my father. I want medical attention. I *demand* medical attention. The Terran military can't hold me here like this."

"The Terran military isn't holding you," Leghef said. "*I* am. They are only giving me a place to keep you where your father can't immediately reach you."

That statement gave Throzath momentary pause. "He will come for me."

"I have no doubt. Unless he died in the attack the Phrenorians launched a short time ago."

That caught Throzath's attention. He focused on her and sat up a little straighter. "You lie."

Leghef had expected that response. The young always denied things that didn't go their way.

She tapped the small keyboard in front of her and queued up the vid files Colonel Halladay had given her.

The large monitor at one end of the room blinked on in a blaze of color and immediately showed vid footage sent from space stations and cargo ships that probably no longer existed. The Phrenorians were a thorough predator species.

Whispered prayers, shouts of disbelief, and curses provided an undercurrent of noise to the vids along with warning Klaxons. The destruction of the space stations and cargo ships made no noise—until the host vessel transmitting the vids was hit. For a short time, deafening thunder filled the recordings, then it cut off abruptly.

Ship after ship after ship.

The hostile confidence on Throzath's face gradually leached away, but he didn't quite give up on it.

Throzath sat up straighter. "This is fake. Like one of the games in the entertainment emporiums. The Terran soldiers made this. But I don't understand why you're trying to fool me."

"I'm not trying to fool you," Leghef said angrily. "The Phrenorians have already done that. Just as they fooled your father into dealing with them. That's what we're here to talk about: the agreement your father had with the Phrenorians that made him their spokesperson."

Throzath grinned at her with the self-indulgent cunning that only young men knew. "We supported the Phrenorians. That's no secret. Everyone on Makaum knows that."

"They do," Leghef agreed. "But they don't know about the arms trade you and your father were involved in. Do you think that knowledge will change people's opinions of you and your family?"

Throzath leaned back, crossed his arms over his chest, and looked petulant. "I don't know what you're talking about."

"I'm talking about the weapon Oeldo had." Leghef didn't try to restrain her anger. Her fury poured out of her, and it was a tool, not a weakness. Her emotions had not been vulnerabilities since she was a child. They were her strength because she knew how to use them to make her resolve stronger.

She leaned on her anger and her need to get answers from Throzath so she wouldn't give in to her concern for Jahup, who was in the jungle fighting for his life against impossible odds, and Noojin, who was lost somewhere in space according to Colonel Halladay. In this room, in this moment, she could allow no distractions.

Her concerns presented a threat to the young man before her. But her anger could break Throzath.

"I didn't give Oeldo a weapon," Throzath said.

"The Terran military know that you did." Leghef tapped the compact keyboard in front of her.

In response, vid of Dr. Gilbride filled the screen. In succinct terms, he laid out the DNA evidence he had gathered from the weapon Oeldo had used in his attack on Jahup. Images of the discovered thumbprint on the old man's elbow showed bright and clear.

"This is your thumbprint," Leghef said. "It was found on Oeldo's body. You were with him only a short time before he was killed."

Throzath shrugged. "I bought him a drink. That old man begged them from everyone. I'll bet he's even begged you on occasion."

Leghef went to the next vid in the sequence. Gilbride introduced and explained the epithelial cells he had found on the weapon.

Most of Throzath's confidence evaporated in that moment, but he was quiet, obviously hanging on to the belief that he could yet escape his present situation.

"I asked you who you saw before you," Leghef prompted. "You didn't answer. You can at least do me that courtesy."

Throzath sneered at her and locked eyes with her. "I see a withered old woman. A leathery bag of bones that believes she is more powerful than she is."

"Allow me to tell you what you don't see." Leghef smiled again, and it was a smile she never let anyone who cared about her and thought they knew her see. There was no joy in it, only fierceness and conviction. "You don't see the girl that I was. The one who followed her father into the jungles to take meat because we lived in poverty and he had no other skills or resources to barter with."

She unfolded the *taruwe* skin to reveal the dozen sharp knives rolled within. Even after all these years, they gleamed.

Leghef slid one of the blades free and the keen edge

caught the light. "My father made these knives from metal he scavenged from the ship that brought us to this planet."

Throzath stared at her and looked less sure of himself.

"He taught me to take meat from creatures he killed," Leghef went on, "even while *kifrik* and *omoro* hunted in the trees above us. I learned to work quickly because the scent of blood drew other predators. I cracked joints with my hands, then I severed ligaments and saved all of the meat I could." She gazed at him over the knife as she turned it carefully in her hands. "Have you ever hunted *sul'gha*?"

Slowly, Throzath shook his head.

"But I'm sure you've eaten *sul'gha*. The meat is considered a delicacy, but it's now illegal because of the way it's taken. We consider ourselves . . . more *humane* these days. However, there are those hunters who still provide it for wealthy customers. Your father bought a lot of *sul'gha* when he was a young man as I recall. And his father before him." Leghef paused. "Do you know anything about how the meat is taken?"

Throzath didn't say anything. She had no clue if he'd heard the whispers that still circulated.

"The meat has to be taken while the *sul'gha* is alive," Leghef said in a low voice. "Once a *sul'gha* dies, it has glands that produce poison. So *sul'gha* are captured, then butchered while still living. The trick is to keep it alive as long as you can so as not to trigger the poison to get a good harvest. I had to learn how to cut around major arteries and organs so as not to kill the *sul'gha*. Every morsel of the meat mattered. A mouthful paid enough in trade to feed a family for a day."

To her surprise, her mouth had gone dry at the mem-

ories. She forced herself to go on and show nothing of
the turmoil inside her.

"The whole time you're taking meat," Leghef said,
"the *sul'gha* screams. Most hunters who trapped them
say they sound like small children. At first, I could
not bear to hear that noise." She swallowed, but hoped
Throzath would think she was only pausing for effect.
"I got over my weakness. My father was a poor man
and he had no sons, so I learned to do what must be
done."

Throzath paled.

"It got so those screams didn't touch me," Leghef
said. "I took meat. Slice after slice, tying off arteries as
I went, because that's how you work your way down to
the bone without killing your prey." She smiled. "I got
so good at my craft that I could hold the still-beating
heart of a hollowed-out *sul'gha* in my hand and take it
before the creature knew it was dead. The heart was
worth the most because it was the hardest to take free
of poison, and I was the most capable butcher anyone
had ever seen."

"Why are you telling me this?" Throzath demanded.

Leghef smiled again. "Surely you're smart enough to
figure that out, Throzath." She turned the knife in her
hand. "Or I can explain it to you as we go. You will tell
me everything you know about your family's dealings
with the Phrenorians."

Throzath turned to one side and threw up. The stink
filled the room. When he was finished, when he had his
breath again and fear for his life burned brightly within
him, he started talking.

FORTY-SEVEN

Kequaem's Needle
Makaum Space
0619 Hours Zulu Time

The first salvage operation went smoothly because, as it turned out, the ship's pilot *was* excellent. Kiwanuka easily understood why the Turoissan was part of Sytver Morlortai's crew.

The assassin also chose his other compatriots well. The Angenen and the Estadyn manning the laser cannons were good choices, and they proved how handy they were with the ship's limited weapons banks when two of the Phrenorian gunships engaged what was left of *Kequaem's Needle.*

The pilot kept up a steady blaze of innovative cursing while she played hide-and-seek among the tumbling sections of wreckage that spread outward from the initial attack sites.

Kiwanuka braced herself by holding on to the back of the seat and opened a vid channel on her faceshield that connected her to Veug. The elint specialist was nearly as innovative with his cursing as the Turoissan was, and his efforts seemed decidedly more heartfelt.

Another onslaught of particle beams chipped away at *Kequaem's Needle*'s thinning shields. Or maybe the ship's pilot had slammed into a spinning piece of debris. That seemed to be occurring more and more as they closed in on the stranded engine section and Cipriano's people.

My people, Kiwanuka corrected herself. All of them were her people. Kiwanuka's stomach was knotted up again, and she knew this time she'd die with it like that if they didn't find a way to get down to the planet.

"Corporal," Kiwanuka said tensely.

Veug punched his keyboard rapidly. "I'm working on it, Staff Sergeant. Tracking everything from the point of the initial attack to now is *hard*. It's like trying to keep your eye on one billiard ball that's able to skip from table to table in a room full of billiard tables while all the other balls are in motion too."

"It's a *space station*," Niemczyk groused. "That's gotta be like finding a *beach ball* on a field of billiard balls."

"Maybe you'd like to try looking," Veug suggested.

"Problems, Staff Sergeant?" Morlortai asked in his annoyingly calm voice.

Kiwanuka still couldn't get used to the Fenipalan assassin. Even though she'd known from the few images of the man she'd seen in his file that he looked more or less normal, she hadn't expected how . . . unassuming and casual he appeared. If she'd passed him on a street somewhere, he wouldn't have drawn a second glance. And she was certain she wouldn't have noticed him at all in a public place like a bar or a mall.

"Nothing we can't solve, Captain," Kiwanuka responded, and hoped that was true. At last count there were four Phrenorian gunships chasing them.

"Perhaps if you told us what you're looking for," Morlortai said, "we could help."

"You and your crew just work on keeping us alive and picking up our people. That alone is enough to keep your hands full."

"We could do more."

Kiwanuka was beginning to believe that was true. Morlortai and his crew were already achieving the impossible by keeping them alive. She decided to try another tack.

"You were hired to kill Zhoh," Kiwanuka said.

Morlortai kept his attention focused on the ship's monitor and didn't reply.

"You didn't decide to do that on your own," Kiwanuka said. "You're a professional, and I'm betting even if you had a personal vendetta against Zhoh, you wouldn't have traveled out to the middle of nowhere to kill him."

"You're correct."

"Tell me who hired you."

Morlortai looked at her as *Kequaem's Needle* took another hit and rolled over. He remained strapped into his command chair while Kiwanuka held on to the deck with her boots and one glove.

"Tell me where we're going after we get our remaining people," he said.

Kiwanuka considered for a moment to let him think the decision was harder for her than it was. "A trade, then. We both get something we want."

Morlortai pursed his lips and hesitated long enough that Kiwanuka assumed he was going to turn her down.

She smiled at him. "You never know, Captain. I could die in the next few minutes and you don't have a next move in mind while the Phrenorian gunships are closing in."

"Hey," the Turoissan called from the helm. "Staff Sergeant."

Kiwanuka maintained eye contact with Morlortai. "What?"

"Do any of your people know enough about Lerskel ships' drives to turn them into bombs?"

That was an intriguing question and Kiwanuka cursed herself for not thinking of it. She passed it along to Cipriano.

"Can do," Cipriano said. "We've already been working on it. A little going-away present from us to the Sting-Tails."

"Glad to hear it, Sergeant." Despite the desperate situation, Kiwanuka smiled when she relayed the news to the Turoissan pilot, and let her know Cipriano and his people were already engaged in that task.

The pilot grinned mirthlessly. "I like that guy. Nothing like being insanely destructive to create breathing space."

Kiwanuka wondered what "insanely destructive" entailed, then thought maybe she didn't want to know because she had enough worries on her plate. Cipriano had something of a reputation for explosives. He and Culpepper had kept a bar crowd thoroughly entertained in Kahl's Lamp the night after Sergeant Richard Terracina had died in the ambush during Sage's first night on Makaum. Kiwanuka hadn't kept track of the conversation, but she remembered some of the highlights.

That hadn't been so long ago. And now the Phrenorian Empire had popped its claws. Glumly, Kiwanuka realized that if Sage hadn't been on the scene, Fort York would have probably already fallen.

Maybe by now it has. The thought pierced Kiwanuka's mind like a laser beam.

Then she realized Morlortai had spoken to her. She blinked. "What?"

"I said you have a trade, Staff Sergeant," Morlortai said. "The destination you're hoping for in exchange for the name of my employer."

"Employers," Kiwanuka said. "I want to know who arranged the assassination of Wosesa Staumar as well as the one or ones for Zhoh."

Morlortai's calm composure slipped for just an instant and he frowned. "Greed isn't becoming."

"It's not greed," Kiwanuka said. "It's desperation."

Kequaem's Needle rocked over hard again and explosions unleashed a crescendo that filled the bridge.

"The (ta)Klar hired me to kill Staumar," Morlortai said. "They wanted to cause confusion in the delicate balance between the Terran military and the Phrenorian Empire troops on the planet. That worked."

On-screen, the stern section of the cargo ship swelled into view. Digital numbers counted down the distance from 123 kilometers. The explosions that had destroyed *Kequaem's Needle* had scattered the ship. The pieces still traveled at extreme velocity.

"Now you give me something," Morlortai insisted.

"We're searching for what's left of the DawnStar Space Station," Kiwanuka replied.

Morlortai's features wrinkled in confusion. "Why?"

"Give me the name of the person who hired you to kill Zhoh."

"Not until you're more forthcoming."

Kiwanuka decided not to press her luck. They were running out of time, and Morlortai wouldn't be able to do what she was thinking without her. "DawnStar sublet space to the Terran military, including a hangar that housed dropships. If we're lucky, not all of them have been deployed."

Morlortai's eyes widened. "That's what you're banking on? That the hangar wasn't immediately destroyed? That a dropship may still yet be housed there?"

"Do you have anything better? I'm open to another solution because this is all I've got."

Morlortai pursed his lips and shook his head. "No."

"Then we'll go with what I have." Kiwanuka shifted and took a new hold on Veug's seat. "In case you're thinking of betraying us at some point, maybe you can get into the hangar without us. Maybe you can even access a dropship. But you're not going to be able to do those things quickly on your own."

Morlortai smiled, but there wasn't a lot of humor in the effort. "All right."

"Now give me the name of who hired you to assassinate Zhoh."

"Blaold Oldawe."

Kiwanuka thought for a moment, racking her brain as *Kequaem's Needle* shivered and shook and sped through space. "Who is that?"

"Zhoh's father-in-law."

That was surprising. "Why would he want Zhoh dead?"

"I don't ask those kinds of questions, Staff Sergeant. All I know is I was paid a lot in advance to take on the job, and there was going to be a lot more once it was done. Unfortunately, the shot I took didn't pan out and events on Makaum, as you have seen, quickly unraveled. We were actually about to head out of system when you arrived." Morlortai spread his hands. "The rest you know." He studied the monitor. "And unless we are very fortunate, this is all going to end within minutes if not sooner."

Kequaem's Needle's reverse thrusters initiated and the escape ship slowed.

The Turoissan pilot skillfully guided her craft into near-docking distance next to the engine compartment. Niemczyk fired a buckyball line from the ship's airlock to the broken section of the cargo ship.

While the Turoissan managed to use the broken section and other debris she'd hauled in via tractor beam as cover, Morlortai's gun crew kept three of the Phrenorian gunships at bay. Cipriano and his people clambered along the line.

That strategy wouldn't last long. The Phrenorian ships doggedly chipped away at the makeshift cover. When the last soldier was aboard *Kequaem's Needle*, Niemczyk sealed the access hatch in the airlock.

"They're aboard," Kiwanuka called to the pilot.

"Roger that," the pilot responded. She fired the ship's thrusters and picked up speed. "Tell your demolitions guy to stand ready with his surprise."

Kiwanuka thought the pilot meant to lure the trailing Phrenorian gunships into position around the engine section. Kiwanuka didn't have much hope for the ploy.

Instead, the pilot latched on to the engine section with tractor beams. The resulting drag on the ship brought *Kequaem's Needle* almost to a standstill and nearly ripped Kiwanuka free despite the magnetic fields generated by her boots and one glove.

"Corporal," Kiwanuka said to Veug.

"Almost, almost," the elint specialist replied.

The Turoissan used the tractor beam drag to throw the ship into a parabolic arc around the cargo ship section. The four Phrenorian gunships tracking *Kequaem's Needle* fired their lasers into the cargo ship section, then brought them to bear on the escape ship as it came around.

The two ship's crew on the cannons accounted for one of the gunships, but the other three lit up in a constant onslaught that vibrated through *Kequaem's Needle* and set off warning Klaxons around the bridge.

Incredibly, the Turoissan fired the ship's thrusters and managed to spin the trailing cargo ship section forward. When it reached whatever trajectory the pilot was looking for, she cut off the tractor beams.

The cargo ship section hurtled toward the three Phrenorian ships that were even now racing in pursuit. Released from the tractor beams, *Kequaem's Needle* sped off on a new tangent.

"Now!" the pilot yelled. She dodged weapons fire with astonishing skill or amazing luck, Kiwanuka wasn't sure. "Have your demo guy blow the charges!"

Kiwanuka broke out of her incredulity that they weren't dead and gave Cipriano the order.

"Fire in the hole!" Cipriano yelled.

Flipping end-over-end, the cargo ship section missed all three Phrenorian ships, and when the small charges Cipriano and his team planted within the engine compartment flared to bright life, it was at least a hundred meters beyond them.

For a moment, Kiwanuka feared that those explosions were all that was going to happen, that something had gone wrong with the demolitions attempt.

In the next instant, a new, white-hot sun punched a hole into black space. A molten bubble of superheated plasma swelled out from where the cargo ship's engine compartment had been. The roiling plasma swiftly cooled in the freezing environment of space, but it overtook the three Phrenorian gunships and closed over them.

And the plasma continued on, chasing after *Kequaem's Needle* like a rampant beast.

"Faster!" the Angenen shouted in his mechanical voice.

Kiwanuka watched the ship's monitor and held her breath. The plasma slowed or the ship picked up speed. She wasn't certain which, but *Kequaem's Needle* gradually outpaced the burning mass.

When it became apparent that they'd outrun the threat, cheers from soldiers and ship's crew swelled to deafening thunder.

Veug had to repeat himself twice to be heard. "Staff Sergeant, I found that piece of DawnStar's space station you wanted. Looks like it's intact."

Kiwanuka stared at the tumbling mass of the space station's corpse sailing through space. "Give the coordinates to the pilot."

And let's hope that hangar isn't empty.

FORTY-EIGHT

Colonel Halladay stood in front of the monitors displaying the rampant destruction going on in low orbit around Makaum. He still had access to some of the comm sats out there, but as the Phrenorian gunships hunted them down, those numbers were dwindling quickly.

Actually, the Phrenorians hunted everything out there.

And there wasn't anything Halladay could do about it. Fort York didn't have a space wing by design and by treaty. Having the hangar on the DawnStar Space Station had been a stretch, but the argument had been made that troops and supplies had to get carried to the planet's surface somehow.

Storm clouds covered the battles that took place in the streets. Soldiers and civilians died in the mud the hammering rain drummed up and sluiced across the plascrete road surfaces. The rain was a blessing, though. The Phrenorians hadn't been able to field their power-suits and tracked vehicles quite so easily.

But when the storm lifted, another was poised to break.

As Halladay watched and waited for a response from Terran Military Command, he tracked the screens' destruction in space as well as on the ground. The Phrenorians would be coming for the fort soon, and there was no way they could hold it.

The best they could hope for was getting the people out of harm's way. Most of them were gone now, fled into the jungle they'd fought to get out of for so long.

Halladay felt bad about that. He'd made a promise to himself and the Makaum people that he would make things better while he was there. Even against General Whitcomb's passive restraints.

Thinking of the general hurt. Halladay had seen vid footage from HUDs of soldiers who had gone to the general's office to attempt to get Whitcomb to safety. The general's office had taken a nearly direct hit from one of the Phrenorian gunships. Flames had swelled up in the office only briefly, then they extinguished as all the air in the room was blown out in a rush. The general had gone out into space with the debris, and the soldier's HUD stopped recording only seconds later.

Later, if he was still alive, Halladay knew he would mourn his commanding officer. He and the general had been together too long for his death not to leave a mark. Even if they had ended up in different places after the assignment to Makaum, there was no forgetting those early years together and all the hardships they'd faced.

The screen showing the encrypted comm from Terran Military Command blinked for attention. It was the response he'd been waiting thirty-four minutes for due to the Gated wormwave transmissions. Even with all the tech, there was unpreventable lag in communications.

Instead of a canned response, though, TMC sent an interactive real-time broadcast. That was risky because the encryption wasn't as tight on real time.

Then again, the least of their worries under present conditions was cyber sec. They were losing space, the sprawl, and on the verge of losing the fort.

And all the soldiers.

The fort morgue held several dead now, soldiers and Makaum citizens and offworlder traders, and the mobile med units fleeing through the jungle were fighting for the lives of others.

General John Rackham stood straight and squared away in a black dress uniform covered in medals. His gray hair was cut high and tight and he wore his scars proudly. He was a legend in the Terran military. He was an excellent soldier and a superb tactician. "Colonel Halladay, I'm sorry we're meeting in the middle of this."

He was also a budding politician.

Halladay saluted the man, had it returned, and hit parade rest like he'd been doing it all his life. Because he had.

"Thank you for your interest, General Rackham."

"My interest always has been and always will be in our soldiers, Colonel." Rackham looked around.

Halladay knew the man was surveying his own screens relaying the vid from Makaum's near-space. His presence at Fort York Tactical Command existed only as an overlay at his end of the connection.

Halladay held back his impatience. He needed to know what was being done. His people were out there dying. The constant barrage of explosions underscored that. "Thank you, sir."

"Your chances of holding on to that fort are nil, Colonel," Rackham said. "I'm hereby ordering you to strike our colors and find some way to survive until we can get help to you."

"Help is coming, sir?" Halladay asked that even though he knew he wasn't supposed to. It had been a reflex.

"I mean for that to happen," Rackham said. "I've said my piece to the Terran Alliance diplomats, and I've pointed out that the Phrenorians are acting on bad faith and their own subterfuge to seize that planet." He paused. "Unfortunately, politics don't move as quickly as battle conditions. They're going to drag it out until every diplomatic way of putting an end to this is explored. That's a direct quote."

Halladay only just kept himself civil. "They saw the vid of the attack on Zhoh GhiCemid? They know that was arranged by Zhoh's own father-in-law?"

"The Phrenorians have another term for it," Rackham said. "One not nearly so endearing. Blaold Oldawe is a Phrenorian politician. He knows how to lie and deny with the best of them."

"The assassin, Sytver Morlortai, confirmed the contract."

"I know that, Colonel, but take a breath and understand the council members aren't going to immediately accept the word of an assassin who has been more or less invisible. *We* barely have a jacket on him."

"Uncle Huang—"

"I've had dealings with Uncle Huang myself," Rackham said. "When we were both younger men. I trust him, but I know he works mostly for his own and his family's benefit."

"Sergeant Kiwanuka risked her life to get that vid to us."

"I know." Rackham's voice softened. "I hope that she's still alive." His gaze drifted across the feeds that Halladay wasn't privy to.

Looking at all the debris strung in space in low planet orbit, Halladay didn't know how that would be possible. But he didn't dare voice that. Saying it out loud would only give the grim possibility weight.

"What about the confession Quass Leghef elicited from Throzath?" Halladay asked.

A faint smile pulled at Rackham's lips. "If the chance should ever present itself, Colonel, I'd very much like to meet that woman. She reminds me of my mother's sister."

"Help me save her," Halladay said, "and these people, and I'll make that happen."

"I'm trying, but I have to be honest. A lot of the council members weren't happy with the Quass's threats. There were rumblings of coercion circling the room."

"There was no other way to get that confession," Halladay said.

The image of the Quass holding the knife and the timber of her voice as she pulled Throzath under her control still floated through his mind. He'd been fully engaged himself, because he hadn't known what the outcome was until he had finished viewing the vid.

"Agreed," Rackham said, "but you're dealing with a lot of politicos who've never held a Roley outside of a public relations fluff piece. They don't like the fact that wars tend to be bloody and messy."

"What about the fortress?" Halladay demanded. "All of the stockpiled weapons?"

Rackham sighed. "Unfortunately, with everything going on during that op, there wasn't much to see. I sold what we had long and hard, Colonel. We just have to wait and see."

Halladay struggled to keep himself from cursing. When he had control of himself, he spoke in a measured voice. "I'll make sure we keep sending vid as long as we can, General. At the least, maybe Charlie Company and Makaum can serve as the catalyst to make the Terran Alliance take a harder line with the Phrenorian Empire."

"Martyrs, Colonel?"

"I'd rather be considered a martyr than collateral damage, sir."

Rackham nodded. "Get yourself out of there, Colonel. Let me see what I can do here."

Halladay resisted the impulse to tell the man to hurry. "Yes sir." He saluted a final time and broke the connection.

Then he turned his attention to the screens and his troop placement, and tried to find some way to shore up Charlie Company's retreat.

Intel Room F
Command Post
Fort York
0642 Hours Zulu Time

Guilt stung Leghef as she sat in front of the computer workstation. Her people were dying in the streets she had helped fund and design.

And she had bullied a boy to the point that she had broken him and knew that he would never again be the same.

She knew that was a necessary thing to attempt to help her people survive the villainy perpetrated by the Phrenorians. But she'd hated her part in all of it. It was something that would haunt her for a long time. Maybe she would never be the same again either.

Working swiftly, she sent messages out to her people and guided them to the groups of Terran soldiers who waited to escort them into the jungle. Most of her people knew about the dangers in the jungle and the paths through it, but they weren't equipped or trained to combat the Phrenorians the way the Terran soldiers were.

Together, she hoped, the two groups would find a way to survive.

Then what? she asked herself.

If the Terran military was unable to give her people the asylum she'd asked for, if the Alliance didn't intercede diplomatically or allow the Terran military to enter the battle, there would be nothing left of Makaum except lives of servitude.

The prospect was unbearable.

The door behind her opened and surprised her. She'd been told it was heavily locked and there were guards posted there to protect her. She turned and looked at the door.

One of the soldiers held the door open for Keladra, and Leghef knew immediately something had gone drastically wrong. Her first thought was that Pekoz had succumbed to his injuries. Then she noticed the bruises on her friend's face.

Leghef waved the soldiers away so that she could speak to her friend in private.

After they had gone, Keladra broke down and cried. Her shoulders shook and tears fell from her dark green eyes. "I am so, *so* sorry," she whispered hoarsely.

Anxiety and confusion threaded through Leghef. She took her friend's hands in her own. "What has happened?"

Keladra looked up at Leghef and struggled to speak. "It's Tholak," she whispered. "He broke into my house, beat Pekoz into unconsciousness, and he has taken Telilu. If you don't come and bring Throzath with you, he will kill Telilu."

Leghef focused on her breathing and forced her mind to operate. Nothing could happen to Telilu. She wouldn't allow it.

She *couldn't* allow it.

"Where is my granddaughter?" she asked.

Tears filled Keladra's eyes. "She's being held out somewhere near Rilormang."

Leghef's heart hurt and her knees weakened and almost went out from under her. "Tholak would not have taken her there." She almost couldn't get the words out.

Rilormang was the First City, the place where the Makaum people learned they had to work together if they wanted to survive. No one went there anymore. Leghef had last seen the place when she was young and traveling with her father taking meat. The dead city still haunted her dreams on occasion.

"Tholak didn't take your granddaughter to that foul place, Quass. He only told the Phrenorians about it. They took her there, and they wait for you."

For the briefest instant, Leghef thought of telling Halladay what had happened. But she knew she wouldn't be allowed.

"I was told," Keladra choked out, "that if the Terrans should accompany you there, your granddaughter's head will be left on the Lorald Stone."

"Then I will go alone," Leghef said. Even as she said

that, she felt certain she and her granddaughter would most likely not live through the situation. But not going was unthinkable.

"With Throzath."

Leghef nodded. "As you say."

Hesitantly, Keladra hugged her, then pulled back. "A group of Tholak's men wait outside, Quass. You will need to go with them. Wear your cloak. The storms have come."

Leghef stepped away from the other woman and walked toward the door.

The soldiers posted outside the door stared at her.

"I am leaving," she said.

"But Colonel Halladay—" one of them said.

"The colonel doubtless has his hands full," Leghef said, and drew upon her diplomatic prowess to brook no argument. "I need to attend to my people. I have done all that the colonel has asked of me. Now I need to go."

"Ma'am," the other soldier said, "meaning no disrespect, but it's dangerous out there."

"I have a group of my people waiting for me outside. I will be fine." Leghef looked at the soldiers. "You are risking more than I am. I'm not a combatant in this confrontation. As Quass, I'll be a valuable prize for the Phrenorians. You and I—and Colonel Halladay— know that. I'll head into the jungle to join my people. When I am safe, I will let the colonel know where to find me."

The soldier was silent for a moment, then said, "The colonel wants to talk to you."

"Quass." Halladay's voice came from a speaker on the soldier's armor.

Leghef assumed the armor had pick-up as well as broadcasting abilities. "Colonel, my mind is made up.

You and I both have things to do and people who are waiting on us to lead them. Talking with me regarding my decision will only waste time for us both. Time that we don't have. Can you understand that?"

"Yes, ma'am." Halladay didn't sound happy.

"You would have evacuated me from the fort soon anyway," Leghef said. "I'm only leaving ahead of you throwing me out. Would you rather I fight you to stay here? With my people who have been wounded? Instead of trusting you and your med staff to care for them?"

"No."

Leghef drew a breath and pushed away her fear for Telilu. "Neither would I. So release Throzath to my custody so I can get him out of this place as well."

"Are you certain you want to do that?"

"I am."

"Then I'll clear the way."

Leghef steeled herself and gave away none of the anxiety that coursed through her. She had gambled a lot over the years as the Quass. She knew how to keep herself centered and let no one see her secret self.

"Thank you for everything you've done, Colonel," she said. "I wish you all the best, and I hope to see you again."

"Yes, ma'am. And thank you. It has been a privilege serving with you."

Leghef took her leave then because she didn't want to have to trust her voice anymore. The thought of Telilu in Tholak's hands, in the clutches of the callous Phrenorians, was too much to bear. She had to go to her, and it took everything in her power not to run for the nearest exit.

FORTY-NINE

Kequaem's Needle
En Route to DawnStar Space Station (remnant)
Makaum Space
0646 Hours Zulu Time

They found us again!" Wiyntan yelled from the helm.

Several of the Terran military soldiers sitting on the bridge's deck were joined by Turit, Daus, Darrantia, and Honiban in creatively cursing the Phrenorians once more chasing them.

Morlortai sat hunched over slightly in his command chair and rocked as the ship's pilot took evasive action. Blue-white plasma blasts blazed through space only meters away.

He tracked the monitor at the front of the ship and glanced at the views of the pursuing Phrenorian gunship provided by the rear vids and their three surviving drones. Primitive fear quivered inside Morlortai, something he hadn't let touch him in a long time, not since he'd quit Fenipal to find a life out among the stars.

"Don't let them catch us," Morlortai advised.

Wiyntan snorted and cursed, then she juked around the broken, slowly spinning remains of a space freighter. Plasma bursts from the Phrenorian ship's forward guns slagged the dead husk of the ship as they ducked behind it.

"Our engines are failing!" the pilot warned. "They've taken too much damage for as hard as I'm pushing them! They're not going to last much longer!"

Morlortai knew that. The ship—their home—was dying around them. Every unaccustomed vibration that quivered through the bridge, every scream of tortured metal, told him that.

"We can't do anything if the engines blow!" Wiyntan yelled.

"If they do," Morlortai said, "we probably won't have to worry about it for long."

Wiyntan screamed in frustration, kept plotting new courses, and pushed the ship till the roar of the engines filled the bridge. When she was desperate, though she hated it and wouldn't admit it, she was in her element. She was the best pilot under pressure Morlortai had ever seen.

"Shields are at seventeen percent and dropping," Honiban said. As usual, his voice was calm. In the years Morlortai had known the man, Honiban had seldom been anything other than composed and collected.

Morlortai nodded but said nothing. There was nothing he could do about the coming failure of the shields except to hope they held together long enough to see them clear.

Another plasma blast struck them and *Kequaem's Needle* jerked from the impact. Morlortai tightened his grip on the seat's armrests and hung on.

"Thirteen percent," Honiban said.

Wiyntan screamed more curses and plotted another course. Despite her best efforts, the distance between them and the pursuit craft kept dropping. The Phrenorian was just too fast.

Morlortai looked at Sergeant Kiwanuka. "You still have a lock on that hangar?"

"We do," Kiwanuka answered tensely.

She was afraid, Morlortai knew. She had to be. Anyone with common sense would be. But she didn't show it. She also didn't hide behind her faceshield. It was open and her face was there for all to see. She looked calm and collected, like everything was totally under her control.

He decided he would hate to play cards against her.

Before Morlortai could ask how far away their objective was, Wiyntan screamed with glee.

"There it is!"

Shifting his gaze back to the forward monitor, Morlortai spotted the huge section of space station dead ahead of them. He tapped his keyboard and pulled up the dimensions of the wreckage. It measured 1187.3 meters on its longest axis, 481.2 meters at its widest, and was 78.5 meters in height. The DawnStar Space Station had been the biggest he'd ever been on. The corp had lost trillions of credits during the attack. Not to mention the staff, guests, and other businesses.

Morlortai was surprised the Phrenorians hadn't already used the large section for target practice.

"I see the docking bay!" Wiyntan called out excitedly. "It's open, though." As quickly as it had come, her excitement vanished. "All of those dropships are probably floating somewhere in space."

"The docking bay being open to space won't matter," Kiwanuka said. "The dropships will be anchored to the deck."

"They're probably all scrap," Wiyntan said.

"All we need is one," Kiwanuka replied.

Kequaem's Needle jerked again as the Phrenorian hit them with another plasma burst.

"A dropship isn't going to be able to take on a Phrenorian gunship," Wiyntan said.

"We're not going to face off with them," Kiwanuka said. "We're going to outlast and outrun them. Those Sting-Tail gunships can't enter a gravity well. If they do, they'll break into pieces. Once we hit Makaum's atmosphere, we're home free. They can't follow."

Morlortai knew it wasn't going to be that easy, but he liked hearing Kiwanuka say it that way.

"Except for the Phrenorians on the ground," Ny'age said. "And that's if we make it safely to a landing."

Wiyntan slipped around more debris as she shot toward the space station remnant. Several pieces of debris floated in front of the docking bay.

"Clear the way!" Wiyntan shouted. "Clear the way!"

Turit and Ny'age shifted their focus from the Phrenorian gunship behind them to the large, spinning sections of ship and space station debris speeding through space on an interception course with *Kequaem's Needle*. Under their attacks, the wreckage broke into smaller pieces.

As Wiyntan zipped into an approach path, she warned, "This is going to be rough."

Rectangular crosshairs formed on the forward monitor. They shrank and fell in on themselves and showed the flight path into the docking area.

Another plasma blast rocked *Kequaem's Needle*.

"I can't slow down much," Wiyntan said. "If I do, we're going to get dusted by the Phrenorians. And if I hit that docking bay wrong, we'll smash across that section like a bug against a transplas screen. I also have to time the spin just right."

Morlortai didn't say anything. Wiyntan was talking to herself in order to stay relaxed. He held on to the armrests and watched the hangar section fill the monitor till he knew there was no turning back.

Just as they were about to slip inside, the Phrenorian fired again. *Kequaem's Needle* jostled just enough to bump into the docking bay opening. Metal shrilled inside the bridge compartment.

The soldiers who weren't belted down in seats were thrown forward. They tumbled past the helm and smashed up against the monitor.

Stabilized in the seat, Morlortai almost cried out because the belts cut into him. *Kequaem's Needle* slammed into two anchored dropships and veered off in another direction just ahead of a plasma bolt that lit up the darkened interior of the hangar in a cascade of blue-white light for a few seconds.

Skidding, throwing sparks that died quickly in the vacuum that existed inside the hangar, the ship rammed into another dropship and came to a sudden, painful stop.

Then full darkness filled the hangar again.

Kequaem's Needle's interior lights went out and Morlortai knew the ship's generator and power supply were destroyed. The ship was now an empty shell and didn't offer any real protection.

Morlortai struggled to take a breath and couldn't. He hit the release on the belts, but they were jammed and didn't disconnect.

"Warning!" the ship's near-AI broadcasted. "Hull breach! Hull breach! Unavoidable oxygen loss occurring now! Get into safety suits! Warning!"

Morlortai was already in his protective suit. He just needed his helmet. As the air inside the command center grew thin, he calmed the fear that filled him and reached to the side of the command chair to grab the helmet. His fingers brushed the helmet but he couldn't reach it.

He tried to call out to Turit or one of his crew, but there wasn't enough air to fill his lungs. The cold from space bit into his exposed flesh. He tried for the helmet again, tried to free himself from the straps, but it was all to no avail. He was trapped in the darkness with the Phrenorian gunship still nearby.

Fort York Airspace
0713 Hours Zulu Time

"Master Sergeant." The tension in Blue Jay 12's voice was palpable even over the jumpcopter's roaring engines.

"Go, Blue Jay 12," Sage responded.

"We're a no-go on landing on a helipad. All of those are either in ruins or are under heavy attack. Colonel's orders are to ignore them, and I'm in agreement with him."

"Copy that," Sage replied, "but you've got to find somewhere to put us out. Up here, we're deadweight and not earning our keep. We need to get into the fight."

"Roger that. When we get you guys off, we've got work to do too. For as long as we're able."

The jumpcopter juked hard left just ahead of a spray of anti-aircraft flak that burst in the air only a few meters away. Shrapnel peppered the jumpcopter's re-inforced plasteel sides with sharp pings.

Sage understood the pilot's fears. He sat in the open jumpcopter doorway as the aircraft streaked across the sky. Below them, under a patchy cloud of black smoke from explosions, not the rain that fell in torrents, Fort York was undermanned and under siege. A staggered line held back the Phrenorians.

Smoking craters dotted the landscape inside and outside the fort's walls. Downed powersuits, Phrenorian and Terran military, sprawled on cracked plascrete streets or were buried in rubble of what used to be homes and buildings.

Dead and wounded citizens, soldiers, and merchants lay in careless abandon in the no-man's-land that existed between the Phrenorian front and the line drawn by the Terran defenders. That space was visibly shrinking, filled with rocket fire from aircraft and TAVs.

Groups of Makaum people and offworld traders sprinted across the deadly patch of ground, but most of them tried for end runs around the combatants.

The survivors all heading in the same direction told Sage the Phrenorians were offering no mercy during the battle. If someone stood in front of the Sting-Tails in battle, that person died. They weren't holding back.

The screaming debris shooting down from the destroyed space stations and ships that got trapped in Makaum's gravity were killed impartially.

A salvo of rockets slammed into the fort's front gates. Bubbles of flames lashed out around them. Two soldiers in powersuits fell back from their positions and were immediately strafed by Phrenorian aircraft.

Some of the old fear from Sage's childhood dawned inside him again. He'd been helpless then, his arms wrapped around his mother as he tried to protect her while she did the same for him.

He shook off the memory and centered himself. He couldn't fight that war, but he could fight this one.

"Master Sergeant," Blue Jay 12 called.

"Go," Sage replied.

"I've got a spot where we can put down without drawing too much enemy fire."

"Show me."

Instantly, a GPS pin dropped onto Sage's faceplate and marked the prospective landing zone in the middle of an offworlder market that was already entrenched in flames despite the heavy rain.

"Not exactly luxury accommodations," the jumpcopter pilot apologized.

"Any port in a storm, Lieutenant." Sage shifted and sent the information to the rest of his team. He addressed them over the unit frequency. "Once we hit dirt, we fight our way to the fort. Every Phrenorian that's in your way gets put down as quick and as hard as you can."

"Copy that, Master Sergeant." Culpepper was busy with the leftover explosives the team had. Pingasa was helping.

"Ready?" Blue Jay 12 asked.

"Roger that." Sage held on and the jumpcopter slid sideways as it lost altitude and dove toward the stricken marketplace.

The aircraft shuddered and skipped as much from the strain it was going through as from the explosions taking place all around them.

The dizzying descent ended in a blast of thruster fire that slammed a wave of mud and small debris against the nearby buildings. Most of the structures lay in pieces. Goods lay out in the open, thoroughly drenched by the rain.

Sage dropped from the jumpcopter as it hovered centimeters above the ground. Ripples skated across the surfaces of nearby puddles despite the pounding rain. His boots sank into the soft earth that had flowed onto the broken plascrete.

Bright green leaves and roots showed in the cracks. The war had started only a little more than an hour ago, and already the planet worked to reclaim land it had grudgingly given up to the Makaum people and the offworlders.

If everything gets destroyed, if everybody dies, Sage thought bitterly, *the Green Hell is going to flourish.*

He turned to the soldiers as they gathered around him. "All right, then. Some of you haven't seen real combat before. Well, you're about to get a look at it up close and personal. So stay together, keep your heads on a swivel, and follow orders."

Their response was immediate, brave and scared and hopeful all at the same time.

Sage assigned Culpepper to take the lead and they ran in single file through the fallen buildings toward where the detonations were loudest.

FIFTY

M ove out!" Kiwanuka released the magnetic fields in her gloves that held her to two of her soldiers who hadn't been safely belted in. She pushed herself up from her seat and scanned the bridge. "Goldberg, get a team and get the civilians out of here!"

"Copy that, Staff Sergeant," Goldberg responded.

Her green-limned silhouette showed on Kiwanuka's faceshield.

"Existing light amplification only," Kiwanuka ordered. "No external illumination. We don't want to advertise to the Sting-Tails that we're still alive until we're ready to evacuate."

She swept the bridge with her gaze and spotted Morlortai struggling in his command chair. He wasn't wearing his helmet and his belts hadn't released.

She cursed and raced over to the assassin as her soldiers guided the rest of the ship's crew out *Kequaem's Needle*'s emergency exit. She located his helmet and jammed it onto his suit. It locked into place immediately and hopefully breathable onboard air pumped into the vacuum.

There was no time to wait and see. He'd live or die and she couldn't do anything more at the moment. She picked up Morlortai and threw him across her shoulders in a fireman's carry. Once she had the exit located, she hurried through it.

"I've got a dropship back here that looks solid," Goldberg announced.

A crimson GPS pin dropped onto Kiwanuka's faceshield. She turned in that direction and followed the green figures ahead of her.

"It's locked!" Goldberg yelled.

"Veug," Kiwanuka said. She swayed around an overturned dropship, caught herself before she fell, and kept going.

"I've got this, Staff Sergeant," the elint specialist answered.

By the time Kiwanuka ran past broken and slagged dropships to reach the one Goldberg had found, Veug was already working on the dropship's security system. Those systems weren't overly complicated, primarily there to keep unauthorized personnel, usually bored soldiers, from joyriding, which had happened. The dropships didn't need tough security because they were usually filled to the brim with Terran military soldiers outside of a hangar.

"Got it!" Veug stepped back and pressed a keypad on the dropship's side.

The cargo hatch opened.

"Get in," Kiwanuka ordered.

Her HUD showed her the Phrenorian gunship jockeying for position at the open bay door.

Warning, the near-AI said. *Hostile is scanning surrounding environment.*

Kiwanuka followed her troops inside the dropship and laid Morlortai on the deck in front of Goldberg. "He was asphyxiating when I found him. If he's alive, keep him that way."

"Copy that, Staff Sergeant." Goldberg dropped to her knees beside Morlortai, who was already showing signs of coming around.

"Veug."

"Yes, Staff Sergeant."

"Get us locked down and pressurize this cabin." That was in case Goldberg had to perform medical procedures that weren't covered by Morlortai's suit.

"Copy that." Veug crossed over to the cabin controls, switched on lights on either side of his helmet, and set to work.

Low light filled the cabin and indicators near the air vents turned green. Environmental systems were set up to run off batteries, not just the dropship's generator.

Kiwanuka made her way up to the front of the dropship. The two cargo ship pilots who had delivered the team to *Kequaem's Needle* at the beginning of the mission hustled into the ship's cockpit ahead of her. Kiwanuka was at their heels.

"Strap in!" one of the pilots bellowed.

Both of them pressed buttons and flicked toggles on the complicated array in front of them to bring the dropship's engines online.

Kiwanuka took the small navigator's seat behind the pilot's and copilot's seats.

"This isn't going to be pretty," the pilot said. "Or by the book."

"If we survive and get down to Fort York," Kiwanuka said, "I'm going to mark it as a win."

"Copy that," the pilot said.

The ship's thrusts came on immediately. The pilot engaged the drive.

"That Sting-Tail pilot knows we're in here," the co-pilot said.

As if in response, the Phrenorian gunship opened fire. Plasma bolts and nuclear-tipped rockets ripped through the dropships still anchored to the deck. Explosions threw brief fire all around them and buffeted the dropship.

"Corporal Veug," the pilot called over the comm.

"Yes, Lieutenant," Veug answered.

"Have you accessed that emergency release?"

Kiwanuka resisted asking what they were talking about. On the monitor, the Phrenorian's bombardment hammered dropships. The reinforced armor glowed cherry-red and ablative armor blew off in chunks. Two of them nearby remained only as broken stumps of the spacecraft they had been.

"Got it now, Lieutenant," Veug assured her.

"Decouple," the pilot ordered.

"Decoupling now."

At first Kiwanuka didn't know what Veug had done or what the pilot had been talking about. Then the dropships on the various monitors available to the dropship showed the other dropships floating up from the deck. The docking clamps holding them in place had opened. The dropship containing the *Kequaem's Needle*'s crew and the soldiers lifted from the deck as well.

Immediately, the pilot engaged the thrusters. The dropship shot forward and banged into the two dropships in front of it, which collided with four or five more dropships. By the time they reached the bay doors, the pilot was pushing at least a dozen of the boxy spacecraft out into the black void at the Phrenorian gunship.

The Sting-Tail pilot fired his weapons. Hit by plasma bolts and rockets, the empty dropships bounced like billiard balls on a well-executed break. Driven forward, deflected by the Phrenorian gunship's weapons, the unpiloted dropships ricocheted in several directions. Another barrage altered their paths and increased their speed, adding to the confusion.

"I wouldn't have thought of something like this," Kiwanuka said. "I guess it's worked before or you wouldn't be here."

The pilot juked the dropship in a fair imitation of the other dropships. Uncertain which target was truly the one he was looking for, the Phrenorian fired at everything that lit up his targeting software.

"How many times do you think someone would get caught out like this?" the pilot asked in disbelief. "This is my first time. I grew up on a ranch in Arizona and have seen cattle stampede. Let's just hope it works."

Once the vessel reached the outskirts of the expanding knot of dropships, the pilot kicked in the large thrusters and headed directly for Makaum through a minefield of debris.

Outside Fort York
0728 Hours Zulu Time

"This way. Hurry."

The gruff man who addressed Leghef was one of Tholak's men. Usually he stood as a bodyguard for Tholak. Today, she supposed, the man served as a kidnapper.

He and three other men, all dressed in offworlder

armor, stood beside a battered crawler covered in mud that sluiced away under the driving rain. Several dents showed in the crawler's armor and Leghef knew it had been near at least one firefight.

They'd waited at the back of the fort for Throzath and her to arrive, away from the battle lines that had been drawn. Most of the Terran soldiers were busy holding the fort against the Phrenorian forces.

"I told you my father would come," Throzath growled at her. He limped at her side.

Leghef made a show of looking around. "Where is he?"

Throzath cursed her and sped past her as he headed for the armored crawler. Once there, he slipped inside.

Around them, crowds of Makaum people and off-worlders ran for the shelter they thought the surrounding jungle offered. The women and children screamed in fear, and some of the men did too. Others howled curses and hurled threats at the Terrans and the Phrenorians.

All of them ran.

Leghef pitied them. Most of them were not hunters and had seldom gone so deeply into the jungle as they were headed now. Staying and entering the jungle without proper training and provisions both offered death.

A group of offworlders spotted Tholak's men loading onto the crawler.

"You there!" the biggest of the group shouted. "Give us that woman!"

The demand surprised Leghef until she recognized Garendy and Tindrau, two hunters who had chosen to work with the Phrenorians as guides and consultants, walking behind the offworlders.

"That's not going to happen," the man in charge of Tholak's group said. Leghef thought she remembered his name was Osler.

The offworlder brandished a weapon and raised it to point at Osler.

One of Osler's men shot the man in the head with the rifle he held. Without pause, even as the dead off-worlder fell, the man shot two more of the group but failed to kill them. Tindrau went down with a bullet in his shoulder.

The offworlders turned and ran. They left their dead comrade behind in the mud. Garendy helped Tindrau get to his feet and run. The crowds flowing around Leghef and her captors gave them a wide berth.

Leghef looked back at the fort and her city, took in all the damage that had been done, and knew that her people would never be the same again. They'd all lived their lives as though the jungles held the most danger.

That wasn't true.

A large mass screamed from the heavens and slammed into the ground and a group of people a hundred meters or more away. Mud, broken trees, shattered bushes, and corpses erupted from the impact area in a wave that fell only twenty meters short of Leghef and her captors.

For a moment, emptiness rang in her ears and she realized she'd gone deaf from the thunder of the explosion.

An armored hand closed around her upper arm with bruising force and yanked her into motion.

The man, Osler, she thought, shoved her into the crawler's rear seat. He sat on one side of her and another man sat on the other side of her. They were there to ensure she didn't get away.

Leghef had no intention of getting away. Not until she was taken to her granddaughter. Once she had Telilu, things would be different. She stared ahead as the crawler chewed through the mud and headed into the jungle as the war raged around them.

Under her silks, she held on to the comm Halladay had given her to use while she was at the fort. She didn't know what kind of range the device had, but it was military issue and she hoped that meant it would transmit for a long distance.

Tholak would be far away from the battles now.

More rockets screamed into Fort York. A few exploded in the air, but several wreaked havoc on the structures within the protective walls.

Leghef hoped, when the time came, if it came, that there would be someone left to respond to her call for help.

FIFTY-ONE

Zhoh caught a flicker of movement coming from an offworlder bodega to his right. Two of his warriors on his strike team, all ten of them working on a door-to-door sweep with him, closed in on the building as part of the effort to herd the fleeing populace back toward Fort York where they would become a human barrier Zhoh intended to use against the Terran military. No beings remained alive behind his warriors who weren't loyal to the Phrenorian Empire.

Zhoh intended to take no chances on subversive elements striking his warriors from behind. Even friendly elements among the Makaum people and the offworlders hoping to strike a bargain were chased into the jungle.

They would return. Or he and his men would bring them back and enslave them.

The lead Phrenorian warrior closed on the bodega fearlessly. A moment later, an offworlder male with a portable Kimer particle beam cannon filled a shattered window. Before the warrior could move, the particle beam blast spread his remains over his partner.

The second Phrenorian warrior tried to dodge and fire at the same time. His blast ripped up pieces of the window frame and hurled goods over the beings inside the building.

Another male fired two rounds from a Kerch burster. Both shrapnel loads struck the warrior and knocked him down. Blood covered him as he tried to rise, but his strength failed him and he fell in the mud.

Zhoh swung his rifle over to aim at the bodega.

Inside the building, another being stepped forward with a Yqueu rocket launcher snugged over one shoulder and aimed into the center of Zhoh's squad.

"Take cover!" Zhoh ordered his warriors.

The group broke formation and sought cover among the overturned vehicles, a large portion of what appeared to be the burned wreckage of a cargo ship that had fallen from space, and other buildings.

Zhoh threw himself behind an overturned cart only a few meters to his left. The primitive vehicle was hitched to the bloody corpses of two *dafeerorg*. Zhoh settled in beside one of them and tried to ignore the acrid stench of the beasts. He didn't know if they smelled worse dead or alive.

The rocket detonated against the cart and the *dafeerorg*. Pieces of the animals and the vehicle blew over Zhoh. Bloody debris and mud covered him.

"Help me," a weak voice cried out in the aftermath of the explosion.

Three meters away, a young Makaum male lay bleeding in the mud. He stretched an arm toward Zhoh. One

of the being's eyes was filled with blood and a flap of
flesh hung from one cheek.

Ignoring the wounded being, Zhoh rose up and
brought his rifle to bear on the bodega. Sheltering
inside the structure wasn't logical. It was one of the
plascrete buildings that had been quickly extruded onto
the site and filled with trade goods.

He fired plasma blasts at the windows and ran toward
the door. Without being told, his warriors provided
suppressive fire to cover his attack.

When he reached the door, he raised a leg and kicked.
It didn't move. Cursing, he reached into his tactical
vest with one of his secondaries and located a shaped
charge. He armed it, slapped it onto the door, and spun
to the side as the beings inside tried to target him with
their beam and projectile weapons. He grabbed another
shaped charge.

The resulting explosion scattered plasteel shards
in front of the bodega, but most of them were driven
inside. Pained screams and curses immediately followed.

Zhoh slung his rifle and drew his pistol. He rounded
on the door, kicked the superheated wreckage out of his
way, and fired at everything inside that moved. A few
beams and projectiles struck him, but his chitin and
armor turned them away.

Two of his warriors followed him inside. They joined
their attacks with his. Eight beings had taken cover
inside the bodega. None of them remained alive.

One of the warriors drew his *patimong* and chopped
the head from one of the dead beings. When he had
the head free, he shoved a slim dagger through the
head's ears, pulled the cord through after it, and tied
the head to his combat harness. The head swung there
and smeared the warrior's thighs with blood.

Zhoh stared at the warrior.

"It is a battle trophy, General Zhoh," the young warrior said. His pheromones were strong over the stink of blood and munitions. "One of my first kills."

Zhoh knew others among his warriors, those who had never been in battle before and those who had more pride than honor, were taking trophies. Tomorrow he would put an end to that. But today he would let it go.

But not without remark.

"Watch yourself, Rilb," Zhoh admonished. "Take care that you don't become overzealous in acquiring your trophies. Collect too many heads and they will become baggage that can get you killed. And if the procurement of one of your collections slows you or causes you to become inattentive, I will kill you myself."

Rilb turned his primaries outward in supplication. "I understand, General. I will be careful. I will not fail you."

Zhoh turned and walked out of the building.

Phrenorian aircars and gunships warred in the slate-gray sky against Terran military jumpcopters. As he stepped out onto the street, a ground-based rocket attack from a block over turned an aircar into an orange and black fireball that smashed into a half-demolished offworlder trade building. The plasteel and plascrete structure fragmented and toppled into the street below.

Zhoh triangulated the location of the ground attack and marked it on his HUD.

Others among his warriors now had heads of humans, Makaum, and other aliens tied to their combat harnesses. The street stank of bloodlust pheromones, and breathing it made Zhoh fill heady.

"General," Mato called over the private frequency he shared with Zhoh. Mato rode in one of the large tracked vehicles and managed small ops that followed Zhoh's battle plan.

Zhoh strode across the street to where the wounded Makaum male lay writhing. "Tell me you have found Sage."

The rage at the loss of the fortress and all its war machines still beat within Zhoh. The way those weapons had been accumulated was dishonorable to the Empire, but they had been his until Sage had destroyed them. Zhoh cursed Rangha, but he recognized Sage's skill and integrity. The Terran master sergeant was an accomplished opponent.

Zhoh intended to kill Sage and take his head. His skull would adorn Zhoh's home in a place of honor.

"I have not been able to find out Sage's exact location," Mato said.

Zhoh curbed an angry response. Given all the tumultuous sorties taking place around him, and the fact that battle was always heated and confusing, he understood that finding Sage was difficult.

But the master sergeant would be found.

"There have been new developments," Mato said.

Zhoh looked down at the wounded Makaum male. Both of the being's legs had been blown off. Shrapnel injuries covered his back. The being would be of no use as a laborer.

Zhoh slipped a knife free of his combat harness and drove it through the being's eyes, ruining the skull so none of his warriors would be tempted to take it.

Zhoh wiped his knife clean of the dead being's blood. "What developments?"

"A story is circulating about the assassination attempt on you." Mato sounded hesitant.

"What story?"

"A recording of a Fenipalan assassin admitting he tried to kill you."

"The Terrans hired this being?" Zhoh considered that and he immediately didn't like where his thoughts took him. "They have their own snipers, just as we do."

"According to the assassin's confession, the Terrans didn't hire him."

That gave Zhoh pause. The whole attack on the Terran military had been predicated on that attempted assassination. It had been the secondary that had connected to the primary. That assumed guilt on part of the Terran military had kept the Alliance out of the Makaum situation.

If that attack were not perpetrated by Sage or another of the Fort York personnel, would that change the Alliance's stance in the matter?

Uncertainty planted a small seed within Zhoh and he didn't like it.

"Does this assassin say who did hire him?" Zhoh asked.

"Yes," Mato answered. "There are even financial records that connect the assassin to his employer. I have sources within the Prime War Board that assure me this recording is being vetted to prove its veracity. After all, this could be a lie propagated by the Terrans."

That didn't make sense, though. In their own way, the Terran military was almost as honorable as a Phrenorian warrior.

"Who was the assassin's employer?" Zhoh asked.

Mato hesitated, which was unlike him, and that weakness vexed Zhoh because he knew it wasn't Mato's way. Mato was guilty of trying to withhold the information to prevent injury to Zhoh.

That was intolerable.

"The assassin was hired by Blaold Oldawe," Mato said.

Zhoh transmitted a shrill hiss over his comm. Instantly, his warriors fell into formation around him. He sent them the tracking coordinates to the site where the rocket attack had come from. The area brought them closer to the fort, and he was ready to take it on by himself if he had to.

"Triarr," Mato said, "this could all be a fabrication."

"This is something Blaold would do," Zhoh said. "If he could rid himself of me, extinguish me here, on a planet the Empire cared nothing about, it wouldn't take long till I ceased to exist. I am not *Laliwu*, not of the preferred bloodline. I am *kalque*. I have no future. I am less than the lowest *cridelrad* in their eyes."

"Not if you deliver this planet, *triarr*," Mato said. "Deliver Makaum to the Empire and you will be given a *Kabilak*. No one can take that honor or that medal from you."

"If Blaold truly hired this assassin," Zhoh said, "he has brought dishonor to himself. The Primes hold him in their favor. Just as they held Rangha in their favor. Both of them are *Laliwu*."

"Rangha is no more," Mato reminded. "And the father of your wife—"

"*Selydy*, you mean, because she is no wife to me."

"—never delivered a planet to the Empire," Mato went on. "Only a few warriors have done that. *Be* one of those warriors, *triarr*, and you will find the salvation you seek."

"I will." Zhoh picked up the pace, running toward his destiny, intent on snatching it back. "I am that warrior."

FIFTY-TWO

Sage took cover in a rubble-strewn alley and watched the huge Phrenorian tracked assault vehicle grind toward the fort. The *Taierne*-class TAV turned the plascrete streets beneath it into powder and shredded the sides of buildings it bumped up against.

The assault vehicle towered two stories tall, thirty meters long, and ten meters wide. Heavily armored and carrying an array of armament, including large particle cannons, two fore and one aft, the war machine was a dreadnought of destruction.

The constant yammering of the tracked treads filled the street and even briefly drowned out all sounds of the storm and the battles being waged around it.

The Phrenorians had fielded six of the units, none of which they were supposed to have by agreement. Sage guessed that the assault vehicles had been shipped in as some kind of equipment, either by the Sting-Tails or third-party black marketers, and reassembled in the Phrenorian Embassy because that's where they'd rolled out of.

A salvo of rockets from Fort York burned through the haze of rain that filled the air. Most of them slammed into the assault vehicle and scattered flames across the armor. At least two of the rockets missed their intended target, or ricocheted off it, and hit nearby buildings. The structures came down in tumbling ruin. However, the ablative armor covering the assault vehicle prevented it from taking anything more than cosmetic damage.

"Master Sergeant," Culpepper called.

Sage's HUD located the man one alley behind him. "I hear you, Culpepper."

"Think maybe the unit can give me and Pingasa some covering fire for a minute?"

"For what?"

"We want to try to stop this thing before it rolls right on into the fort."

"Copy that." Sage gave the command to the rest of the team and told Culpepper to signal the attack.

"Now!" Culpepper said.

Sage swung out around the corner of the building and fired gel-grenades at the Phrenorian assault vehicle. He knew they wouldn't do any good because the rockets hadn't done much damage. Thankfully, the jumpcopters had carried ammo and supplies to restock what his team had burned off shutting down the fortress.

The other soldiers peppered the war machine with weapons fire and more grenades. The small explosions cascaded across the assault vehicle and did nothing more than leave smoke that was quickly washed away in the downpour.

The war machine halted for a moment, then fired

both forward cannons. The rounds struck the building where Sage had taken shelter as well as the one on the other side of the street where Murad had his team. Chunks of plascrete and warped plasteel became missiles that knocked the armored soldiers down.

Sage flew across the alley and through the wall on the opposite side. Plascrete dust settled over him and the wreckage of the electronics goods store he'd been blown into. He struggled to get his breath back as he knocked plascrete and transplas from him and sat up. He deployed the two drones from his suit to get a better view of the street action.

Behind the war machine, a small army of Phrenorian warriors were racing to their location on foot. Sage guessed that someone aboard the assault vehicle had sent for them.

He checked on the five soldiers with him and discovered Corrigan was unconscious.

"Escobedo," Sage said, "you and Robinson transport Corrigan out of here. Find someplace to lie low till her brain's unscrambled."

"Copy that, Master Sergeant." Escobedo pulled one of Corrigan's limp arms over her shoulder as Robinson did the same.

Sage strode to the hole his team had made in the wall, marveling that the building hadn't come down on top of them, and watched as the war machine came straight at them. Evidently the pilot had decided to plow through the building.

Then Pingasa and Culpepper, identified on Sage's HUD, sprinted from the alley. They each carried a satchel charge. The assault vehicle's rear cannon swiveled to pick them up, but it was too late. Pingasa and Culpepper threw the satchel charges onto the treads as they spun up under the war machine's mudguard. The olive-drab packages vanished under the assault vehicle's skirt.

The rear cannon fired and opened a crater that could have swallowed a supply crawler in the cracked street. Pingasa and Culpepper were knocked from their feet for just an instant, then they were running away from the group of Phrenorian warriors who had just arrived.

The satchel charges under the assault vehicle's skirt exploded. One of the tracked treads broke and slapped at the war machine as it turned. The other continued to function. One broken tread was all that was needed to bring the assault vehicle to a stop.

Sage pinged the Phrenorians with a laser targeting marker beaming from his left glove. He opened a comm channel to Fort York.

"Yes, Master Sergeant." The young man at the other end of the connection sounded harried.

"Can you target a strike on my position?"

"On the assault vehicle?"

"Negative," Sage said as he pumped depleted uranium rounds into the Phrenorians. "We've stopped the assault vehicle. The Sting-Tails have mounted a squad of foot soldiers that intended to follow that assault vehicle right into the fort. I've lit them up for you."

"Copy that, Master Sergeant." The tactical officer sounded relieved. "Be advised that you have birds in the air."

Sage bellowed a warning to his troops to grab shelter. He took cover behind one of the building's fractured walls as beams and bullets chopped into the plascrete around him.

Another salvo of rockets struck the street, only this time they were on top of the Phrenorian warriors. Body parts and plascrete flew everywhere. Smoking craters occupied space where they had been.

"Target confirmed," Sage said. "Thanks for the assist."

"Thank you for taking out that assault vehicle. We couldn't make it happen."

"You can thank Pingasa and Culpepper when we get out of this," Sage said.

He ran out into the street. Some of the surviving Phrenorians continued fighting, but the battle didn't last long. All the Sting-Tails died because they wouldn't surrender. Culpepper and Pingasa clambered up the assault vehicle and tossed in explosives.

"Do you see that?" Lieutenant Murad demanded as he gazed at the dead enemy. "Do you see what they have?"

The sight of human heads strung around the waists of most of the Phrenorian warriors wasn't new to Sage. He'd been on other worlds and seen it happen.

"They're not supposed to do that," Murad said. "They're not allowed."

"Yeah," Sage said. "I know. But the Phrenorians here are outside the rules of engagement now, Lieutenant." He clapped the younger man on the shoulder hard enough to get his attention. "C'mon. We don't have time to gawk. Let's get someplace where we can do some good. They need us at the fort."

Murad nodded, then gave the command to move out.

Sage ran slack behind his group to cover their retreat from any latecomers to the push.

Halladay buzzed Sage's comm for attention. "Master Sergeant?"

"Yes, Colonel," Sage replied.

"I wanted to share some news with you," Halladay said. "I don't want this getting out to anyone yet. In case it doesn't happen. But I also don't want anyone caught by surprise and not know what's going on if I buy a bullet in here somewhere."

Halladay had already let it be known that he wasn't leaving the fort until the last soldier was ahead of him.

"I'm confiding in you," Halladay continued, "because you're the most senior soldier at this fort and you work closely with Quass Leghef, who will continue, hopefully, to serve as a go-between for the Alliance."

"Yes sir." Sage trotted toward the fort. The walls were only a hundred and twenty meters away.

Bodies littered the streets, the shattered buildings, and the fence line along the fort. Sage didn't try to sort them out. There would be time for that later, and it would be a job to do.

If he lived through the next few hours.

"The Alliance's oversight committee regarding the military situation on Makaum is considering changing their stance on how they're going to handle their part of this fiasco. The surprise attack by the Phrenorian Empire isn't sitting well with them right now."

Sage didn't comment, although he had plenty he could have said, because it wouldn't have done any good. Halladay wasn't the person he would have wanted to speak to.

"There's also the matter that the war is shifting this way and Makaum is going to play a significant part in resources. The Alliance now desires those resources."

"They aren't even concerned about the people out here dying," Sage growled. "If they had been, they would have done something a long time before this."

"You're preaching to the choir, Master Sergeant. Chairman Finkley, father of Major Finkley, who is currently AWOL somewhere out in the jungle and will be facing charges if we live through this present situation, wants his son alive."

"It's good to know the committee cares about someone."

"Chairman Finkley believed his son would be safe once we left Makaum. Now that it looks unlikely that Major Finkley is going to get out of this alive, the congressional leader is throwing his weight behind the shift." Halladay sighed. "I haven't yet informed him I'll be bringing charges against the major."

Sage stepped through the gate and entered the fort. Soldiers stood behind barricades, braced and ready for the next onslaught.

"I don't want this getting out, Master Sergeant," Halladay said. "That's why I'm not telling anyone else. It might not happen. I don't want our soldiers to know the Alliance turned its back on them." The colonel sounded achingly bitter. "But if they do mount a rescue operation, we're going to have to move quickly."

"Yes sir," Sage said. He didn't get his hopes up. The politicos did what they wanted to when they got good and ready. "Just tell me where you need me, Colonel."

"I need you to get to Quass Leghef, Master Sergeant. When the Alliance makes its move, they're going to want to talk to her. They believe she's the linchpin to hold the Makaum people together."

"Yes sir. Where is she?"

"Out in the jungle," Halladay replied. "I'm tracking a handset comm I gave her earlier. She left the fort ten minutes ago after some kind of dustup that left some dead men behind."

"What happened?"

"We're not sure. We've got some scratchy vid of the encounter, but no aud, and nobody I've got access to knows those people. The Quass was going into the jungle to join up with some of her people, but there are pockets of them scattered throughout the Green Hell."

"Understood, sir."

A still image of Quass Leghef ghosted onto Sage's HUD as he flagged down a crawler. The young private braked so quickly in front of Sage that he threw mud all over him.

The young driver got out of the vehicle. "Sorry, Master Sergeant."

Sage waved the apology away. He pinged Jahup, Pingasa, Culpepper, Escobedo, and two other soldiers to round out his team. He didn't want to take all of the soldiers.

In the still image, Quass Leghef stood with a group of men. Sage recognized one of them as Throzath, but he didn't know the others. He pushed the image on to Jahup and switched to a private frequency.

"Do you know these men?"

Jahup only needed a moment. "They work for Tholak."

That news left a bad feeling in Sage's stomach. He relayed the news to Halladay.

The colonel cursed. "I knew something was wrong when she asked for Throzath's release. I should have been paying more attention."

"You had a lot of balls in the air at the time, sir," Sage said. Rockets punched holes in the parade ground and Quonset buildings only meters away and he ducked. "And the Phrenorians can be insistent about getting attention."

"I know. Find her, Master Sergeant, and get her someplace safe so she can talk to the politicos when the time comes. I'm sending you the Quass's comm protocol. You can track her down using that."

"Copy that, sir."

"I'm sending Murad orders now that he's supposed to go with you. Bring him up to speed."

"Yes sir."

Murad took the seat next to Sage and looked at him expectantly.

"Stay safe out there, Master Sergeant."

"Will do, sir. You do the same." Sage accelerated and switched to his private frequency with Murad. The lieutenant listened without interrupting as Sage pulled up the Quass's location on his HUD.

FIFTY-THREE

Without warning, the crawler stopped amid a towering copse of flowering *atceri* trees. Leghef gazed out the window at the surrounding jungle.

Purple blossoms as big as a person's face sprouted on all the hundred-meter-tall trees. Heavy growth interlaced the branches so tightly that only a little of the rain reached the jungle floor.

The *atceri* bloomed only during the rains, and the trees soaked up the rains through the blossoms, which drank like greedy mouths. Even the bark sopped up water as spillover threaded down the massive trunks. Under the canopy of rain, blossoms, and branches, the open area reeked of the *atceris'* fragrance, so sweet it was near to rot.

Osler slid out of his seat but held up a hand to stay Leghef before she attempted to get out as well.

"Where is my granddaughter?" Leghef demanded.

"Wait," Osler commanded.

"I will not." Leghef pushed up, but the man still sitting beside her pulled her back down.

"You will," Osler said. "You're not in command. Not out here."

Leghef held back a retort. Threats would do no good here. And they wouldn't bring her to Telilu.

A moment later, another crawler burst through the foliage and came to a stop in front of the one Leghef was in.

Throzath got out and limped to meet the other vehicle. "Father."

The crawler driver sprang out and opened the vehicle's rear door. Massive and burly, a once-proud warrior now gone to seed, Tholak stepped from the crawler. His broad head was shaved clean and he wore a dark beard shot through with gray that Leghef would have sworn wasn't there days ago. Scars from past narrow escapes from beasts he hunted because he chose to, not because he had to, looked gray against his tanned skin.

Tholak embraced his son momentarily, then ushered him into the vehicle. He turned his attention to Leghef and crossed the intervening distance with a cold smile.

"Leghef," he greeted flatly.

"You took my granddaughter." The cold rage in Leghef's voice surprised her. She hadn't heard it in a long time.

"I did," Tholak admitted.

"I want to see her."

Tholak took the seat up front with the driver and closed the door. "I'm going to take you to her."

Osler resumed his seat beside Leghef and the crawler jerked into motion.

"Why have you done this?" Leghef demanded.

"Because I want to keep my fortune," Tholak said.

"How are you going to do that?"

"I have made arrangements with the Phrenorians. When I give them the people they want, I get to keep my wealth and standing, and I'll get a percentage of the shipments they take from this planet."

The thought horrified Leghef. "You can't do that, Tholak. Our people have fought for every breath they've taken on this planet. Generations have spilled blood to provide us the lives we have now. The Phrenorians will turn them—turn *us*—into slaves."

Tholak shook his head. "Not *us*. Never *us*. I won't accept that, and I have the word of the Phrenorian Empire that I will be appreciated."

"They're lying to you, and you're too stupid to realize it. You'll serve right alongside the people you're enslaving. If the Phrenorians don't kill you."

Tholak laughed. "That's not going to happen."

The crawler bounced over the uneven ground. Leghef studied the jungle and realized she knew where they were heading.

"You're bringing them to Rilormang?" Leghef stared at Tholak. "You know what that place means to our people."

"Rilormang saved us once," Tholak said. "It can save us again."

"Turning them into slaves isn't saving them."

Tholak's face grew red. "You think having them die fighting the Phrenorians for the Terrans is a better death?"

"You argued with me not so long ago against offworlder presence on our planet," Leghef said.

"I argued against the Terrans because I knew they would embroil us in their war. And they have. Do you know how many of our people I have seen lying dead in the streets or their homes?"

Leghef's voice was steel when she spoke. "Not nearly so many as I have. You were among the first to leave and hide out in the jungle."

Tholak reached across the seat and backhanded Leghef so fast she couldn't move in time to get away. Her head snapped back and her cheek felt like it had been infused with fire.

For a moment, Leghef was beyond thinking. Her hand flashed to the knife she'd secreted in the sleeve of her dress. She swept the blade toward Tholak's neck, intending to sever the carotid—and stopped herself just short of that when she realized killing him would get Telilu killed.

If her granddaughter was even still alive.

Instead of slicing Tholak's carotid, the blade scored his cheek to the bone. Blood gushed down his face and dripped through his beard.

Osler grabbed her wrist then, and she didn't fight him. Fighting would only have made things go worse for Telilu and herself. She screamed quietly inside her own mind while Tholak clapped a big hand to the wound on his cheek.

"Didn't you search her?" Tholak yelled.

Osler plucked the knife from Leghef's hand and pocketed it. "We did."

"Not well enough."

"She's an old woman."

"She used to *hunt*!" Tholak roared. "You're lucky to be alive." He ordered the driver to pull over and for the guards to search her thoroughly.

They yanked Leghef from the crawler and pressed her against it. Tholak stood on the other side of the vehicle while one of the men attended his wound with a spray-on sealer that Leghef and her fellow hunters would have given almost anything for back when she was young.

The search was thorough and insulting, and when they turned up the comm, she cursed her weakness. She should have stayed her hand, should have waited for a better opportunity. Now, if Telilu *were* dead, Leghef would be unable to avenge her granddaughter.

Osler showed Tholak the comm unit. "She had this."

Tholak glared at the man. His face was bloodstained around the spray-on patch. Leghef knew the wound hurt, and she hoped it got infected. Contagion was another thing that often came with the *atceri*. Of course, back in those days, the hunters hadn't had the offworlder meds. Tholak would survive.

"Destroy it and tie her up."

Osler dropped the comm to the ground and stomped on it with a military-grade boot that had come from an offworlder store. Then he took a plastic strap from a bag at his hip and bound Leghef's wrists together.

"Is my granddaughter alive?" Leghef demanded. She tried to keep her voice from breaking, but it did anyway at the end.

"She is," Tholak said. "She will be until I gut her in front of you if you don't do what I say. You're fortunate you still have a role to play in this." He turned to Osler. "Put her back in the crawler."

FIFTY-FOUR

Zhoh stood beside the damaged TAV and reviewed the vid Mato had captured from the war machine. It played on a loop inside his handheld viewer. Although the Terran military combat armor didn't reveal faces out in the field, Zhoh felt certain one of the soldiers had been Sage. The big pistol sheathed on the soldier's chest announced that.

Seething, Zhoh shifted his attention to Fort York. He triggered the magnification function of his ocular and switched his focus to that eye. Somehow, in spite of everything he'd thrown at it, the Terran fort still stood.

Under other circumstances, he might have felt gladdened by the tenacity of his opponents. Strong enemies made strong warriors. A battle could not be truly won unless at some point it came close to being lost.

Most of the assault vehicle's crew was dead. Zhoh

had dispatched one of the warriors himself because he would not recover from his wounds, and warriors were not going to be pulled from battle to ferry him back to the hospital in the embassy.

War brought about acceptable losses. He was still determined to take Makaum and seize the glory that came with that accomplishment.

He raked the fort with his gaze. The assault on the east had stalled out and was, in fact, now giving ground before the Terran soldiers.

Zhoh checked his battle strategies to see who was responsible for that assault. He opened his comm.

"Colonel Nalit, report."

No answer was forthcoming.

"Colonel Nalit," Zhoh called again. Then he flipped to the frequency he shared with Mato. "Is Nalit dead?"

"I don't know, General." Mato sounded harried. "I have tried to locate Nalit and Warar, but neither of them is responding to comm hails."

"The east side attack is being beaten back."

A group of jumpcopters streaked through the airspace and laid down a salvo of missiles that routed the Phrenorians there.

"I'll check on that."

Zhoh hailed both Nalit and Warar, but got no response. He searched for their armor transponders in the nearby neighborhoods, where they should have been, and was surprised when there was no sign of them. Then he realized that the two warriors weren't on the battlefield.

As a jumpcopter fired rockets at his location, he took cover and opened his comm to Mato again. The warheads slammed against the TAV and unleashed firestorms that curled and twisted. Some of the slower-moving or less-aware warriors got caught in the blast.

A few of the warriors not caught in the blast attempted to use spray foam to extinguish their burning comrades even though the injured could have extinguished the flames by rolling in the surrounding mud and puddles. Other warriors fired their weapons at the jumpcopter as it screamed by overhead.

Zhoh watched as two of the warriors who were on fire succumbed to their injuries. Their would-be rescuers turned from them.

The jumpcopter came back around for another approach. Scrambling quickly, Zhoh lowered himself through an open hatch and slid behind the controls of one of the anti-aircraft guns. He readied the particle cannon and tracked the jumpcopter. When the aircraft was within range, he fired.

The rapid particle beam pulses tore the jumpcopter to pieces. Plasteel rained down and pelted the street and nearby structures. A large chunk of it struck the TAV hard enough to make the tracked assault vehicle shudder. Since he wasn't securely belted in as he should have been, Zhoh banged against the seat and the control console.

With the skies clear, Zhoh heaved himself up from the gunner's seat and crawled back out of the hatch till he stood on top of it. Patchy smoke crawled up from the wreckage and wrapped across the TAV.

"General," Mato called, and only then did Zhoh realize his second had been calling for him.

"I'm here," Zhoh answered. "Locate Nalit and Warar."

"Searching through satellites," Mato replied.

Zhoh climbed down the TAV till he reached the rubble-strewn, muddy street. He moved among his wounded warriors and gave two of them merciful deaths.

"I have them," Mato said. Confusion crept through in his voice. "This doesn't make sense."

To Zhoh, wherever the two lieutenant colonels were made perfect sense. They were betraying him. Ignoring his leadership and following someone else's orders. Neither of the two was strong enough to defy him. Not even working together.

"Where are they?" Zhoh demanded.

"At a place called Rilormang."

Zhoh searched through what he knew of Makaum, but the name failed to make a connection for him. "What's the significance of that location?"

Mato paused for just a moment. "All I can find in our records of Makaum history is that Rilormang holds special cultural importance to the Makaum beings."

"What's out there?"

An image of an impenetrable jungle popped up on Zhoh's handheld viewer. The area looked like so much of the jungle that he'd already seen on the planet.

"What about the terrain underneath the trees?" Zhoh asked.

"We have no records of it," Mato answered. "There is some mention of caves in that area. Something called the Caves of the Glass Dead."

"That isn't in our records?"

"No, *triarr*. If it were, I would be able to find it."

Zhoh pondered that and grew quickly frustrated. "Nalit and Warar would not go there for no reason."

"A group of beings who serve Tholak, a Makaum government representative, took the woman leader there."

"Tholak served General Rangha," Zhoh said, remembering the being with acute disapproval.

"Yes. Tholak was a primary outlet for Rangha's black market weapons business here on the planet, and he arranged for Rangha to get weapons on- and offplanet to trade with others."

"Why would Tholak take the woman?" Zhoh asked.

"She is quite well-regarded among her people."

"If Tholak has her, perhaps he believes he can persuade her, or coerce her, into standing with him."

That made sense, and it was exactly what Tholak had promised he could do. Had the obnoxious being found a way to deliver on that promise? The likelihood was inconceivable, yet Tholak had taken Leghef.

"Can you locate Tholak?" Zhoh asked.

"I'm running a sweep for him now, but currently I'm turning up no signals anywhere."

"The abduction of Quass Leghef and the disappearance of Nalit and Warar are not a coincidence." The certainty of that grew inside Zhoh.

"One of our spies still inside the fort says that Colonel Halladay has tasked Master Sergeant Sage with finding Leghef."

That got Zhoh's attention immediately. "Do you know where Sage is?"

"No, but our spy told me he headed north."

"Get me a transport ship," Zhoh said. "I'm going to kill those traitors and Tholak, and Sage if he arrives there, and I'm going to take Leghef and back the Alliance down. I *will* bring this world to its knees and deliver it to the Empire."

FIFTY-FIVE

The Nyslora Lowlands
10 Kilometers North of Makaum Sprawl
0821 Hours Zulu Time

Two hundred meters from where the comm protocol signal had remained stationary until eight minutes ago, Sage pulled the crawler to a halt and got out. He retrieved his Roley from between the seats and readied the weapon.

"Jahup," Sage said, "you're on point."

The young man nodded, but Sage could read the nervous energy bouncing around inside him. His grandmother was in unfriendly hands and that couldn't be ignored.

"We go slow," Sage said, "and we go careful. If they don't see us coming, we've got an advantage. We'll be more in control of what we do, and we can take away whatever it is they think they want to do." He swept his team with a glance. "Everybody ready?"

"Yes, Master Sergeant," Jahup said, and the other soldiers echoed him.

"Then let's move out."

Jahup took the lead and Sage followed him. The rest of the soldiers followed in a staggered line about three meters apart. Culpepper ran slack.

The jungle became a maze of foliage and brush. Hardly forty meters into the approach, Sage was certain he wouldn't have been able to make it back out on his own. Pins marked the crawler, the last known location of Leghef's comm, and his team.

Twenty-three meters from the comm marker, Sage settled the team into a loose semicircle around the clearing. Other than the crawler tracks that had torn along the muddy ground and the several *kifrik* shifting restlessly in the canopy high above, there was no sign of life.

"She's not here." Anxious concern and confusion carried in Jahup's voice. He broke cover and walked out into the clearing. "No one's here." He turned to Sage. "We've lost her!"

"Take it easy, soldier," Sage said as he walked out into the clearing. "We're going to find her."

"How do you know that?" Jahup demanded.

"Because not finding her is unacceptable." Sage ordered the others to fan out and search the area.

Jahup stood in the middle of the crawler tracks.

"Tell me what you see, Jahup." Sage wanted to keep the young man thinking about logistics and not getting buried in fear. "You're a hunter. You know this jungle. What happened here?"

Turning slowly, Jahup said, "There were two crawlers. One came the way we did, from the fort. The other came from the west."

The soldiers spread out and scanned the terrain while staying alert for a possible attack.

"What's to the west?" Sage prompted.

"Some of the bigger farms," Jahup answered.

"Are any of them owned by Tholak?"

"Yes."

"Then chances are that other crawler belonged to Tholak." Sage followed Jahup over to that set of crawler ruts.

"Yes," Jahup said. "But there are no signs of them traveling back that way. There's just the one set of tracks."

"Okay, so we know they didn't take your grandmother that way." Sage turned toward the north. "That means they went that way, because there are no tracks to the east, and we came from the south along the only set of tracks, so they didn't go back in that direction either."

"Hey, Master Sergeant," Culpepper called. "I found something."

Sage shifted over to the corporal's point of view through his HUD and saw the comm fragment in Culpepper's big hand.

"Somebody smashed that comm," Culpepper said. He stared down at the ground and the boot prints stood out in the soft dirt. "It wasn't an accident."

"They found it on her," Jahup said. "That must be what happened."

"Yeah," Sage said, "but they didn't leave her here. They took her, and they headed north, Jahup. What's out there?"

Jahup shook his head. "Sacred lands. We don't go there anymore. We don't even hunt there. It's called Rilormang."

"Why would they go there?"

Jahup turned to face Sage. "I don't know."

"Then let's get the crawler and go find out," Sage replied. "We can't be far behind them."

Rilormang
The Sulusku Highlands
28 Kilometers North of Makaum Sprawl
0832 Hours Zulu Time

A small army of Phrenorian warriors bivouacked beneath the towering trees in front of the Caves of the Glass Dead. They stood armored and carrying weapons around fast attack crawlers equipped with firmpoints for heavy weapons.

As she got out of the crawler, under Osler's watchful and angry gaze, Leghef couldn't believe how small the caves were. The last time she had seen them, the mother of her mother had brought her there to explain what the place meant to the Makaum people. The visit had been short, filled with reverence and awe.

Leghef remembered it most because the mother of her mother had wept and she had not because even after being given the explanation for why the place was kept, she still didn't understand. The Caves of the Glass Dead were part of the Old Stories, the ones that were put away and only occasionally brought out to scare children who misbehaved.

Osler shoved her from behind, nudging her in Tholak's direction. "Keep moving."

Leghef raised her bound hands before her because she was afraid she was going to fall on the uneven terrain. She managed to keep her footing and stumbled till she achieved a more natural stride.

Tholak joined two Phrenorians who stood apart from the rest of their kind. Leghef knew from that separation that these two were the ones who held the power in the group.

"Inside the caves," Osler commanded.

Throzath stood a short distance away and leaned against the other crawler. He wore a sidearm belted around his waist now and glared cold threats at Leghef as she passed.

"You and me, old woman," Throzath said, "we're not finished."

Leghef ignored him. The young man would never have as many fangs as a *tasdyno*, be as big as a *jasulild*, or be as quick as a *kifrik*. She had held her own against all those things. She didn't fear Throzath.

She stepped inside the main cave and was on the verge of demanding to know where her granddaughter was when Telilu dashed from a back corner near the entrances to the other caves that led underneath the Sulusku Highlands.

"Mother of my father!" Telilu rushed toward Leghef with her arms spread wide.

Her green-tinted hair was pulled back and hung to the middle of her back. She wore a yellow jumper and trail boots, not enough protection for where they were. She carried her small doll under one of her arms.

"Daughter of my son!" Relief swept Leghef and brought tears to her eyes when Telilu wrapped her thin arms around her, but she refused to shed them. She wouldn't let Telilu see her crying and become confused. For now she just enjoyed their brief respite together and didn't think of what might come next.

Leghef managed to wrap her bound arms over the girl's head and hugged her back.

Telilu released Leghef and stepped back. "I was so scared."

"I know," Leghef said, "but you must be brave."

Telilu stared at the plastic straps that bound Leghef's wrists. "Why are you tied up?"

Out of habit, Leghef smoothed her granddaughter's hair. "We're not among friends."

Telilu frowned. "I knew that when they took me from Kalcero's house. They hurt Pekoz and Kalcero's mom and left them lying on the floor bleeding."

Anger tightened Leghef's throat, but she made herself speak. "I'm sorry you had to see that."

Telilu hugged Leghef again. "I wanted to go for help, but they wouldn't let me."

"These are not good men."

"I know that. They are friends with the bug men, and the bug men have been killing people in the streets and in their homes. I never liked them, but I hate them now."

A sharp stab of pain shot through Leghef's heart. Her granddaughter's innocence had been ripped away so casually, and it was something she had fought all her life to protect.

Now it looked like Telilu's innocence wouldn't be the only thing that Leghef couldn't protect.

"They're going to be sorry when Noojin finds out I've been taken," Telilu promised.

"Noojin?" Leghef tried to make sense of that.

"Yes," Telilu said with confidence that astounded Leghef as they stood in the midst of men and aliens who would do them harm. "Noojin will know I have been taken, and probably that you've been taken, and she will tell Jahup. Then they will get the master sergeant and bring the Terran soldiers to save us."

Before she could ask her granddaughter how Noojin would know she had been taken, much less where she was, Tholak approached her. The sight of his swollen, injured face gladdened Leghef's heart.

Unconsciously, Leghef slid Telilu behind her, not wanting the girl anywhere around Tholak.

"I brought you here to talk to our people," Tholak said as he stood before her.

"I have nothing to say to them," Leghef said.

Impatience tightened Tholak's features, and the injury made his scowl lopsided. "You're going to say what I tell you to say."

Leghef ignored him.

"You're going to tell them," Tholak went on, "to come out of the jungle and submit themselves to the Phrenorians so that they can live."

"I will not!"

Tholak acted as though he hadn't heard and pressed on. "You're going to tell them that the Phrenorians will be generous, that living directed, *useful* lives—"

"As *slaves*!"

"—will be better than dying out here," Tholak went on. "And you will address the Terran Alliance. You will tell them that we reject their offer of help. They are to order the soldiers here to depart from Makaum and stop battling the Phrenorians until such time that arrangements can be made to ship the soldiers offplanet."

Rage filled Leghef so that she couldn't have spoken if she wanted to. She knew Tholak was lying. Or the Phrenorians were lying. Master Sergeant Sage, Colonel Halladay, none of those brave soldiers would be allowed to slip away. The Phrenorians wouldn't permit it. They would make examples of them, things to frighten their enemies with.

Finally, she could speak. "You do this here, Tholak? Here where our ancestors came together, set aside their differences, and sacrificed themselves so that we might live as one community against all the death that continually stalks us on this world?"

"Our people will know this place," Tholak said. "They will respect what you say here."

"They are fleeing for their lives."

Tholak frowned. "And we have to stop that. You know as well as I do that our people have grown too soft to live out here. If they don't have a home, and the Phrenorians are generously offering them one, they will die."

Even as she wanted to argue, Leghef knew it was true.

"Now," Tholak said, "let's go. You have a vid to make and we've got to make certain it reaches the right hands."

He nodded to Osler and the big man shoved Leghef deeper into the cave. All the old fears of ghosts and darkness crowded in on her as she walked to the back of the cave.

The Glass Dead were there, and she shivered as she remembered how they had looked when she was just a girl.

FIFTY-SIX

Nyslora Lowlands Airspace
19 Kilometers North of Makaum Sprawl
317556 Akej (Phrenorian Prime)

Seated in the troop section of the transport aircraft, Zhoh used relaxation techniques his combat instructors had taught him in his first year of training to get himself focused to take the lives of other warriors in the heat of battle. He held his *patimong* in his top secondaries, crossed his primaries over his chest, and concentrated on the feel of the smooth grain of the *daravgane* the weapon had been forged from.

> The blade will not fail.
> The warrior will not fail.
> The battle plan will not fail.

That was the most basic foundation of the Warrior's Code. Everything worked together, like primaries and secondaries, like *chelicerae* and tail, like blade and poison.

Centered, he took out his handheld viewer and studied the terrain below the transport aircraft. Endless emerald jungle streamed in all directions. Winged lizards skated along the treetops. Only the GPS pin let him know where their destination was.

He put the device back in his harness and glanced at the warriors belted into the transport section around him. All of them sat quiet and resolute. They were better trained than the raucous Terran soldiers Zhoh had seen. He believed in their abilities and their training.

Still, Zhoh knew that even though those Terran soldiers remained individuals, they could become a cohesive force. Master Sergeant Sage had commanded them in such a manner and brought them to a single purpose.

Fighting alongside Sage after the Cheapdock debacle had been surprisingly fulfilling.

Killing Sage and mastering Makaum would be more fulfilling.

Mato buzzed for his attention over the comm.

"Yes," Zhoh responded.

"There is an encrypted communication coming in from General Belnale," Mato said. "I have no idea what it is about."

That surprised Zhoh. Comms aboard a transport ship weren't hardened enough to ensure no one would intercept exchanges. General Belnale was taking a risk.

"You told him where I was?" Zhoh asked.

"He already knew, *triarr*, and the general became even more insistent that I put him in contact with you when he learned your location."

"You told him my intent?"

"No. But I think he knows."

Zhoh thought about that, and he didn't like where his suspicions led him. Abandoning his leadership role in the attack on Fort York and going after Nalit and Warar wasn't something Belnale would approve.

"Triarr?"

Zhoh realized he'd gotten locked in his own thoughts. "Put General Belnale through."

"At once."

Almost immediately, General Belnale's voice boomed into Zhoh's hearing. "General Zhoh, turn that ship around and return your attentions to the battle against Fort York."

"I can't do that."

Belnale hissed his displeasure. "You cannot undo what is being done."

"Do you know that my lieutenant colonels have deserted their posts?" Zhoh asked.

"Yes."

"Do you know why?"

Belnale hesitated, and Zhoh knew the answer was going to be bad.

"They are following their orders, General," Belnale said.

"What orders? The orders they should be following came from me."

"They have other orders."

"What are those orders?" Zhoh demanded, but he knew. He only wanted it spoken aloud.

Belnale didn't hesitate then, and he didn't mince words. "They're making arrangements with a Makaum being to negotiate surrender of the planet to the Phrenorian Empire."

"I am going to *take* this planet."

"There is doubt, General Zhoh, of your competency."

Zhoh's anger mounted. His pheromones stank of it. "I will kill any warrior that dares say I am incompetent."

"As would I. And maybe you'll get your chance. But until such time occurs, you have to follow orders."

"Who are Nalit and Warar meeting with?"

"A being who says he can unite the Makaum beings."

"Are you talking about Tholak?" Zhoh could scarcely utter the man's name.

"Yes."

Zhoh had to respect General Belnale's candor. Lying was something a Phrenorian only did as a combat strategy when dealing with an opponent.

Only a true *Phrenorian,* Zhoh amended. Nalit and Warar were not, by his standards, true Phrenorians.

"Who gave those spineless *cridelrad* this order?" Zhoh asked.

"The Prime War Board," Belnale answered. "I was not part of that decision. I was outvoted." He spat and cursed. "I don't like the way the other generals are choosing to win this war. This way, negotiating and subterfuge, is not . . ."

"This way is not honorable," Zhoh said, because he knew his superior couldn't bring himself to denounce the action of his fellow generals in such a manner. Zhoh had no such compunctions. "We don't win wars through deception, General Belnale. We win them through martial superiority and determination. Straightforward things. That is what makes a Phrenorian warrior. We are not diplomats."

"This was my objection as well, General Zhoh, and I went on record to state that. But we have taken losses in the war with the Terrans lately that have been unexpected. The majority of the War Board wants to deliver a planet, *that* planet, as a symbol of our power, and to show other planets why we are to remain feared."

"Then it should be done the *right* way!"

"The War Board fears they have made a mistake."

"What mistake?" Zhoh demanded.

"They allowed you to lead the army there."

Zhoh took a moment to collect himself. "They did not choose me. I won the honor of leading this army by right of combat."

Belnale spoke plainly. "The Alliance believes you lied about the assassination attempt on your life and started the war on Makaum for your own purposes."

Zhoh couldn't believe what he was hearing. "What purposes?"

"To regain your lost honor."

"I didn't *lose* my honor," Zhoh protested. "It was stripped from me."

"The story being told is that you hired your own assassin and have tried to pin it on Blaold Oldawe."

Zhoh's mind spun. So *that* was what this was about. A last-ditch effort to save Blaold Oldawe's name and family honor. He cursed himself for getting blind-sided.

"That's not true," he said, but he knew it was true if the War Board said it was true.

"The assassin is currently in the hands of the Terrans," Belnale went on.

"The War Board is saying the Terrans can make the man say anything," Zhoh said. Dread closed in on him.

"The War Board doesn't want that story being told. They want to control what is being told."

"What is their story?"

"That you hired your own assassin to start the war and regain your honor, then implicated Blaold Oldawe to strike back at him for naming you *kalque*."

Zhoh's thoughts spun dizzyingly.

"The War Board also faults you for losing the stock-pile of weapons that were on Makaum," Belnale continued. "Their story will be that you accumulated those weapons to become wealthy, then let the edge you had to win this war slip through your primaries."

"I didn't stockpile those weapons."

"You didn't tell the War Board about them," Belnale accused.

Zhoh could say nothing in his defense that would reflect on him honorably. He had not told because that was the dishonorable thing to do.

"I know why you didn't say anything," Belnale said. "You wanted to protect the Empire."

Zhoh ran his secondaries over his *patimong* and tried to regain himself. "Yes. That is exactly why I said nothing. I have not lost this war. I can still win it. I *am* winning it. Fort York can't stand."

"The Alliance is shifting. If they do, if they send warships to Makaum, the ships we have there won't be able to stand against them. And the Empire doesn't want to lose any more dreadnoughts. There have been too many losses in other places. On top of that, Makaum must be taken. The Empire needs that planet's resources to beef up their armies and navies."

"Then I will get it for them."

"General Zhoh, the War Board has already chosen its champions."

Zhoh saw what Belnale was not saying in that moment. "I'm not going to be allowed to win this war."

"No," Belnale said. "That honor will go to Nalit and Warar."

Anger filled the air around Zhoh. "Warriors who work in the shadows with beings who betray their own kind," he snarled. "Is this who we are becoming?"

"The war costs the Empire," Belnale said. "They want to win by any means necessary."

"Even at the cost of honor?"

"They plan to keep their honor," Belnale said. "If this

tactic doesn't succeed, they will place the blame for the loss on you."

Zhoh couldn't believe it. "To save Nalit and Warar."

"They come from important families. Their honor must be kept intact for the good of the Empire."

"I am *kalque*," Zhoh said. "Worthless because I chose to mate with the wrong person."

"You chose that female so you could move up in the Empire," Belnale stated bluntly. "Instead of making your way up the hierarchy on your own, you chose a shortcut."

The words hammered Zhoh because he knew that was true. He had brought that dishonor—Sxia and their feeble brood—onto himself.

And that dishonor had grown.

Desperation, something that was so new to him that he almost didn't recognize it, ate through Zhoh like acid.

"Do the right thing," Belnale urged. "Go back. Take your place in the battle with Fort York. If you die there, you will know honor again."

"And if I don't?"

"It would be better for the Empire if you did, Zhoh."

"Because the Empire will still get their scapegoat if the battle for Makaum is lost, and—should Tholak truly get the Makaum beings to agree to side with the Empire—I will no longer be an embarrassment."

"Yes."

Zhoh thought furiously and knew those were not the only two options. "No, there is another way."

"Zhoh—"

Zhoh broke the comm connection and took a moment to himself. Then he said, "Mato?"

"Yes, *triarr*?" Mato was quiet.

"You heard?"

"Yes."

"I am not going to die quietly for the Empire," Zhoh said. "I am a warrior. I was born to fight. I *choose* to fight. I will fight the Empire if I must to regain what was taken from me by those who did not deserve to do so."

"I will fight with you, *triarr*."

Zhoh knew that it wasn't loyalty that bound Mato to him in that moment. It was his own survival. As Zhoh's second, Mato would be held accountable for Zhoh's "failures" as well. He would be reduced to *kalque*.

"Good," Zhoh said. "Then let's win this war and claim our glory. We'll take it from the Empire itself if we have to."

FIFTY-SEVEN

Once it hit the Makaum atmosphere, the dropship bounced like a rock skipping water. At least that was how it felt to Noojin as she clung to the webbing that held her in her seat. The fact that she would die in an atmosphere rather than the vacuum of space was oddly comforting.

For a moment she thought the Phrenorian gunship had finally gotten a target lock on them and was in the process of chipping away at the dropship's armor, but the *John Lee* had escaped.

"The Sting-Tail gunship is falling back," the dropship pilot whooped. "He doesn't want any part of the gravity well in that ship."

"We're due for some good news," Kiwanuka said.

Noojin relaxed a little and hoped that meant they might reach ground safely. But even as she thought that, she remembered that the fort was under attack and the Makaum sprawl was a battlefield. She wanted to see Jahup, and in the next instant she realized she didn't know if he was even still alive.

A moment later, the dropship leveled out and became tolerable except for the lesser gravity as the *John Lee* controlled the long fall to the ground far below. Then they would be in the thick of it.

Kiwanuka opened a link to the fort and Noojin listened in.

"Attention, Command. This is Sergeant Kiwanuka aboard the dropship *John Lee*. We're returning from space and are seeking orders."

"Good to know you're still alive, Sergeant Kiwanuka," a woman said.

"Thank you, Command."

Noojin scanned the intel feeds on her HUD as her armor relinked to the ground-based satellites and she tried not to be sick. The fort had taken critical losses and couldn't possibly hold up much longer without some kind of assistance.

"Colonel Halladay left standing orders that you were to be transferred over to him as soon as you showed back up," the woman said. "I'm connecting you now."

Kiwanuka continued scrolling and the reflections glowed softly against her face inside her helmet.

When the yellow dot first showed up on Noojin's HUD, she thought it was one of the links to Fort York. Then Telilu's name flashed under it and she remembered the doll and the transponder she had given to the girl.

Telilu was only supposed to use it if she were in trouble.

Noojin tried to connect with Quass Leghef's home, but the ping failed to go through. Noojin had forgotten about the scenes of destruction still playing on her HUD. When she looked at all the fires and destroyed buildings where the sprawl had once stood, her stomach cramped and she wept silently to herself. Fearfully, she opened the signal and tracked the source, expecting to find it somewhere in the craters and fallen buildings below.

But it wasn't there. It was way north of the sprawl and out into the jungle, and that made no sense.

Something else has gone wrong!

With that realization sharp in her thoughts, Noojin approached Kiwanuka.

"Kjersti," Noojin said in a strained voice, remembering too late that they were in the field and that wasn't how she was supposed to address the staff sergeant. "Something's wrong."

"What?" Kiwanuka asked.

"It's Telilu." Noojin rocked as she leaned against the dropship's bulkhead and held on to cargo netting. "When the Phrenorians arrived, she got worried. She couldn't sleep at night. She was afraid that they would try to steal her away. I put an emergency transponder in her doll and told her I would monitor it, that all she had to do was press it and I would know."

"All right," Kiwanuka said.

"Once we reached the atmosphere, my armor lit up with the signal because I'd patched it through on my personal network," Noojin went on. When she tried to continue, her voice gave out and she had to work to keep speaking. "The transponder wasn't strong enough to broadcast where we were. There were no repeaters for personal sat systems in space."

"Telilu is probably fine. She most likely pressed the transponder during a time when she was scared. There's plenty to be afraid of down there right now."

"I know that," Noojin said. "I told myself that, but where Telilu is just isn't making sense."

"What do you mean?"

Noojin forwarded the information from her HUD to Kiwanuka's. "That's the Sulusku Highlands," she said. "There's no reason for her to be there."

"A lot of people bailed from the sprawl after the attack started," Kiwanuka said. "She's probably in one of those groups."

"No," Noojin said desperately. "You don't understand. Telilu wouldn't go there. No one would. She's somewhere on sacred grounds. We stay away from them. Not even this attack would make Telilu go there."

"Is she talking about the Sulusku Highlands?" Colonel Halladay asked.

"Yes sir." Kiwanuka quickly explained the transponder's signal and how Noojin had it.

Just as quickly, Halladay explained about Sage's assignment tracking Quass Leghef. Noojin's fears grew.

"Sage told me he was following a trail the last time I talked to him," Halladay said. "He's been comm silent for a while because he's in close to where he believes Quass Leghef is being held by Tholak. Jahup mentioned something about a place called the Caves of the Glass Dead."

"I've never heard of a place called that," Kiwanuka said.

"Neither have I," Halladay said. "Whatever Sage is on to out there, I'm betting it's bigger than eight soldiers can handle."

Noojin made herself speak. "The Caves of the Glass Dead is where the different groups of Makaum people first came together and realized that they had to live as one. No one goes there." She hurried on because she couldn't stop herself. "What about Jahup?"

"He's with Sage," Halladay said.

The hard knot that had formed in Noojin's chest softened somewhat, but the location of where Jahup was headed and where Telilu was, and possibly Quass Leghef was as well, left her with sour bile at the back of her throat.

"We have to go there," Noojin said.

"You are," Halladay said. "Staff Sergeant, do you think your commandeered transport can get you there?"

"Yes sir."

"We need Leghef somewhere we can keep her safe," Halladay said. "Important negotiations are taking place among Alliance members and she needs to be part of that. Leghef is key right now, Staff Sergeant. Find the master sergeant, find Leghef, and get her to safety."

"Copy that, sir."

The comm went dead as Kiwanuka gave the dropship pilot the new orders.

Noojin resumed her seat and concentrated on pulling herself together. When they arrived, Jahup, Telilu, and the Quass would need her at her best.

Rilormang
The Sulusku Highlands
28 Kilometers North of Makaum Sprawl
0837 Hours Zulu Time

Crouched behind a boulder on a small rise above the entrance to the cave system where the crawlers had parked, Sage surveyed the motley group that had assembled there.

Despite the fact that they were working together in

some capacity, the Makaum people and offworlder mercenaries clustered in their groups apart from the Phrenorian warriors standing guard over the cave entrance.

There was no mistaking who was in charge. The Sting-Tails ran the operation and everyone knew it.

Jahup crouched only a couple meters away from Sage. Despite the younger man's worries about his grandmother, he remained calm and listened. He was, Sage knew, going to be a good soldier.

As long as he survived the war taking place on Makaum.

That seemed doubtful because they were currently outnumbered four to one, and three-fourths of those were Phrenorians.

So far, there had been no sign of Leghef. And there was no way they were leaving the area without her.

Sage opened a burst comm transmission to Jahup. This close in to the Phrenorian network, he didn't want to chance a long-distance link to the fort. He had also cut his HUD link to Fort York as well because that would have shown up on any Phrenorian signal sweeping the immediate vicinity.

He didn't want to know how bad things had gotten at the fort, and he was certain things were worse, because he didn't want to be torn in two directions.

One mission at a time, Sage reminded himself. A soldier lived longer that way.

"What are those caves?" Sage asked.

"The Caves of the Glass Dead," Jahup answered softly.

"That doesn't tell me much, Jahup."

"I don't know much." Jahup paused and breathed out. The whisper-soft noise carried over the comm connection. "The older people rarely talk about this place, and even then only in bits and pieces. What I do know is that it was here the Forging was accomplished."

"What is the Forging?"

"Do we have time for this? My grandmother is in there, and we have no idea what's being done to her."

"We need to know what we're dealing with to get some idea of what's being done to her," Sage replied. "I know this is hard, Jahup. It's everything I can do not to rush in there myself. The only thing that's stopping me is that I'm about as certain as you can get that we'd be KIA before we reached those caves. I need the intel. So do you. So does your grandmother. We only get one chance at this."

"Back a hundred years ago, maybe more," Jahup said, "our people were split into small, roving groups of no more than a hundred and fifty people."

Sage was familiar with hunter/gatherer groups. Several tribes still existed like that in Colombia when he'd been a boy. The free ones did. It was the only way to escape enslavement by the narco-barons growing coca plants. If they were good, if they were careful, a group of a hundred and fifty people could live off the land while living a nomadic lifestyle.

"Groups were predatory," Jahup went on. "They had to be. Some of them became cannibals."

"Because it was easier to hunt their own kind than to hunt the monsters hunting them," Sage said.

"Yes. Those were the Dark Times, and the cannibals were called *Oszage*, which in our language means 'stealer of the future.' Each life they took withered our greater family."

"Nobody's ever mentioned that," Sage said.

"No one will," Jahup said. "That's why this place isn't talked about. There's too much bad history here. In those days, not so long ago to people my grandmother's age, and the previous generation, our ancestors feared each other and they lived small lives without any promise of a better or safer existence."

The Makaum men opened the back doors of a cargo crawler and crowded around.

"Then the three brothers were born," Jahup went on. "Dendene, Nytai, and Risal. All of them became leaders of their own groups. Their family line stretched back to Shipfall, when the generation ship transporting our people crashed onto Makaum. They grew up together, then the day came when their father split them up, establishing each of them with their own group. They didn't like having to live apart. No one did. But the brothers vowed to find a way to live as one large tribe. They carried knowledge their father had given them regarding farming, and they planned the crops they would raise."

The Makaum men hauled crates from the crawler and placed them on the ground. They brought out crowbars and put them to work opening the protective cases.

"So they found a place, where we live now, and set up their farm," Jahup said. "After they were attacked by two groups of the *Oszage*, the brothers formed warrior bands, which became the hunters of our people, and tracked the cannibals down. Then they invited the other groups they found to the farmland. Slowly, they grew their population and their ability to produce enough food for everyone. Eventually, after much hard work and bloodshed, they had all of the groups together as they had dreamed. That was called the Forging, where they forged all the groups into one large group."

"So what is the Glass Dead?" Sage asked.

"The brothers." Jahup sounded distracted. "According to my grandmother, the brothers live in the cave."

"They 'live in the cave'?" Sage repeated. "Didn't you say this was a hundred years ago?"

"At least. Probably closer to two hundred. I learned how to hunt. I didn't care about history because incidents in the past weren't what killed you. It was what you met in the jungle that did."

When the Makaum men were finished uncrating their cargo, three self-propelled satellites about the size of a full-grown man stood on the ground. They were globe-shaped and had four fins and a thruster. Onboard containers of lifting gas, usually hydrogen or helium, provided lighter-than-air mobility.

With all the rivers and oceans on the planet, hydrogen would be readily available and, with offworld technology, extraction and usage would be simple enough for satellite suppliers.

"What are those devices?" Jahup asked.

"Low-orbit satellites," Sage answered. "I think I know what Tholak and the Phrenorians want with your grandmother." He pinged Culpepper. "Do you see those sat systems?"

"Roger that, Master Sergeant," Culpepper replied.

"I don't want those to get airborne."

"Copy that, but making that happen isn't going to be easy."

"The last easy assignment you had was this morning when you brought a mountain down, Corporal."

"Oh, yeah, that."

"Get back to me when you have an idea."

"Oh, I've already got an idea because I figured you might ask me something like this. I have to warn you: it'll be loud and visible. Nothing subtle about it."

"I've learned not to expect subtle from you," Sage said. "But make sure it's effective."

"Copy that. I'm always effective."

FIFTY-EIGHT

The Caves of the Glass Dead
Rilormang
The Sulusku Highlands
28 Kilometers North of Makaum Sprawl
0841 Hours Zulu Time

A re they asleep?" Telilu whispered.

"Some say they are," Leghef said.

The three men, all of them old and bearded but somehow still strong and fierce, stood in a loose semi-circle at the end of the cave. Strong offworld lanterns hung around the cavern and chased away the darkness.

When Leghef had last been there, visitors had burned torches. Black soot still marked the walls in the places where the torches had hung, and a black smudge coated the uneven, rounded cavern roof.

The place was smaller than Leghef remembered, but it was no less fearsome.

"Others," Leghef went on, "believe that one day, should we need them, they will wake and come to help us."

"Why?"

"Because we are their children. We are the future they promised their people."

Telilu looked pointedly at Tholak and the two Phrenorian officers conversing at the passageway entrance they'd come through.

"Then why aren't they waking up now?" her grand-daughter asked.

"Maybe because they know we can take care of ourselves," Leghef said in as brave a voice as she could manage.

The three brothers—Dendene, Nytai, and Risal—stood with weapons in hand: a sword, a spear, and an ax. Nytai wore a laser pistol at his hip. That weapon was a replica of a true pistol that had survived the wreck of the generation ship and generations of hard use.

All three men looked like they'd been carved from yellow gold stone. In reality, after death each man had been painstakingly coated in *moschon* sap, a resin that was used to preserve and strengthen furniture surfaces, and their youth returned to them through the hands of talented sculptors. They stood on carved stone pedestals that looked like miniature jungles.

Around them, on the walls, scenes from the stories of the brothers, of the generation starship, and some of the monsters they had discovered in the jungle were rendered in bas-relief. Each scene was meticulously carved out of the rock and stippled with ore-based paint so the images stood out in bright color.

"Why are they here?" Telilu asked.

"So that people remember them and all the good things they did," Leghef said.

"Just like they will remember Leghef is the mother of your father, child," Tholak said as he approached. "After she reunites our people."

Even though her hands were still bound, Leghef stepped in front of her granddaughter so Tholak could not easily get to her.

Tholak grinned at her to show how ineffectual he believed her to be. He stopped just out of arm's reach.

"My men are setting up a sat-relay station," he said. "In a few minutes, we will be ready for you to make an impassioned plea to the people who are hiding out in the jungle."

Some of Tholak's men carried in protective cases. They placed them on the cavern floor, opened them, and unpacked the electronic equipment within. A small generator whirred to life in one corner of the cavern and powered it all as the men engaged the different pieces.

"Even if I were to do what you say," Leghef said, struggling to get the words out, "how do you expect those people to hear you?"

"Because the Terran military supplied all of those groups with comms," Tholak replied. "Military-grade units keyed to frequencies Fort York uses for public service announcements. We're going to appropriate those frequencies and deliver your message."

He reached into his coat and took out a small hand-held device. When he punched it on, script filled the screen and Leghef recognized it was a speech.

"This message," Tholak said. "The one that will unite our people to submit to the Phrenorian Empire and ask them for protection from the Terran Alliance."

"I won't do it," Leghef said. "You might as well go ahead and kill me."

Telilu's eyes rounded in fear and she grabbed Leghef tightly. "No!"

Tenderly, Tholak reached out and brushed Telilu's hair. The girl drew away from him.

"You will do as I tell you," Tholak growled menacingly, "or I'll slice this child to pieces in front of you." He grinned coldly. "You weren't the only one who learned to take meat from a *sul'gha*, Leghef. Tell me: do you think I can keep her alive long enough to remove her still-beating heart?"

Rilormang
The Sulusku Highlands
318991 Akej (Phrenorian Prime)

Zhoh spotted the first traitorous Phrenorian guard posted along the outer perimeter of the sec line Nalit's and Warar's warriors had established around the caves. The transport ship had dropped them on a hilltop four hundred meters away and he'd led his warriors toward the caves through the jungle.

As he peered at the warrior over his rifle, there was an instant when Zhoh considered ordering the private before him to stand down, but he didn't trust that order to be obeyed. The warriors who were out here had disobeyed his orders already by abandoning their battle assignments.

Instead, Zhoh pulled the particle beam rifle he carried to his shoulder, took aim at the center of the warrior's chest as the private lifted his own assault rifle, and squeezed the trigger.

The initial blast knocked the warrior backward.

Zhoh fired again, still inexorably walking forward, and the second blast reduced the warrior's cephalothorax into a mass of broken chitin and torn tissue. The warrior was dead by the time he hit the jungle floor.

Three more traitors dodged to the sides and situated themselves behind rocks and trees. Still, they vacillated before firing even though one of their own now lay dead.

"Don't hesitate," Zhoh commanded his troops. "These warriors are traitors to the Empire. They have forsaken their duties and don't deserve to live. Kill them all."

He took cover as he moved and marked his targets automatically. Farther down, the traitors guarding the mouth of the cave sought shelter and immediately returned fire. Whatever hesitation they might have had disappeared. The Makaum people and the offworlder mercenaries ran for protection.

Zhoh scanned the battlefield but couldn't find Nalit or Warar. He guessed they were inside the cave. Even now they were hiding, unwilling to risk their lives.

"Ashtasu," Zhoh called over his comm. "Release the drones."

The corporal in charge of the drones wasn't visible, but the units came online an instant later, and after that they took to the air. Eight of them, in two diamond patterns, flitted through the trees. They were the length of one of his primaries and armed with laser rifles and particle beam weapons.

"*Triarr*," Mato called over the comm link they shared. "I have the drones. As I get information you need, I will relay it."

"Find Nalit and Warar," Zhoh commanded. "I want to see them dead at my feet."

"I will."

Zhoh looked at the surrounding jungle. "And find the master sergeant. Perhaps we arrived here before he did, but he will be along."

"I'll alert you as soon as I see him. What do you want done with the low-orbit sat relays?"

"Can you block their signals for now?" Zhoh fired at a traitor who was exposed for an instant.

The particle beam blast pounded the traitor's back. Unconscious or dead, he rolled down the small hill's incline near one of the crawlers.

"No," Mato answered. "Not with the drones we have there. I can destroy them."

"Don't do that." Zhoh took a grenade from his combat harness and threw it toward a crawler where three humanoids had sheltered. The grenade sailed true and plopped to the ground just beyond the crawler.

The explosion blew one of the beings out of hiding and left him lying limp. The other two staggered out with cuts and burns over most of their exposed bodies. One of them no longer had a face or eyes and stumbled blindly while crying for help.

"Leave the sats," Zhoh said. "Let them get them into the air if they can. Can you use the equipment aboard the transport ship to hijack control of them?"

"Yes. I'll have those pilots get the aircraft into the sky."

"Nalit and Warar won't have time to enact their treacherous plan," Zhoh said. "When I get Leghef, I will have her talk to the Terran Alliance and bend the humans to our will."

"I will let you know the instant I have control of those sat systems."

In the clearing, the satellites lifted from the ground slightly, then slowly rose.

With the chronometer working against him, Zhoh called his warriors to him. The time to move against his enemies was upon him.

Pride swelled within Zhoh as his warriors formed up on him. He led the way toward the cave and took out another warrior and two other beings as he went.

Behind him, the heavens suddenly cracked open and a huge object crashed through the canopy a hundred meters away. As it fell, it tore down trees, branches, and leaves in its path. More of the fierce rainstorm swept through the jungle in torrents around it. Something landed on him and knocked him to the ground.

FIFTY-NINE

Kiwanuka held on to the safety webbing as the *John Lee* plummeted through the jungle. The dropship bounced haphazardly as it tore through towering trees five meters in diameter. Judging from the clangor, the dropship was causing a huge amount of damage.

"We're definitely not on stealth mode," the pilot said bitterly. "And you better like where we set down because you're not going to have a choice."

"I choose alive, Lieutenant," Kiwanuka replied.

The dropship stopped with a massive thud, but it didn't wobble. The vessel didn't sit straight either. Kiwanuka freed herself from the webbing, seized her Roley, and stepped into the transport compartment.

"Everybody all right?" she asked as she glanced over

the soldiers and civilians scattered across the compartment.

The soldiers answered back immediately, sounding
shaken but steady.

"Then let's get into the fight." Kiwanuka nodded to
Goldberg. "Open that bay, Corporal."

"Copy that, Sergeant." Goldberg tapped the keypad
beside the hatch.

"A word, Staff Sergeant."

Kiwanuka turned to face Morlortai, who only looked
slightly worse for the wear. "You're alive."

"I am." The assassin nodded. "Thanks to your quick
action, and to the medical treatment I received."

Not much medical treatment had been necessary.
Otherwise the Fenipalan wouldn't be up and around so
quickly.

"What do you want?" Kiwanuka asked. "I don't have
time to stand around talking."

"Nor do we," Morlortai assured her. "As I understand it, we're surrounded by a larger, hostile force in
the middle of nowhere. I suggest we continue our truce.
We have a common foe, and our goal is to survive. We
can work to help each other."

Kiwanuka hesitated.

"The offer is genuine," Morlortai said. "I'm the best
sniper you'll ever see."

"You haven't seen me shoot," Kiwanuka said.

Morlortai showed her a trace of a smile. "My apologies. However, wouldn't *two* amazing snipers be better
than one?"

"How can I trust you?"

"Because you need to," Morlortai said. "Because we
already have one agreement regarding freedom for my
crew and me, and I believe you will honor that. We could
leave you here as soon as that hatch cycles open. We

could disappear into that jungle and take our chances in getting off this planet. Instead, I'm offering you a small, well-trained unit that specializes in surgical operations."

"There's nothing surgical about what we're doing out here," Kiwanuka said grimly. "We're all going to get bloody in this."

"As you say." Morlortai nodded. "But put a sniper rifle in my hands and perhaps you'll see for yourself."

The hatch opened at the same time Kiwanuka opened the dropship's weapons locker. Armor and weapons hung neatly there despite the harsh landing.

"Suit up," Kiwanuka said. She slid a Yqueu sniper rifle free and handed it to Morlortai, who inclined his head. She claimed another for herself. "Veug?"

"Yes, Staff Sergeant."

"Get these people checked into armor and weps. Even if they can't handle all the suit systems, the near-AIs and armor will provide protection."

"Yes, Staff Sergeant."

"And don't be all day about it."

"No, Staff Sergeant." Veug approached the weapons locker, sized up Morlortai and his crew, and handed out armor.

Kiwanuka extended her hand to Morlortai. "An agreement, then."

"Yes," he replied, and shook her hand. "You'll be glad that you did this."

"Make sure that I am," Kiwanuka said. "Let me know when you're in the field."

"I will. Good luck, Staff Sergeant."

Kiwanuka sprinted out of the dropship and took stock of the blasted and broken impromptu landing site. Shattered trees and branches lay all around them. The *John Lee* stood awkwardly on landing gear that had crumpled on one side.

The dropship listed to the side and was pockmarked with damage from Phrenorian weapons fire sustained in space. The hull was slagged in places where the ablative armor had been torn away on reentry.

The *John Lee* would never fly again without some serious time in a repair bay.

Any landing you can walk away from, Kiwanuka reminded herself.

The HUD showed that they were three hundred meters from the caves and where the GPS pin Noojin's sec system showed Telilu was.

"Noojin," Kiwanuka said. "You're with me. We're going to get Telilu and Quass Leghef."

"Copy that, Staff Sergeant," Noojin said. Despite the attempt to be brave and efficient, the fear in her made her voice crack. She cradled her Roley in her arms.

Kiwanuka opened a comm link to Fort York. "Command, this is Staff Sergeant Kiwanuka. We're on-site and everybody knows we're here." She stared at the impenetrable jungle around them. "I suggest we ping Master Sergeant Sage and let him know too. That way we can coordinate."

"Roger that," Halladay said. "Putting you through now."

With Noojin flanking her, Kiwanuka ran for the explosions ahead of them. Several trees collapsed, and she was willing to bet Culpepper was behind it.

0852 Hours Zulu Time

The tall trees toppled in perfect synchronization from the hill overlooking the cave mouth. From what Sage could tell, the trees had been ripped free of the earth.

They also fell toward the cave mouth on the other side of the small clearing.

At first, Sage thought Culpepper had misjudged the amount of explosives he'd used, that the corporal had used too much, because the trees *flew* several meters. After a brief reflection, Sage was certain he had seen the trees leap from the ground like they'd been fired from a cannon.

Broken roots shot through with white flesh trailed muddy loam as the trees sailed through the air. The trees were at least three meters in diameter and a hundred meters tall. They had to weigh thousands of kilos. *Each.*

In all the battles he'd witnessed, Sage had never seen anything like the sight before him. On worlds where he'd fought the Phrenorians, whole archologies—a thousand stories and more—had fallen, but never in the controlled way the trees took flight. They sailed like perfectly placed projectiles, which he supposed they were under Culpepper's guidance, and crashed onto the sat systems rising slowly and heading for the canopy high overhead.

All three units became scrap under the massive trees when they landed. Tremors raced through the ground and shook a cascade of water from the interlaced branches that formed the canopy. The fat drops fell over everything.

"Waa-hoo!" Culpepper exulted.

In spite of the situation, Sage grinned at the success. The timetable for whatever Tholak and the Phrenorians had been planning was at least set back, if not derailed.

"Well done, Corporal." Sage raised up enough to survey the clearing. The Phrenorians and Tholak's men huddled in confusion. "The rest of you send these Sting-Tails running or bury them where they stand."

Sage switched over to the frequency he shared with Murad. "Sir, with your permission, Jahup and I are going after Quass Leghef. Provided she's still alive, I mean to bring her back that way."

"Copy that, Master Sergeant," Murad said. "Good luck. I'll keep our soldiers on task here and see if we can't come up with an exfil."

"Thank you, sir." Sage looked over to Jahup and switched to the comm channel between them.

The younger man's body language radiated calm and readiness that probably no other soldier on the mission had. Jahup was in the jungle and fighting for his life. He was in his element.

"Me and you," Sage said. "We're going after your grandmother."

"Copy that, Master Sergeant."

"You stay on my six. Close. Don't let anything get between us."

"I won't."

"Nothing that isn't us lives, Jahup. Do you understand? Everyone down there except your grandmother is an enemy, and we don't have time for prisoners or mercy. No time for questions or guesses."

"They won't get any mercy from me," Jahup said. "I didn't come here to give it. Or expect it. Those who took her are going to die. All of them."

Sage took a breath to center himself. "Then let's do this." Popping up, he sprayed a salvo of grenades at the locations he'd noted where the Phrenorians and Tholak's mercenaries were grouped to drive them to cover. When the grenades detonated, he sprinted forward, taking advantage of all the confusion the falling trees and grenades had created.

A group of Makaum men taking cover behind a crawler spotted him and fired their weapons at him immediately. Bullets and beams ripped into the ground at Sage's feet and were blunted by the armor.

Sage ducked to one side, fired a trio of gel-grenades at the area where the crawler's solar batter array was located, and hunkered down behind one of the fallen trees. Projectiles ripped splinters from the tree trunk and lasers scorched the bark into flames. Streamers of smoke rose above the tree and got ripped apart in the rain.

The gel-grenades went off and were followed almost instantly by the solar batteries cooking off with sharp detonations. The roar of explosions blocked out all other noise in the clearing. Shrapnel from the vehicle ripped through the surrounding countryside with sharp pings.

Standing again, his assault rifle to his shoulder, Sage climbed over the tree high enough to settle the Roley onto the rough bark. He fired depleted uranium rounds into a solitary man running from the burning crawler. Flames clung to the man's body despite the rain. When the bullets hit him, he fell into a large puddle, both he and the flames extinguished.

Nothing else around the crawler moved.

"Master Sergeant Sage," a woman called over his comm.

Sage vaulted over the tall tree and dropped to the ground in a crouch. He kept going forward toward the cave and blasted suppressive fire and grenades to keep a group of Phrenorians pinned behind a stand of boulders near the cave entrance.

The Phrenorians concentrated their fire on the tree and pinned Sage in place. Splinters and bark ripped free of the trunk. Flaming chunks fell away from the tree.

"Kiwanuka?" Sage asked as he placed the voice.

"Roger that," she said.

Sage ducked behind a tree with a trunk thick enough to offer him brief shelter while he searched for his opponents' positions. He pumped ammo back into his assault rifle from the armor and peered around the tree. "You're back from space?"

"I am," Kiwanuka answered. "Colonel Halladay ordered us to help you out. I brought my team with me, as well as a complement of talented civilians."

"What civilians?"

"Morlortai and his crew."

Sage placed the name with difficulty as he spotted a man's leg sticking out from behind a boulder. He squeezed off a burst of depleted uranium rounds and the leg came apart in a rush of blood and bone. When the man fell, Sage tapped two more rounds through the man's head.

"After their ship got destroyed by the Phrenorians, we gave Morlortai and his crew a ride home on a dropship. Helping us is their way of paying back the favor."

"Some favor," Sage said dryly. "If it hadn't been for them, you wouldn't have been up there."

"We made it back."

"Yeah, but a lot of people didn't." Sage peered around the tree trunk and ducked back just before a grenade attached to the bark. The explosion of flames roasted the bark and set off warnings inside his suit. "Where is your dropship?"

"Crashed getting us here. The *John Lee* is going to need some skilled people to get it back online. We're not going to get any help there."

"Copy that," Sage said. "Jahup and I are on a rescue mission to get Quass Leghef. She's inside the cave with Tholak and some of his hired muscle, and maybe some of the Phrenorians."

The tree shivered under the continued assault. Another explosion tore into the trunk.

"We're stalled out here," Sage said. "Can you clear the way?"

"I've got this, Master Sergeant," Kiwanuka said coolly. "I didn't survive a Phrenorian space attack just to get back here and watch you die. I've got the second-best sniper on Makaum with me."

Sage grinned at that. He released the drones from his armor and the views instantly became another layer of the transparencies he was tracking on his faceshield. He sent them out to map the area. One of them got ensnared in a *kifrik* web that he didn't see until it was too late. A *kifrik* slid along the wet strands and attacked the foreign thing trapped in its web.

The second drone zoomed along the terrain until Sage spotted Zhoh racing for the cave entrance. Before Sage could recover from his surprise at seeing his opponent there, the Phrenorian general blasted the drone with his assault rifle.

The view transparency from the drone blinked out of existence from Sage's faceshield.

"Zhoh is here!" Sage roared.

He stood and took a step from behind the tree just as a particle beam cannon fired a blast at his position. The concussion knocked him from his feet and he spun across the muddy turf. His view of the battlefield flipped again and again as he rolled.

Zhoh fired blasts into the Phrenorians in front of the cave, knocked them out of his way, and he disappeared into the cave. The sight of Zhoh killing his own warriors confused Sage. He pushed his questions regarding that out of his mind as he reeled in his scattered senses. Phrenorians were the enemy. He intended to put his sights on as many of them as he could.

Sage hitched up against a copse of young trees and managed a sitting position. He still held the Roley. The assault rifle was covered in mud, no longer as clean and shiny, but he knew it was still lethal.

Four Phrenorian warriors shot at him from behind rocks and the trees Culpepper had blasted down and two of the burning crawlers. Bullets and blasts hammered Sage's armor.

Warning! the near-AI said. *Get to cover, Master Sergeant. The damage the armor is sustaining is reaching critical levels.*

Only a few meters away, Jahup lay pinned down by enemy fire. Two more Phrenorians crept up on his position.

Sage pushed himself up, pulled the rifle to his shoulder, and put the sights over one of the Phrenorians only to watch the warrior's cephalothorax burst in a spray of chitin and soft tissue. The Phrenorian fell even as another spun sideways when a heavy-caliber round smashed into him.

Trusting Kiwanuka's skills, Sage pushed himself up and ran for the cave entrance. Without being told, Jahup followed at his heels.

SIXTY

The Caves of the Glass Dead
Rilormang
The Sulusku Highlands
28 Kilometers North of Makaum Sprawl
0855 Hours Zulu Time

Thunder echoed into the cavern from the jungle outside. Telilu jumped and cried out in fear. Her arms squeezed Leghef harder.

Tholak's attention wavered for just a moment. His grip tightened on the knife he held as he glanced back over his shoulder.

Leghef was focused, drawing on all those old skills she'd been raised with that had kept her from getting killed taking meat out in the jungle. She stepped forward and threw her hands over Tholak's blade. She slid the plastic restraining strap holding her wrists together as quickly as she could, hoping to sever it.

When she could slip the plastic binding no farther, when the strap pressed into Tholak's forearm and the movement caused him to shift his attention back to her, Leghef pulled her hands back again and hoped the strap would part. The cold kiss of the blade against her left wrist brought a hot rush of blood down her hand.

But the strap parted and her hands were free. She didn't try to run, didn't try to flee, because she knew those things wouldn't be possible with Tholak and Osler standing practically on top of her. Instead, she grabbed Tholak's hand and twisted. For a moment, she thought her blood would prevent her grip from holding, then Tholak's wrist turned, his hand opened, and he yelled in pain and warning.

Leghef scooped the knife from Tholak's hand and her mind formed a plan of action just ahead of her body's response. For a moment she feared that she was too old, had lived too soft, had forgotten too many things.

But the knife's hilt, even through the blood coating her hand, felt right, strong and true. She slashed Tholak's throat and crimson bubbles frothed at the wound.

A shocked look filled his face and he took an instinctive step back to avoid further injury. It was too late, though. His mind just hadn't accepted that.

Leghef placed her hand in the center of Tholak's chest and pushed. He stumbled back and fell, and Osler's attention was diverted by his employer's blood for too long.

Osler tried to bring his pistol up, but Leghef blocked the attempt with her free hand, stepped inside the man's reach, and drove her stolen knife home in her opponent's left eye. Osler stood there for a moment, like he was thinking about what he was supposed to do next, but he died before he made up his mind.

Unable to retrieve the knife because it had gotten stuck in bone, Leghef released the hilt and plucked the pistol from the dead man's hand. As Osler fell, the Phrenorians turned to her, saw what had happened, and reached for their weapons.

Leghef pulled Telilu's hands from around her waist and shoved her toward the small passageway at the back of the cavern.

"Run, Telilu!"

Leghef followed, expecting to feel a bullet tear through her or a beam burn a hole through her or a particle blast shatter her organs and knock her from her feet. Hoarse shouts of surprise and agony rang out behind her as she slipped into the passageway after her granddaughter.

There was another way out. If they could get there in time, it was possible they could disappear into the jungle.

320776 Akej (Phrenorian Prime)

Zhoh ran into the cavern and raked his gaze over the glassy figures at the back and the two Phrenorian lieutenant colonels who stood before him. The glassy figures failed to hold his interest when his enemies were so readily available.

"Traitors!" Zhoh raged. He slung his assault rifle over his shoulder and held his *patimong* ready. He raised his primaries before him to use as clubs or to tear into the warriors.

Nalit raised a beam pistol and took a half-step back, something no warrior would do in the face of an opponent. Zhoh shot his left primary forward and caught the wrist of Nalit's secondary just behind his hand. Then he squeezed and snipped off the lieutenant colonel's hand. The severed fist and the pistol dropped to the worn stone floor as Nalit screamed in agony.

Mercilessly, Zhoh swung the *patimong* at Nalit's cephalothorax. When the shock of the blade meeting chitin and cleaving it ran along his arm, satisfaction flooded Zhoh. His pheromones drenched the air around him as savage joy filled him.

It was good to kill his enemies. That was what he'd been born for. To break them and take their lives, no matter who they were.

Zhoh struck again and again and spattered Nalit's blood against the cave wall. He wanted to beat out of himself the weakness that had sent him chasing after Sxia and the promise of advancement she had offered in the Empire. Choosing to pursue that was his downfall.

It hadn't been her weak bloodline. It was his own covetous nature. He knew that now. He struck again, knowing that if he hadn't sought the prestige a union with her would bring that it would have been years before he garnered enough attention and support to get where he wanted to be.

He had stepped away from the order the Empire existed on.

Yet, his crimes were less than Rangha's black market dealings. They were less than Blaold Oldawe's hiring of an assassin to kill his son-in-law.

And they were less than the subterfuge the War Board wanted to do to throw Zhoh like waste before a *krayari* beetle.

He didn't deserve that and he refused to let that be all he was given. He would take what he wanted, and he would start taking it here, on this planet. He would create his own Empire.

Zhoh struck again, only then realizing that he was

hacking into a corpse. Gore and broken pieces of chitin covered him, Nalit, and the wall and floor.

Releasing Nalit, Zhoh stepped back. His warriors stared at him in awe as they guarded the doorway into the cavern.

Warar stood only a short distance away. He held two pistols in his secondaries but didn't raise them. Zhoh's warriors had him covered with their weapons, so if he moved, he would die. His pheromones stank of fear and indecision, and Zhoh gloried in seeing the warrior stripped down and left wanting.

At the same time, his anger blazed. These were the warriors the Empire had put their trust in. He wondered what they would think if they saw Warar now.

"You're no warrior," Zhoh accused. "You're no Phrenorian who lives only to advance the Empire. You're the reason so many are weakening. Your bloodline fouls our future. You could have stood with me and helped me take this planet."

"The War Board didn't want you as their hero," Warar said in a false show of bravado.

"You could have shared the glory I am going to receive," Zhoh taunted.

Warar stood straighter, but the fear stink on him grew worse. "Don't talk to me about being weak. And don't talk to me about any glory you think you're going to get. You're *kalque*. You have no future. Even if you take this planet, the War Board will strip—"

Zhoh stepped up to the warrior then, seized Warar's face with his *chelicerae*, and injected him with venom. With a quick flick of his primaries, he snipped off Warar's secondaries, which were holding the beam pistols. Ignoring the thunder of gunfire and explosions coming from outside the cave, he fended off his opponent's attempts to break free until Warar went limp.

"Triarr," Mato called over the comm, "you must capture the woman. Already, it appears the Alliance may be ready to reverse its decision to pull out of Makaum. Public sentiment throughout those systems is becoming volatile. Several planets in the Alliance are demanding that action be taken. You must take control of that situation now."

Zhoh dropped the corpse and turned his attention to the passageway at the back of the cave. Since Leghef was not in the room it was likely she had fled in that direction.

"I will," Zhoh said. He ordered some of his warriors to remain behind and guard the cave entrance. Then he ran toward the passageway. "Have the transport ship ready to relay a comm link."

He peered ahead, knowing that the old female could not have gotten far. He would catch her.

And when he did, there would be a reckoning.

SIXTY-ONE

Sage reached the cave mouth, posted up beside it, and whipped his head around to peer inside. A round smacked into his head and rocked it back on his shoulders. He pulled his head back as his faceshield flickered uncontrollably. Disjointed images rolled through his vision so fast and sharp he had to close his eyes against them.

"Are you all right?" Jahup stood slightly behind Sage.

"Yeah," Sage said. "Yeah, I'm good. Rookie mistake. Should have known someone would have been watching."

He took a breath to clear his head and opened his eyes. The transparencies shifted and blended. Some came to the top and others cycled down. The layers shuffled like cards in a deck till it all became confusion.

Warning, the near-AI said. *Helmet has experienced critical damage and is malfunctioning. Some services may be off-line or unreliable. Defensive properties being estimated. Replacement necessary.*

His reflection on Jahup's faceshield showed the tear that ran the length of the side of his helmet. Sage swore, then felt fortunate that the round hadn't cored through his head. Either the ammunition the Phrenorians were using was some kind of armor-piercing bullet he hadn't heard of, or his armor integrity truly was breaking down faster than he'd realized.

The Phrenorian who stepped out of the entrance after Sage showed in the reflection too.

Jahup fired immediately, but his rounds flattened against the Phrenorian's abbreviated armor and only succeeded in driving their opponent back. Off balance, the Sting-Tail fired into the air.

Sage spun and dropped his Roley to hang by its sling. He grabbed the Phrenorian's weapon barrel in both hands and shoved hard backward. Driven by the armor's extra muscle and speed, the Phrenorian bounced off the other side of the cave entrance hard enough to stagger him.

Inside the cave, caught from the corner of Sage's own vision because the HUD wasn't providing the 360-degree view he was used to, four other Phrenorians held their fire, unwilling to kill one of their own too hastily. But they tracked Sage with their weapons, lighting him up with their red targeting lasers.

Sage slammed his head into the Phrenorian's mouth, crushed the warrior's *chelicerae* into bloody smears, and stunned him. He yanked the Phrenorian's rifle away and ducked back across the entrance. He swung the rifle and broke it while more explosions went off out in the clearing.

Before the Sting-Tail returned to his senses, Sage ducked back across the entrance. A couple of rounds tore more gouges across his armor and the heat of a laser felt like it was going to cook his right forearm.

Then he gripped the Phrenorian's chest armor in one hand and yanked him around to present as a shield to the other Sting-Tails. Some rounds and laser blasts smacked into the Phrenorian and he shuddered with the impacts. At least one of the rounds slashed a furrow across Sage's right calf.

He yanked a high-explosive grenade from his ammo rack, popped the pin, and pushed the weapon behind the Phrenorian's chest armor while his opponent was too dazed to know what was going on.

Setting himself as a fulcrum, Sage whirled and threw the Phrenorian into the four warriors within. He spun back behind the corner of the cave entrance, yanked two more grenades—a tangler and a fragmentation explosive—pulled the pins, and flipped both into the cave.

He grabbed his Roley and readied the assault rifle.

"Ready?" he asked Jahup.

"Ready, Master Sergeant."

The comm sounded scratchy inside Sage's helmet, but he could hear.

All three grenades went off in quick succession, one followed by two more almost a heartbeat later.

Sage ducked around the cave entrance behind the Roley and stayed low. Water sluiced into the cave from outside and collected into a pool that splashed around his boots. Smoke and debris from the explosion created a small cloud within the immediate area.

Ahead of him, the Phrenorian he'd booby-trapped

lay leaking his guts out onto the floor. Chitin and tissue clung to the walls and ceiling. Two Phrenorians writhed in a tangled heap on the stone floor. Sage thought only one of them was alive, but to make sure, he put rounds through the cephalothoraxes of both and stepped over their bodies as they went still.

"Sage," Kiwanuka called. "Noojin and I are on your six."

The fourth Phrenorian bled profusely and shiny bits of metal gleamed in his flesh. He pointed his rifle and fired at the same time Sage did. The Roley's depleted uranium round ripped into the Phrenorian, knocked off chunks of chitin, and exposed vulnerable organs beneath that glistened.

The Phrenorian's round pierced Sage's right thigh and came out the other side.

Sage fired again as he ignored the rush of pain and continued forward till the Roley's barrel was almost touching the Phrenorian. As he stepped around his opponent, Sage threw a shoulder into him and knocked him backward. The Sting-Tail was dead when he reached the ground.

You are critically wounded, the near-AI said.

The fiery pain in Sage's leg almost crippled him. He forced himself to walk and followed the Roley across the room and into a passageway on the other side of where Tholak lay dead beside another man who was equally dead. Throzath huddled nearby and held his empty hands up.

"Don't shoot!" the young man begged. "Don't shoot."

"Take him into custody," Sage ordered.

Jahup threw Throzath on the ground, pulled his hands behind him, and bound his wrists and ankles. Sage stood guard until the task was completed.

Your femur is broken, the near-AI went on. *You*

cannot go on. You must seek immediate medical attention.

"Negative," Sage growled. "Not till we wrap this mission. Fix it."

"Master Sergeant," Jahup said, not privy to the conversation with the suit, "you're bleeding."

"It'll be okay," Sage replied. Perspiration covered his brow and his vision blurred a little. *It's the pain,* he told himself. *Push through it. You've been here before. People are counting on you.*

"Fix it," Sage growled at the near-AI. "Fix it now."

Complying. Administering pain management suite. Applying coagulant. Applying synthetic blood.

A warm glow filled Sage and made his tongue thick. He tried to call up the suit's enhanced nightvision to cut through the dark that filled the passageway, but the vision enhancement suite was off-line. He called for the suit's external lights and was relieved when the beams strobed from his chest plate and illuminated his surroundings. Only three of the four lights were working and he assumed he'd lost one of them along the way.

Sage entered the passageway, limped unsteadily, and crashed a shoulder into the rock wall. He righted himself with effort and continued.

"Sage," Jahup said, "you're wounded. You need to stop."

"We'll stop when your grandmother is safe," Sage replied. "Keep moving."

Stabilizing broken femur.

Sharp pain bit into Sage's leg despite the drug cocktail jackhammering away in his bloodstream. His brain was as light and insubstantial as a cloud and it bounced around inside his skull. His eyelids weighed five hundred kilos. It was everything he could do to keep them open.

From previous experience, he knew the suit had drilled screws into his leg to pull the bone together for support. His thigh suddenly felt tighter as the upper leg armor clamped down around his flesh and bone to give it added strength and structural reliability. His footing became more certain, but he grew aware that he was listing to one side due to the drugs muddying his reflexes.

Broken femur stabilized, the near-AI reported. *Chances of procedure being successful are at twenty-seven percent. Significant damage to the soft tissue around the femur remains ongoing. Unable to resolve an accurate assessment of internal damage.*

"Cut the narco-suite and clear my head," Sage ordered. He picked up the pace now that the leg felt more certain. It wasn't the leg, though. It was the armor holding him together.

Warning! Washing the painkillers from your system will result in potentially debilitating pain.

"The pain isn't going to kill me," Sage barked, "but not being able to see something, or react to something, when I need to will. Override protocol. *Clear my head!*"

A cool wave of meds entered Sage's bloodstream and swiftly cleared away the effects of the narcotics.

The downside was the onslaught of agony that came on so fast it caught him off guard and took his breath away. Every move was excruciating, but the armor moved his leg like there was nothing wrong with it. He kept the pain at bay through sheer willpower.

His stride evened out and he lurched into a run and forced himself to close the distance between himself and Zhoh and Leghef. The woman was up ahead, totally at the Phrenorian's mercy.

The passageway twisted back and forth and up and

down. Several times Sage had to duck under low-hanging ceiling sections. The ripped side of his helmet caught on stone twice. He remained aware that the external lights he was using would mark him for the Phrenorians as he approached them.

"Master Sergeant," Murad called.

"Go, Lieutenant," Sage responded.

"Be advised that we have spotted a Phrenorian transport ship on the other side of this hill. Judging from your GPS location, it's almost on top of you."

Sage bounced off an acute turn, recovered from the pain, and spotted daylight ahead of him. "That must be the ship that brought Zhoh here, sir. We'll be sharp."

"Sergeant Kiwanuka is on her way to your twenty," Murad said. Weapons fire cracked and screamed in the background. "She is bringing a small group with her."

"Copy that," Sage said.

He stepped from the passageway and out into the jungle that washed up against the hill, once more in the Green Hell with death all around him.

321212 Akej (Phrenorian Prime)

Zhoh searched for the female as he ran through the forest. Anxiety chafed at him when he couldn't immediately see his prey. In the passageway and the caverns, he'd been more confident that he would locate them. There were fewer places to hide. The constant background of noise, of combat, and the storm crashing and falling rain all around hadn't been there.

Now, with the rain cascading down from the canopy high overhead, it was almost as if the planet itself was hissing spitefully at him. He steeled his resolve. Makaum had been just as much of an opponent as the Terran military.

And his commanding officers.

Zhoh caught a trace of the female's spoor then and he followed it. She was afraid. He could taste that in her scent. So was the child. He knew having the child was good. She would provide leverage over the female.

He would not underestimate the female because of her age or size, though. Tholak had made that mistake and had paid for it.

He put a primary out to turn more sharply around a thick tree and once more tasted the female's spoor. She was closer now. She had been injured. He smelled the blood on her and that odor made Zhoh's senses come even more to life.

He lengthened his stride, cut through a copse of trees and broke several saplings doing so, and spotted the two figures ahead of him. His warriors pounded after him, their large peds slapping against the wet ground and gathered puddles.

This isn't rain, Zhoh told himself. *This world is weeping. It knows I have beaten it.*

He gloried in that. Visions of him receiving the *Kabilak* in the Grand Halls of the Empire on Phrenoria became more real. The fantasy was taking his *patimong* and killing Blaold Oldawe and Sxia immediately after the presentation.

But all things were possible.

Lannig *changes everything,* he reminded himself. Makaum was merely another molting time, another instance of growth and strengthening.

He ran.

Ahead of him, the female tripped and fell. She

sprawled on the muddy ground. The child stopped and struggled to get the female to her feet, but it was already too late.

Zhoh stopped in front of them, towered over them, and reached down for the female. She was moving, so she was still alive, and that allayed some of the fear he'd suddenly felt when he remembered how frail she was.

The child turned to him, screaming and crying, and batted at the secondaries that Zhoh extended to pick up the woman.

Irritated at the show of defiance, Zhoh backhanded the child and she flew backward. Immediately, he regretted the blow. She would be of no use to him as leverage if she were dead. He looked at her and noted the rise and fall of her chest and the throbbing pulse in the hollow of her neck.

The old female rolled over and brought up a pistol Zhoh hadn't known she possessed. She fired twice at point-blank range and both bullets smashed into him before he could wrest the weapon from her grip.

She screamed in desperate frustration and fury.

"Stop!" Zhoh commanded. "I won't kill you, but I can injure you in many ways that will make you wish you were dead."

She screamed again, an inarticulate explosion that was so primitive it impressed Zhoh. When he had seen the female on several occasions, she had always been calm and composed.

Zhoh waved to one of the warriors at his back.

"Restrain her," he commanded. "Restrain the child."

Two warriors bent to perform those actions.

Zhoh opened a comm link to Mato. "Send the transport ship down to my location."

"At once," Mato said. He sounded distracted. "There is news coming in just now from the Alliance meeting."

As he waited, Zhoh watched tree branches overhead roast into ashes under an onslaught of laser fire. The opening grew quickly and revealed more and more of the transport ship.

"Triarr," Mato said. "It has been confirmed. The Alliance is sending a Strike Wing of space fighters and a carrier to aid Makaum. The Empire has recalled the dreadnoughts. We are to be abandoned."

"Get out of there!" Zhoh ordered. "Leave the buildings! That will be the first place the fighters hit!"

The Empire filled its facilities with explosives designed to reduce any site they built to smoking, radiated ruins rather than let any potential information fall into enemy hands. The signal to self-destruct the embassy and the outlying labs would be sent at any moment. Mato would be lost.

"There is no time," Mato said stoically. "Kill the Terrans, *triarr*! Kill as many of them as—"

The comm link ended and Zhoh stood there in the rain as the transport ship burned through the leafy canopy. He didn't hear the explosions that killed Mato, but they echoed in his head all the same because he had heard them before.

He turned his attention to the female before him and rage swelled within him.

SIXTY-TWO

Rilormang
The Sulusku Highlands
28 Kilometers North of Makaum Sprawl
0902 Hours Zulu Time

Ignoring the pain that seared his injured leg and the fact that his HUD was off-line and he was reduced to only his own vision, Sage sprinted and followed the Phrenorian tracks through the jungle. His breath scoured the back of his throat and he knew his body was burning more oxygen as he increased his demands of it and it worked to manage his injuries.

Jahup matched him stride for stride and Sage knew the younger man was holding back deliberately in spite of his grandmother's situation. Jahup was a hunter. He knew strength lay in numbers when facing a larger or more dangerous quarry.

Sage cut around a tree and had no chance to stop himself before he ran into the ambush set by three Phrenorians. The Sting-Tails opened fire from the brush. Rounds hammered Sage's armor, set off warnings, and blew away patches of the outer layer.

Knocked from his feet, breathless, Sage rolled into a kneeling position and brought the Roley to his shoulder. He bracketed the nearest Phrenorian and opened fire.

Jahup was there before Sage could yell a warning. The younger man ran up a tree till gravity took hold again, and flipped backward over the arc of bullets that hammered the trunk and pursued him. As he turned in the air, Jahup opened fire. Sage's rounds ripped his target's cephalothorax to pieces.

The second Phrenorian shivered from the impacts of Jahup's rounds. Sage partially blinded the third warrior with a gel-grenade that covered several of its eyes. As Jahup landed in a crouch, the Phrenorian blew up.

The concussion knocked Sage and Jahup from their feet, but they got up quickly and ran toward the hovering transport ship.

Bullets and beams hosed the jungle around Sage and Jahup as the crew aboard the Phrenorian ship opened fire. Dodging quickly, Sage and Jahup went to ground behind trees. Sage got his Roley up and fired, but the Phrenorians stood behind heavy armor.

He cursed in frustration, knowing he was so close but that he wouldn't reach Leghef or Zhoh before the Phrenorian general escaped with his captive.

"Sage," Halladay called over the comm, "the Phrenorians are pulling out of the system. The Alliance is sending ships to support us. If you people can hang on a little bit longer, we'll have reinforcements."

Sage looked for the transport ship's weaknesses he could exploit, something—anything—that would give him an edge so he could force it to turn away. "That's good news, sir."

Jet engines provided vertical takeoff and landing capabilities. The wings held two massive engines for forward thrust, and two more engines mounted in back of those and to the side at ninety degrees for vertical lift.

Engines were delicate. Any wing or cavalry or powersuit squad griped about that constantly. The rule of thumb was that for every hour of operation in the field, the wrench jockeys had to spend three hours in maintenance and repairs.

The basso report of a heavy-caliber sniper rifle roared over the constant intake of the transport ship's engine. A moment later, one of the Phrenorian gunners toppled from the ship.

The sniper rifle boomed five more times. Two more Sting-Tails fell from the transport ship.

"Kiwanuka?" Sage called.

"Affirmative," Kiwanuka responded.

"Can you take out the pilot?"

"Negative," she answered. "I've already tried. The cockpit's reinforced. Even these enhanced fifty-caliber rounds won't penetrate. And even if I did, there are automated systems on board."

The transport ship continued dropping as it burned its way down to the ground. The pilot carefully avoided the tree line during the descent.

Spurred on by an idea, Sage brought the Roley to his shoulder, slipped his finger over the grenade launcher trigger, and fired three rounds into the trees nearest the transport ship.

When the grenades exploded, they reduced tree branches into kindling that was sucked into the roaring jet engines. Harsh grinding immediately followed. One of the engines released a cloud of thick, black smoke and exploded a moment later.

Out of control, the transport ship slid sideways, hit

the trees, and a second engine exploded. The ship dropped like a rock, flipped over when it hit, and broke into pieces. A half dozen Phrenorians stumbled out and took defensive positions around the wreckage of their aircraft.

"Kiwanuka," Sage said, "can you—"

"We've got this," Kiwanuka replied. "We'll protect your six while you get Leghef. Jahup's little sister, Telilu, is out there too. She has a tracker. That's how we found you."

"Copy that."

Two innocents were on the line. Sage pushed the dread and uncertainty he felt from his mind and focused on the task at hand. Even without an exfil, Zhoh could disappear into the jungle.

Hoping to take Zhoh by surprise, Sage pushed up and ran forward. Jahup must have had the same idea, because he was up only a half-step later.

A small figure lay on the ground ahead.

Cold fear wormed through Sage's stomach for a moment, then he saw that the figure was still breathing.

"Telilu!" Jahup yelled. He ran for the girl and crouched beside her. He reached for her and a round cored into his back and knocked him forward.

Spinning, knowing he'd made a mistake, Sage brought the Roley up and looked over the sights at Zhoh standing behind a copse of trees. The Phrenorian warrior held Leghef before him, using her as a shield. He pointed a big pistol at Sage.

"It's over, Zhoh," Sage said. "Your people have probably already let you know the Alliance is sending support to Makaum. They're not going to let this planet go. They're going to protect these people."

"Is that what they're doing, Sage?" Zhoh's tone was mocking, which surprised Sage because the modulators didn't normally have that much complexity. That kind of interpretation took years of speaking. "Only hours ago, the Alliance was still behind you getting your people out of here and leaving the planet."

"That's above my paygrade," Sage said. "I'm a soldier doing my job, and my job right now is to save that woman."

Small arms fire cracked in the distance and Sage knew Kiwanuka and her team were hard-pressed standing against the survivors of the Phrenorian crash.

"Why save her?" Zhoh mused. "Why is this being any more important to the Alliance than any other they have let die?"

"She's important to me," Sage said.

Zhoh moved one of his primaries reflexively. "What if you can't save her?"

"I'll kill you."

"A Phrenorian would have already killed me. Even if it meant killing her as well."

"I'm not you," Sage said. "You already knew that. That's why you're holding on to her."

"Perhaps she's worth something to the Alliance as well."

"Do you have a way of asking them?" Sage challenged. "Because I'm not making that offer for you."

"Even at the risk of her life?"

"If me and you can't come to an arrangement right here, right now, involving the Alliance diplomatic corps isn't going to help. They won't offer you anything more than I'm willing to offer you."

Zhoh hissed distastefully. He straightened himself and stood taller. "What do you have to offer?"

"Let the woman go and you can live."

"You're talking about surrender to a Phrenorian warrior of the Empire?" Zhoh's *chelicerae* twitched. "The only reason we understand that concept is because we crossed paths with humans. We don't even have a word for that in our language."

"I hear you don't have a word for *mercy* either." Sage shifted slightly and tried not to get noticed.

Two other Phrenorians stood to one side of Zhoh. Both held their assault rifles at the ready, but neither appeared too eager to use them.

"But mercy is something I'm willing to offer," Sage continued. "You just need to let the woman go and lay down your weapon."

"What would you do if our situation were reversed?" Zhoh asked. "Would you accept . . . *mercy*?"

"No," Sage stated flatly. Rain ran down his faceshield and made his vision blurry. "The Empire doesn't recognize mercy, and they have no use for prisoners."

"Maybe you're wrong about that." Zhoh paused. "Do you know what I was wrong about?"

Sage wanted to keep Zhoh talking. As long as the Phrenorian was talking, he wasn't going to kill Leghef. "What?"

"Our stories," Zhoh said, "are not so different, Master Sergeant. I arrived on this backwater planet under a cloud of disgrace. Some small part of it was my own fault. I was too covetous of a higher position within the Empire. I wanted to grow more quickly. The parents who gave birth to me marked me with their low-caste colors. I was marked, and would never rise above where I was. Only through skill and bravery did I change that. *Lannig* changes everything."

Sage remembered the phrase from the briefing he'd had on the Phrenorians.

"I knew that if I was patient," Zhoh said, "I could again take control of my future. Except the mate binding I agreed to robbed me of what little future I had. I became *kalque*. Do you know what that means?"

"No."

"It means, in the eyes of the Empire, I was nothing, no one, and I would never know any kind of life that I deserved. I was fated to die on the battlefield of some planet somewhere far from my homeworld. The Terran military sent you here for the same reasons."

"I fought to get here," Sage said.

Zhoh hissed. "In a nowhere, out-of-the-way place like this?"

"There are people here who needed protecting," Sage said. "I signed on to do that."

"Insignificant people!" Zhoh shouted. "None of them worth a drop of your blood because you are a warrior!"

Sage waited, knew that they were getting to it, and still wasn't sure what was going to happen.

"You had such small goals," Zhoh said, "and you rose to every occasion. You *earned* the attention of the Alliance even though you didn't pursue it. Tell me, Master Sergeant, do you believe in your Alliance? What it does? What it stands for?"

"Not everything," Sage said, "but most of it. I know that it's not perfect. We're working on it."

"Then I commend you for your belief, and I hope you keep it till your dying day." Zhoh paused. "It is a horrible fate for a warrior to have to die for an entity that doesn't even know who he truly is."

"With me, it goes the other way around," Sage said. "I know what I'm willing to die for. *Who* I'm willing to die for. Most of those people are unknown to me, but I want them to have their lives and for their families to be safe. I'm not looking for glory."

"Nothing else exists for a warrior!"

"You're wrong," Sage said. "There's home. I carry

my home with me, from the mountains where I grew up, and I find a piece of that home and my mother's people and my father's people on every world where I've followed a flag."

Zhoh was quiet for a moment. "I don't have a home. Not anymore. I was stuck serving a dishonorable general who put personal gain before the needs of the Empire. I became mate-bound to a female whose father wanted only to have someone he could blame for the deformed children he knew she would have—which he had, but his child didn't show her malformations. That Empire that I have served so long, and for which I wanted to be a bigger part of, wants to cover up all of that and to lay the blame upon me for losing this world."

Sage didn't know what to say to that.

"So you see," Zhoh said, "your offer of mercy, if I were to take it, would be wasted. I have nowhere to go even if I were permitted to leave this planet, or if I escaped from whatever penal colony the Terran Alliance put me on."

"That's tomorrow," Sage said. "That hasn't even been talked about. Let's just focus on this moment."

"Let's do that, then," Zhoh agreed, "because that much I have figured out." He drew his *patimong* with one of his secondaries. "I'm going to kill you, Master Sergeant, because I am a warrior, because I recognize in you a greatness we call *Genyard*."

The syllables that came through the modulator on Zhoh's chest were unintelligible to Sage.

"Do you know what this means?" Zhoh asked.

"No," Sage replied.

"Pity," Zhoh said. "The title is one of the Empire's greatest honors and seldom is given. It translates to 'warlord' and refers to a warrior so skilled in battle that all others automatically follow him." He paused. "To me, that is what you are. Killing you will be a great honor."

"I take no honor in killing you," Sage said. "You're a good soldier and a good officer. We're just on opposite sides of this war."

"It's more than that," Zhoh said. "You could never do what I do. You would hesitate to end those who are weak or injured or unable to defend themselves."

"You took my side when I faced DawnStar's sec team."

A rough noise came from the translator and Sage guessed that it was what passed for laughter among Phrenorians.

"You impressed me then," Zhoh said, "and I was looking for a battle myself that night. No, you're weaker than I am, but still *Genyard*, so taking your life will still bring me glory. After I destroy you, I am going to kill every soldier I can until I am finally brought down. That way I can die with the glory a warrior should have."

Sage aimed at Zhoh's cephalothorax and squeezed off a single shot because he didn't want to risk hitting Leghef. But Zhoh moved too quickly and the round only ripped the bark off the tree trunk behind him and exposed the white flesh.

Zhoh flung Leghef to the side and she went down with a cry of pain. When she rolled, Sage saw no wounds. While Sage was distracted, Zhoh pumped two rounds from his pistol into him.

Pain ripped through Sage's chest and stomach, but he had the Roley up and firing. His first burst took out one of the Phrenorians caught flatfooted to Zhoh's right. The general's sudden movement had taken his two warriors by surprise as well. A half dozen rounds struck Zhoh, but Sage couldn't tell how much, or if any, damage had been done.

The Sting-Tail Sage shot dropped to his knees. Jahup shot the other one, then tried tracking Zhoh, but by then the Phrenorian warrior was on top of Sage. The forward momentum and the Phrenorian's greater weight took them both to the muddy ground.

Zhoh pressed his pistol against Sage's faceshield. Shifting his weight to the side, Sage mostly dodged the first bullet and caused it to ricochet from him. The second one smashed into his helmet and set off another wave of alarms in the armor.

Boosting nanobots in bloodstream, the near-AI announced. *Suturing chest and stomach wounds. Bullets will have to be removed later. Narco-suite—*

"No!" Sage shouted. "Override! No painkillers! Keep my head clear!"

Unable to bring his rifle up, Sage released the weapon and levered an arm between Zhoh and himself. Several of the Phrenorian's secondary arms grabbed Sage's arm and attempted to pin it against his body. Sage's blood covered both of them.

Zhoh threw himself to the side again and just barely avoided Jahup's shot. The bullet plunged into the muddy ground only millimeters from Sage's head.

Sage's strength flagged as he fought to break Zhoh's holds. He knew he was getting slower. He barely blocked Zhoh's primaries as he bludgeoned Sage with them.

Bracing his feet against the ground, he put his weight and muscle into a short jab that connected with Zhoh's cephalothorax, split the chitin there, and knocked him back. Blood sprayed from his damaged face.

Zhoh hissed and clicked in rage. He tried to bring his pistol around, but Sage blocked it with an arm, and caught it by the barrel. Zhoh fired and the round slapped into the mud. Before the pistol could be pulled back out of Sage's hands, he ripped the weapon free of Zhoh's grip.

Zhoh hammered one of his primaries down on Sage's head and agony filled his vision. The faceshield fractured over Sage's face and made seeing details more difficult. Pain became the bedrock of his world and the abyss of unconsciousness waited at the fringes.

Sage grabbed the claw as Zhoh drew it back up. He held on tightly while Zhoh pushed at him with his other primary. Concentrating, Sage used all his added strength to twist the primary. Cartilage popped and chitin cracked as the wrist tore, then the primary popped free.

A thin feeling of success threaded through Sage for an instant. He worked at bucking Zhoh off him, but the Phrenorian clung with all of his secondaries.

Zhoh opened his remaining primary and locked it around Sage's helmet. He squeezed and the suit's alarms screamed in warning. Sage's head throbbed as the pressure increased.

"This is how it is, Master Sergeant," Zhoh said. "That moment of death on the battlefield when you realize you've spent everything you have trying to vanquish your enemy—only to fail."

Zhoh's tail arced over his shoulder and stabbed into Sage's chest armor. The sharp pain told him it had penetrated, and the agonizing burn—though it felt as if it was coming from a long way off—let him know he'd been envenomed.

The suit's near-AI screamed something, but he couldn't make out the warning.

He concentrated on his right arm as he reached down for the Smith and Wesson .500 Magnum. He curled his fingers around the pistol's butt and fought to bring it up while the burning pain spread across his chest.

Zhoh realized what Sage was doing too late. The Magnum's barrel shoved against the Phrenorian's cephalothorax and he rolled the hammer back.

"I'm not going to be the first one to fail," Sage promised.

He pulled the trigger and Zhoh shook with the impact as a crater opened up and evacuated soft tissue in a spray that briefly challenged the falling rain. Zhoh's hold on him loosened.

Sage grabbed Zhoh's tail and yanked it from his armor and his flesh. The burning caused by the poison continued, but he shoved the Phrenorian from him, rolled over to his side, and pushed himself up on his free hand. His knees were weak and his broken leg trembled even encased in the armor, but he made himself stand. He held the pistol at the ready.

Zhoh struggled to get to his feet, but failed. He had no strength left, and even that was fading.

"I pray we meet on another battlefield after this one," Zhoh said. Blood covered him as his heart pumped it out. "Maybe . . . maybe if you had lost as much as I have . . . maybe you would see that you and I are more alike than you think. You revealed that the night you went looking for that confrontation with DawnStar."

Guilt pinged Sage because he knew that might be true. He had gone there to draw out Velesko Kos, and he had deliberately hunted the criminal element on Makaum to stir up the action. He'd been looking for his own war all this time.

"You see it now, don't you?" Zhoh's voice was all but gone. "You see . . . how we are . . . the same. So nearly the . . . same. Goodbye, *Genyard*."

The Phrenorian shivered and was still. Sage swayed

on his feet, barely able to keep his balance. Pain felt distant, but only because there was so much of it.

Nearby, Jahup crawled off a Phrenorian. The younger man held a long-bladed knife in one hand and was covered from head to boots in mud and blood.

Two other Phrenorians lay twitching in the death throes. Jahup had had his hands full.

"Are you okay?" Sage asked.

"I am." Jahup knelt and cleaned his blade with a fistful of grass, then returned the weapon to a sheath on his combat harness. "Zhoh?"

"Dead."

Jahup reached down and picked up his Roley. Limping, obviously in pain, he approached Sage. "And how are you?"

Sage bent down to pick up his assault rifle, struggled through the spinning that cycled through his head, and straightened back up with difficulty.

"Still standing," Sage answered. "As long as I can do that, I'll be all right."

Combatting Phrenorian venom. Administering Phrenorian anti-venom. Dumping reserve nanobots into bloodstream. Sutures holding. Resecuring broken femur.

Across the clearing, Leghef pushed herself to her feet. Jahup ran to her and they were joined by Telilu.

Noojin came out of the jungle and ran to the little family. They all embraced each other.

Kiwanuka strode out of the jungle holding the Yqueu sniper rifle. She looked complete and ready. She walked over to stand by Sage.

"You've certainly looked better, Master Sergeant," she said.

Sage smiled through the broken faceshield. "Well, you've never looked better, Staff Sergeant Kiwanuka."

"I'll bet you say that to every soldier that's saved your

life." Kiwanuka glanced up at the sky. "Colonel Halladay sent us a ride."

Four jumpcopters flew in a diamond formation and hovered over the opening the Phrenorian airship had made in the canopy.

Sage realized his auditory enhancements were gone because he hadn't heard the airships' approach. "It's a good thing the colonel's not making us walk back. I don't think I would make it."

"You'd make it," Kiwanuka said. "I'd carry you if I had to."

"I appreciate that, Staff Sergeant." Dizziness cascaded through Sage's skull and he tried not to waver, but the suit wasn't as responsive as it normally would have been. He was about to fall when Kiwanuka reached an arm around his waist and helped support him.

"I got you," Kiwanuka said.

Sage wrapped an arm over her shoulders. "Maybe we could make it look like we have each other." He smiled conspiratorially. "I don't want the younger soldiers thinking I'm too hurt to do my job. If there's any kind of a fort left, I have to help the colonel put it back together."

Kiwanuka cleared her faceshield and smiled back at him. "There's still a fort, Master Sergeant, and you're just the soldier to put it back together."

Sage hoped so.

EPILOGUE

Sage sat at a table in the corner of Uncle Huang's Noodle Shop and gazed through the transplas window at all the new construction taking place in the sprawl.

A Navy Seabee wearing a production powersuit walked slowly along an alley where strong defoliant had killed out grass and trees only that morning. The yellowing leaves fluttered in the wind, popped free of the stems, and blew away.

Taking aim with his extrusion arm, the engineer pumped plascrete the color and consistency of bread dough into forms that sketched out a two-story building. His extrusion arm was connected to a large, industrial-grade crawler that carried a tank of ready-to-use plascrete.

Other crews worked throughout the city. The newly built spaceports, some of the first of the new construction, stayed busy with arriving shipments. The Alliance had been generous with the help.

Several Makaum and offworlder children stood in the street and watched in awe. Sage marveled at the sight. That street and alley had run with blood only two months ago. People had died there.

Yet now, after the Terran Navy Construction Battalions had arrived to aid in the rebuilding of the sprawl, picturing the area as a war zone was difficult.

They'd also extruded a prison early on, the first of its kind on the planet, to hold career criminals who had shown their colors during the invasion and the Makaum supporters of the Phrenorian Empire. Throzath was now a guest there. His case would be decided in a few weeks after the court system got squared away.

"What are you thinking?" Kiwanuka asked.

She sat across from him. Like him, she wore a newly minted AKTIVsuit. The Alliance had been quick to resupply the Terran military as well. Gilbride had gotten a number of specialists and surgeons added to his roster only days after the Phrenorian attack. People and the sprawl both were still being put back together.

"I'm just amazed," Sage said.

"At what?" Kiwanuka lifted an eyebrow and looked innocent. "How quickly the Seabees can hose up a building?"

Sage smiled, and he realized it was easier to do that these days even though training the new recruits at the fort made for long, hard shifts. "No. I've seen that lots of places."

"Then what?"

"How quickly the people come back after something like this."

"You've seen that lots of places too."

"I know," Sage agreed. "And it never ceases to amaze me." He looked out the window. "Especially the kids. They lose families, lose homes, get maimed and scarred for life, and everything's still new to them. They're always excited to see it."

Out in the street, the kids talked and mimicked the extrusion suit operator's ponderous stride and the way he held his arm out. Some of the other Seabees laughed at the kids. One of the Navy men reached into the truck and took out a bag. He called the kids over and passed out chocolate bars, which were still considered a delicacy.

Especially since they were free.

Eating the chocolate, the kids went back to watching as the building took shape.

"They're kids," Kiwanuka said, nodding at them. "The biggest part of any future we have. They're why we do what we do."

"All the fighting and killing?" Sage asked.

He had been haunted by more nightmares lately, but he thought they were a by-product of the meds he'd been given while Gilbride and the surgeons had put him back together. He'd dreamed more of Sombra de la Montaña those past few days as well, but he was pretty sure that was caused by Jahup, Noojin, Telilu, and Leghef coming to see him when he'd been in the med bay, and during the dinners they'd invited him to. He remembered his old family while he got used to the new one. Kiwanuka had gone with him to the dinners, and her presence had made those times more enjoyable.

"We don't fight and kill," Kiwanuka said. "Our job here is to preserve and protect. Don't get that mixed up."

"Kind of hard to do one without the other."

"Have you fired a shot since we kicked the Phrenorians off Makaum?" Kiwanuka asked. "Other than in training?"

"No."

"There you go."

Sage nodded. "It's hard to imagine it staying that way."

Kiwanuka looked at him. "It can stay that way as long as you want it to, Master Sergeant. Colonel Halladay—excuse me—*Brigadier General* Halladay is planning on keeping you at Fort York as long as you will stay."

Sage was surprised. "When did that promotion happen?"

"It didn't. Not yet. But Bryce in the *brigadier general's* office told me the paperwork had been put through the proper channels."

Sage nodded. "Halladay is a fine officer. He deserves it."

"Brigadier General Halladay also pushed through paperwork for me. I'm going to be a master sergeant."

Sage smiled at her. "Congratulations, *Master Sergeant* Kiwanuka. You deserve it too."

"Thank you." Kiwanuka smiled. "He also has something planned for you. With Quass Leghef's help."

"No."

Kiwanuka kept talking. "Sergeant Major of the Army—"

Sage shook his head. "No. They only give that title to soldiers who are going to be out of the service in a few years. And it goes to the oldest sergeant in the Terran military at the time. That's not me."

"Maybe you're closer to being the oldest sergeant than you think you are."

Sage mock-frowned at her. "You're not doing yourself any favors here, *Master Sergeant.*"

Kiwanuka smiled. "Keep calling me that. I like the sound of it."

"It gets old after a while."

"I'll let it." Kiwanuka scooped up noodles with her chopsticks. "Anyway, Quass Leghef pointed out that you are the most senior sergeant on Makaum. She pushed the advancement with Halladay. They're both confident it will go through."

Sage didn't comment. Leghef was a power cell when it came to getting her desired results.

"With the war moving out here," Kiwanuka said, "Command is considering bumping Fort York up to a major training and recruiting facility. There's room to expand here, put in barracks and family housing."

"Sounds like they're planning on turning Fort York into a big operation."

"They are. And it will take someone who knows what he's doing to run an operation like that."

Sage considered the changes and realized he'd taken to training the new soldiers more than he'd thought he would. Those men and women knew they needed training to survive, and they knew the war was coming this way.

He'd come to Makaum looking for a war. Now the war was coming to him. It was a sobering thought.

"I'll have to think about that," he finally said.

"Planning on ducking out when the going gets tough, Master Sergeant?" Kiwanuka asked.

"They need to have the right person for that job," he replied. "I'm not sure I'm it."

"You are." Kiwanuka reached across the table and put her hand on his. "You *are*. At the least, you can be that person until a better one comes along." She grinned.

Sage nodded. "Maybe."

They were silent for a moment and Kiwanuka took her hand back. He missed her touch. He'd grown used to it lately. They ate. Sage used his chopsticks to pick up more noodles. It was a dish he hadn't tried before. Kiwanuka had suggested it.

"Do you know what you're eating?" Kiwanuka asked.

"Luosifen," he said. "You're the one who suggested it."

"It's a traditional Chinese dish, a specialty of Liuzhou, a city in Guangxi in southern China. They make it out of river snails and pork bones and a bunch of herbs. Black cardamom, tangerine peel, licorice root, and other things I can't remember."

"River snails?" Sage looked for them in the noodles.

"Don't tell me snails would be the worst thing you've ever eaten."

"No."

"There aren't any snails in that dish," Kiwanuka said. "Uncle Huang told me he substitutes *jasulild* for the snails and the pork bones."

"If Pingasa *had* gotten eaten by one of those things, people might not order this for a while."

Kiwanuka grinned. "He still tells that story to everybody who will listen. Sometimes he buys beers so he can tell it again to people he already knows."

Sage laughed, and it was a good sound, one that he didn't recognize as his own. That surprised him and he thought maybe it was the imported beer they were drinking.

Out on the street, a crawler paused outside the safety margins imposed by the Seabees. Noojin sat behind the wheel in civilian dress and Jahup sat in the passenger seat. They held hands between them. After a moment, they rolled on.

"I guess they got their relationship worked out," Sage observed.

Kiwanuka nodded. "Nearly losing someone will do that to you. They're as happy as two young people can be. I helped them with their paperwork that would allow them to see each other while serving." She looked up at Sage. "I was wondering if I should put in paperwork myself."

Sage looked at her.

"We eat an awful lot of meals together these days, Master Sergeant, and we've been known to keep each other company late at night."

Sage's ears burned and he had to stop from laughing at himself and accidently hurting Kiwanuka's feelings.

"Our *togetherness* has been noticed," Kiwanuka went on. "With my promotion in the pipeline, I don't want to mess things up. Plus, I'm happy with where we are. Maybe it's time for you to figure out if you are."

"I'm happy," Sage said. And it was the first time he could say that truly in a long time. "Let me know when you want the paperwork to hit Halladay's desk."

"All right."

Sage leaned across the table and kissed her, something that they hadn't done in public. When he pulled away, Kiwanuka looked at him in surprise.

"People are going to talk," she said.

Outside, the children had turned their attention from the construction site and were laughing and pointing at the two of them. They kept saying a word Sage didn't understand.

"They already are," Sage said, and nodded.

Kiwanuka pulled a face at the kids and they roared with laughter.

"What are they saying?" Sage asked.

"It's a Makaum word that comes from some of their oldest history. It means 'Warlord.'"

"Warlord," Sage repeated, and he remembered that final battle with Zhoh, what the Phrenorian warrior had told him about them being more alike than Sage wanted to admit. He wasn't comfortable with the title then, and not now. It came with too much blood, too much loss, and too much selfishness on his part.

"Yes," Kiwanuka said. "Jahup has told the story of Zhoh calling you that a lot. After the way you fought for the Makaum people, that's how they refer to you, only in their language. I think Quass Leghef had a hand in that. And I'm sure Noojin and Jahup pushed it along."

Sage didn't care for it and wondered if there was a way to make it go away. "*Warlord* sounds a tad ostentatious, don't you think?"

"*Master sergeant* isn't in the Makaum vocabulary. If you don't like it, you can let them know." Kiwanuka shrugged. "Or maybe it will go away all on its own."

Sage doubted that. Stories had a way of insisting on being told. But maybe one day it wouldn't bother him so much.

Across the street, the Seabee engineer was already shooting the second floor. The plascrete gleamed in the bright afternoon air.

All his adult life, he'd jumped around space, spending short amounts of time in different systems, always chasing the war. Before that, he'd been a military brat after Sombra de la Montaña. The idea of settling down in one place had seemed foreign to him.

But now he knew he didn't like the idea of leaving Makaum. Not when there was so much work to do and he was living with the people who deserved it.

"I'll talk to Halladay," Sage said.

"Good." Kiwanuka leaned across the table and kissed him this time.

The kids laughed and pointed again, their mouths stained with chocolate.

"Get a move on, Master Sergeant," Kiwanuka said. "Finish your *jasulild* noodles and let's find something to do with the rest of this free afternoon. We're not going to get many of them."

Sage knew that. But he knew they'd make the most of the ones they got.